I0691340

THE TOUCHSTONE OF
FORTUNE

Being the Memoir of Baron Clyde, who lived, thrived, and fell in the Doleful Reign of the so-called Merry Monarch, Charles II

CHARLES MAJOR

1st WORLD
LIBRARY
Literary Society

The Touchstone of Fortune

Charles Major

© 1st World Library, 2009
PO Box 2211
Fairfield, IA 52556
www.1stworldlibrary.com
First Edition

LCCN: 2009923367

Softcover ISBN: 978-1-4218-8818-7
Hardcover ISBN: 978-1-4218-8917-7
eBook ISBN: 978-1-4218-8719-7

Purchase *"The Touchstone of Fortune"*
as a traditional bound book at:
www.1stWorldLibrary.com/purchase.asp?ISBN=978-1-4218-8818-7

1st World Library Literary Society

Giving Back to the World

"If you want to work on the core problem, it's early school literacy."

- James Barksdale, former CEO of Netscape

"No skill is more crucial to the future of a child, or to a democratic and prosperous society, than literacy."

- Los Angeles Times

"Literacy... means far more than learning how to read and write... The aim is to transmit... knowledge and promote social participation."

- UNESCO

"Literacy is not a luxury, it is a right and a responsibility. If our world is to meet the challenges of the twenty-first century we must harness the energy and creativity of all our citizens."

- President Bill Clinton

"Parents should be encouraged to read to their children, and teachers should be equipped with all available techniques for teaching literacy, so the varying needs and capacities of individual kids can be taken into account."

- Hugh Mackay

To My Wife

CHAPTER I

DAUGHTERS AND POVERTY

Goddess Fortune seems to delight in smiling on a man who risks his all, including life, perhaps, on a desperate chance of, say one to one hundred. If her Ladyship frowns and he loses, his friends call him a fool; if he wins, they say he is a lucky devil and are pleased to share his prosperity if he happens to be of a giving disposition. Lucky? No! He has simply minted his courage.

The most remarkable illustration of these truths that has ever come to my knowledge is my friend George Hamilton, the second son in this generation of the illustrious House of Hamilton, Count Anthony being its present head. The younger son was penniless save for the crumbs that fell from his elder brother's table, and Count Anthony was one who kept an eye on the crumbs.

George, who was of an independent nature, accepted Anthony's grudging help reluctantly. Therefore when Charles II was restored to the English throne in 1660, the younger Hamilton, who had been with the king in exile, was glad to assume the duties of Second Gentleman of the Bedchamber in Whitehall Palace. With the pension attached to this office, winnings at cards and other uncertain revenues from disreputable sources, George was enabled to maintain himself at court where debts were not necessarily paid, where honesty and virtue were held in contempt, and where vice of all sorts was not only the daily stock in trade but the daily stock of jest and pleasure, boasting and pride; for what is the use of being wicked if one hides one's light under a bushel?

Hamilton was a favorite with those who knew him well and was respected by those who knew him slightly, not because of his virtues, for they were few, but because he was strikingly handsome in person, moderately quick of wit, generous to an enemy, kind to every one, brave to the point of recklessness, and decent even in vice, if that be possible. He was no better than his friends save in these easy qualities, but while he was as bad in all other respects as his surroundings, the evil in him was due more to environment than to natural tendencies, and the good—well, that was his undoing, as this history will show. A man who attempts to 'bout ship morally in too great haste is liable to miss stays and be swamped, for nothing so grates on us as the sudden reformation of our friends, while we remain unregenerate.

But to write Hamilton's history I must begin at the beginning, which in this case happens to be my beginning, and shall conclude with his "hundred to one" venture, which closed his career and mine, at least in England.

*   *   *   *   *

The Clydes, of whom I am the present head, have always had great respect for the inevitable and have never permitted the idealization of a hopeless cause to lead them into trouble solely for trouble's sake. So it was that when my father of blessed memory saw that King Charles I and his favorites were determined to wreck the state, themselves, and their friends, he fell ill of the gout at an opportune moment, which

Charles Major

made it necessary for him to hasten to Germany to take the cure at the baths.

My revered father was the twenty-second Baron Clyde, Edwin by baptism, and I, his namesake, am, or rather was, the twenty-third and last baron of our line, having lost my title by reason of entanglement with the desperate fortunes of George Hamilton.

My father had been a staunch supporter of Charles I, not only because Charles was our divinely appointed king, but also because his Majesty was a lovable person in many respects. His misfortunes were the result of bad advice, false philosophy, and a heart too kind. Kindliness in a king is a dangerous virtue, and a royal conscience is like a boil on the elbow, always in the way. Aside from his kindliness there were only two other qualities necessary to insure King Charles I the loss of his head, and he possessed them— stubbornness and weakness. A good king need have but two virtues, strength and love for his people, but if he would reign comfortably, these virtues must be supplemented by a strenuous vice,—sure death to his enemies.

So when my father saw that fidelity to King Charles's hopeless cause meant hopeless ruin, he took the gout and went to Germany. Absence from England enabled him to desert the cause he loved, but could not help, and more, it saved him the humiliation of being compelled to join the Cromwell forces,— a cause which he could have helped, but hated. Therefore he saw to it that his gout remained with him during the entire Cromwell interregnum, and he died at Aix-la-Chapelle just before the recall of Charles II to the English throne.

I inherited my father's title and a part of his estate; a great portion of the latter having been granted to the accommo- dating husband of one of Charles II's friends.

I returned to England with the king, and, as balm to my wounded estate, was made Second Gentleman of the Wardrobe in that modern Sodom, Whitehall Palace, Westminster, where lived Charles II, who was said to have been appointed and anointed of God, king of our glorious realm. God makes some curious mistakes, if human opinion is to be accepted.

The name Lot was unknown in Whitehall, but Mesdames Potiphar, Salome, and Delilah were met at every turn, while Davids and Johns, eager to be tempted, and Samsons, stooping to be shorn, hedged the king about with anything save divinity.

That interesting Frenchman, Comte de Grammont, is accredited with saying that during his residence in England he knew but one woman in Whitehall who was both beautiful and pure,—Frances Jennings, maid of honor to her Grace, the Duchess of York, the Duke of York being James, brother of Charles II, and heir presumptive to the English throne.

I am proud to say that this beautiful Frances Jennings was my mother's brother's child. In early youth I had lived in her father's house and was more her elder brother than her cousin.

I suppose De Grammont was wrong in his sweeping assertion, but he was right in his judgment of Frances, for though she was admittedly the most beautiful woman— perhaps I should say girl, for she was very young—at court, she—. But what befell her is a part of George Hamilton's history and shall be told all in its turn.

*　*　*　*　*

Frances Jennings and her younger sister Sarah, who after-ards became the first duchess of the present House of Marlborough, were the daughters of my uncle, Sir Richard Jennings, of Sundridge, near St. Albans. With a fidelity more creditable to his heart than to his head, Sir Richard had clung to the cause of Charles I, had lost his entire fortune, and in the end was forced to bend his neck to the yoke of Cromwell to save his life. When Charles II returned to the throne, he easily forgave Sir Richard his enforced apostasy, but failed to return his estates, forgiveness being so much easier than restitution to an indolent selfish nature.

So it was that at the time this story opens, which was several years after King Charles's return, Sir Richard and his two daughters were living almost in poverty at Sundridge, hoping for help from the king, though little expecting it. Without assistance furnished by myself and a former retainer of Sir Richard, one Roger Wentworth, who had become a prosperous tanner of Sundridge, my cousins and my uncle would have been reduced to want. But Wentworth and I kept up a meagre household, and I was on watch at court to forward my uncle's interest, if by any good fortune an opportunity should come. At last, after long waiting, it came, though as often occurs with happiness delayed, it was mingled with bitterness.

I think it was in the year 1662 or '63—it may have been a year or two earlier or later, I cannot say at this distance of time—the Duchess of York, who, with her husband, lived in Whitehall Palace with King Charles, announced her intention of choosing her maids of honor by personal inspection. She declared that, barring the fact that the maids must be of good family, beauty would win the golden apple, as it had in olden Greece. On hearing this news, I saw the opportunity for which I had waited so long. If beauty was to be the test, surely my cousin Frances would become a maid of honor, and once at court, if she could keep her head and her heart, the fortunes of her house were sure to rise, for the world has never known so good a beauty market as Whitehall was at that time.

There was no question about my cousin's beauty. Would she be able to make it bring a price worthy of its quality? To do this, she must have the cunning of the serpent, the virtue of a saint, and the courage of Roland himself. She must not be fastidious, though she must be suspicious. She must not be a prude, though she must know that all is evil about her. Lastly she must have no heart, though she must learn the rare art of being tender to the right person at the right time.

I was sure that Frances was equipped with the mental and moral qualities necessary in so dangerous a field as Whitehall Court. Among those qualities was her knowledge that she was beautiful; not that she believed it as a matter of vanity, but knew it simply as a matter of fact. That knowledge would give her self-confidence and would help her to value justly the flattery of men, which was sure to be her portion to overflowing. She would know that flattery was her due, and therefore would not be too grateful for it, gratitude being a dangerous virtue in a woman. She was as dear to me as if she were my sister, and I hesitated bringing her to terrible Whitehall. But desperate conditions need desperate remedies, so I determined to lay the matter before my uncle and let him and my cousins decide the question for themselves.

With this object in view, one bright spring morning, I took horse at the Leg Tavern in King Street, Westminster, and rode to Sundridge to spend a few days with my uncle, hoping to interest my beautiful cousin in the Duchess of York's announcement concerning the choice of her maids. I knew that Sir Richard would protest against Frances's going to

Whitehall, but I hoped, with the help of my cousins, to override the old gentleman's feeble will. While I saw clearly the dangers the girl would encounter; I had faith in her strength, and felt sure the chances of making her fortune were worth the risk. In other words, I was staking a human soul which was infinitely dear to me, against wealth and station—a hundred to one chance, even with the Fates smiling. When one considers how seldom the long odds are taken and how often they win, one cannot help believing that courage is the touchstone of Fortune; the criterion by which the capricious Goddess measures her votaries and distributes her smiles.

I made my journey to Sundridge and arrived there in the afternoon near the hour of three, finding my uncle and my cousin Sarah at home, but Frances abroad.

"She walks a great deal nowadays," remarked my uncle, and Sarah assented with—"Yes, a great deal," having, I fancied, more significance in her manner than in her words.

"There has been hardly a pleasant afternoon in a month that she has not been abroad with her book," continued Sir Richard.

"Her book," murmured Sarah, who was a laconic young person, much given to observing conditions about her and equally prone to keep her conclusions to herself.

"She refuses all company," remarked my uncle, who did not seem to catch the sceptical inflection in his younger daughter's voice, "and I sometimes fear she wishes to be alone because she is brooding over our misfortunes."

"Brooding!" murmured Sarah, with slightly lifted eyebrows.

"Even when she is at home she sits all day long at the window and sighs," said Sir Richard, dolefully.

"Sighs," concurred laconic Sarah.

There are so many symptoms which, in a young woman, may seem to indicate the disease of love that one making a hasty diagnosis is likely to fall upon that malady, it being prevalent in spring, both of the year and of life. I had believed that my cousin's healthful vanity and quiet strength of character would, in a measure, keep her safe from this troublesome spring disorder, but my uncle's account of her doings led me to fear that perhaps her wholesome armor of self-conceit was not so invulnerable as I had hoped.

Later I spoke my half-formed doubt to Sarah, who answered:—

"I don't know what she is doing. I attend to my own business; that is, unless I see profit in meddling elsewhere."

"Ah, but this is your business and mine if we love your sister, as you will say when you learn the object of my visit," I answered, hoping to loosen her cautious tongue.

Sarah's eyes opened wide with a question in them, but her lips remained sealed, and I would not satisfy her curiosity, which I knew was at boiling-point, until she had made a direct request. Her manner had resolved my doubts into fears, so as she did not speak, I continued:—

"But you must be able to form an opinion as to what your sister is doing. You are with her all the time, and every young girl instinctively knows the symptoms of love, even though she may never have felt them."

"Not I!" she answered, with sharp emphasis.

"Oh, but you may suspect or surmise," I insisted.

"Suspect sometimes. Surmise never. Waste of energy," answered Sarah, who, of all the persons I knew, had energy to spare.

"It would be a crime, a horrible crime," I continued, hoping in time to extract her opinion, "if your beautiful sister were to throw herself away on any man to be met hereabout."

"Horrible!" acquiesced Sarah, earnestly.

"Then why don't you watch her, and, if need be, prevent such a mistake?" I suggested.

"Not necessary," answered Sarah.

As she failed to explain, I asked, "Why is it not necessary?"

"Because she is not a fool," returned Sarah, indicating by her manner that I might find her meaning if I could.

A moment's thought carried me to her conclusions, and I laughed because I was answered and pleased, being convinced that Sarah, at least, did not consider her sister in danger. Then I caught Sarah in my arms and kissed her, saying:—

"A kiss! That's for wisdom, cousin!" Sarah's was a drawing personality.

"A slap! That's for impudence!" answered Sarah, suiting the action to the word, though there was a smile in her eyes.

Later in the afternoon Frances came home radiant and offered me her cheek to kiss. She was delighted to see me, though I noticed short lapses from attention, which seemed to indicate preoccupation. But I had learned my lesson from Sarah and soon came back to my belief that Frances was not a fool, and that whatever malady her symptoms might indicate, she would never permit it to inure her.

After talking with my uncle and my cousins a few minutes, I said: "I have had a long ride and want a good supper Come, Frances, let us go out and buy all the good things in Sundridge."

Sir Richard said nothing, and a faint shadow of humiliation came to Frances's face, but practical Sarah settled the question by saying:—

"Go with him, Frances, and see that he buys enough. You know we have had barely a crust in the house the last fortnight, and not a farthing in all that time with which to buy one. We have a warm welcome for you, Baron Ned, but welcome after a long ride is a mere appetizer. I'll fetch a basket—yes, two!"

The name "Baron Ned" was a heritage from the days of my childhood, and doubtless it will cling to me till the day of my death. I have never objected to it on the lips of my friends, but rather, have always liked it.

Sarah's good common sense set us all laughing, and when she brought in two large baskets, Frances and I went forth to buy our supper.

When we were a short way from the house, I said: "I've come to spend several days with you, my cousin-sister. Are you not delighted?"

"Yes," she answered, cordially enough, but without the old-time gladness in her manner.

"And my purpose in coming concerns you," I continued.

She started perceptibly and blushed, but after a moment brought herself together and asked laughingly:—

"You don't want to marry me, brother Ned?"

"No, no," I answered. "We're far too dear to each other to spoil it all by marriage, and my station in life, to say nothing of my small estate, is in no way up to your value. It would not be a fair exchange. Your husband shall be at least a duke, with not less than forty thousand pounds a year. That, by the way, is a part of my mission in Sundridge. No, no, I do not bring an offer!" I said, hastily, noticing that she drew away from me in her manner, "I simply hope to pave the way to such an offer some time in the future, and want to warn you against doing anything that might forestall good fortune."

I had hardly finished speaking when her manner of drawing away became so pronounced that I feared I might lose my race by going too fast, so I quickly sought to right myself by saying with marked emphasis:—

"I am not going to pry into your affairs."

A telltale blush came to her cheek as she interrupted me with a touch of warmth: "I have no affairs."

"I am sure you have not," I answered soothingly, "though a girl as beautiful as you are is sure to attract men, and is quite as sure to have little affairs. But they are of no more importance than a laugh and a sigh."

"Yes, yes, of course. Of no importance—not the least," she answered, blushing exquisitely, and unconsciously telling me there was an affair.

"No, no," I continued earnestly. "I do not want to pry. I am simply going to suggest a project which perhaps you may turn to your advantage. Marriage has no part in it save that the greatest good fortune that can befall a woman is to marry well, which I hope will be the ultimate result of what I shall propose. If a young woman's friends do not put her in a position to marry the right sort of a man, they fail in their duty to her."

"I hate the word 'marriage,'" returned Frances, impatiently.

"Ah, but it is a woman's privilege, the one great purpose of her life," I insisted. "Why pretend otherwise? I don't believe in the drag-net process of getting a husband, but in England a girl must be seen before she is married, and her chief concern should be to be seen by the right man."

"I should detest the right man," returned Frances, now grown almost surly.

"Yes, yes, now, perhaps. But the suggestion I have to make, if acted upon, will do all these things for you and will give you the opportunity to detest the 'right man' intelligently if you feel so inclined when you meet him. I have taken it upon myself to come all the way to Sundridge with a suggestion, because of the love I bear you and because you have no mother to do these things for you. As for dear Uncle Richard —well, you know, he can't."

"No, no! father is old and of late has been failing rapidly. Sarah and I can look for no help from him. On the contrary, we must help him. I have thought of nothing else, night or day, for years. Tell me what it is you have to suggest. What you have had to say to us has always been for our good. We should have starved these last five years had it not been for you and good old Roger Wentworth. Tell me, Baron Ned, what have you come to offer me?"

I had intended telling Frances privately of the Duchess of York's announcement, but after my talk with her I concluded to wait and to make the statement in the presence of her father, so I answered:—

"I am not ready to tell you just now, but I'll do so before I return to London."

"Then return at once, Baron Ned."

"If I do, you'll never hear it," I answered.

"In that case, stay. But tell me as soon as you can, for pent-up curiosity is killing to a girl," said Frances, with a doleful little smile.

"Does nothing else trouble just now?" I asked.

She turned to me in surprise, blushed and answered: "Yes. My poor, dear father. Yes—father. Of course there's nothing else. Why do you ask?"

"Just to be asking," I replied.

At that point we came to the shop where we were to buy our supper, and I was glad to change the subject. I had learned definitely that there was a man in the case, and my task would be to put him out if I could. The man who first enters a young girl's heart is hard to dislodge, and the worst part of the terrible business is that even she herself may be unable to expel him her whole life through.

When supper was well under way that evening, I took the opportunity to set my great ball rolling, and said:—

"Uncle Richard, I have come from London for the purpose of offering a suggestion which may eventually be of advantage to all of you."

Sarah put down her knife and fork to listen; Frances held hers in suspense, and Sir Richard looked up quickly, asking:—

"What is it, nephew? We all thank you in advance."

A cold bath is better taken quickly, so I plunged in.

"The Duchess of York has announced her intention to choose four maids of honor by personal inspection. Aside from the fact that they must be of good family, they will be taken solely on account of their beauty, the most beautiful to win."

Frances dropped her knife and fork and sprang to her feet, exclaiming:—

"I'm going to see the duchess! Thank you, cousin Ned! I'll be a maid of honor!"

"Of course—beauty!" observed Sarah, resuming her supper with a dry laugh.

"Your sister can win on the terms offered, if anyone can," said I, turning sharply on Sarah.

"I am sure of it," returned Sarah. "I laughed only because *she* is so sure."

Frances then turned to her sister, not reproachfully but earnestly: "Sure?" she exclaimed. "Of course I am sure. I know myself. You have a far better mind than mine, but I have—well, I know what I have. I don't believe I am vain, but I know, sister, that you and I must rebuild the fortunes of our house, or worse will come to us than we have ever known. You are sure to do your part because you have intellect—brains. *You* know you have. Is it any less a matter of vanity for you to know yourself than it is for me to know myself? I know what I have, and I intend to use it."

Sarah assented by the monosyllable, "Right!" while Frances ran to the head of the table, knelt by her father's chair, and said:—

"It is all for dear old father's sake."

Sir Richard brought his daughter's head to his shoulder, affectionately smoothed her hair for a moment, and spoke with quavering earnestness:—

"It is not to be thought of one moment. Whitehall is a nest of infamy, and the king, I am told, is the worst man in it. I gave all I had to his martyred father, and now the son does not even so much as refuse to make restitution. He simply gives lying promises and leaves me to starve. I am surprised, nephew, that you come to us with this proposition."

"In that case, dear uncle, it shall be dropped at once," said I, expecting, however, to take it up at another time.

Frances was about to insist, but a glance from Sarah stopped her, and she remained silent. I knew it would require a great deal of sound argument to bring Sir Richard to our way of thinking, but I was sure that Sarah could soften him and that, at the right time, I could finish our helpless antagonist.

Meantime the love affair of Frances, if there was one, should be looked into, if Frances did not object too seriously. In truth, I was a very busy man, solely with the affairs of other people.

Being so engaged in telling of other people's affairs, I have not had time to mention the fact that I had a love affair of my own, that is, if I may call that a love affair which involved only one person—myself. She who I hoped would one day be the party of the second part was Mary Hamilton, sister to Count Anthony and George Hamilton, mention of whom was made at the outset of this history.

I myself may have been lacking in morals, but at my worst I was a saint compared to George Hamilton and his friends, Lord Berkeley, young Wentworth, and the king's son, James Crofts, Duke of Monmouth. There was, however, this difference between George and his friends: he was gentlemanly picturesque in wickedness; they were nauseous in the *filthiness* of vice.

After I became a suitor for the hand of George Hamilton's sister, I had closed my eyes to his shortcomings and, for some time prior to my Sundridge visit, had sought to further my cause with her by winning her brother's help. I had known Hamilton many years before, when we were all exiles in Holland and France, and had always liked him. In fact, we had been friends from our youth, and while in latter years I had not seen much of him, having avoided him because of his vicious mode of life, I had found no difficulty in taking up our old intimacy. At the time of which I am writing I was sure that he was my friend and had given him good reason to think the same of me. There was an attraction about him that was winning and irresistible even to men. What must it have been to women?

Charles Major

I speak of this friendship between George Hamilton and me at this time because of the great strain its bonds were soon to have; so great that I am still wondering why they did not break. To close this mention of my own love affair, I would say that at the time of my visit to Sundridge I had reasonable cause to hope for a favorable termination. Not that I expected ever to kindle a fiery passion in Mary's breast, for she was not of the combustible sort, but I believed she liked me, favored my suit, and I hoped would accept me in the end. While she was very pretty, she was not of so great beauty as to mislead her family into expecting that she would catch an earl by fishing in a duck pond, and, barring the earl, I should be a husband more or less satisfactory to her and her family. George was my friend in the matter, and to him I believed I owed much of my prospects of success. Soon the relation of my own love affair to that of my cousin Frances will be apparent.

My second day at Sundridge was spent with my uncle and my cousins, Frances remaining at home with us. Adroit Sarah had talked with her father about the maid-of-honorship and had found an opportunity to tell me that while he was not yet persuaded, he was at least in a receptive mood, ready to listen to what I had to say. In the evening Frances and Sarah went off to bed early, leaving Sir Richard to the mercies of myself and a flagon of wormwood wine which I had brought in as an ally from the Black Dog Tavern.

At first when I broached the subject of Frances becoming a maid of honor, he turned away from me, saying:—

"I fear, nephew, I fear! I confess that I did not expect the suggestion to come from you; you know the court even better than I do. My dear boy, we might as well send the little girl to the devil at once."

"Whitehall is no heaven, I admit," I answered. "But you don't know Frances. She will be as safe at court as she is in your house. The devil is everywhere, uncle, if one chooses to seek him."

"That is true, Ned."

"And Frances will not seek him anywhere. Of that I was sure before I determined to suggest this matter. It is true she has seen nothing of life beyond the pale of your influence and protection, but you are well along in years, uncle, and must face the truth that your daughters will have to confront the world without you, sooner or later—later, I hope."

"That terrible truth is my only reason to fear death," returned Sir Richard, sighing and leaning back in his chair.

"Yes, it must be a terrible thought to you," I answered, cruelly, for the purpose of forcing my dear old antagonist into the right way of thinking. "But it is your duty to your daughters to face it squarely, and if possible, to let it help you in preparing them to meet the world. They may, if they will, find evil everywhere; they may avoid it anywhere. Frances, with her marvellous beauty, is sure to meet good fortune at court, and good fortune is a great moral preservative of women."

"Bad doctrine, Ned, bad doctrine," said my uncle, shaking his head.

"But good truth," I answered. "Vice, like disease, breeds best in poverty."

"You have just admitted that Whitehall is a nest of vice. Wealth has not prevented it there," returned my uncle, beating me in the argument for a moment.

But I soon rallied: "Wealth will not help those who want to go wrong, but it has saved many a woman who wanted to be good. However, all this argument is impertinent. Frances is strong, and she is good, and you may rest your mind of all fear that she will ever be otherwise. Hers is not only the virtue of goodness, but of stubbornness and pride."

"I believe you are right, nephew," returned my uncle, smiling for the first time that evening. "Stubbornness is a good thing in a woman, and my Frances has a store of it 'that might surprise one knowing her but slightly."

"Yes," I replied. "And now, while her beauty is reaching its climax, is the time for her to make the most of it. I know the world, uncle, and I know the court, only too well, I am ashamed to say. But above all, I know my cousin, and knowing also the evil state of your fortune, I unhesitatingly urge you to seize the opportunity presented by the Duchess of York. She is a good woman and my dear friend. Frances will be under her care and mine. Of my care I need not boast. It shall be that of a brother. But Frances will need no one's care for long. She will soon find a husband, rich and of high rank, and then—"

"Would you send my girl out angling for a husband?" asked Sir Richard.

"Yes, if you insist on putting it so," I replied. "What is every girl doing? What else is every good mother doing for her daughter? Marriage is the one way in which a gentlewoman may find settlement in life. Frances has no mother. Let us help her to win the happiness she deserves. 'Angling' is an ugly word, and in Frances's case is not the right one. Great men and rich men will soon be angling for her. Let us place her where the bait is worth taking. Let us not mince matters, but admit between ourselves that we are sending Frances to court to make a good marriage. No one less than a rich duke or a wealthy earl will satisfy me. If you wish to allow a mere jealous fear in your heart to blight her prospects, she will be the sufferer, and hereafter may thank your folly for her misfortune."

Sir Richard remained silent a moment or two and then spoke tremulously: "The saddest thing about age is its hesitancy, its doubts, its fears." Here the tears began to stream down the old man's cheek as he continued: "Through all my misfortunes Frances has been my joy, my solace. Sarah is a good daughter, but she lacks the ineffable tenderness, the calm, ready sympathy of her sister. If evil were to befall Frances, my heart would break—break." He covered his face with his hands and sobbed, murmuring as though to himself: "My God, I fear! I fear! She is my all—all! The king has taken everything else, and now you ask me to give her to him."

A great lump came to my throat, but in a moment I was able to say: "Do not fear, uncle, do not fear! Rather, rejoice! Let me be your staff, your courage, your strength! Think it over till morning, and then give your consent with the full assurance that it will mean happiness for the girl whom you and I so dearly love."

The old man rose, took my hand, held it in his feeble grasp for a moment, and went to his room without another word.

As I was going down the narrow passageway to my bedroom, Frances opened her door and asked: "What does father say? I know it almost kills him."

"Yes," I answered. "But he will consent in the morning."

Tears came to her eyes and she gave me her hand, saying: "Thank you, brother Ned. We are wounding him only for his own sake. If it were not to help him, all the wealth in the world would not tempt me to give him this pain nor to go to Whitehall, for I fear the place."

As she stood at the door, candle in hand, her low-cut gown exposing her beautiful throat with its strong full curves, its gleaming whiteness and the pulsing hollow at the base, her marvellous hair of sunlit gold hanging in two thick braids to below her waist, her sweet oval face of snowy whiteness, underlaid with the faint pink of roses, her great luminous eyes with their arched and pencilled brows, and the tears pendant from the long black lashes, I could not help knowing that there was not in all Whitehall beauty to compare with hers. And when her full red lips parted in a tearful smile, showing a gleam of ivory between their curving lines, I knew that if our king were an unmarried man, she could be our queen, but barring that high estate, I felt sure that a score of titles and great fortunes would lie at her feet before she had been a month in Whitehall. That is, I knew all this would happen if she kept her head. The king himself would be her greatest danger, for in a way, he was handsome of person when he kept his mouth closed, and even a little beauty in a king, like a candlelight in a distant window, shines with magnified radiance.

I went to bed that night having great faith in my cousin's strength and discretion, but my confidence was to receive a shock the next day.

CHAPTER II

A MAIDEN ST. GEORGE

After breakfast the following morning, while Sir Richard and I were sipping our morning draught in the dingy little library, he brought up the subject of the night before.

"As you justly observed, Baron Ned," my uncle began, restraining his emotion as best he could, "sooner or later my daughters will have to face the world alone. I am of no help to them now, and perhaps shall be no loss when I am gone, but it is like taking the heart out of me to send my beautiful girl to this unholy king; the wickedest man in the vilest court on earth. But it must be done. God help me and save her!"

"I will not go!" cried Frances, running into the room from the hallway, and kneeling by her father's chair.

"I fear you must, Frances," answered Sir Richard. "There, there, we'll say it is settled and let it rest a few days, so that we may grow used to the thought before making our plans in detail."

＊　＊　＊　＊　＊

After dinner I missed Frances, and when I asked Sarah where

she had gone, I received answer in one word: "Walking."

"Alone?" I asked. Sarah smiled.

In a moment I said, "I think I, too, shall go walking."

"The Bourne Path is pretty," suggested Sarah.

"Will you come with me?" I asked.

Again Sarah smiled, shaking her head for answer, and I set off, taking my way down the path which wound beside a rocky bourne, a distance of several miles in the direction of Hamilton House, one of the country places of Count Hamilton.

When I reached a point perhaps half a league from Sundridge, I saw a lady and gentleman walking leisurely ahead of me. Her hand was on his arm, and his head was bent toward her, evidently in earnest conversation. Her head drooped prettily, indicating a listening mood, and the two seemed very much like lovers in the early wooing stage. At once I recognized the beautiful figure of my cousin Frances. The gentleman I did not know, seeing only his back, though there was something familiar to me in the tall, straight form, the broad shoulders, and the graceful carriage of the head. He was a cavalier, every inch of him, from his long, dark, slightly curling hair to the golden buckles on his shoes. He carried his beaver hat in his hand, dragging the rich plume on the ground.

I hastened forward, but they were so interested in each other that they did not know of my presence till I asked:—

"Cousin, won't you introduce me?"

Frances turned with a little scream, and the gentleman spun around quickly, putting on his hat and dropping my cousin's hand, which he had been holding. At first my surprise deprived me of the power to think, but soon I recovered self-control, and said:—

"Ah, there is no need to introduce me, cousin. I already know Master Hamilton."

"Yes," stammered the gentleman, holding out his hand, "Baron Ned and I know each other well."

I did not take his hand, and when I saw anger mounting to his eyes, I explained with the best smile at my command:—

"I do not take your hand, sir, because I have that to say to my cousin which will greatly displease you. I am glad to have the opportunity of saying it in your presence, as I dislike speaking ill of a man behind his back."

"You need speak no ill of Master Hamilton either in his presence or behind his back, if you intend to do so on my account," interrupted Frances, throwing back her head defiantly.

But I was not to be halted in my duty. Here was a future duchess in danger of being lost to the world for the sake of a vicious, penniless gambler, having neither title, estates, nor character.

"I do not ask your permission, cousin," I answered, bowing and smiling, for it is well to keep one's temper in such a case. "What I shall say is the truth, word for word, and Master Hamilton himself shall be the arbiter."

"Speaking the truth may be a great impertinence," remarked

Frances, trying to hide her anger under an air of carelessness.

"True," I returned. "And what I have to say will confirm your position. Shall I speak now before Master Hamilton, or shall I say what I have to say in your father's presence and send to Master Hamilton later a full account of my remarks?"

"For my part, sir, I shall be glad to hear whatever you have to say now," interrupted Hamilton, with an angry gleam in his eyes and a poor attempt at a smile playing about his mouth.

I would say here that I was confronting one of the bravest men in England and one of the best swordsmen in the world. While he was not prone to seek a quarrel, he certainly had never avoided one because of fear of his antagonist.

I took advantage of my cousin's silence and, turning to Hamilton, said: "If I speak one work of untruth, you are at liberty to give me the lie." Then turning to Frances, I continued: "What I have to say, cousin, is this, Master Hamilton is one of the most disreputable men at court."

Frances drew back, startled, and Hamilton grasped his sword hilt, drawing the blade half from its scabbard.

I bowed, smiled, and said: "Tut, tut, Hamilton! A lady should never see a naked sword blade. Later, later, of course, at your pleasure! I shall be found at my uncle's house in Sundridge during the next three or four days. After that you know my lodgings in the Wardrobe at Whitehall. I shall be delighted to receive your messenger, if it is your pleasure, after you have heard what I have to say."

His sword disappeared, and his smile broadened to a grim laugh: "You're right, baron. Pardon my haste. There's ample time, ample time."

Turning to my cousin, I took up my thread: "Master Hamilton is penniless, which is no small failing in itself. Therefore he lives by gambling, which might be excusable if he did not cheat. In gambling, you know, cousin, the mere law of chance will not put much money in a man's purse. Good luck is but another name for skill in trickery. If one would thrive by cards and dice, one must be a thief."

There was another angry movement by Hamilton, which I interrupted, smiling, bowing, and saying, "Let us talk this matter over calmly, smilingly, if possible."

"I'll smile when I can," returned Hamilton, made more angry, if that were possible, by a paradoxical inclination to laugh. "Proceed, baron, proceed! I am becoming interested in myself."

Frances gave a nervous little laugh, looked first to Hamilton, then to me and back again, as though she would ask what it all meant, and I continued:—

"As I have said, Frances, Master Hamilton and his friends live by cheating at cards and other games in a manner to make all decent men avoid play with them. They pluck strangers and feather their purses from new geese who do not know their methods. They also derive considerable revenue from passe women who have more wealth than beauty, are more brazen than modest, and more generous than chaste."

"I'll not listen to another word!" exclaimed Frances, looking up to Hamilton in evident wonder at his complacency.

"Just one moment longer, Frances," I insisted. "Master Hamilton's intimate friends have been known on more than one occasion to stoop to the crimes of theft, robbery, and even murder to obtain money, and have escaped punishment only because of royal favor. I do not say that Master Hamilton has ever participated in these crimes, but he knew of them, did not condemn them, helped the criminals to escape justice, and retained the guilty men as his associates and nearest friends. Add to this list the fact that Hamilton is a roue and a libertine, to whom virtue is but a jest, and with whom no pure woman, knowing him, would be seen alone, and I believe I have drawn a picture of a man who is in no way fit to be your companion in a lonely stroll. On the other hand, he is a brave man, a generous enemy, a staunch friend, and a ready help at all times to the needy. Now I have finished what has been a disagreeable though imperative duty. Doubtless it has been disagreeable to you, also, Master Hamilton, but—"

"On the contrary," he interrupted, in low tones, and with bowed head.

"But, of course, I am ready to stand by my words," I continued. "And now, sir, you may, if you wish, say to Mistress Jennings that I have lied. Doubtless she will believe you, in which case it shall be my pleasure to send a messenger to you, thereby saving you the trouble of sending one to me."

I put on my hat and awaited his reply. His hat was in his hand, and his face was bent toward the ground, his air of ironical politeness having left him. Frances turned to him and was about to speak, but, noticing the peculiar expression in his face and attitude, remained silent. After a long pause Hamilton spoke without lifting his eyes:—

"I suppose no other man ever received such an arraignment in cold blood as I have just heard from Baron Clyde." Then turning hesitatingly to my cousin, "But I am sorry to say it is true, Mistress Jennings, true in every word."

He looked into my eyes, again bowed his head, and spoke after a long silence: "Baron Ned, I can almost find it in my heart to thank you for having done your duty so bravely. I have known for some time that I am not fit to be this lady's companion and that I have no right to seek her friendship."

I bowed low, without speaking, and after another long pause he looked up to me again as he asked:—

"Now will you take my hand?"

"Gladly, George," I answered, giving him my hand, which he held for a moment and dropped without a word, a strange smile playing about his lips.

Naturally enough, Frances was at a loss how to act. Tears of vexation came to her eyes, and she turned from us to dry them with her handkerchief. She failed to find the handkerchief, so she turned to George, who, seeing her need, drew it from his pocket where she had left it for safekeeping. The first favor a young girl shows to a man when she finds herself in a "coming on disposition" is to hide some of her intimate personal belongings in his pocket. The little incident of the handkerchief caused us all to laugh and went a long way toward making us easy.

Hamilton's frankness had taken part of the wind out of my sails, and his open confession had at least paved the way for absolution, which I feared might be followed by disastrous results, since to forgive always makes the heart grow fonder.

Presently Hamilton turned to Frances, saying: "You may better appreciate your cousin's fidelity to your interest when I tell you that in speaking thus frankly to you, he placed himself in danger of two misfortunes, both of which, probably, he felt sure would befall him. Please do not think that I boast, but it is true, nevertheless, that my sword point is considered one of the most dangerous in England. Doubtless Baron Ned expected to be called upon to stand by his words. Furthermore, he is a suitor for my sister's hand, as you may know, and of late has sought my friendship, in part, no doubt, for the purpose of forwarding his cause."

At this point he turned toward me and smiled. I, too, smiled, though not joyously, for I thought surely this affair would ruin all my chances with Mary.

"Therefore," continued Hamilton, "he had much to lose in arraigning me, and nothing to gain but your welfare. You must see that it was unselfishly done. If there is gratitude in your heart, give it here." He placed his hand on my shoulder and, after a long pause and an apparent effort, finished what he had to say: "Forget me. I am unworthy to speak your name or to have the great joy of hearing you speak mine."

This was taking the wind out of my sails at a great rate. In truth, it was taking the sails themselves, though I believed he was not speaking for sake of the advantage. In a moment he bowed low, sweeping the plume of his hat in the dust, saying as he left us:—

"Farewell, Mistress Jennings, and thank you, Baron Ned. You say I am a staunch friend. You have still to learn the whole truth of your praise."

Turning instantly, he hastened away from us down the Bourne Path, and though we waited for him to look back, he disappointed us, and soon was lost as he passed beyond a bend. Frances was weeping gently, and I, too, felt a lump in my throat, not because of what I had said or done, but because of the unexpected good I had found in Hamilton, whom I had always liked; good, which up to that time I had never suspected, having always seen him in the shadow of a throne.

When Hamilton had disappeared, I asked Frances if we should return to Sundridge, and she answering by a nod, we started home, each of us heavy-hearted, one of us weeping pathetically. Her heart had just received its first sharp blow, and I pitied her, for the first one hurts.

After walking a little way in silence, I remarked, "There is no reason why we should add to your father's troubles by telling him of this affair."

"Nor Sarah," sobbed Frances. "She is like a wasp—all sting." After a long pause devoted to drying her eyes, she continued, "But it has not been much of an affair."

"I am not asking what it has been, Frances," I returned, speaking tenderly, for I knew her heart was sore. "I have no right to ask."

"Yes, you have the right to ask," she replied, earnestly. "You have earned it to-day, if never before. I'll tell you all about it. You see I did not know—I did not think it possible—that he was the evil person you described. To me he seemed as high-minded as he was gallant and handsome."

"He is high-minded in many respects," I said, "and might have been a decent man in all respects had he lived under other conditions. He is far the best of what is known at court as 'the Royal Clique,' and is an angel of goodness compared with the king and his despicable son, James Crofts, Duke of Monmouth. Do you want to tell me where and how you met Hamilton?"

After a moment's silence she began her pathetic little

narrative, hesitating at first, but gathering courage as she spoke:—

"I first saw him on the street in St. Albans, more than a month ago. Of course I did not look directly at him, but I saw him and knew that he was looking at me. I have been used to being stared at by men since I was a child of twelve—I am past eighteen now, you know—and learned long ago not to resent an impertinence which is alike unavoidable and, in a poor way, flattering. But there was this difference: when he stared at me I blush to say I liked it, nor should I have repulsed him had he spoken to me. He was the first man I had ever seen that had really attracted me. You are not a woman, therefore you cannot understand me fully. You see, a man goes to a woman; a woman is drawn to a man, usually, I suppose, against her will. I know little about the subject, this being my first, and, I hope, my last experience, but—"

"And I, too, hope," I interrupted.

"Yes," she continued quickly. "But do you know I can almost understand the feeble, hopeless resistance which the iron tries to exert against the magnet. But, cousin Ned, it is powerless."

Here she brought her handkerchief to her eyes, and I exclaimed regretfully, "Oh, Frances, I am surprised and sorry!"

"Yes, yes! I, too, was surprised, and was so sorry that I wept through the whole night following my first sight of him, and between shame for what I felt and longing to see him again, I suffered terribly. I prayed for strength against this, my first temptation, and then my heart shrunk in fear lest I should never again be tempted. The next day I walked out on the Bourne Path toward Hamilton House and met him. To my shame I confess that I looked at him. He stopped, bowed low before me, and asked if he might introduce himself, since there was no one else to do that office for him. He said that soon Lord St. Albans would be up from London and would introduce him to my father. But having seen me the day before at St. Albans, he was unable to wait; therefore, he was at that moment on his way to Sundridge, hoping to see me. He seemed confused and shy, but from what you say, I fear he was not."

"Oh, yes, he was," I interrupted, in fine irony. "George Hamilton is as shy and as modest as the devil himself."

"I fear it is true," she answered smiling faintly and sighing.

I could see plainly that she did not look upon satanic modesty as a serious fault in itself, and I fear it is not objectionable to her sex. It is the manner of brazenness more than the fact which is offensive. George's modest-faced boldness was both alluring and dangerous.

As she progressed she grew eager in her narrative, and after two or three false starts, continued: "Then he said that Count Hamilton, our neighbor, was his brother. I was silent for a moment, but presently was so foolish as to say that I had seen him at St. Albans and had asked a shopkeeper who he was. You see I was confused. I had not at all intended to say that I had seen him, and certainly would have concealed the fact that I had asked about him. But I said what I said because I could not help it."

"On that ground it may be excusable," I suggested.

"No, no," she protested. "It can be excused on no grounds. But I did it, and it can't be helped now. Without waiting for permission, he turned, and we walked together almost to

36 Charles Major

Hamilton House. I suppose, under the circumstances, he considered it best not to ask for a permission which might have been refused, and from his standpoint doubtless he was right. Take without asking seems to be man's best method with woman. When I saw we were approaching Hamilton House, I turned about for home, hoping, yet fearing, that he would not go back with me. But he did."

"Yes, you were sure to be disappointed in that respect," I answered. And she continued hastily:—

"Yes, he walked all the way with me. Before reaching Sundridge stile, I asked him to leave me. That was another mistake, for it gave to our meeting a clandestine appearance. He said my word was law to him, and that he would obey, though to do so, that is, to leave me, was pain, you understand."

"Yes, I can understand that he did not want to leave you," I answered. But I saw that she had not finished, so I remained silent, and in a moment she continued:—

"He had been so respectful to me throughout that I thought him a modest, well-behaved gentleman, and—"

I laughed, interrupting her to explain: "All art, Frances, all art. You'll find much of that manufactured modesty at court. It is the trump card in the game of love and is but a cloak for brazenness."

"Yes, I so found it," she answered, drooping her head, "for when he was about to leave me at a secluded spot, he took my hand and would have kissed me without so much as 'By your leave,' had I not caught his intent before it was too late. I drew away, inclined to be angry, and said, 'Sir, one may overrun one's course by going too fast.'"

"That truism, under like circumstances at court, would have made you famous," I said, pleased alike with her naivete and her wisdom.

"I tried, with fair success, to appear offended," she continued, blushing deeply, "but the awful truth certainly is that I was not. I suppose it is true that women like boldness and do not find wickedness in men as distasteful as mothers say it is."

"On the contrary," I remarked, growing more and more delighted with her wisdom, innocence, and candor.

"Yes," she continued, blushing exquisitely, "even since you have told me how wicked he is, I am not sure that I like him less, though I fear him and shall avoid him as I should a pestilence."

"Ah, but will you, can you, Frances?" I asked.

"Indeed, yes, brother Ned, and if you doubt me, you don't know me," she returned.

"But do you know yourself?" I asked.

"Yes, now I do, thanks to your bravery," she answered.

"But you saw him many times after his first bold attempt," I suggested.

"Oh, it was easily forgiven," she returned, naively. "Yes, I have met him almost every day since then. The days I did not see him seemed to be blanks in my life. After his first boldness, he was always courteous. He never again became familiar, but seemed to try only to convince me of his regard in most respectful terms, and—and I listened all too willingly, but made no answer save what I could not conceal in my manner. That, I fear, was answer all too plain. But now you have opened my eyes, and I see clearly. I owe you a debt of gratitude I can never repay."

"If you go to court, this affair will have been a good lesson," I returned encouragingly. "For there you must learn to despise the proffered love of men, whether it be pretended or real, until one comes who is worthy of you in person, wealth, and station."

"Yes, I shall," she answered earnestly. "But here we are at home. As you suggest, let us not speak of this poor little affair."

"By no means," I answered, as I opened the gate.

"And Baron Ned," she said, holding me back for a moment, "have no fear that I shall lose my heart at court to the detriment of my fortune. I may not consider myself—only my father and my house. It is my duty to make him happy, and I am going to do it without regard to any other purpose in life. My having known Master Hamilton will not only keep other men out of my heart, but will help me to know them and will lead me to fear them when I go to court."

Later in the evening my cousin and I walked out in town, and I had a long talk with her, partly concerning Hamilton, a theme to which she always returned, and partly concerning conditions she would meet if she became a maid of honor. And my faith in her grew as we talked.

That night I went to sleep convinced that my beautiful cousin was strong enough and shrewd enough to evade all the pitfalls of Whitehall, and that her experience with Hamilton had been the one thing needful to make her keenly alive to her danger. I felt that she was safe, but—

Near the hour of two o'clock the next afternoon, Sir Richard and I, returning from a short walk, did not find Frances at home, so I made my way to the Bourne Path, thinking it hardly possible that in the face of yesterday's events Frances could have gone to meet Hamilton. Still one can never tell; therefore I took the benefit of the doubt and set forth to make sure.

When perhaps two miles from Sundridge, the day being warm, I climbed to a ledge of rock on the shelving bank of the bourne, twelve or fifteen feet above the path, and sat down to rest in the cool shade of a clump of bushes. Below me, perhaps five or six feet above the path and far enough back among the bushes to be hidden from passers-by, was another rocky shelf or bench, admirably fitted to accommodate two persons.

Sarah had told me, after much questioning, that Frances had left home only a few minutes before Sir Richard and I had returned. I had walked rapidly, and as I had not overtaken her, I concluded I was on the wrong scent.

Within ten minutes I discovered that I was not on the wrong scent, for, much to my surprise, sorrow, and disgust, I saw Frances and Hamilton come around a turn in the path, push aside the bushes as though they knew the place, enter the dense thicket bordering the path, and sit down on the rocky bench beneath me. My first impulse was to speak, but for many reasons I determined to listen. Silence reigned below me during the next minute or two, and then Hamilton spoke:—

"You must deem me a coward, Mistress Jennings, since I did not call your cousin to account for what he said yesterday?"

"No," she answered. "It was brave of you to refrain. It must be a great deal easier for a gentleman to resent an insult than to endure it. My cousin said as much to me yesterday evening. He said he had always known that you were brave, but that he had not expected to find in you the moral courage to bear his words with equanimity. He also said he was glad he did not have to meet you in a duel, because you were so greatly his superior with the sword. It was brave of you not to challenge him. Perhaps it was on my account you desisted."

"No, it was because I respected him far more than any man I have ever known, and because he told the truth. Do not speak of my bravery in the same breath with his. He was as cool as though he were telling an amusing story."

"He certainly was," returned Frances, laughing softly and closing with a sigh.

"But he had truth on his side, and truth is a great stimulant to courage," remarked Hamilton.

Frances sighed again, diligently studying her hands resting listlessly on her lap.

"Yes, he told the truth," continued Hamilton. "That is why I sent the letter to you early this morning, asking you to meet me for the last time—the last time, Frances. This is not a mere promise to lure you on, but the truth, for I have learned my lesson from Baron Ned, and with God's help, I, too, shall hereafter protect you from all evil, including myself. It is not the Hamilton of yesterday who is speaking to you, but a new man, born again in the fierce light your cousin threw upon me. I feared you might resent his effort to protect you, and I wanted to tell you again that he spoke nothing but the truth, and that he did his duty where another man less brave would have failed."

Frances sighed audibly, and I was sure her eyes were filled with tears.

"Hereafter I shall be as honest with you and as brave for your welfare as Baron Ned was yesterday," said Hamilton, his voice choking with emotion. "I see you now for the last time, unless—" He stopped speaking for a moment and, taking her hand, continued hesitatingly, "Does the thought pain you?"

"I suppose I should say no," answered the girl, withdrawing her hand. "But you see, I, too, have a little moral courage, and, in the face of an inevitable future, do not fear to say, yes, the greatest pain I have ever known."

He moved toward her with evident intent to embrace her, but she rose, saying calmly, almost coldly:—

"Master Hamilton, do you wish me to leave you?"

In Hamilton's place, I should have preferred trying to embrace St. George's dragon rather than the girl standing before him.

Hamilton bowed with humility and said: "Please do not fear. Sit down and hear me out. I shall not detain you long."

She sat down, seeming to feel that notwithstanding her recent admission, there was no danger of further unseemly demonstration on Hamilton's part.

"I want to say," continued Hamilton, "that while Baron Ned spoke the truth, I have never been guilty of the crimes which it is said some of my friends have committed. I am unworthy enough in every respect, but I am innocent of murder and robbery. I shall mend my ways from now on. I don't ask you to believe in me, but when I am at all worthy of your kind regard, I shall tell you, and you *may* believe me, for from this day forth I shall try to be as truthful as Baron Ned. No man can be more so."

Frances sighed and answered, "I hope so."

Hamilton again took her hand, which she now permitted him to retain, and continued: "If I am ever so fortunate as to gain wealth and position worthy of you, I shall kneel at your feet, if you are free to hear me. If the good fortune never comes, this will be our farewell."

"I hope the good fortune will come soon, for your sake, and—" But she did not finish.

"Yes, yes, and—and—?" asked George, pleadingly.

"Yes, and for my own sake," she answered, turning her face from him, probably to hide the tears that were in her eyes.

"I shall see that good fortune does come," said he, "but I do not ask you to wait an hour for it. If happiness comes to you in the right man—I cannot finish. Good-by!"

He rose, bent over her, kissed her hand, and was about to leave her hastily, evidently in fear of himself. But she clung to his hand and, drawing him down to her, offered him her lips. At first he seemed to draw away, but unable to resist, caught her in his arms, kissed her, and fled.

Frances thrust aside the bushes and watched him as he walked rapidly down the path. When he turned, just before reaching the bend, she kissed her hand to him, murmuring as though speaking to herself, "Good-by, good-by!" Then she sat down and covered her face with her hands.

After a short time she rose, dried her eyes, and started home, and in a few minutes I climbed the hill and took a short cut to Sundridge. I reached home before Frances, and, notwithstanding all I had seen, was fully convinced that she would be as safe in Whitehall Court as in her father's house.

* * * * *

That evening Frances and I walked out together, and I, feeling stricken in conscience, confessed that I had witnessed the interview between her and Hamilton. She was surprised, and at first was inclined to be angry, but she had so little vindictiveness in her nature and was so gentle of disposition that her ill-temper was but the shadow of anger, and soon passed away. Then, too, her good common sense, of which she had an ample fund, came to her help and told her that whatever I had done was for her own good. So the rare smile, which was one of her greatest charms, came to her face, like the diaphanous glow of a good spirit, rested for a moment on her lips, mounted to her eyes and faded slowly away, as though it would linger a moment to ask my forgiveness.

"I am glad I witnessed the interview," said I, drawing her hand through my arm to reassure her, "for notwithstanding all that happened, I now feel sure you are to be trusted."

"But am I?" she asked, showing a self-doubt which I wished to remove.

"Yes, you will have no greater trial at court than the one through which you have just passed. You have combated successfully not only your own love, but the love of the man you love."

"Ah, Baron Ned, don't!" she exclaimed, in mild reproach, shrinking from the thought I had just uttered so plainly.

"It is always well to look misfortunes squarely in the face," I answered. "It helps one to despise them. The thing we call bad luck can't endure a steady gaze."

"It will help me in one respect,—this—this—what has happened," she returned, hanging her head.

"In what way?" I asked, catching a foreboding hint of her meaning.

She hesitated, but, after an effort, brought herself to say, "I shall never again have to combat my own heart, and surely that is the hardest battle a woman ever has to fight."

"Because your heart is already full?" I asked.

She nodded "Yes," her eyes brimming with tears.

Her heart was not only full of her first love, which of itself is a burden of pain to a young girl, but also it was sore from the grief of her first loss, the humiliation of her first mistake, and the pang of her first regret for what might have been.

"It will all pass away, Frances," I returned assuringly.

"Ah, will it, Baron Ned? You know so much more about such matters than I, who know nothing save what I have learned within the last few weeks."

"I feel sure it will," I answered.

"I wish I felt sure," she returned, trying to smile, but instead liberating two great tears that had been hanging on her lashes.

After pausing in thought a moment, she said: "But I believe I should despise myself were I to learn that what I have just done had been prompted by a mere passing motive. I shall never again see him as I have seen him. Of that I have neither fear nor doubt, but this I cannot help but know: he is the first man who has ever come into my heart, and I fear that in all my life I shall never be able to put him out entirely."

"But you may see him at Whitehall," I suggested. "What then?"

"If he remains there, I shall not. But when he learns that his presence will drive me away, I know he will leave," she answered.

"I believe you estimate him justly. Did you tell him you were going to court?" I asked.

"No," she answered, "because I am not sure that I shall go."

"Then we'll not tell him," I suggested.

"Nor any one else?" she asked.

"By all means, no one else," I replied. "I am sure you will win in this beauty contest, but you might fail, in which case we should be sorry if any one knew of the attempt."

"I shall not fail," she answered confidently, though not in vanity.

"But Hamilton said he would return to the siege when he had made his fortune," I suggested.

"Of that I have no hope," she returned dolefully, "and I shall put him out of my thoughts if I can, as soon as I can."

"It must be done now," I returned emphatically.

"Ay, it is easy to say 'now,' but 'now' is a hard, hard time. It is much easier to do a difficult thing to-morrow. But do not fear, Baron Ned. It shall be done, and I shall marry a duke or an earl, loathing him."

She was almost ready to weep, so, believing that she would like to be alone, I left her.

Within half an hour she was at home, sitting in a low chair by her father's side, laughing, happy, and beautiful, with that rare, indefinable home charm a woman may have which is as far beyond the mere beauty of hair and skin and eyes as the sparkle of a bright mysterious star is beyond the beauty of the moon's pale sheen.

With all my cousin's marvellous beauty, her rarest charm lay in her gracious manner, her unobtrusive vivacity, and her quaint combination of Sarah's Machiavellian wisdom with the intense femininity of Eve. Add to these qualities the unmistakable mark which a pure heart leaves on the face, and we complete the picture of one who in a short time was acknowledged to be without a peer in Whitehall, the most famous beauty court the world has ever known.

Before I left Sundridge it had been agreed among us all that Frances should go to London, though the plans had not been arranged nor the time fixed. There was no need of haste, as the choosing of the maids would not be closed for two months or more. I left with my uncle funds necessary for the purchase of gowns, and the payment of other expenses, and, with his consent, undertook to notify the Duchess of York that Frances would seek to enter her Grace's service in the near future. Then I went back to London, and when next I saw my cousin it was in the shadow of a tragedy.

My uncle's humble friend, Roger Wentworth, the leather merchant of Sundridge, had a brother living in London, who was also a leather merchant, Sir William Wentworth. He had been Lord Mayor at one time, and had been knighted by the king because of a loan made by the city to his Majesty. Sir William was an honest, simple man, who cared little to rise above his class, but he had a wife who thrilled to the heart whenever she heard the words "Lady Wentworth," and experienced a spasm of delight whenever she saw her name in the news letters or journals.

Sir William had a son, also, who imagined himself to be ornamental, but laid no claim to usefulness of any sort. Lady Wentworth concurred heartily and proudly in her son's opinion of himself and encouraged his uselessness to a point where it became worthlessness. But Sir William took no pains to conceal his disappointment and disgust. Young William held a small post at court, and, being supplied with money by his mother, was one of the evil spirits of the set composed of Crofts, Berkeley, Little Jermyn, the court lady-killer, and others too numerous and too vicious to mention. Wentworth was goose to these pluckers and was willing to give his feathers in exchange for their toleration.

*   *   *   *   *

Shortly after I left Sundridge, Sir Richard learned that Roger intended journeying to London in the course of a month to buy leather, so he asked him to take Frances with him. To this request Roger gladly and proudly assented. He usually travelled a-horseback to London, but this being a state occasion, he brought out his old coach, a huge lumbering concern, and had it painted a brilliant green in honor of his fair passenger-to-be. Roger also promised Frances the services of his sister-in-law with the Duchess of York, a help so great, in Roger's opinion, that it could not be over-estimated.

I had been at home more than a month before Frances started on her journey. I did not know when she expected to leave Sundridge, as we had agreed that she should notify me as soon as she reached London.

I had seen George on several occasions after my return from Sundridge, and although he said little about himself, I knew from others that he was at least trying to quit his old way of life and to avoid his evil friends. Soon after my return to court he went to France, and I did not see him again for several months, although he came home, most unfortunately, and spent a day or two in London at the time of Frances's arrival, of which he knew nothing until after his return to France.

All that took place at Sundridge after I left there and the occurrences on my cousin's journey to London, I learned from her and from Hamilton afterwards, though I shall write them down now in the order of their happening.

Early one morning Roger presented himself at my uncle's house with the huge green coach drawn by two horses so fat that they could hardly breathe, driven by an old servant, Noah Sullivan, who was so fat that at times he could not breathe at all.

The season was fair for travelling, and barring a heavy rain, the road to London would be good. But it had a bad reputation for highwaymen, and no cautious man with anything to lose cared to risk a journey after dark, especially near London, save with a guard. Roger was taking with him a thousand pounds in gold; therefore it was desirable that he and his fair passenger should reach the city before nightfall. To do this with the fat horses, he must start early,—a fact of which Frances had received due notice.

On the appointed morning she was ready when the coach drove up. Her box was placed in the boot, and she took a seat beside her old friend Roger, giving vent to the tears she had held back so bravely while saying good-by to her father and Sarah, who were to move up to London in case she remained at court.

Wheezy old Noah on the box cracked his whip, the fat horses in the traces pulled and grunted, the coach creaked and groaned, the wheels turned and Frances had set forth, a maiden St. George, to fight the dragon of Whitehall, compared to which the old-time monster was but a bleating lamb. Roger had hoped to be in his brother's house long before sundown, but when he reached that justly famous halfway house, the Cock and Spur, Noah insisted that the fat horses were so badly winded that a rest of several hours was necessary before they could proceed a step farther. Roger argued with his Master of Horse, but to no purpose. The fat horses rested till near the hour of five, when Noah yielded to his master's importunities and the journey was resumed. Meantime an unexpected rain had begun to fall, which increased in violence as night approached. The road grew heavier as the journey progressed, and the wheezy horses required rest so frequently that Roger began to fear for the safety of his gold and his fair passenger.

Supper time approached, but Roger was so anxious to reach London before dark that he asserted his right as master and refused to stop at an inn where Noah had drawn up the horses, insisting that they be fed. Considerable time was lost in argument with Noah, but at last they took the road once

Charles Major

more, which by that time had become very heavy. Night fell without twilight, because of the storm, and the travellers were overtaken by darkness just as they reached the most dangerous part of the road within less than a league of London.

The road grew heavier with every turn of the wheels, the horses wheezed dismally, and Roger groaned inwardly. He kept his head out of the coach door most of the time, looking for trouble, and found it before his journey's end. Noah lighted the great lanthorn and hung it in front of the dashboard, his only cause of anxiety being the horses, until a greater arose.

CHAPTER III

IT IS HARD TO BE GOOD

There is an infernal charm about sin which should have been given to virtue, but unluckily got shifted in very early human days. And so it was that George Hamilton had troubles of his own in this respect. When he left Frances Jennings at Sundridge, he was aglow with good resolutions, all of which were to be put into immediate practice, and many of which he carried out in part by strong though spasmodic effort when he returned to court.

His attempts to be decent at first filled his friends with surprise, then disgust, then raillery. The untoward thing had never been tried at Charles II's Whitehall, and it furnished a deal of talk between routine scandals. In fact, it was looked upon as a scandal in itself.

This new phase in one of the king's own subdevils soon fell under the notice of his Majesty, who asked George one day if he would like to have an easy benefice in the church where he could meditate on his past and build for the future.

"And pray for Lady Castlemain's unbaptized children, your Majesty?" asked George, whereupon the king shrugged his shoulders and turned away. Lady Castlemain and Charles were—well, there had been talk about them, to say the least.

The court ladies laughed when George declined to drink himself drunk or refused to help his former companions fleece a stranger. Nell Gwynn told him that even his language had grown too polite for polite society, and, lacking emphasis, was flat as stale wine. In truth, it may well be said that George had set out to mend his ways under adverse conditions. But he *had* set out to do it, and that in itself was a great deal, for there is a likable sort of virtue in every good intent. He had reached the first of the three great R's in the act of repentance, Recognition; Regret and Recession being the second and third—all necessary to regeneration. I had faith in his good intentions, but doubted his ability.

Hamilton and I had become fast friends, and by his help my suit of his sister Mary had prospered to the extent of a partial engagement of marriage. That is to say, Mary's mother, an old worldling of the hardest type, had thought it well to secure me and to keep me dangling, to be landed in case no better fish took the hook. I was aware of the mother's selfish purposes, but did not believe that Mary shared them, though I knew her to be an obedient child. This peculiar condition of affairs somewhat nettled me, though I do not remember that I was at all unhappy because of it.

But to come back to George. One day, a fortnight before Frances's arrival in London, while he and I were watching the royal brothers, King Charles and the Duke of York, playing pall-mall, I expressed my doubts and fears of his ultimate success in reformation so long as he remained in any way associated with Crofts, Berkeley, Wentworth, and others of the vicious clique.

"Yes, I know it is an uphill journey," returned George, laughing with a touch of bitterness, "but think of my reward if I succeed!"

"Do you mean my cousin?" I asked.

"Yes, but I have little hope," he replied, though perhaps he had more hope than he expressed.

I had told him of her intention to come to London, hoping that he would leave before her arrival, as he did, though neither he nor I knew when she was coming. So I asked:—

"Don't you know that she will be carried off by some rich lord before you are half good enough for her?"

"I suppose so," he answered, with a sigh.

"You must know that she is coming for that purpose," I returned, wishing to take all hope out of him.

He winced perceptibly and answered after a long pause, nodding his head in the direction of the king: "There is the only man I fear—the king. But rather than see her the victim of any man, by God, I'll kill him, though it cost me my life the next moment!"

I was touched by the new light in which I saw him and took his arm in friendliness as I said, "I judged you wrongfully at Sundridge."

"You were right," he answered impatiently. "You awakened in me not only a sense of my duty to Frances, but a knowledge of my obligation to myself."

"But are you so sure of my cousin, even barring other men?" I asked, hoping to sow the seeds of doubt.

"Yes," he answered, with emphasis. "As sure as a man may be in such a case."

"Well, George," said I, "it warms my heart to say that I hope you will gain wealth, station, and mode of life worthy of her, and that in the end you may win her. My candid opinion is, however, that you will have to do it quickly. She will accept none of these creatures at court, of that you may be sure, but there are many worthy gentlemen in England who are rich and of great name, who have business at court and will see her and want her. There is Dick Talbot, Duke of Tyrconnel. He is a fine fellow, enormously rich, and—"

"A mere lump of meat," interrupted Hamilton, angrily. "She could not love him."

"No," I answered. "Nor do I think she will try. But it is better in the long run that a woman respect a man, not loving him, than to love, despising him. Respect is likely to last; all sorts of love may die. But in any case it is Frances's intention to marry a fortune for her father's sake, even though she has to close her eyes in doing it."

"I'll try to prevent that misfortune," he answered gloomily. "But if she learns to love a man worthy of her, I shall take myself out of her way forever. Let us stand together, Baron Ned, and help this girl to happiness for life, without respect to myself. You see I'm not all bad. In truth, I am becoming self-righteous. I have left the ranks of the publicans and sinners and have become a Pharisee. I tell you, Baron Ned, nothing so swells a man in the chest as the belief that he is not as other men are."

His righteousness, at least, was not devoid of bitterness, and it is possible that a part of his aversion to his former friends and to the king grew out of his jealousy of them for Frances's sake.

"There is no good reason why you should allow your righteousness to become offensive, as that of the ranter, who hates rather than pities iniquity because, in his opinion, God is a God of vengeance," I suggested ironically. "But rather let your virtues grow as the rose unfolds and—"

"Oh, be damned to your raillery! I'm not going to be too decent!" he retorted, finding nothing to amuse him in my remark. Nor did he become too decent, as will appear all too soon.

If, for a time, Hamilton's life did not conform to our desires, we must not condemn him too harshly, for the evil which we try to throw off clings like a bur, while the good we would keep must be tied on. Thus much I say in anticipation. In the end he gained the battle with himself, though his victory won him the king's hatred, put his life in jeopardy, and brought him misfortune such as he had never before known.

Soon after the foregoing conversation, George went to Paris and remained a few days with King Louis, whom he had known since early youth. His evil star brought him back to London the day before Frances left Sundridge, though, he knew nothing of her departure. I did not know of his return, nor did I know of his remote connection with the terrible events attending her arrival till long after they happened.

*   *   *   *   *

While Frances, Roger, and the fat horses were struggling through the mud, the darkness, and the rain, a band of congenial spirits were gathered about the huge fireplace in the taproom of the Leg Tavern in King Street, Westminster, a stone's throw from Whitehall Palace. There was my Lord Berkeley, the king's especial crony, who possessed all his royal master's vices without any of his Majesty's meagre virtues. He imitated the king in dress, manner, cut of beard, and even in the use of Charles's favorite oath, "Odds fish!" an expletive too inane even to be wicked, being a distortion of the words "God's flesh." There was young Crofts, the king's acknowledged son, Duke of Monmouth by grace of his mother's frailties. He was a living example of the doctrine of total depravity in what purported to be a man. There was John Churchill, a very decent fellow in a politic way, though in bad company. He afterward married my laconic cousin Sarah, whose shrewdness made him the first Duke of Marlborough, and last, I regret to chronicle, was George Hamilton, resting from his labors at self-reform. Soon after dark another congenial spirit, the most pusillanimous of them all, young William Wentworth, Sir William's son and Roger's nephew, entered the taproom dripping with rain. Before going to the fire, he called Crofts and Berkeley to one side. Placing his arms about their necks, he drew their faces close to his and made the following remarkable communication in a low whisper:—

"At the supper table, to-night, my worthy sire let slip the information that my good uncle of Sundridge had been expected this afternoon. He had not arrived when I left home fifteen minutes ago, but probably is stuck in the mud a mile or two outside of London on the St. Albans road."

"Let him stick! What is it to us?" asked Crofts.

"Thus much it is to me," answered Wentworth. "He has with him a thousand pounds in gold, while I, his gentleman nephew, have not a jacobus to my name. Now the question becomes one of mere humanity. Shall we allow my good uncle to stick in the mud, or shall we sally forth like good Samaritans, relieve him of a part of his load, and make travelling easier for the dear old man?"

"As men and Christians, we must hasten to his help," declared Crofts.

"But how about Hamilton and Churchill?" asked Berkeley, whose courage was not of the quality to make a good highwayman. "Crofts has invited them here for a feast with us. How shall we get rid of them? Hamilton has become a mere milksop, and Churchill always was too cautious and politic for this sort of a game. Not only will they refuse to go with us if we tell them of our purpose, but they will try to keep us from going."

"Let us take them with us," suggested Crofts. "They won't go if we tell them our purpose, but they will not peach if we take them with us upon some other excuse. We'll walk ahead of them, and—but come with me to the fire. I have a plan. All I ask you to do, Wentworth, is to shake out your cloak, hang it before the fire, and speak of the rain and the bad night outside. I'll do the rest! I'll fetch them! Come!"

Laughing boisterously, the three swaggered over to Hamilton and Churchill, who were sitting by the fireside. Wentworth took off his coat, held it before the blaze to dry, and said, with a terrible oath:—

"Bad night without! Never saw it rain so hard! Raw and cold for this time of the year!"

Crofts ordered a fresh bowl of Rack punch; then, turning to Wentworth, asked:—

"Raining? Who cares for a little rain? I like to be out in it. By the way, I have a wager to offer! Ten pounds to the man to the table; winner to take the lump!"

"Hear! Hear!" cried everybody.

"Let us all walk out on the St. Albans road without our cloaks, the last man to turn homeward wins the entire stake."

"Good!" shouted Wentworth. "I must owe my ten pounds to the pot until to-morrow."

"And I'll take the wager! Here's my money!" said Berkeley, throwing ten pounds to the table.

"Will you go?" asked Crofts, addressing Hamilton.

That evening George was in a mood for any adventure having action in it, for he was nearly out of money. He did not suspect the real purpose of the absurd wager, and after a moment's consideration of the forty pounds to be won, declared:—

"I'll win the pot if I have to go to Edinburgh!"

"And you, Churchill?" asked Crofts.

"You're a pack of fools, but I'll go," replied Churchill, knocking the ashes from his pipe.

They drank their bowl of punch and immediately set off for the St. Albans road.

"The Oxford road is nearer than the St. Albans. Why not take it?" asked George.

"You said you were going to Edinburgh," returned Wentworth, "and, besides, the St. Albans road is our wager, and that is the one we'll take, unless you want to turn back and forfeit your stake."

To the St. Albans road they started, Crofts, Berkeley, and

Wentworth walking perhaps two hundred yards in advance of Churchill and Hamilton. The rain was pouring down in torrents, and the night was so dark that Hamilton and Churchill could not see the advance guard, though they heard a deal of talking, laughing, and cursing ahead of them. This order of march was what Crofts and his friends desired, for of course the wager was not on their minds. They were hoping for something greater, and would have been glad to release Churchill and Hamilton had they offered to turn back. But lacking that good fortune, the valiant three evidently hoped to meet the coach and rob it before the others came up, in which case Crofts and his friends would deny the robbery, if accused, and would divide the gold into three parts instead of five.

When nearly two miles from the city, Crofts, Berkeley, and Wentworth met Roger's coach and delivered the attack as silently as possible. Just the manner in which it was done I have never learned, since Hamilton himself did not know the particulars of it, and Frances told me it happened so quickly that it was over almost before she knew it had begun. She said the horses had stopped, which was not a matter of surprise to her, as they had been resting every few minutes, and that a man wearing a mask entered the coach, rummaged the cushions, and was backing out with the bag of gold in his hand when Roger seized him.

The robber was almost out of the coach, but Roger clung to him with one hand while he drew his pistol with the other and fired. Then the man tossed the bag of gold to one of his friends on the road, drew his sword, thrust it in Roger's breast, and the poor old man fell back on the coach floor at my cousin's feet. She heard some one call to Noah: "Drive on if you value a whole skin!" and Noah, awaiting no second command, lashed the horses with his whip until they plunged forward at a clumsy gallop.

Hamilton and Churchill, being perhaps two hundred yards down the road, knew nothing of the trouble ahead till they heard the pistol shot, when they ran forward, supposing their drunken friends were fighting among themselves. They had not taken many steps when a coach passed them, moving rapidly. As it passed, George heard a woman scream faintly, but immediately the coach dashed out of sight. The light from Noah's lanthorn had fallen on Hamilton's face, and Frances had recognized the man of whom she had been thinking and dreaming all day.

I did not know, however, till long afterwards that she had seen him, nor did he suspect that she was in the coach.

When Hamilton and Churchill came up to the robbers, Hamilton asked:—

"What was the trouble?"

"The damned old fool in the coach shot at me," answered Crofts.

"How came he to do it?" asked Churchill, suspecting the truth.

"I do not know," returned Wentworth. "He must have taken us for highwaymen, for he thrust his head out of the door and fired a pistol at Crofts, who was nearest the coach."

"Yes," said Crofts. "And he was about to fire again, point blank at my head, when I drew my sword and quieted him. Matters have come to a pretty pass when gentlemen can't walk out on the public road without becoming a target for every frightened fool that travels in a coach. I'll learn who this fellow is, and will see that he becomes acquainted with the interior of Newgate or dangles to a rope on Tyburn."

"Shall we declare the wager off?" asked Wentworth, turning to Churchill and Hamilton.

"By all means," answered Churchill.

All being willing to return, they started back to London, Wentworth, Berkeley, and Crofts falling behind. The story they had told was not convincing, but when Hamilton expressed his doubts to Churchill and intimated his belief that a robbery, if not a murder, had been committed, Churchill answered cautiously:—

"Perhaps you are right, but the less we know or think or say about this affair, the better it will be for you and me. As for myself, I shall leave London for a while to avoid being called as a witness in case the matter is investigated. If we try to bring these fellows to justice, they may turn upon us and swear that we did the deed, in which case we might hang, for they are three to two; a good preponderance of testimony. But in any case the king would see that no evil befell his son and his friends. Therefore if we are wise, we shall remain silent and take ourselves out of the way for the time being."

The next day, as I afterwards learned, George made the mistake of returning to France, not that he feared punishment for himself, but because he did not want to speak the unavailing truth and thereby bring upon himself the king's wrath, nor did he want to bear false witness to protect the criminals.

Near the hour of ten o'clock that night, Noah drew up the fat panting horses before Sir William's house. The porter, who had been watching all day, opened the gate, the coach entered the courtyard, Noah uttered a hoarse "Whoa!" and almost fell off the box to the ground. As soon as he could get on his feet again, he went to the coach door, spoke to Frances, ran to Sir William, who was waiting at the top of the house steps, candle in hand, to welcome Roger, and spoke but one word: "Dead!"

Frances hurriedly came from the coach, and Sir William went to meet her. Holding out her hands to him, she cried:—

"Oh, Sir William, they have killed your brother! Robbed him and killed him!"

Frances was incoherently explaining to Sir William when Lady Wentworth came down the steps and led her into the house. Then the doors were opened wide, and poor old Roger's body was carried reverently to the best parlor.

The following morning, when I was notified that Frances was at Sir William's house, I went to see her and learned the particulars of the tragedy, though she said nothing at that time about having recognized any of the highwaymen, and seemed strangely reluctant to talk about the affair.

On the fourth day after Roger's death he was buried in Saint-Martin's-in-the-Fields churchyard, good Sir William taking the only means in his power to express his love for his brother by an elaborate funeral. Never were there more beautiful hatchments seen in London. They bore Roger's humble coat-of-arms, half in white and half in black, to denote that the deceased had left a widow. Never were there more nor finer white mourning scarfs distributed among the mourners, and never in the memory of man had so much burnt sherry been served at a funeral.

These extraordinary arrangements attracted a great deal of attention throughout London and caused Roger's murder to be talked about far and near. The result of this publicity was that the city authorities set on foot an investigation which soon brought Wentworth, Crofts, and Berkeley under suspicion. The sheriffs, however, kept their suspicions to themselves, and I heard only faint whispers of what was going on.

After the funeral Lady Wentworth invited Frances to be her guest for a week or two, and upon my advice the invitation was accepted.

Two or three days after the funeral, while Frances and I were walking out together, she complained of young Wentworth's attentions.

"To-day he put his arm about me," she said, laughing, though indignant.

"And what did you say and do?" I asked.

"I simply remarked that I disliked the touch of half-witted persons, whereupon he declared that he had wit enough to be offended. Then I told him he should thank heaven for the small favor and pray God to help him use it."

After cautioning her to secrecy, I told her of the ugly whispers that were abroad connecting young Wentworth, Crofts, and Berkeley with the murder of old Roger.

"No, no!" she cried, greatly agitated. "I saw the two men who did it. I saw them in the light of Noah's lanthorn. Neither of them was young Wentworth."

I at once grew interested and asked her to describe the men she saw.

"No, no, no!" she cried vehemently, almost hysterically. I

thought she was going to weep, so I said in haste:—

"Don't weep, Frances! You must forget."

She looked quickly up to me and answered: "I am not weeping. There is not a tear in me. I have wept until I am dry."

"But your grief is unreasonable," I returned. "Roger was your friend, I know, but his death does not call for so great sorrowing."

"No, no, it is not that, Baron Ned. You don't know. I can't tell you. Please do not speak of this terrible affair again."

I supposed it was her horror of the tragedy that had wrought upon her nerves, usually so strong, so I dropped the subject, and it was not brought up again until after many weeks, when circumstances made it necessary for me to break silence.

*   *   *   *   *

While Hamilton was away, the murder of Roger Wentworth was freely discussed in London and was brought to the king's notice by a deputation of citizens who told his Majesty very plainly that certain of his friends were under suspicion.

The king pretended that he had not heard of the crime, expressed his grief, was moved to tears by the recital, promised to do all in his power to bring the offenders to justice, and dismissed the Londoners with many brave, virtuous words. As soon as they were gone, he joined a cluster of friends, among whom were Crofts, Wentworth, and Berkeley, to whom he repeated, with many witticisms, the complaints of the city delegation. With what he thought was fine comedy, he reiterated his firm determination to bring the criminals to justice with despatch that should have nothing of the law's delay. Closing his remarks on the subject, he said with a wink and an affected air of severity:—

"Gentlemen, I insist that you make an effort to be more careful of my tanners in your frolics. Even tanners' hides have their uses. Waste them not! Again I say, waste them not!"

"Not even for a thousand pounds, Rowley?" asked Crofts.

"Ah, well, of course, a thousand pounds is—well, it is a thousand pounds," answered the king, laughing.

It may be surmised from the king's words and manner that he intended taking no steps to bring the offenders to justice, and that he knew who they were. The London people soon discovered his real intent and began in earnest on their own account.

When the net began to draw too closely about the culprits, the king interfered and gave the London courts of justice to understand that further proceedings against Wentworth, Crofts, and Berkeley would cause a royal frown. The Londoners were not willing to drop the matter, even at the risk of royal displeasure, so the king caused it to be hinted to the London officials that Crofts, Berkeley, and Wentworth were innocent, but that possibly Hamilton was the guilty man. No mention was made of Churchill, he being at the time the Duke of York's most intimate friend.

Hamilton was away from home and was friendless, all of which gave his accusers the courage to fix suspicion on him, though they did so without taking the responsibility of making the charge themselves.

So it was that when George returned to England, several weeks later, he found trouble awaiting him in many forms.

$$* \quad * \quad * \quad * \quad *$$

My cousin's presentation to the duchess was made in private and was a success in every respect. I asked Mary Hamilton to accompany Lady Wentworth, Frances, and myself on this occasion, and she graciously consented. Lady Wentworth insisted on making the presentation, so one morning I called for my cousin and her chaperone, took the Wentworth barge at Blackfriars water stairs, and proceeded by river up to Westminster stairs, where we disembarked. I left my companions in a bookstall in the Abbey and went to fetch Mary, who lived near by in a house called Little Hamilton House, under the shadow of Great Hamilton House, which was the home of Count Anthony.

Mary was waiting for me, so she and I hastened to the bookstall, took up Frances and Lady Wentworth, went back to the barge, and then by water to Whitehall Garden stairs. There we left the river, walked to the Palace, and proceeded immediately to the parlor of her Grace, the Duchess of York, whom we met by appointment.

When we entered her Grace's parlor, she rose, came to meet us, paused for a moment, gave one glance to Frances, and, without a word of presentation, offered her hand to my cousin, saying:—

"I need no introduction to Mistress Jennings. Her beauty has been heralded, and I know her. I understand she wishes to do me the grace of becoming one of my maids of honor?"

"Yes, madam," returned Frances, kneeling and kissing her Grace's hand. "I hope you may do me the grace of accepting my poor services."

"Oh, do not kneel to me here among ourselves," said the duchess, smiling graciously. "It is you who grant the favor, and, without more ado, I heartily welcome you to our family."

Thus, almost before she knew it, Frances's beauty had won, as we had been sure it would, and she was a maid of honor in Whitehall Palace to her Grace, the Duchess of York, sister-in-law to the king.

"The Mother of the Maids will instruct you in your duties, chief of which you will find easy enough, that is, to be beautiful," said the duchess, taking a chair and indicating that we were to be seated.

Frances, Mary, and Lady Wentworth took chairs, but nothing short of a broken leg or tottering age would have justified me in accepting the invitation to sit.

"Before I send for the Mother of the Maids," said the duchess, graciously, "let us talk a few minutes about ourselves and other people."

Her suggestion being taken by silent consent, she asked Lady Wentworth about Sir William's health and was graciously inquisitive concerning many of her Ladyship's personal affairs, to her Ladyship's infinite delight. She talked to Mary and to me for a moment, and then turned to Frances, of whom she asked no personal questions, but spoke rather of her Grace's own affairs and of life at court, dropping now and then many valuable hints that had no appearance of being instructions.

Presently her Grace said, "Now we have talked about

ourselves, let us talk about other people."

We all laughed, and Frances inquired, "Will your Grace kindly tell us whom we may abuse and whom praise?"

"Oh, abuse anybody—everybody. Praise only the very young, the very old and the halt; abuse all able-bodied adults, and laugh at any one in whom you see anything amusing," answered the duchess.

"Not the king and—" laughed Frances.

"The king!" interrupted her Grace, with a tone of contempt in her voice. "Every one laughs at him. He's the butt of the court. Do you know his nickname?"

"No," returned Frances.

"Yes, yes," interrupted Lady Wentworth, laughing nervously. She did not want to be left out of the conversation entirely, so she chimed in irrelevantly.

"We call him Old Rowley in honor of the oldest, wickedest horse in the royal mews," said the duchess, laughing. "You need not restrain yourself. Soon every one at court will be talking about you, the men praising your beauty, and insinuating ugly stories about your character, and the women wondering how any one can admire your doll's face or find any wit in what you say. Remember that the ordinary rule of law that one is deemed innocent until proved guilty is reversed in Whitehall. Here one is deemed guilty till one proves one's self innocent, and that is a difficult task. Ah, my! It has been many a day since we have had any convincing proof! Eh, Lady Wentworth?"

"Yes, yes, your Grace! Many a day, many a day! Ah, we are

a sad, naughty court, I fear," answered my Lady, with a penitent sigh. Her chief desire was to be a modish person; therefore she would not be left out of the iniquitous monde, though her face, if nothing else, placed her safely beyond the pale of Whitehall sin. One of the saddest things in life is to be balked in an honest desire to be wicked!

"Yes, you won't know yourself when your character comes back to you, filtered through many mouths," said the duchess, laughing. "But don't take offence; retaliate!"

"My cousin will have to learn the art, your Grace," I suggested.

"Ah, I have a thought!" cried the duchess, turning to Frances. "Nothing succeeds like novelty here at court. Be novel. Don't abuse people save to their faces, but don't spare any one then. Remember that a biting epigram is the best loved form of wit among us Sodomites. We love it for its own sake, but more for the pain it gives the other fellow. We like to see him squirm, and we have many a joyous hour over our friends' misfortunes. Turn yourself into a mental bodkin, and you will find favor among us, for it is better to be feared than loved in our happy family."

"Ah, how beautiful!" cried Lady Wentworth, determined to be heard, even though never addressed.

"But as I have said," continued the duchess, "try, if you can, to be novel, and be a bodkin only to the victim's face, save, of course, in the case of a new bit of racy scandal. That must be used to the greatest advantage as soon as possible, for scandal, like unsalted butter, will not keep."

The duchess laughed, as though speaking in jest, but she was in earnest and spoke the truth.

"But I must learn the current faults of my friends-to-be," suggested Frances, laughing, "so that I may not fall into the unpardonable error of repeating an old story. Stale scandal is doubtless an offence in the ear of the Anointed."

The Anointed was the king.

"That is true," returned the duchess, seriously. "Old scandals bore him, but if, by good fortune, a rich new bit comes your way, save it for our Rowley, whisper it in his ear and forget it. Leave to him the pleasure of disseminating it. He dearly loves the 'ohs' and 'ahs' of delight incident to the telling of a racy tale. But I'll take you in hand one of these days and tell you how best to please the king, though your beauty will make all other means mere surplusage. To please the king, you need but be yourself; to please my husband, the duke, is even an easier task. He is everybody's friend. They will be wanting to divorce the queen and me for your sake. Two such fools about pretty women the world has never known before and I hope never will again. To see the two royal brothers ogling and smiling and smirking is better than a play. I used to be disgusted, but now it amuses me. So if my husband makes love to you, don't fear that I shall be offended, and if the king makes love to you, as he surely will, have no fear of the queen. She is used to it."

"I shall try to please every one," said Frances.

"No, no, no!" cried the duchess. "That would be your ruin! A dog licks the hand that smites it. We're all dogs. Every failure I have known at court has come from too great a desire to please."

Frances laughed uneasily, for she knew she was hearing the truth, disguised as a jest. After a moment's silence, she asked:—

"May I not at least try to please your Grace? And may I not seek your advice and thank you now and then for a reprimand?"

"Yours is the first request of the sort I have ever heard from a maid of honor, and I shall take you at your word," said the duchess. "I'm not posing as the head of a morality school, but if I may, I shall try to be your guide."

Lady Wentworth was almost comatose with pride—"pride on the brain" Frances afterwards called it.

Presently her Grace continued seriously. "The king will make love to you on sight. If he fails in obtaining a satisfactory response, he may affect to be offended for a few days, during which time my husband may try his hand. Failing, he will smile and will withdraw to make room for Rowley's return attack. Rowley's return will be in earnest, and then will come your trial, for the whole court will fawn upon you, will lie about you, and beg your favor for them with the king."

"Surely it is a delightful prospect," returned my cousin, smiling.

"Oh, delightful, delightful!" ejaculated Lady Wentworth in a semilucid interval.

"Now I'll send for the Mother of the Maids," said her Grace, "who will show you to your rooms and instruct you in the duties, forms, and ceremonies of court. I suppose you dance the country dances. They are the king's favorites. He calls the changes."

"Yes, your Grace," answered Frances.

"And the brantle and the coranto?" asked the duchess.

"Yes, your Grace."

"And do you play cards?"

"Yes, your Grace, but I loathe games."

"Ah, I see you're equipped," said the duchess. "But here comes the Mother of the Maids."

The duchess presented Frances to the Mother, who presently led her forth across the threshold of a new life, destined to be filled with many strange happenings.

After leaving the Duchess of York, Frances and the Mother of the Maids entered the Stone Gallery, half the length of which they would have to traverse before reaching the door that entered the narrow corridor leading to the apartments of the maids of honor. Midway in the gallery, a man, evidently in wine, accosted Frances without so much as removing his hat.

"Ah, ah! Whom have we here?" he asked, winking to the Mother of the Maids.

Frances was astonished and a little frightened, but she soon brought herself together and retorted:—

"What is it to you, sir, whom we have here?"

At once it occurred to Frances that the impertinent man was either the king or the duke, but she hid her suspicion.

"Much it is to me, fair mistress," returned the gentleman, taking off his hat and bowing. "The sun shines for all, and when one dare be as beautiful as yourself, all men may bask in the radiance and may ask, 'What new luminary is this?'"

"You may bask to your heart's content," retorted Frances, laughing, "but you must know that it does not please the sun to be stopped by an unprepossessing stranger."

The Mother's face bore a look of consternation, and the gentleman threw back his head, laughing uproariously.

"Ah, my beauty, but I would not remain a stranger. If I am unprepossessing, it is because I am as God made me and I cannot help it. But I can help being a stranger to you and would make myself known, and would present my compliments to—"

"To the devil, who perhaps may like your impertinence better than I like it," retorted Frances, turning from him angrily and hastening toward the opposite end of the gallery.

When Frances reached the door of the corridor, she looked back and saw the Mother of the Maids listening attentively to the gentleman. He was laughing heartily, and when the Mother left him, Frances noticed that she courtesied almost to the floor, a ceremony little used save with the king, the queen, the duke, and the duchess.

When the door of the gallery was closed behind Frances, she asked the Mother:—

"Who is the impudent fellow?"

"He? Why, he—is—why, he is Sir Rowley," answered the Mother, hesitatingly, and Frances knew that she had won her first round with the king, though she kept her knowledge to herself.

CHAPTER IV

A SMILE AT THE DEVIL

In the evening the duchess gave a little ball in her parlor to present Frances to the king and to the queen, if her Majesty should attend, to the Duke of York, and to others living in Whitehall immediately connected with the palace household.

I went to the ball early, wishing to be there before Frances arrived, to help her if need be over the untrodden paths of court forms and etiquette. Soon after I entered her Grace's parlor, Mary Hamilton came in with her mother, and I joined them. I should have been glad to see a gleam of joy in Mary's eyes when I approached, but I had to be content with a calm, gracious "I'm glad to see you, baron."

Presently the Duke of York arrived with the duchess on his arm, and they took their places at the end of the room opposite the musicians' gallery. Mary and I hastened to kiss their hands, and, withdrawing to a little distance, awaited Frances's arrival. After the others in the room had paid their respects to her Grace, she beckoned me to her chair and said:—

"Your cousin will arrive presently. I have just seen her. Look for a sensation when she comes. She is radiant, though her gown is as simple as a country girl's."

"I hear you have brought us a great beauty, baron," remarked the duke.

"Yes, your Highness. We who love her think so," I answered.

"You'll be wanting to be made an earl for your service in bringing her, eh, baron?" said the duke, laughing. Then bending toward me and whispering: "A word in your ear, Clyde. You may have it if you play your cards right and are persistent in importunity."

"No, your Highness. I ask for nothing save favor to my cousin," I replied.

"She is like to have enough of that and to spare, without asking, if she is half as beautiful as she is said to be," returned his Grace.

"Of that your Highness may now be your own judge," I returned. "Here she comes."

At that moment Frances entered on the arm of the Mother of the Maids, and the duke, catching sight of her, exclaimed:—

"God have pity on the other women! Half has not been told, baron. There is no beauty at court compared to hers. Earl? You may be a duke!"

While Frances and the Mother were making their way across the room to pay their respects to the duke and the duchess, a buzz of admiration could be heard on every hand, and Mary whispered to me behind her fan:—

"If the king were unmarried, I would wager all I have that

your cousin would be our queen within a month."

Count Grammont, who was standing behind me, leaned forward and whispered, "Your cousin, baron?"

"Yes, count," I answered.

"Mon Dieu!" he returned, shrugging his shoulders. "You will soon be a duke. We may not call her the queen of hearts, for already we have one, but surely she is the duchess of hearts. I wish I might present her in Paris. Ah Dieu! She would make quickly my peace with my king!"

Poor Grammont's one object in life was that his peace might be made with his king. He lived only in the hope of a recall to Versailles.

Frances made a graceful courtesy, as she kissed their Highness's hands, and, when the brief ceremony of presentation to the duke was over, turned to Mary and me, glad to have a moment's respite beside us. She said nothing, but I could see that for the moment the gorgeous scene about us had bewildered her. The vast mouldings of gold, the frescoed cupids, nymphs and goddesses, the wonderful paintings, the brilliant tapestries, all fairly shone in the light of a thousand wax candles, while the polished floor of many-colored woods was a mirror under her feet, reflecting all this beauty.

The powdered and rouged courtiers, arrayed in silks, gold lace and jewels, seemed more like creatures from a land of phantasy than beings of flesh and blood. The men with their great curled wigs, their plumed, bejewelled hats and glittering gold swords, seemed to have stepped from the pages of a wonderful picture-book, and the women, whose gorgeous gowns exposed their bepowdered skin halfway to their waists, measuring from the chin, and whose lifted petticoats made a proportionate display, measuring from the feet, surely were brought from some fair land of folly and shame.

I touched Frances's hand to awaken her, and whispered: "Show neither wonder nor interest. See nothing, or these fools about us will laugh."

She laughed nervously, nodding her head to tell me that she understood.

"But I must look. I can't help it," she said.

"You must see it all without looking," I suggested, and Mary helped me out by saying:—

"It is all tinsel, not worth looking at. That is the quality of all you will see at court; gold foil, king and all."

Presently I saw the gentlemen removing their hats and tucking them under their arms, so I knew the king had entered, and felt sure he would soon come up to salute his hostess, the duchess, near whom we were standing.

I told Frances that she was about to meet the king, and admonished her to keep a strong heart. She smiled as she answered:—

"I think I have met him already." Then she told us briefly of her encounter with the tipsy gentleman in the Stone Gallery.

She had entirely recovered her self-possession and was prepared to meet calmly the man who was a demigod to millions of English subjects.

The queen did not come with the king, so he loitered a

moment among the courtiers before making his way to the duchess, but the delay was short, and soon he presented himself. The duchess rose when he approached, but hardly allowed him time to finish his bow till she took his arm, turned toward us, and smiled to Frances to approach. I touched my cousin's arm, gently thrusting her forward, and the next moment she was courtesying to the floor before the man who believed, in common with most of his subjects, that he owned by divine right the body and soul of every man in England, together with every man's ox and his ass, his wife and his daughter, and all that to him belonged.

The king raised Frances, still retaining her hand, and bent most gallantly before her.

"I have met Mistress Jennings," said he, smiling, "and she told me to pay my compliments to the devil."

The king laughed, so of course the courtiers who heard him also laughed. Instantly the news spread, and one might have heard on every hand, "The new maid told the king to go to the devil." But as the king seemed to be pleased, the courtiers were, too, and the new maid of honor became a person of distinction at once.

The king's unexpected remark disconcerted Frances for a moment, and her confusion added to her charm. In a moment she recovered herself, courtesied, and said:—

"I beg your Majesty not to remind me of my terrible mistake. I thought you were a bold cavalier, and of course did not know that I was speaking to my king. I offer my humble apology. Pray do not pay your compliments to the devil, but keep them for me, your Majesty's most devoted subject."

"Odds fish!" exclaimed his Majesty. "I'm glad of the

reprieve. I did not want to go to the devil, but Odds fish! I'd be willing to do so for a smile from my most devoted subject."

"Merci, sire!" answered Frances, with a courtesy and smiling as graciously as even a king could ask.

"If my most devoted subject will honor her king by asking him to dance the next coranto with her, he will do his best to make amends for his boldness earlier in the day, for he is naturally a modest king."

"A modest manner and a bold heart, I fear, your Majesty," returned Frances, making the most pleasing compliment she could have paid her sovereign. "May I be honored with your Majesty's hand for the next coranto?"

"It is my will," graciously answered the king.

The ball opened with a brantle which his Majesty danced with the duchess, Frances remaining, meantime, with Mary and me, awaiting the coranto with the king, a royal favor which would win for her the envy of many a lady, as the king seldom danced.

When the brantle was finished, the king worked his way over to Frances, and when the bugle announced the coranto, she was saved the embarrassment of seeking him, as she must have done had he not been by her side.

An altogether unexpected ordeal awaited Frances, for when the French musicians began to play and his Majesty led her out, she found herself and the king the only dancers on the floor except the Duke of York with Mistress Stuart, and the Duke of Monmouth with his father's friend, Lady Castlemain. Every one else stood by the wall, many of the

Charles Major

ladies hoping to see the new maid fail, and all of the gentlemen eager to behold her and to comment.

The coranto is a difficult movement to perform gracefully. It consists of a step forward, a pause during which the dancer balances on one foot, holding the other suspended forward for a moment, then another step, followed by a bow on the gentleman's part and a deep courtesy by the lady.

I confess that I was uneasy, for Frances was a country girl, and the coranto was the most trying, though, if well done, the most beautiful of all dances.

Mary clasped my hand in alarm for Frances and whispered: "I do hope she dances well. The lack of grace in a woman is inexcusable. She had better not dance at all than poorly."

Mary's hopes were realized at once, for the king and Frances had not been on the floor three minutes till the gentlemen began to clap their hands softly, and in a moment a round of applause came from the entire audience, as often happened in those informal balls.

The king turned to Frances, saying: "They are applauding your dancing. Take your bow."

"No, it's all for your Majesty," she returned.

"No, no, my dancing is an old story to them. It is your grace they are applauding."

"Spare me, your Majesty," she pleaded, laughing.

As the applause continued, they stopped dancing for a moment, and Frances made her courtesy to the audience. Thereupon the applause increased, and she courtesied again, kissing her hand as she rose from the floor.

The girl was in high spirits, and laughed as she talked to the king, who smiled on her in a manner that caused my Lady Castlemain to remark:—

"The young milkmaid's affectations are disgusting." Other equally flattering remarks were to be heard from women of the Castlemain stamp, but the men were a unit in praising the new beauty.

Of course the king soon declared his undying love for her, and she answered, laughing:—

"If your Majesty will swear by your grandmother's great toe that you have never before spoken to a woman in this fashion, I'll listen and believe, but failing the oath, you must pardon me if I laugh."

"I hope you would not laugh at your king?" he asked.

"Ay, at the Pope," she retorted, "if I found him amusing."

"But if I swear by the sacred relic you name, never again so long as I live to speak in this fashion to any other woman, may I proceed?" returned the king.

"I would not be a party to an oath whereby my king would be forsworn," she answered.

To which the king replied: "I shall say what I please to my most devoted subject. Am I not the king?"

"I am content that you say what you please if you grant me the same privilege," answered Frances.

The king laughed and said he would gladly grant the privilege in private, but that in public he had a "damnable dignity" to uphold.

* * * * *

After the dancing was over for the evening, the king offered Frances a purse of gold to be used at the card-table, but she declined, and as nearly every one else went to the tables, the duchess granted leave to Frances, Mary, and myself to depart.

Mary and I went with Frances to her parlor adjoining her bedroom, where we remained for an hour or more talking over the events of the night. Mary had heard one in the ballroom say this and another say that. Frances had heard all sorts of remarks, some of them kind, others spiteful. I had heard nothing but praise of my cousin, and all that we had heard was discussed excitedly and commented on earnestly or laughingly, as the case might be.

Frances was in high spirits till by an unlucky chance Mary spoke of her brother George, of whose acquaintance with Frances she knew nothing, and instantly my cousin's eyes began to fill. I saw that the tears would come, despite all her efforts, if something were not done to stay them. Therefore I spoke of her father's joy when he should hear of her triumph, and my remark furnished an excuse for her weeping. In the course of an hour Mary and I left Frances and went to the card-tables, where we found Mary's mother, who at that time, happening to be winner in a large sum, was ready to quit the game, so we all walked home across the park with linkboys.

* * * * *

During the following month or two Hamilton was abroad, neither I nor any one else at court so far as I knew having heard from him. After a time the rumors connecting his name with Roger's death reached my ears, but I paid no heed to them, believing them to have been made of whole cloth, for I did not know that he had been present when the crime was committed. But one day my cousin's actions and words set me thinking.

Roger was only a tanner; therefore after a deal of stir in the matter of his death with no result more tangible than vague insinuations from Crofts and his friends, the investigation by the London authorities was dropped, at least for a time. Roger's tragedy was forgotten or was put aside, save in so far as it was kept alive by Crofts, who felt that it was well to keep the person of George Hamilton as a fender between himself and the crime.

So, as frequently happens when a bad man turns good, Hamilton's troubles began to gather and were awaiting his return. I did not know where he was (though I afterwards learned he was in Paris), and therefore was unable to warn him. In fact, I knew little that was worth telling him at the time of which I am writing, since I did not believe he was really in danger. I did not even know that he was aware of the Roger Wentworth tragedy.

Meantime Frances was making progress at court, of which even I, with all my hopefulness, had little dreamed. What she desired above all else was money for her father. Sir Richard and Sarah had moved up to London to be near Frances and were living in a modest little house at the end of a cul-de-sac called Temple Street, just off the Strand near Temple Bar.

The opportunity to get money soon came to Frances in the form of an offer by the king of a small pension which would

84   Charles Major

have placed her and her father beyond the pale of want. But the king's manner in offering it had caused her to refuse.

She had fallen into the wholesome way of telling me all that occurred touching herself, which during this time consisted chiefly of the efforts of nearly every man of prominence in Whitehall, from the king and the duke to bandylegged Little Jermyn, the lady-killer, to convince her of his desperate passion. She laughed at them all, and her indifference seemed to increase their ardor.

One day Frances met me in the Stone Gallery as I was coming from my lodging in the Wardrobe over the Gate, and asked me to walk out with her. I saw that something untoward had happened, so I joined her and we went to the park. When we were a short way from the palace, she told me of the king's offer and tried to tell me of his manner, the latter evidently having been meant to be understood by Frances in case she wished to see it as he doubtless intended she should. She saw it as the king intended, but the result was far from what he expected.

"I turned my back on him," she said angrily, "and left him without so much as a word or a courtesy, and I intend to leave Whitehall."

"By no means!" I exclaimed. "Accept or refuse the king's pension as you choose, and pass serenely on your way, unconscious of what he may have implied. If you remain at court, you must learn not to see a mere implied affront, and perhaps to smile at many an overt one. Before you came you had full warning of what would happen. Don't see! Don't feel! Don't care! Be true to yourself and smile at the devil if you happen to meet him. He has no weapon against a smile. One escapes many a disagreeable situation by not seeing it, and one always finds trouble by looking for it."

"Your philosophy wearies me," she answered petulantly.

"In that case, I'll confine my remarks to facts and to a mere statement of your duty. You must have money. Accept the king's pension and laugh at him."

"I'll not take your advice," she retorted angrily. "I'll return to my father's house at once. He was right. A decent woman has no business at court."

"Since you speak so plainly, I'll do likewise," I rejoined, growing angry. "You came to court to make your fortune by marriage. That is a bald, ugly way to state the case, but it is the truth. Admit it."

"I fear I must," she answered, hanging her head.

"You surely could not ask greater progress toward your desire than you are making," I continued. "You came into favor at a bound, and have been growing each day, not only with the king, but with all the court, including the queen, the duchess, and the duke. Every one loves you and, better still, respects you, which is a distinction few beautiful women enjoy nowadays. Dick Talbot, the Duke of Tyrconnel, the richest unmarried nobleman in England, is eager to marry you, and would ask you to be his wife if you would but throw him a smile."

"I hate him!" she retorted impatiently. "An overgrown Irish fool. One would as well marry a bull calf!"

"But he is as decent as any man I know, and will meet all your purposes in coming to court in the matter of wealth and station. I don't know that it is a misfortune for a woman to marry a man she can rule."

"Yes, it is," she answered. "She always despises him. I should prefer one who would beat me to such a man."

"But if you intend to carry out the purpose you had in coming to court, you—"

But she interrupted me, speaking slowly, almost musingly: "The purpose I had, perhaps, but not the one I have. I did not know myself. I did not know. I doubt if any girl does. I don't want to marry any man."

"Is it because another man fills your heart?" I asked, speaking gently. "Tell me, my beautiful sister, tell me. I'll find no fault with you. I'll help you if I can."

I received a sigh for my answer, and another and another, as she walked by my side, hanging her head. But when I urged her to speak, she raised her eyes to mine, and there was a cold, angry glint in them as she asked:—

"Do you mean—?"

She did not mention Hamilton's name, but I knew whom she meant and answered:—

"Yes."

A long pause followed, during which I was unable to read the expression on her face, but presently she spoke, her voice trembling with anger or emotion, I knew not which:—

"I hate him! If he were to touch my hand, I believe I should want to cut it off! I hate him—that is, I try to hate him."

Her words and manner caused me uneasiness in two respects: first, it led me to fear that she loved Hamilton; and second, in view of the rumors I had heard connecting his name with Roger Wentworth's death, it flashed upon me that possibly he was the man she had recognized by the light of Noah's lanthorn. Either of these surmises, if true, was enough to mar my peace of mind, but together they brought me trouble indeed.

I had come to look for a speedy accomplishment of my cousin's good fortune, and also to regard Hamilton as my dearest friend among men. Still I was helpless to remedy these evils if they really existed. What I did at the time was to insist, first, that Frances regain her senses as soon as possible, and second, that she say nothing of her intention to leave Whitehall for at least ten days. To my first request she replied that she had never been so completely in possession of her senses as at that present moment, and my second, she positively refused to consider.

The best of women want their way, at least in part, so I said, "I abandon my first request as unreasonable."

She looked up to me, hardly knowing whether to laugh or to frown, but she chose the former, and I continued, "And as to my second suggestion, I amend it to, say, five or six days."

"Three!" she insisted. So we let it stand at that, each with a sense of triumph.

We returned to the palace, and soon I had an opportunity to ask the king for a word privately. He graciously consented, and led me to his closet, overlooking the River Thames. From this closet, on the second floor, a privy stairs led down to a door which opened on a small covered porch at the head of a flight of stone steps falling to the king's private barge landing at the water's edge. When I noticed the narrow stairway, I had no thought of the part it would one day play in the fortunes and misfortunes of Frances, Hamilton, and myself.

On the king's command, I sat down near him, and he asked:—

"What can I do for you, baron? I do not remember your having ever solicited a favor of me, and I shall be delighted to grant what you ask, if I can."

"I seek no favor, your Majesty," I returned. "I simply want to tell you that my cousin, Mistress Jennings, has just informed me of her intention to leave Whitehall, and I wonder—"

"No, no," cried the king, interrupting me. "She shall not go! Why is she discontented here?"

"I am not sure that I can tell your Majesty," I answered evasively. "I am loath to see her go, and, knowing well your kindliness, hoped you would be willing to urge her to remain."

"Gladly," replied the king. "She is the most beautiful ornament of our court, and we must not lose her. I don't mind telling you for your own ear that I suspect the cause of her sudden resolution and respect it."

He laughed, and after a long pause, continued:—

"I forgot that she was fresh from the country, and that she still retained part of her prudish ideas, so while walking with her yesterday on the Serpentine, I offered her a pension, to which she is justly entitled, adorning our court as she does. But I fear she took my honest efforts at gallantry too seriously. My dear baron, the girl shall have her pension without the slightest return on her part save one of her rare smiles now and then. Say to her, please, that the king sends his apology and eagerly awaits an opportunity to offer it in person."

"I thank your Majesty," I answered, rising and bowing, "and feel sure you have done all that is needful to keep my cousin at court. She has certain prudish standards which I fear are too easily shocked, and is as self-willed as—well, as a beautiful woman—"

"Ought to be," interrupted the king, laughing and finishing my sentence.

I wanted him to suspect that his gallant speeches would be repeated to me, hoping that the knowledge might temper them.

After talking a moment longer with him, I asked permission to withdraw, and at once sought Frances. When I found her in the parlor of the duchess, I drew her to one side and told her of my interview with the king.

"You have tamed the lion," I said, "and you may accept the pension without harm to your sensitive dignity. But please don't make a fool of yourself again by taking such a matter seriously. Keep your head, keep your heart, keep your temper, and thrive. Lose either, and have the whole court laughing at you. I'm sorry Hamilton is so fixed in your heart that you cannot dislodge him, but this good may grow out of the evil: you may judge other men dispassionately."

A great sigh was her only answer.

*   *   *   *   *

Frances took my advice, along with the king's pension, and

soon learned that as good wine needs no bush, so true virtue needs no defence.

A brief account of Frances's triumphs and adventures at court is necessary before this history can be brought to the point of Hamilton's return; that is, to the time when I knew he was in London.

Her first great triumph was over the heart of the king, to whose lovemaking she learned to listen and to smile; not the smile of assent, but of amusement.

Soon our august monarch became silly with love of the new beauty, and with her help often made himself ridiculous. On one occasion, a few months after Frances's installation as maid of honor, he left a love note in her muff which she pushed out at one end as she thrust her hand in at the other. She was careful to do this little trick in such a manner that those who saw the king place the note in her muff should see it fall out. It was picked up by an inquisitive soul, reached the hands of the "lampooners," and appeared in biting verse in the next issue of the *News Letter*.

When the king complained to Frances of her ill-treatment of his note, she declared, with a great show of astonishment, that she had not seen it, which was literally true, since she had only felt it. She said that it must have fallen to the ground as she took up her muff, and tried to make it appear that she was greatly disappointed.

"I would not slight so great an honor as a letter from my king," she said demurely.

"No, no," returned his Majesty, laughing. "Our most devoted subject would not slight her king's message. I believe you did it intentionally."

"In which case your Majesty will leave no more notes for me in public," answered Frances. And the king's choice lay between taking offence and looking upon the affair as a jest. He was too far gone in love to take offence, so he chose to laugh.

On another occasion, at the queen's ball, the king asked Frances to walk out to the garden with him.

"It is dark, your Majesty, and I fear the dark," she replied. "Let us walk there in the daytime, so that every one may see how graciously my king honors me."

He could not coax her out, so he said: "Very well, my prudish Miss Solomon. Have your way and break my heart."

"To do either would please me," she retorted. "I like to have my own way, and there are few women who would not be delighted to break a handsome king's heart."

Frances having captured the king, every other man at court was her admirer. She could have had her choice of a husband from among the noblest and richest men of the land, but she showed no one especial favor. If one imagined that she smiled with marked graciousness on him, he soon learned that others were equally fortunate, and after a time each accepted his smile from her and took it for granted that his failure to receive greater favor was because of the king's success. All praised her discretion, though many believed that she was concealing adroitly what she would not have the world suspect. With all her circumspection, it soon became the common talk at court that she was the king's new favorite, though there was no reason given for the rumor save the belief that the king was not to be resisted.

*　*　*　*　*

　　　　　　　Charles Major

The Duchess of York and I knew the truth concerning Frances, but all Westminster and London talked of the new star at Whitehall who was outshining Castlemain, Nell Gwynn, Stuart, and the host of other luminaries who had scintillated with scandal ever since the king's return to Britain's throne.

One morning, shortly after the king's last-mentioned conversation with Frances, she met Nell Gwynn in the palace garden, and was surprised when Nelly addressed her as "Little Solomon."

"Where did you learn the name?" asked Frances.

"From its author, the king," answered Nell. "Come home with me and I'll tell you all about it."

They took Nell's barge and went to Westminster water stairs, where they walked across the park to her house in Pell Mell.

Frances cordially hated Lady Castlemain and the king's other brazen friends, but, after having met Nelly several times, she had learned to love the sweet, profane, ignorant girl because, despite her apparently evil life, there was honesty, kindliness, and truth in Nelly's heart.

When the two young women were seated in Nelly's cozy parlor, she began to open her heart to Frances.

"Yes, the king told me how he invited you to go to the garden with him one evening, and how he dubbed you 'Little Solomon' when you refused."

"Ah, did he?" asked Frances, surprised at the king's willingness to speak of his rebuff.

"Yes," returned Nelly, surprising Frances still further by a soberness of manner rarely seen in the laughing girl.

After a long pause, Nelly continued: "Do you know, I hate the fat Castlemain woman. And the bow-legged Stuart hussy! She seems to be proud of her crooked shanks and exhibits them on every possible occasion. There is something about extreme ugliness that drives it to exposure, on the principle, I suppose, that murder will out. And there's ugly Wells! I hate her, too! Her charm, like that of the Puritan's face, lies wholly in her damned ugliness. I hate them all, though I do not fear them, but oh, Mistress Jennings—" Here she leaned forward and grasped Frances's wrist almost fiercely, "The human heart is a strange thing, at least mine is, for I love you, but oh, I fear you!"

"No, no," cried Frances, at a loss just what to say.

"Yes," continued Nell, insistently. "Let me tell you! Of late I can neither eat nor sleep because of the dread that you will rob me of the king's love. I can do nothing but pray and swear. He does love me more than he loves all the world, because he knows I am true to him! And his love is meat and drink and life itself to me! If you could see but one little part of my love for him, if you could know that I worship him, God help me! as I should worship only my Maker, if you could understand that if you were to steal him from me, you would take my life, my very soul,—if so poor a thing as I can have a soul,—you, who may choose and pick men at will, would leave his love to me!"

"You need not fear, you need not fear," said Frances, soothingly.

"He is not true to me," continued Nelly, impetuously, "and I know it. But I do not care. I have his love, and with that I am

94   Charles Major

content. I would not ask fidelity. I care nothing for the wealth he gives. I accept only a meagre portion of what he offers, and have refused honors and titles which would be a burden to me. I want only the man, Charles Stuart."

She began to weep softly, drying her eyes and trying to laugh. "He's not much of a man, and I know his weaknesses better than any one in all the world knows them. But he is all to me, and I beg you to leave me this part of a man, for you only, of all women I know, can take him from me."

"I would not take the king from you, even to be his queen, if that were possible. I promise that I shall not rob you of his love. It is the last thing in the world I want. You say you love me. I believe you and give you like return. Every one loves you, Nelly."

"Ah, I thank you—Frances," answered Nelly, hesitating at the name.

"Let us seal a pact of friendship," said Frances. "We shall need each other's help in this vile court that takes its quality from its king."

"Yes, truly he is vile," returned Nelly. "But women of my class, born and bred in the slums of life, do not measure a man by his virtues, but by their love of him. I know not how it is, nor why, but this I know, we love because of what we give, and the more we give, the more we love."

"I fear the same is true of all women," answered Frances, with a sigh. "If a woman could but say to her heart, 'Thou shalt' and 'Thou shalt not,' there would be fewer unhappy women in this world."

"Oh, do you, too, know that awful truth?" exclaimed Nelly,

eagerly bringing her hands to Frances's shoulders. "Tell me all about it. There is nothing sweeter than to hear the troubles of a friend. They help to make our own seem smaller. Tell me."

"I cannot," answered Frances, now as woebegone as Nelly herself. "It is too terrible even to think upon, yet I think of nothing else. A woman may love a man to the point of madness and still hate him."

"But it is not the king you love?" cried Nelly, in alarm.

"No, no, Nelly. You have my word. But let us talk of something else," answered Frances.

"No, no, let us talk about you," insisted Nelly, whose curiosity was equalled only by her good nature.

"Not another word," returned Frances. "Don't you want to go to the barge for a ride on the river?" And Nelly eagerly assented.

When they were seated in the barge, Nelly's waterman asked her where he should take them, and she proposed going to the Bridge, leaving the barge at the Bridge stairs, and walking up Gracious Street to the Old Swan Tavern for dinner. Frances liked the plan and accepted Nelly's invitation to dinner—and to trouble.

CHAPTER V

THE FIGHT AT THE OLD SWAN

On the way down to the Bridge, inquisitive, irresistible Nelly drew out of Frances a meagre statement of her case. Although Nelly could not write her own name, she was excellent at putting two and two together, and on this occasion quickly reached the conclusion that there was a man whom Frances had good reason to hate, but loved.

Without suspecting that Roger Wentworth's death bore any relation to Frances's trouble, Nelly soon began asking questions about the tragedy, and learned that Frances had recognized one of the highwaymen. When Frances refused in a marked and emphatic manner to describe the man she had seen, or to speak of him beyond the first mention, Nelly began again with her two-and-two problem, and, as the result of her second calculation, reached the conclusion that the highwayman Frances had recognized and the man she loved and hated were one and the same person. However, Nelly had the good taste to keep the result of her calculations to herself, and dropped the subject which seemed so distasteful to her companion.

When Frances and Nelly reached the landing at the water stairs just above the Bridge, they left their barge and walked up Gracious Street (called by some Grace Church Street, though, in fact, it should be Grass Church Street) to the Old Swan Tavern on the east side of the street, a little above Eastcheap.

The Old Swan was a picturesque structure, beautiful in its quaintness, sweet in its cleanliness, and lovable in its ancient air of hospitality. Its token, a full-grown swan, was the best piece of sign painting in London. Its kitchen was justly celebrated. The old inn was kept by Henry Pickering, a man far above his occupation in manner, education, and culture. He had lived many years in France, where he had married a woman of good station, and where his only child, Bettina, whom we called Betty, was born and lived during her early childhood. Pickering's wife died in France, and his fortunes failed, so he returned to England, bought the Old Swan, and soon became rich again.

The Old Swan Tavern must not be confused with the Old Swan wharf and stairs, which were a short distance below the Bridge.

Neither Frances nor Nelly had ever visited the old tavern before, so, being unacquainted with the private entrance, Nelly marched bravely into the tap-room and asked Pickering to show them to a quiet dining room.

Two unescorted ladies of quality taking dinner at even so respectable a house as the Old Swan was an adventure well calculated to shock the judicious, but Nelly did not care a straw for appearances, and Frances hardly knew how questionable the escapade was.

When Pickering had seated his beautiful guests in the small dining room adjoining the tap-room, he returned to the bar and sent his daughter Betty to serve them. She was a beautiful girl of eighteen, who had returned only a few months before from France, where she had spent three or four winters in a convent, her summers having been spent with her father.

There was no fairer skin nor sweeter face than Betty Pickering's. The expression of her great brown eyes, with their arching brows, was so demure as to give the impression that somewhere back in the shadow of their long, thick lashes lurked a fund of laughter and harmless mischief as charming as it was apparently latent. Her form was of the partridge fashion, though not at all too plump, and her hands, which were white and soft as any lady's, were small and dimpled at every knuckle. Her little feet and ankles—but we shall stop at the ankles.

Betty was unusually rich in dimples, having one in each cheek and a half score or more about her lips and chin whenever she smiled. She was well aware of the beauty of her dimples and her teeth; therefore, like a sensible girl that she was, she smiled a great deal, both from feminine policy and natural inclination. In short, Bettina was a Hebe in youth and beauty, and soon after I learned to know her, I learned also that she was an earthly little angel in disposition. It may appear from the enthusiasm of this description that there was a time in my life when I was in love with her. I admit it— desperately in love with her.

To have Betty's services at the Old Swan was a favor enjoyed only by her friends and guests of the highest quality. She was not an ordinary barmaid, though she had friends whom she delighted to honor. Among these were Hamilton and myself, we having visited the Old Swan frequently prior to the time of Hamilton's going to France.

Frances and Nelly had chosen a table in a secluded corner of the private dining room, and were waiting somewhat impatiently when Betty went in to serve them.

"Will my ladies eat from table linen—extra, sixpence?" asked Betty, bending her knee in what might have been called a perpendicular courtesy. Had she been sure that her customers were of high rank, she would have saluted them with a low bow, omitting to mention the extra charge for the linen. But as Frances and Nelly were not escorted by a gentleman, she was not sure of their station.

"Will we eat from table linen?" demanded Nelly, in apparent indignation. "Now, damn the girl! Just hear her! From what else, in God's name, hussy, should we eat? From a trough? And mind you, if there is a spot on it as large as my smallest finger nail, I'll tear it to shreds!" She winked to Frances, perhaps to show Betty that she was only chaffing, for in all the world there was no kinder heart than Nelly Gwynn's.

Betty at once concluded that her guests were great ladies, perhaps from Whitehall itself, for surely none save ladies of the highest or lowest rank would use the language that came so trippingly on Nelly's tongue. So Betty made a deep courtesy, smiled, and answered:—

"Yes, my ladies, it shall be as spotless as a maid of honor's character. It cost five shillings the ell."

"Is that the best you can do?" demanded Nelly, laughing despite herself at Betty's reference to the maids of honor. "Never in all my life have I eaten from anything cheaper than guinea linen, and I know I shall choke—choke, I tell you! Odds fish! this is terrible!" Then turning to Frances: "But it serves us right, duchess, for leaving the palace."

"Yes, your Highness," returned Frances. "But you insisted on coming to the place."

Betty was almost taken off her feet! A princess and a duchess! So her third courtesy was nearly to the floor, as she asked:—

"What will your Highness and your Grace have to eat?"

"A barrel of oysters, a lobster broiled—make it two lobsters —a dish of raw turnips, with oil, vinegar, and pepper, a bottle of canary, a bit of cheese, and a pot of tea. But Lord! I suppose you never heard of tea! It's a new drink, child, recently brought from China."

"Yes, your Highness," answered Betty, very proud that the Old Swan could furnish so new a beverage. "We have some excellent tea of my father's own importation."

"Then fetch it, and in God's name, be quick about it! Doubt-less you could be quick enough in running after a man!" said Nelly.

"In running away from him if I wanted to catch him," answered Betty, casting down her eyes demurely, as she courtesied and left to give the order in the kitchen.

Nelly's love of fun brought trouble before the dinner was over.

When Betty left her guests, she went to her father in the tap-room and told him that a princess and a duchess had honored his house, whereupon Pickering began to swell with pride. As friends dropped in from time to time, he informed them that a princess and a duchess were waiting for their dinner in the small dining room, and followed up the extraordinary announcement in each case by asking proudly:—

"Show me another tavern this side of Westminster that entertains guests of like rank. If they were to drop into the Dog's Head, old Robbins would *drop* dead. And on what would he serve them? I would wager a jacobus to a farthing that he hasn't a tablecloth of real linen in his house, and as for forks, why, he never heard of them. Your fingers and a knife at the Dog's Head! The Old Swan serves its guests of high rank with five shilling linen and silver forks. Silver, mind you, hammered from unalloyed coin by Backwell himself. If any of you happen to be at the Dog's Head, drop a hint that you saw a princess and a duchess in the Old Swan's small dining room."

If a guest doubted Pickering's statement concerning the quality of his guests, he led them to the door of the small dining room, where the sceptic was relieved of his doubts, for Frances and Nelly looked their assumed parts convincingly.

Soon after Nelly's dinner had been served, a handsome gentleman entered the tap-room, sat down at a table, and tapped with his sword-hilt for service. His doublet and trunks of rich velvet, his broad beaver hat with its long flowing plume, and his silken hose, had all been elegant in their good days, but now they were stained, shabby, and almost threadbare in spots. His shoe buckles showed vacant jewel holders, and his sword hilt was without a precious stone, all giving evidence that their owner had been dealing with pawnbrokers. He was shabby from head to feet, though he bore himself with the convincing manner of a gentleman.

Pickering sent the barboy to wait on the newcomer, but the boy returned immediately and whispered:—

"Ye made a mistake in sending me, master. Better send one of the maids or Mistress Betty. The gentleman is more than he seems to be."

"What did he say?" asked Pickering.

"'Ee didn't say nothing," answered the boy. "'Ee looked at me."

At that moment Betty came in, and Pickering nodding toward the stranger, she went to serve him. When she stopped by his table, she made a perpendicular courtesy, and asked:—

"How may I serve you, sir?"

"You may bring me a bit of cheese, Betty, and a mug of your father's famous beer," said the gentleman, giving his order modestly.

"Very well, sir," returned Betty, making another stiff courtesy to "a bit of cheese and a mug of beer." But while her knee was bent, she caught a glimpse of the man's face beneath the drooping brim of his hat, and the stiff courtesy instantly changed to a bow as she exclaimed softly:—

"Ah, Master Hamilton, I did not know you. We have not seen you at the Old Swan this many a day, and—and you are very much changed, sir."

"You are not changed, Betty, unless you have grown prettier, if that be possible," returned George Hamilton.

"Thank you, Master Hamilton," answered Betty, laughing softly, and bringing her dimples and teeth into fine display. With all her profound respect for the high rank of her lady guests, Betty's smiles, while waiting on handsome George, were of a far rarer quality than those given to rank and station in the small dining room. In Hamilton's case, she could not suppress the smile nor restrain the soft laugh incident to her surprise. The warm glow in her eyes and her murmured words of modest welcome came of their own accord, because she was kind of heart and as bewitching a bit of humanity as one could possibly want to caress.

At different times I had imagined that Betty was in love with Hamilton, and had suffered strange twinges of jealousy on account of my fear; twinges that surprised and angered me, for my heart had no business going astray after a barmaid. She had always been kind to me, with a shy fluttering in her manner from which I should have taken comfort had she not been freer and easier with Hamilton.

Betty's manner with me should have given me a hint of the way her heart was tending, even at that early time, but Hamilton was so much more likely to attract a woman than I, and his manner was so much more offhand and dashing than mine that I thought it impossible for such a girl as Betty to think twice of me while she might have been thinking of him. But I was wrong, as will unfold later; wrong, greatly to my trouble and surprise.

I should be delighted if I could discover the standards whereby women measure men. Ugly John Prigg is adored by a beautiful wife, from whom no other man can win a smile. Stupid little Short possesses a tall rare Venus, and cadaverous Long a bewitching Hebe. Bandy-legged Little Jermyn, of Whitehall, he of the "pop eyes" and the rickets head, he with neither manner, presence, brains, rank, nor money, save what he steals and begs, is beyond doubt the lady-killer of our court, so what are we to do about it all but wonder and "give it up"?

"While you have changed for the better, if at all," said

Hamilton, "I also have changed for the better, and sadly for the worse, in some respects. There is a paradox for you, Betty. I'm better and I'm worse. Do you know what a paradox is"?

"I'm not sure, Master Hamilton. Perhaps Lord Monmouth is one," answered Betty, laughing, and coming so close to the truth that Hamilton concluded she knew the word. "He has been coming here of late, and has been trying to make love to me."

"And succeeding, Betty?" asked George.

"Ah, no. I've stopped waiting on him. He hasn't money enough to buy the shadow of a smile from me, even though he is the king's son."

"I commend your discretion, Betty," said George. "But if Monmouth and his friends have been coming here, the Old Swan must be having rare company."

"Yes," returned Betty, with a touch of pride. "A duchess and a princess are now taking dinner in the small dining room. There! You may hear the princess laughing now! She is a merry one."

"A princess, say you, Betty?" asked George. "Nonsense! That is Nelly Gwynn laughing. I should know her laugh in the din of battle."

"Nelly Gwynn?" cried Betty, joyously. There was not in all England a duchess nor a princess half so great in Betty's opinion as Nelly Gwynn. She was the queen of all London east of Temple Bar, and dearer to the City's heart than any one else at court.

George, too, liked Nelly, and when Betty left him to fetch the pot of tea from the kitchen for the ladies, he determined to go to the private dining room and see the king's sweetest sweetheart, from whom he knew he would hear all the news of court, including perhaps a word about Frances.

Taking his hat from the floor, Hamilton entered the small dining room and hurried toward the princess and the duchess. Frances sat with her back toward the door, so that she did not see him as he approached, nor did he see her face. When Nelly saw him she rose hastily, stretched out her hands in welcome, and exclaimed:—

"Well, well, handsome George, as sure as I'm not a bishop's wife! How are you, my long-lost love?"

She stepped forward to meet him, gave him both her hands, stood on tiptoe to be kissed, and when that pleasing operation had been finished, said:—

"Come with me. I want to present you to my hated rival, the king's latest love. Mistress Jennings, this is my dangerous friend, Master George Hamilton."

Nelly's words were my cousin's first warning of Hamilton's presence, and her surprise, nay, her consternation, deprived her, for the moment, of the power to think. Hamilton bowed low before my cousin and said:—

"I have the great pleasure of knowing Mistress Jennings."

Anger came to Frances's help, and she retorted: "You are mistaken, sir. You have not the pleasure of knowing me, nor have I the humiliation of knowing you."

She turned again to her dinner. Nelly whistled in surprise,

and Hamilton said: "I beg your pardon." Then turning to Nelly: "I thought I knew the king's new lady love, but it seems I was mistaken. Adieu, Mistress Gwynn." And turning hastily, he left the room.

As George was resuming his chair at the table in the tap-room, three roystering, half-tipsy fellows, wearing the uniform of the King's Guard, entered, flung themselves into chairs at the long table and called loudly for brandy. Hamilton did not know any of them, though he knew by their uniforms and swords that they were in the king's service.

Soon after the guardsmen were seated, Betty came from the kitchen carrying a pot of hot tea and a bottle of wine for Nelly and Frances. As she was passing the newcomers, one of them rose, seized her about the waist, and tried to kiss her. But the girl belonged, flesh and blood, to the class of women with whom kissing goes strictly by favor, so she dashed the hot tea in the fellow's face and went her way with the bottle of wine. Though the tea was hot, it cooled the fellow's ardor, and he sat down, cursing furiously. Pickering tried to quiet him, saying:—

"A little less noise, please, gentlemen. A duchess and a princess are dining in the next room."

"A duchess and a princess?" exclaimed one of the men. "We should like to see the duchess and the princess that would dine here. By God! A duchess and a princess! Come, gentlemen, let us introduce ourselves."

Accordingly the three of them made a dash for the door of the small dining room and entered. Immediately a series of screams came from the princess and the duchess, announcing that the intruders were introducing themselves. Instantly Hamilton drew his sword and hastened to the rescue. When he entered the room he saw one of the men embracing Nelly and another trying to seize Frances. His first attention was given to the man with Frances. He struck him with the hilt of his sword, stunning him for the moment, but the fellow soon recovered, and the three ruffians drew their blades.

Finding himself assailed from all quarters, George made a dash for a corner of the room, where his back and flank were protected. In telling me of it afterward, Frances said that she and Nelly were so badly frightened that they could neither move nor scream. The deafening noise of the clashing swords, the tramping of the heavy boots on the bare oak floor, the blasphemous oaths of the drunken ruffians, and the stunning din of battle almost deprived her of consciousness.

After a time all that she could see was Hamilton's face behind the curtain of flashing swords, and all that she could hear, even above the din, was his heavy breathing. He had thrown off his doublet and was fighting in his shirt sleeves, desperately, and it seemed hopelessly. Soon the blood began to stream down his face, and the white linen of his shirt was covered with red blotches.

No man can stand long against odds of three to one, but, for what seemed a very long time to Frances, Hamilton defended himself gallantly, and seemed to be giving back as much as he received.

But the fight could not have lasted much longer, and sooner or later, George would have been cut to pieces, had not little Betty entered the fray. No weapon had she, not even a teapot, but she ran bravely in, knelt behind one of the ruffians, and when an opportunity came, seized him by the foot, bringing him down to the floor with a thud. Quickly another foot was in Betty's deadly grasp, and another man fell, leaving only one assailant standing, whom Hamilton soon routed. The two men on the floor attempted to rise, but Betty clung to their feet, and George's sword quieted them.

When George was satisfied that the ruffians would not try again to introduce themselves to the duchess and the princess, he wiped his sword on Betty's five shilling table linen, remarking:—

"I thank you, Betty dear. You came into the fight just in time to save my life. Another half minute and I should have needed a coffin." He was breathing heavily and spoke with great effort.

When George had sheathed his sword, he started to leave the room without speaking to Frances or Nelly, but before he reached the door, Frances called out faintly:—

"Master Hamilton! Please wait, Master Hamilton!"

For the moment she forgot the cause of her hatred of him, forgot that he had been implicated in Roger's murder, as she supposed, forgot everything in all the broad world save her love for him, and that he had just been at death's door in her defence.

Hamilton stopped a little short of the door, and Frances ran to him, calling softly: "Oh, sir, wait! Forgive me! I do know you! A moment since I did not know you, but now—Oh, I must have made a terrible mistake! I have judged you wrongfully. I do know you! I do know you!"

Hamilton bowed and smiled grimly through the blood which was trickling down his face, then standing proudly erect, answered:—

"Mistress Jennings is mistaken. She does not know me, nor

have I the honor of knowing the king's new favorite."

Here Betty cut the conversation short by saying: "I'll fetch a barber-surgeon, while father takes you to a room."

"You'll do nothing of the sort for me," objected Hamilton. "My wounds are mere scratches. I'll go to the pump. It is the only surgeon I shall need. Fetch a barber for the men on the floor there."

George went to the pump in the courtyard, followed by Betty, after whom came Nelly and Frances. Betty was proceeding to wash George's wounds, when Nelly offered to take the towel from her hand, but the girl refused with a touch of anger, saying:—

"Please do not interfere, Mistress Gwynn. You and the duchess stood by gaping while he was fighting to protect you. He would have been dead by now if he had waited for help from either of you. I advise you to leave the Old Swan, but don't forget to pay your bill to the barboy."

"Never mind the bill," said Pickering, who was at the pump handle. "But please take my daughter's advice and go."

"Go where you may find guinea linen. Persons of your quality make too much trouble at the Old Swan," interposed Betty, who was not in a good temper.

At first Nelly was inclined to resent Betty's sharp words, but in a moment she returned softly:—

"You're right, girl. You have earned the privilege to scold."

"And please forgive us," said Frances, to which Betty did not reply.

"Where are your wounds?" asked Nelly, addressing George. "Off with your clothes and let us see."

"Not here, Nelly, not here," he answered, bending over the tub in front of the pump. "My wounds are mere trifles. Only a scratch or two on the scalp and a pink or two on the arms. Take Betty's advice. Leave at once. This is no place for your friend. The society of our virtuous monarch doubtless will be far more congenial."

Nelly hesitated, and George, seeing that Frances was about to speak, turned upon her, almost angrily:—

"Please go before greater trouble comes. I could not hold out for another fight. I am almost finished. Let the king fight the battles of his friends. The ruffian that escaped will return with re-enforcements, and I am not able to fight them again."

"Oh, but she is not the king's friend, as you suppose, as my idle words might lead you to believe," returned Nelly, pleadingly.

George rose from the tub over which he was standing and answered: "Show your gratitude for what I have done by going at once."

Seeing that George was in earnest, Nelly left the courtyard, leading reluctant Frances by the hand. Hamilton's supposed crime had been forgotten, and I believe would have been forgiven had he permitted Frances the opportunity at that time.

When Frances and Nelly reached the street, Frances said, "I must see him again to tell him that I am not—"

"What I am," interrupted Nelly. "Do not fear to speak

plainly. I am content with myself. But I shall take measures at once to convince George that you are what you are. I'll set you right with him."

"I'll return and explain for myself," insisted Frances.

"He will refuse to hear you. If you wish, I'll leave you at the barge and go back to explain to him."

Frances consenting, they went back to the barge, and Nelly, returning to the tavern, sought Betty. Hamilton was not to be seen, and in reply to Nelly's inquiries, Betty told her that he had fainted at the pump and had been taken upstairs to a room.

"His wounds are deeper than he supposed," said Betty, "and the loss of blood has been very great. We have sent for a surgeon."

"I'll go to see him," said Nelly.

"No," returned Betty, shaking her head emphatically. "Father says that fever may set in, and that Master Hamilton must not be disturbed. You cannot see him."

"Have your way, Betty," answered good-natured Nell. "And Betty dear, I was only teasing you about the table linen."

"I understand. Just a little sport with the barmaid," returned Betty, a note of sarcasm ringing sharply in her usually soft voice.

"Yes, Betty. I'm sorry. Forgive me. Here are two guineas."

"I don't want them," answered Betty, clasping her hands behind her.

"Again forgive me," said Nelly. "I have been wrong altogether in my opinion of you. You are a good, beautiful girl, and I'm coming back to see you very soon."

"Please don't come on my account, Mistress Gwynn," returned Betty.

"No, I shall come on my account," replied Nell, coaxingly. "I'll go now for fear of making more trouble for you, but I intend to be your friend, and you shall be mine. When Nelly makes up her mind to have a friend, she always has her way. Good-by, Betty."

Betty courtesied, and Nelly left the Old Swan, returning at once to Frances, who was waiting in the barge. On their way back to the palace neither Frances nor Nelly spoke after Nelly had told what she had heard at the inn. Usually Nelly was laughing or talking, or both, and when a woman of her temperament is silent, she is thinking. In this instance her thinking brought her to two conclusions: first, that Hamilton was the man Frances loved and hated; and second, that it was his face she had recognized on the night Roger Wentworth was killed.

The dangerous element in these calculations was that they were sure to reach the king's ear as soon as Nelly found an opportunity to impart them. It were treason to withhold from his Majesty such a tearing bit of scandal. She had no reason to suspect that the telling of what had happened and of what she had deduced would bring trouble to Frances and George. She simply knew that the king would be vastly pleased with the story, and her only purpose in life was to give him pleasure. How well she pleased him in this instance and the result of her innocent effort to make him happy will soon appear.

The day after the adventure of Frances and Nelly at the Old Swan, I had business with Backwell, the goldsmith, and when I had disposed of my matters, I walked over to the Old Swan near by to eat a grilled lobster, a dish for which the inn was famous. I knew nothing of the trouble that had occurred the day before, not having seen my cousin, nor did I know that Hamilton was in London, not having seen nor heard from him since Frances's arrival at court.

By far my greatest motive in going to the Old Swan was to see Betty, whose beauty and sweetness had begun to haunt me about that time.

If Mary Hamilton had shown me the least evidence of warmth, my admiration for Bettina, perhaps, would have remained merely admiration. But in view of Mary's admirable self-control, I found myself falling into a method of thought morally then prevalent with all modish men. I confess with shame that I hoped to have Mary for my wife and Bettina to love me and to be loved. I did not know Betty then, and have regretted all my life that once I looked upon her as—well, as a barmaid. While I thoroughly realized that she was an unusual girl in many respects, still I held to a theory then prevalent that barmaids were created to be kissed.

When I reached the Old Swan, I chose a table in a remote corner of the tap-room, ordered a lobster from one of the maids, and, while waiting for it, drank a cup of wormwood wine.

The place seemed dingy and drear with its great ceiling beams of time-darkened oak, its long, narrow windows of small square panes, its black fireplace, lifeless without the flames, and its dark, grim mahogany bar stretching halfway across the south side of the room. The white floor, well sanded and polished, seemed only to accentuate the general gloom, and the great clock, ticking solemnly behind the bar, seemed to be marking time for a funeral dirge. But suddenly all changed to brightness when Betty entered. Pickering was talking to me, standing between me and the girl, so that she did not see me when she first came into the room. She stepped behind the bar for some purpose and called to her father, who started to go to her, but before he reached her she looked up and saw me. In a moment she was by my side, smiling and dimpling in a manner fit to set the heart of an anchorite a-thumping.

"I came for a lobster, Betty," I said, taking her hand, "and to see you. I was afraid you might forget me."

"The Old Swan is likely to forget you, Baron Ned," she answered, withdrawing her hand, "if you don't come to see us oftener."

"Ah, Betty, you're a mercenary bit of flesh and blood. Always looking out for customers," I returned, shaking my head.

"Yes," she replied, laughing softly. "And—and very sorry when certain customers come so seldom."

Had she spoken glibly, her words would have meant nothing, but there was a hesitancy, a pretty fluttering in her manner which pleased me, so I was emboldened to say:—

"I hope I am one of the 'certain customers,' Betty."

Again she laughed softly, as she answered, "Yes, Baron Ned, *the* certain one."

"Do you mean, Betty, that I am the 'certain one' for the Old

Swan or for Betty?" I asked.

She was standing near me, and I again caught her hand, but it was not a part of Betty's programme to be questioned too closely, so she withdrew her hand, saying, "I must go."

On former occasions I had put forth what I considered adroit efforts to steal small favors from the girl, for, as already intimated, I considered her merely a barmaid; but I had failed, and the conviction was dawning on my mind that either she was not an ordinary barmaid or that I was the wrong man. The first assumption would make me all the more eager, but the second would deter any self-respecting man from further pursuit. My fears inclined me to accept the second, and resulted in a dim sort of jealousy of the right man, who, I suspected, was Hamilton.

When Betty started to leave me, I caught her skirt to detain her, and said: "When George Hamilton used to come here, I was jealous of him, and feared that he might be the 'certain customer.' But I am glad that he has left England."

The girl blushed as she answered, "No, no, Baron Ned, there is no other 'certain customer.'" But she checked herself, evidently having said more than she intended, and continued hurriedly: "But Master Hamilton has not left England. He is now in the Old Swan. He asked me to say nothing of his presence in London, but I know he would want me to tell you."

"Yes, yes, of course he would, Betty. Where is he?" I asked.

"Upstairs in bed," she answered.

"Is he sick?" I asked, rising.

"No and yes," she replied. "He is suffering from his wounds, and the surgeon says the fever is mounting rapidly to his head."

"His wounds?" I exclaimed.

"Yes, lots of them," she answered. "But I hope none of them are serious, save for the loss of blood."

"Wounds? Blood? Tell me, Betty, tell me! Has he been in trouble?" I asked, deeply concerned.

"You see it was this way, Baron Ned," she began, leaning back against the table and smoothing out her apron. "Yesterday while Mistress Gwynn and another lady, a duchess, were eating their dinner in the small dining room, three drunken ruffians came in and tried to kiss them. Master Hamilton, who was here at this very table, heard the disturbance, so he drew his sword, ran to the rescue, and he and I beat the fellows out. He fought beautifully, but one man can't stand long against three, so I upset two of the ruffians by tripping them—pulled their feet from under them, you know—and Master Hamilton's sword did the rest. One of them ran away, and the other two were carried to the hospital on stretchers. One of the ruffians had tried to kiss me a few minutes before, and I had almost drowned him with a pot of tea. If he ever returns, I'll see that the tea is boiling."

"It seems that every one is wanting to kiss you, Betty," I remarked.

"Not every one, but too many," she rejoined.

"And you don't want to be kissed, Betty?" I asked.

"Well, not by the wrong man," she answered, laughing softly and tossing her head emphatically.

"I wish I were the right man," I suggested.

"There is no right man—yet," she returned, laughing and dimpling till I almost wished there was not a dimpling stubborn girl in all the world.

"Betty, you're a bloodthirsty little wretch," I said, shaking my head sorrowfully. "You scald one man and help Hamilton to kill two."

"Oh, they will not die," she answered seriously. "I was haunted by the fear that they might, so I got up in the middle of the night, took father and one of the boys with a link, and went to the hospital, where I learned that they will recover."

"Show me to Hamilton's room, Betty, and bring two lobsters there instead of one. He and I will have dinner together," I said, turning to go with her.

"He doesn't seem to want to eat, though I doubt if his lack of appetite is owing wholly to his wounds," she replied, as we were leaving the tap-room.

"How long has he been here?" I asked.

"Since yesterday noon," she answered. "He came just in time to find trouble. An hour ago I took a bowl of broth to him and a plate of sparrow-grass, but he said dolefully that the food would stick in his throat. I told him he was not wounded in the throat. Then he said it was in his heart, and that such a wound kills the appetite. I believe he's in love, Baron Ned," she concluded, leaning toward me and whispering earnestly.

"With you, Betty?" I asked.

"No, no, with some one else."

"Would it make you unhappy?" I asked.

"To be in love?" she asked, arching her eyebrows.

"No. For him to be in love," I said.

"If he is unhappily so, I should be sorry," she answered.

"And you would not be jealous?" I asked.

"Ah, Baron Ned!" she returned, protestingly.

CHAPTER VI

SWEET BETTY PICKERING

When we knocked at Hamilton's door, he answered, "Come," and I entered, Betty closing the door behind me, leaving George and me together. He was lying on the bed, his head and arms bandaged, and a feverish gleam shining in his eyes. I went toward him, offering my hand. He rose and sat on the edge of the bed, but did not accept my greeting. I was about to speak when he lifted his hand to interrupt me, saying coldly:—

"Well, Clyde, what do you want?"

"I want to see you and help you, if I can," I answered, in surprise.

"Now that you have seen me, you may go," he returned.

I did not know the cause of his ill feeling, though I knew that something had happened to turn him against me, so I stood my ground and answered:—

"I shall go if you insist, but before I go, please tell me in what manner I have offended you. Neither you nor I have so many friends that we can afford to lose one without an effort to save him. The world is full of men and women, but a friend is a gift of God. I thought you had forgiven me what I said at Sundridge. Your time to take offence was then, not now."

"I hold no ill will for what you said then in my hearing. It is what you have done in so cowardly a manner since I last saw you, and at a time when I was not present to hear or to resent it."

"But what have I done?" I asked.

"You should know. I don't," he answered, sullenly.

"If neither you nor I know what I have done to offend, how are we to settle this matter? How may I apologize or make amends?" I asked.

"You can't," he returned.

"Ah, but I can and I will, George Hamilton," I answered, determined not to let him put me off without knowing wherein I had offended. "Save what you heard at Sundridge, I have neither done nor said anything unfit to come from a friend. If any man has reported me otherwise, he has lied. If any woman—well, she is mistaken."

"No one has reported you otherwise or any wise," he answered.

"Then tell me the cause of your grievance, and I may be able to explain or deny. You perhaps know by this time that I always speak the truth to you, so out with it, George. Let us settle this matter, whatever it be—one way or the other. Friendship should not be left to dangle between love and hatred. It sits squarely on the heart of an honest man, or is cast out candidly and above board. Shall I sit down?"

"Yes," he answered, rising from the bed, drawing the rug up over his shoulders, and taking a chair not far from where I was sitting. "I saw your cousin—"

"When and where?" I interrupted.

"Yesterday, in this house," he replied.

"Did she come to see you? And did you permit her to come?" I asked, finding it my turn to be angry.

"No, she did not come to see me, nor had I anything to do with her visit to the Old Swan. She was eating dinner with Nell Gwynn, and—"

"Was she the duchess, of whom Betty told me?" I asked, interrupting him.

"Yes, the Duchess of Hearts, as I hear she has been dubbed at court," he answered, with an angry gleam in his eyes and a sharp note of contempt in his voice.

"And was it for her you fought?" I asked, feeling as though I was reading a page from a story-book. "Betty told me about it, but you tell me, please?"

"Betty usually exhausts a subject, so there is no need to tell you about the fight," he said. "It was really a small affair, and my wounds are nothing to speak of. I suffered more from other causes."

"Yes, yes, George. Tell me all about it," I returned, drawing my chair nearer to him. "I fear a mistake has been made, a misunderstanding of some sort, though I cannot imagine even the sort. Now, tell me."

"I came up from Sheerness on a Dutch boat and landed at Deptford yesterday morning," he began hesitatingly. "After sending a messenger on business in which I was deeply interested, I came to the Old Swan to get a bite to eat and to find a bed. While waiting in the tap-room for my dinner, I recognized Nelly's laugh and went into the private dining room to see her, hoping that she might drop a word concerning another person. I should not have gone to see her, for while in France I had heard from De Grammont, with whom I have had some correspondence, that I was out of favor with the king and that Crofts had been trying to fix on me the guilt of a crime which he himself committed.

"Grammont wrote me, also, of the triumphs of Mistress Jennings, the new beauty of the court, but I paid little heed to the gossip, though I confess I was thrown into great fear by what he wrote about her. I knew also that the king would help Crofts make trouble for me, so I felt it was just as well that my presence in London should remain unknown. But I did go in to see Nelly, and, much to my surprise, found the other person."

It was to my surprise, also, but I said only: "Yes, yes, George. Your story is growing interesting. Proceed!"

After a moment, he continued: "Nelly offered to present me to the other person, whom she designated as 'the king's new favorite.' Naturally I said that I already had the honor of knowing Mistress Jennings. Then your cousin looked up to me and remarked calmly that I was mistaken; that I did not have the honor of knowing her, nor she the humiliation of knowing me. So I made my bow, went back to the taproom, and in a moment the fight occurred, of which you already know."

"But what has all this to do with your grievance against me?" I asked.

He turned his face away from me, looked out the window for a minute or two, and answered: "These are my causes of offence, Baron Clyde. You have brought your cousin, your own flesh and blood, to Whitehall to sell her to the king, and—"

"That is a lie, Hamilton!" I cried, springing to my feet, "and, by God, you shall answer for it as soon as you are able to hold a sword!"

"I shall be very willing," he returned, though it was evident he was somewhat cooled by my anger. "But since you would know the cause of my ill-feeling, sit down and hear what I have to say."

I resumed my chair, and he continued: "I can see no reason for your cousin's strange aversion to me save that you have used well the time of my absence in traducing me, hoping doubtless to smooth the king's path by removing me from her thoughts."

What he said did little to allay my anger until I looked into his face and saw that by reason of his fever and his great trouble, he was not responsible for his words. I had been on the point of giving him the lie the second time, but after a moment's consideration, my anger changed to pity, and I said:—

"Forgive me, Hamilton. I am sorry I spoke in anger. You did not lie. You have been simply jumping at conclusions."

"Perhaps," he answered wanderingly.

"But if I tell you, upon my honor, that you are mistaken, will you believe me?" I asked, still feeling a touch of irritation.

He did not answer, so, thinking to give him one more chance, I continued gently: "I have neither harbored an unkind thought of you nor spoken an unkind word of you since the day we parted at Sundridge. On the contrary, I believed that the hot moment there had welded a friendship between us which would last all our lives through."

He walked over to the window, stood looking out a moment, then came back and resumed his chair before me.

"I do not favor your suit with my cousin to any greater extent than I did when we were at Sundridge," I continued, determined that there should be no misunderstanding of my position in that respect, "though since that time I have learned that you are a far better man than I had ever supposed. I have not recommended my cousin to the king, nor is she his favorite in the sense you seem to believe. I do not know the cause of her aversion to you, and, sir, I have nothing else to say except that I take it for granted that you know I speak the truth. This is my explanation. It is for you to say whether you accept or reject it."

I rose, giving him to understand that I was ready to take my leave, but he motioned me to resume my chair. After gazing vacantly out the window for a moment, he covered his face with his hands and answered:—

"I accept your explanation gladly, Baron Ned. I have wronged you. I have been in such turmoil of mind and conscience for so long a time that I am hardly responsible, and now I suppose I am in a fever because of the loss of blood."

I resumed my chair, the difference being settled between us, and in a moment we began to discuss the cause of Frances's sudden change.

It must be remembered that I knew nothing all this time of Hamilton's remote connection with Roger Wentworth's murder. The dimly hinted rumors that had reached my ears I had put down to Crofts's desire for a scapegoat, and the conversation between Frances and Nelly, and Nelly's conclusions, all came to me after this interview with Hamilton.

Failing to reach any conclusion after a long discussion of the subject, Hamilton and I began to speak on other topics, and I asked him where he had been and what he had been doing.

"I have been at the French court, gambling furiously, and hoarding my money," he answered. "I have not even bought a suit of clothes, and have turned every piece of lace and every jewel I possessed into cash."

"I supposed you were leaving off some of your old ways, gambling among them," I remarked, sorry to hear of his fall from grace.

"And so I have," he answered. "But I wanted a thousand pounds to use in a good cause, and felt that I was doing no wrong to rob a very bad Peter in France to pay a very good Paul at home. I have paid the good Paul, and am now done with cards and dice forever."

"I'm glad to hear you say so, George," I returned.

"Yes, I'll tell you how it was," he continued. Then he gave me an account of the killing of Roger Wentworth, the particulars of which I then learned for the first time. I allowed him to proceed in his narrative without interruption, and he finished by saying: "I learned that same evening that a thousand pounds had been stolen from a traveller. I suspected Crofts, Wentworth, and Berkeley of the robbery, but I did not know certainly that they had committed the crime, since I did not see them do it. The next morning I learned that a man had been killed by highwaymen, and as I felt sure that the murder had been committed in the affair I had witnessed, I went to France because I did not want to be called to testify in case criminal proceedings were instituted. In France I learned that the murdered man was young Wentworth's uncle.

"Of course, I did not receive a farthing of the money, but I almost felt that I was accessory before the fact because I had not hastened to prevent the crime, and after the fact because I had made no effort to bring the criminals to justice. Churchill told me flatly that I should be alone if I tried the latter, and said that he was not so great a fool as to win the enmity of the king by attempting to bring the law upon Crofts. You know Churchill's maxim, 'A fool conscience and a fool damned.'"

"There is wisdom in it," I answered.

"I suppose there is," returned Hamilton. "I wanted the thousand pounds to pay Roger Wentworth's widow, so I won it in France, brought it to England, and yesterday sent it by a trusted messenger to Sundridge. Of course the widow does not know where it came from."

"It was like you, George," said I. "One does not do a thing of that sort for sake of a reward, but, believe me, the reward always comes."

"It was the right thing to do," he answered. "But instead of the reward comes now the keenest grief I have ever known, the loss of the small regard in which I was one time held by the only woman I ever loved or ever shall love."

He stopped speaking, but I fancied he had not finished, so I did not interrupt him. I had so much to say in return that I did not care to begin until I had a clear field. He was becoming restless, and I could see that the fever was mounting rapidly. After a long pause he continued:—

"But, in a way, the loss of her regard is the least of my troubles, and I should bear it with equanimity, for if I am honest with her, I would not desire to keep it, as I can bring her no happiness. It is the loss of my respect for her, the knowledge that I was wrong in deeming her better than other women, the humiliation of learning that I was a pitiable dupe in giving my love to one who could give herself to Charles Stuart, that hurts."

I saw that he was trying to suppress his excitement, but it soon got the better of him. He rose from his chair, drew the rug closer about him, and walked rapidly to and fro across the room a minute or two. Being near my chair, he bent down to me, looked wildly about him to see that no one was eavesdropping, and whispered:—

"I intend to kill the king just as soon as I'm out of this. Then God or the devil, I care not which, may finish me."

At that moment Betty came in, followed by one of the maids carrying our dinner. I asked George to eat with me, but he refused and lay down on the bed, drawing the rugs up to his chin and shaking in an ague. The maid left us, but Betty remained, evidently expecting to wait on us and incidentally to talk, for she dearly loved to relieve her mind.

As much as I liked Betty, I asked her to leave us, and when

she was gone, I drew my chair to George's bedside, leaving the dinner to cool.

"First, I want to tell you again," said I, "that Frances is not the king's mistress, nor ever will be."

"Do you know, or do you believe?" he asked.

"I know," I answered, and followed up my assertion with a full account of her life at court, the king's infatuation, at which she laughed, his offer of a pension, which at first she refused, the respect in which every one held her, and the wisdom with which she carried herself through it all.

"Ned, you're as great a fool about her as I was," he returned, shaking his head. "Do you suppose Charles Stuart would give her a pension with no other purpose than kindness or justice? Be sane! Don't be a fool!"

"I say nothing of his purposes; I speak only of her conduct. But I shall not argue with you. If you find any pleasure in your opinion, keep it," I answered, knowing that I could not reason with a man who was half crazy.

"I shall," he replied sullenly.

"But there is another matter in which I believe you will agree with me," I continued. "I have discovered the cause of my cousin's ill feeling—of her change respecting yourself."

He rose from his bed, demanding excitedly: "What is it? Tell me, tell me!"

"You have just told me that you and Churchill were walking at a considerable distance behind Crofts and the others when Roger Wentworth was killed."

"Yes, yes," he returned. "Perhaps as much as two hundred yards."

I watched his face closely to study the effect of my next bit of information, and after a long pause, asked, "Do you know that Frances was in the coach?"

"No, no! Hell and furies! In the coach when Wentworth was killed? My God, tell me all about it, man!" he cried, clutching my arm, and glaring at me with the eyes of a crazy man.

"Yes," I answered. "And she tells me she recognized one of the robbers by the light of the coach lanthorn, though she refused to describe the man she saw and will not be induced to talk about him. Possibly you were the unlucky man. If true, can you wonder that she hates you?"

He sat down on the edge of the bed, musing, then fell back on the pillow with a great sigh, and muttered as though speaking to himself:—

"I can wonder at nothing save my marvellous ill luck. This tale points a moral, Baron Ned. If one belongs to the devil, one should stand by one's master. Hell is swifter in revenge than heaven in reward."

"It is only the long run that tells the tale," I answered, taking his hot hand to soothe him. "Heaven always wins, and your reward will come."

"Ah, yes, the long run is all right if one can only hold out," he answered, gripping my hand and breathing rapidly. He was almost in delirium. "But I'll take the short run, Baron Ned." Here his voice rose almost to a scream: "I'll take the short run, Ned, and will kill the king! Then to hell after him by way of Tyburn Hill!"

He sprang to me, grasped my shoulders fiercely, and spoke as one in a frenzy: "I was right, Ned. She is all I thought she was at Sundridge. When I first knew her I doubted my senses. I did not know there was a pure woman outside of a convent, but when I learned to know her I changed my mind. Now comes this accursed Charles Stuart! His house has been a bane to England ever since the spawn of the Scotch courtesan first came to London. But his reign will be short!"

He was becoming delirious, so I induced him to lie on the bed while I went downstairs to find Betty. When I found her, I told her that the fever was mounting to Hamilton's brain, and that I feared he would soon become violent.

She sent a boy to fetch a physician, then turned to me, saying:—

"I'll go up to him. I believe I can quiet him."

So we went back to George's room and found him out of bed, prowling about like a caged wild thing, tossing his arms, and shouting his intention to kill the king.

"You must go back to bed, Master Hamilton," commanded Betty in her soft, low voice.

He caught her around the waist and said, laughing, "You're a good girl, Betty."

"I hope I am, sir. But you must go back to bed," she answered.

"And you're pretty, too. Pretty and good don't usually go together," said George, drawing her close to him.

"No, but you must go back to bed, Master Hamilton, or you will be very ill," she pleaded.

"I'll go for a kiss, Betty," he answered, bending over to take it. But she put up her hands to ward him off.

"I'll give you the kiss, Master Hamilton, if you insist. But it will be only a bribe to induce you to do what is for your own good, and if you take it, I shall never come back to your room again."

"Ah, Ned, here's another good girl!" exclaimed George, releasing Betty. "There are two of them in the world! Who would have suspected it? Keep your kisses for your husband, Betty."

"Yes, Master Hamilton," she answered demurely, giving me a luminous glance, all unconscious of its meaning. The glance was my first hint that perhaps Betty had at times been thinking of me.

"All right! Here's to bed, my girl," said Hamilton.

She smoothed the bed covering and turning to leave the room, said, "I'll come back when the physician arrives."

I could easily see that Hamilton was going to have what the old women call a "bad night," so I asked Betty to sit with him, and she consenting, I went by river to my lodging in Whitehall, where I collected a few necessary articles in a bag and returned quickly as possible to the Old Swan. When I reached George's room, I found Betty at her post. The physician had given Hamilton a quieting potion, and he was resting, though at intervals he broke out, shouting his intention to kill the king.

During nearly two weeks Hamilton lay moaning and raving, sweet, dear Betty rarely leaving his side for more than a few minutes at a time. I, too, clung to my post faithfully, but at least a part of my motive in doing so was selfish, being the joy I found in Betty's company. At the end of two weeks George began to recover rapidly, and I was dismissed along with the physician.

When I returned to Whitehall, I found that my Lord Sandwich, under whom I held my place as Second Gentleman of the Wardrobe, had been seeking me. The king had gone to Sheerness on business of the navy two weeks before, and the Earl of Sandwich, being at that time Lord Admiral, was to go down the river on a summons from his Majesty. Much against my will, I was compelled to go with him, and, by reason of this enforced absence, was away from London during the next month or two, when I very much wished to be there.

I saw Frances only twice during George's illness, and as she made no inquiries about him, I concluded that sober thought had brought back her old aversion. Therefore I did not mention his name nor try to correct her error, feeling that it was better for her to remain in her present state of mind.

I was convinced that Hamilton's threats against the life of the king were but the ravings of a frenzied brain, and that he had no intention of killing Charles, but I also felt sure that trouble would come of it, since he had been overheard by several persons. The treason was certain to reach the king's ear, and if it did, Hamilton's life would be in jeopardy. But of that in its turn.

* * * * *

Immediately on my return to London I went down to the Old Swan to see George, of course having Betty in mind. In truth, Betty had been in mind most of the time and much to my regret ever since the day I left her.

Even if I had not been plighted to Mary Hamilton, I could not have asked Betty to be my wife. She would not be happy in my sphere of life, and I could not live in hers. The painful knowledge of this truth did not in any way help me to put her out of my thoughts, but rather made my longing for her all the greater. Since I had learned to know her well, I thought I meant honestly by her. Still she was a barmaid, and I could not always bring myself to respect her as she deserved. Time and again I resolved in all sincerity never to see her again. Since I could not marry her, I would gain nothing but unhappiness myself and perhaps misery for her by continuing my suit.

But when back in London, I persuaded myself that it was my duty to see George, and tried to shut my eyes to the fact that Betty was the real cause of my anxiety.

When I reached the Old Swan, I soon found Betty, and there could be no mistake in my reading of the light I saw in her eyes.

After talking with her a minute or two in the tap-room, I asked her to tell me of Hamilton, and she said hesitatingly that he had left the inn nearly two months ago.

"Do you know where he is?" I asked.

She answered hesitatingly, "N-o-o-o."

I saw that she did not want to be questioned, so I remained chatting with her for an hour, and returned to Whitehall, very proud that I had restrained my tongue during the interview.

* * * * *

On the afternoon following my interview with Betty, I was sitting in my room adjoining my Lord's private closet in the Wardrobe, trying in vain to think of something besides Betty, when I heard a peal of merry laughter, which I recognized as Nelly Gwynn's. Immediately following, I heard the deep, unmistakable voice of the king. They had just entered my Lord's private closet, between which and my room there was a loosely hung door, permitting me to hear all that was said.

"Ah, Rowley," said Nell. "You have been away from me a long weary time, and I know you have forgotten me."

The king denied the charge, and doubtless took his own way to convince her.

"While you have been away, I have found a new friend to console me," said Nelly.

"Ah!" exclaimed the king, with suddenly awakened interest.

"Yes," returned Nelly.

"Is your new friend a man or a woman?" asked Charles.

"A woman, of course, oh, jealous heart! You know there is but one man in the world for me—your ugly self."

"Who is your friend?" asked the king.

"I'll give you three guesses. You admire her greatly," said Nelly.

"Indeed, it must be the Bishop of Canterbury's lady," suggested his Majesty.

"Surely!" exclaimed Nell, with a merry laugh. "But guess again."

When the king had exhausted his three guesses, she said triumphantly, "My new friend's name is Frances Jennings."

"Ah, indeed!" exclaimed the king. "She will have nothing to say to my friends, Lady Castlemain and others, and I supposed she would be too nice and proper to choose you for her friend."

"No, no," returned Nelly. "She is my first friend among the court ladies. We have had several rare adventures together, and don't you know, I have discovered that she is in love."

"With whom?" demanded the king.

"With your friend and mine, George Hamilton," returned Nelly.

"Ah, well, he is in France, and we shall see that he remains there," said the king.

"No, he is not in France. He is in London," said Nelly. "I saw him at the Old Swan just before you left for Sheerness, nearly two months ago."

"Odds fish!" swore his Majesty. "We'll find a mission for him abroad."

"You'll have to find him first," said Nelly. "I've been down to the Old Swan to see him, but the girl there tells me he left the tavern long ago, and I suspect he is at his brother's house near St. Albans. But I'll tell you further."

Then she told the king what Frances had said about a

mysterious man whom Nelly asserted Frances both hated and loved. She told him also that Frances had recognized one of the highwaymen who had robbed Roger Wentworth, and closed her narrative with an account of my cousin's refusal to recognize Hamilton and her eagerness to explain to him after the fight.

"So you see, Rowley dear, I put this and that together and concluded that Frances Jennings loves George Hamilton because she can't help it, and hates him because she recognized him as one of the murderers of Roger Wentworth. She did not say that this is all true, nor will she talk on the subject, but one may see through a millstone with a hole in it."

"Perhaps Hamilton's complicity in the crime may save us the trouble of sending him abroad," said the king. "We may be able to hang him instead."

"Surely you would not hang him for so small an offence? The murdered man was only a tanner!" cried Nelly, fearing she had brought trouble on Hamilton by her gossip.

"Of course, if there were no reason save the demands of grasping justice, we should not trouble ourselves to look into the matter," said Charles, "but stern justice, if used and not abused, is often a ready help to kings."

Charles laughed, doubtless showing his yellow fangs, as was his habit when uttering a cruel jest, and Nelly began to coax him, hoping to avert the unforeseen trouble she had set afoot. At last the king promised that he would take no steps against Hamilton, but I knew that royal promises were never worth the breath they cost in making.

* * * * *

As soon as Nelly and the king left my lord's closet, I hastened to the river and took a boat for the Old Swan, intending to find Hamilton and to warn him.

When I told Betty that I wanted to see Hamilton on an affair of great urgency, she admitted that she knew where he was, and that she had refused to tell me when I asked her the last time because he had exacted a promise from her to tell no one.

"But I shall see him," said Betty, "and if you will come back to-morrow, I'll tell you where he can be found if he consents."

During the last month or two a *News Letter* had been circulated by thousands throughout London and Westminster, in which the character of the king had been assailed with great bitterness. At first Charles paid no attention to the new journal, but soon its attacks got under his skin. I was told that efforts had been made to discover the publisher and his printing shop, but that nothing could be learned save that the sheets were left at taverns and bookstalls by boys who declared they found them in bundles in the churchyards.

It was impossible to find even the boys. The bookstalls and taverns were ordered not to sell the *News Letter*, but the people hated the king so bitterly that the circulation increased rather than diminished after the royal interdict, and as the sheets sold for the extravagant price of one shilling, it was impossible to stop the sale, since every one who handled them was making a rich profit.

Judging from many articles appearing in the *News Letter*, I suspected that Hamilton was a contributor, if not the editor. If either, he was piling up trouble, should he be discovered.

On leaving the Old Swan, I went back to the palace and met Frances at the Holbein Gate, cloaked and bonneted, ready to go to see her father.

I offered to accompany her, and we took a coach at Charing Cross for Sir Richard's house.

My conscience had troubled me because I had done nothing to clear Hamilton of her unjust suspicions. Up to that time I had found no opportunity to speak to her privately after my return from Sheerness, nor had I fully made up my mind to try to convince her that George was not guilty of Roger's death. But when she and I entered the coach to go to her father's house, I broached the subject:—

"You remember, cousin," I began, "what I said to you in Hamilton's presence on the Bourne Path?"

"Every word," she replied. "It was all true, and I shall be grateful so long as I live."

"But what I said at that time did not seem to cause you to hate him?" I continued, wondering what her reply would be.

"No," she answered, with slight hesitancy. "It did not."

"Is the aversion you now feel toward him the result of what I said at that time?" I asked.

"No, no," she returned quickly. Then suddenly checking herself, she demanded, "Why do you speak of my aversion to him, and what do you know about it?"

I told her that I knew all the particulars of her meeting with Hamilton at the Old Swan, of her refusal to recognize him and of the fight that ensued. I told her of my talk with him, at the beginning of his sickness, two weeks before I left for Sheerness, and then without giving her time to guard against surprise, I asked:—

"Do you believe he was implicated in the Roger Wentworth tragedy?"

She looked at me a moment, and answered defiantly: "I do not believe it. I know it. I have not spoken to any one else about it, nor shall I speak of it again, but I saw him, and of course I hate him." She turned her face from me, and I fancied there were tears in her eyes.

"You know that I do not favor Hamilton as your suitor?" I asked.

"Yes," she answered, still with averted face.

"And if I were to tell you that you were wrong, that Hamilton had no part in the robbing and killing of Roger Wentworth, would you believe me?"

"No, no!" she exclaimed, turning to me quickly, with an angry gleam in her eyes. "I tell you I saw him, and I thank God that at last I know him as he is! After he had fought so bravely to defend me at the Old Swan, my heart softened for a moment, and I forgot that he was a murderer. He is brave and strong, but—why should you try to excuse him now, when you spoke so plainly at Sundridge? I thought you were too severe then; now I know that you told me only a part of the terrible truth. My softened mood lasted only a short time after I left the Old Swan, and I cared not whether he lived or died."

Hoping to put her right, I told her of the wager at the Leg Tavern, which in my opinion fully explained George's presence on the St. Albans road, but she declared that it was a flimsy excuse, and said she did not want to talk further on the subject.

Knowing that I could not convince her at that time, I bore away from the topic and called her attention to the impropriety of taking dinner unescorted at a public house.

"I know all about it, cousin," she returned, "but a good character is of no value in Whitehall. It is an incumbrance. As to my conscience, you need have no fear. When I first came to court, I supposed I should encounter dangers. I was mistaken. I am as safe here as I should be in my father's house. All the pitfalls and snares are to be seen by any one who wishes to see them. It is the sleeping spider that catches the fly, not your bold, brazen hunter, clumsily alert."

I did not want to be preaching constantly to Frances, so we talked on other subjects till we reached my uncle's house, where I remained, singing, dancing, and very merry with Frances, Sarah, and Churchill, till we heard the night watch call, "One o'clock and raining!"

Churchill and I slept at Sir Richard's and returned to Whitehall the next morning.

During the following week I went to see Betty frequently under the pretence of wishing to see Hamilton, but she told me (honestly, I believed) that he had left the Old Swan and that she did not know where he was. So I repeated my visits every day, each visit growing longer and I growing fonder. Betty, too, seemed to be looking for my visits with a degree of pleasure that both pleased and grieved me, for with all my longing for the girl, I never lost sight of the fact that if I were the right sort of man, I should not wish to gain her love to an extent that would mean sorrow to her.

If I were the right sort of man? The question has always set me wondering. The man who never doubts that he is the right sort of man may be put down as all bad, though the right sort of man is not necessarily all good.

CHAPTER VII

THE EYE OF THE DRAGON

One morning, a week or more after my visit to my uncle's house, with Frances, she came to my closet in the Wardrobe greatly excited, and told me that a sheriff had come to take her to one of the London courts of law.

"Here is the paper he gave me," she said, handing me a document which proved to be a subpoena. "I have committed no crime, and I can't imagine what it all means."

After examining the subpoena, I explained: "You are wanted merely as a witness before a jury of inquiry engaged in investigating a crime of some sort. It may be Hamilton's fight at the Old Swan, or it may be the Roger Wentworth affair. Perhaps some one is trying to fix that awful crime on Hamilton. But I tell you, Frances, he is innocent."

I had not, at that time, explained to her that Hamilton and Churchill were two hundred yards behind Crofts and his friends when the robbery was committed, having felt that it was just as well not to make Hamilton's innocence too clear.

We of the court considered ourselves exempt from processes of this sort while in the palace. Therefore I carried the paper to the king, whom I found at cards in his closet.

"What is it, Clyde?" asked his Majesty.

For answer, I handed him the subpoena, and when he had glanced over it, he returned it to me, saying:—

"Please tell the sheriff for me that Mistress Jennings will appear before the court of inquiry this afternoon at two o'clock."

"It is a disagreeable business for a lady, your Majesty," I remarked, bowing. "But if it is your desire—"

"Yes, yes, Clyde! Come with me," he interrupted, leading me out of the room to a corridor. "You see it is this way. We of the palace have so frequently set the law at defiance of late that the citizens are beginning to grumble. In this instance I should like to make a great show of compliance. We'll make it easy for your cousin by going with her. And Clyde, if you will say to the duchess for me that I should deem it a favor if she and one or more of her ladies will accompany us, I doubt not she will be glad to go."

"But, your Majesty, what has my cousin done that she should be dragged before the courts of law?" I asked, pretending ignorance of the real nature of the summons and hoping to ascertain whether the king knew anything about the present occasion.

I gained the information I wanted when he replied instantly: "Oh, she is not to be tried. She has done nothing. She is called only to be questioned concerning a crime now under investigation." Then hedging quickly, "That is, I suppose such is the purpose of the subpoena."

The king's manner and his evident knowledge of what was going on convinced me that Hamilton was the subject of inquiry, and I greatly feared an effort was being made to charge him with Roger Wentworth's death or to arraign him because of his threats against the king's life.

I was about to leave the king when he stopped me, saying "Please go to my Lady Castlemain's lodging over Holbein's Gate and ask her to go with us down to London. And Clyde, have my barge at the Bowling Green stairs at one o'clock so that we may take our leisure going down the river and still reach the law courts on time. Our punctuality will flatter the city folk."

At one o'clock, according to instructions, I went to the royal barge waiting at Bowling Green stairs, where presently came the king, the duchess with one of her ladies, Frances, my Lord Clarendon, and my Lady Castlemain, the last named bearing in her arms a young baby. In a barge which was to follow us were several gentlemen of the court and a halfscore of the king's guardsmen. Evidently the occasion was to be in the nature of a frolic; poor Frances to furnish the entertainment.

On thinking it all over, I was convinced that the investigation, whatever it should turn out to be, had been instigated by the king.

When we entered the barge, Frances clung to my hand and sat down beside me, but the king, who was sitting with the duchess on one hand and Castlemain on the other, beckoned Frances to sit beside him. She went to him reluctantly, and he moved toward the duchess, making room for Frances between himself and Castlemain. But that fair lady objected and moved up to the king, indicating by a nod that Frances might sit on the spot her Ladyship had vacated.

But the king said, "You are to sit by me, Mistress Jennings."

"She'll do nothing of the sort," exclaimed Castlemain, with an oath. "She'll sit on the other side of me or in the bottom of the barge, or in the river, I care not which."

"You shall make room, or I'll have you put out of the barge," said the king, displaying a flash of temper.

Immediately a torrent of profanity and piercing screams came from her Ladyship.

"Let any man lay hands on me," she cried, turning to the king, "and this brat of yours goes into the water!"

"Sit down, in God's name, sit down and have your way," said the king, waving his hand to the man on the wharf to throw the warps aboard.

The duchess laughed and offered to give her place to Frances, but of course my cousin refused and came back to me.

* * * * *

When we reached the courtroom, we found it filled with men, women, and children, most of them belonging to the lower walks of life and all of them eager to see the king, whom they seemed to know was coming.

As we entered, the High Sheriff, in his gown, rose and cried: "Oyez! Oyez! His Majesty is now in presence!" Whereupon the audience rose and remained standing till the king left.

We had entered by the public door, the king doubtless wishing to display himself as fully as possible to the people.

As we passed down the aisle to the bar, I caught the eyes of a man garbed as a Quaker. He wore a thin gray beard, and his white hair hung almost to his shoulders. His bearing and expression were truly sanctimonious, and had the gleam in his eyes been in keeping, I should not have taken a second glance at him. But it was not, so as I came close to him I noticed him carefully and saw that he was observing me. At once I thought of Hamilton, and although I was not at all sure of my ground, I dropped my hat near him, as an excuse for stopping, and, while bending toward him, whispered:—

"Dark spectacles shade the eyes."

If the man was not Hamilton, my remark would mean nothing; if he was, it would give him a valuable hint.

When the king and the duchess were seated, the judge spoke from the bench, calling the attention of the good people of London to the fact that his gracious Majesty had given to the court information which, it was hoped, would lead to the arrest of the man who had committed the heinous crime of robbing and killing Roger Wentworth on the king's highway. The judge said that his gracious Majesty, loving justice as perhaps no other king of England had ever loved it, had come in person to offer as a witness one of the fairest ladies of the court, by whose testimony it was expected the guilty man might be brought to justice.

During this speech, which was much longer than I have given it, I noticed that the king was restless, and I suspected that, in his heart, his Majesty was cursing the judge for a fool.

When the judge sat down, the Grand Jury was summoned, and in a few minutes the wheels of justice were ready to turn. In proceedings of this nature, there is no prisoner at bar;

therefore no one is in court save the crown by its counsel, the purpose being only to obtain information upon which a true bill or indictment may be found against some one suspected of the crime under investigation.

After all was ready, the sheriff escorted Frances to the witness stand, and the judge asked her to place her hand on the Bible. She did so and made oath that she would true answers make to all questions that should be put to her touching her knowledge of the robbery and murder of one Roger Wentworth.

When she had made oath, the king's counsel said: "You may state to the court whether you were acquainted with one Roger Wentworth, a tanner of Sundridge, during his life." To which question Frances answered that she had known Roger since her childhood.

The king's counsel then put several preliminary questions which led up to the time of Roger's murder, after which he asked:—

"You may state to the court whether you saw the faces of any of the highwaymen."

"I did," answered Frances.

"Are you acquainted with one George Hamilton?" asked the lawyer.

"Yes," answered Frances. And my heart almost leaped out of my mouth in fear that her next word would mean death to an innocent man.

"You may state whether George Hamilton was one of the highwaymen who attacked and killed Roger Wentworth."

Frances paused for perhaps ten seconds, but the time seemed an hour to me, and I remember wondering how the Quaker felt.

"No," she answered, in a voice clear as a bell and without a flutter of hesitancy.

It could easily be seen that her answer surprised the court and the king's counsel, and as the king glanced up to Crofts, who was standing by his side, I noticed a queer expression which seemed to say that the evidence was not what they had expected.

The king's counsel held a brief whispered consultation with the judge, who spoke privately to the king, and suddenly Frances was told that the proceedings were over. Evidently the king had refused to have her questioned further, fearing, no doubt, that she might testify to having recognized the real culprits.

After the court had risen, we were perhaps ten minutes making our way from the courtroom, and when we came to the coaches which were to take us to our barge, I saw the Quaker standing near by. He wore colored spectacles. He was Hamilton. As I passed the Quaker, I said to Frances loud enough for him to hear:—

"I shall go to see Betty each Sabbath evening hereafter."

Frances looked up in surprise at my apparently senseless remark, but I did not explain its significance, and she remained in ignorance of the fact that Hamilton had just heard her make what she supposed to be a false oath for his sake. Soon after we reached the palace, my cousin and I walked out to the park, and after a long meditative silence, she asked:—

"Was I guilty of a great sin in making a false oath on the book?"

"No," I answered. "Because you swore to the truth, not only in the spirit, but in the letter. Hamilton was not one of the highwaymen who attacked and killed Roger Wentworth."

"Ah, but I saw him and recognized him," she answered.

"Why, then, did you make oath that you did not?" I asked.

"I have been asking myself the same question over and over," she returned. Then after a long pause. "I deliberately swore falsely. I did recognize him by the light of the lanthorn. I wish I had never seen him, but having known him as I did at one time, I almost wish that I could have remained in ignorance of his guilt. Would that the lanthorn had been dark so that I could not have seen him."

"I do not deny that you saw him, Frances, but I do deny that you saw him attack Roger Wentworth. Hamilton was two hundred yards down the road when Roger was killed. If not, he has lied to me, and, with all his faults, I have always found him truthful."

After a moment she answered musingly: "I believe you are right. Noah had whipped up the horses, and we must have covered at least a hundred yards or more before I saw Master Hamilton's face. I fear I have committed a great sin against him, and this day came near committing a greater. I was on the point of answering 'yes' to the lawyer's question, when some motive prompted me to say 'no,' and to make false oath. I wish I were dead. I have wronged him cruelly, and you are to blame."

The last sentence was purely feminine logic, which is always interesting but usually inaccurate.

She began to weep, and I took her hand to soothe her, as I asked gently: "Tell me, Frances. Tell me all your trouble. Speak it out. Let me be your other self. Perhaps I can help you."

After a long pause she began her pathetic story: "I cannot blind myself to the truth. It is because I cannot stop thinking of him. The creatures that infest this court are but foils to show me that he is a man, even though he be a bad one, while they are mere imitations. I have often heard you say bitingly that women do not hate wickedness in men as they should—"

"I fear it is true," I interrupted dolefully.

"I suppose it is," she continued. "And one might go further and say that no woman ever loved a man only because he was good. Too often goodness is but the lack of courage to do wrong or the absence of temptation. If a man has no qualities save goodness to recommend him, I fear he might go his whole life through not knowing a woman's real love. We are apt to turn from the nauseating innocuousness of the truly good and to thank God for a modicum of interesting sin."

"I'm sorry to hear this philosophy from you, cousin, for it smacks of bitterness, and I regret to learn that you have not thrown off your love for Hamilton, though I have long suspected the truth."

"Yes, yes, Ned, the truth, the truth! I, too, am sorry. But it can't be helped, and I want to tell you all about it," she said, clasping my arm. "I—I am almost mad about him! The king and the courtiers are harmless. It may be that my love exalts

Master Hamilton and debases others by comparison, but it is as I say with me, and I fear it will ever be. He may be bad, but he is strong, brave, and honest. He is a man—all man—and I tell you, Baron Ned, a woman doesn't look much further when she goes to give her love."

My eyes were opening rapidly to qualities in my cousin that I had never suspected, so after a moment I asked in alarm:—

"But surely you would not marry Hamilton?"

"No, I cannot marry him because of father," she answered, shaking her head dolefully. "I must marry a rich man. More than a month ago the Duke of Tyrconnel asked me to be his wife, as you know. He seems to know that he must buy me if he would have me, so he tells me that he has forty thousand pounds a year, and offers to settle ten thousand a year on me if I will marry him. I asked for a fortnight in which to consider his offer, and when the time was up I begged for another, which he granted, kindly saying that he did not want me to answer till I was sure of myself, even though the delay cost him a year's happiness. The time is almost up, and I must ask another extension; but I shall eventually take him, and then God pity me, for I know I shall die."

"No, no, Frances," I returned, trying to conceal my delight. "You will be happy with Dick Talbot if you will thrust the other man out of your heart."

"Thrust the other man out of my heart!" she exclaimed. "It was never done by a woman. She may be cured, I suppose, by time and conditions, but she can't cure herself. A woman's heart is like a telescope. It magnifies the man of her choice, but reverses and becomes a diminishing glass for all others. But I shall accept Tyrconnel just as soon as I grow used to the thought of living with him. Soon you will have accomplished your purpose in bringing me to court."

"My purpose?" I asked in surprise. "Was it not also your purpose?"

"I suppose it was, but I hate myself for having conceived it. I'm learning to hate every one, the king more than any man, unless I except that little wretch, Jermyn, the court lady-killer. What a despicable thing your lady-killer is! Doubtless God created him to show by comparison the great worth of worms, snakes, and other reptiles."

"What has Little Jermyn been doing?" I asked, amused at her vindictiveness.

"He has crushed so many hearts that he deems himself irresistible, and of late has been annoying me. If by any chance he finds me alone, he importunes me to make a tryst with him and save him from death because of a broken heart. I usually answer by walking away from him and try to show him that he is beneath even my contempt, but his vanity is so great that he imagines my manner to be the outgrowth of pique or a desire to lead him on. Therefore when others are present, he gazes on me with down-bent head and eyes upturned from beneath his bulging forehead, as though he would put a spell upon me."

"Well, let him gaze. It can't harm you," I suggested.

"No, but it makes me ill," she answered. "Three nights ago I was standing with the king and several ladies and gentlemen, waiting for the country dance to begin, for which the king was to call the changes. This Little Jermyn came up to the group, and, without speaking a word to any one, fixed his upturned eyes on me."

"That was a sin," I said, laughing, but she ignored my interruption.

"For a time I paid no heed, but soon his gaze so nauseated me that I could not restrain my anger, and said, loud enough for him and the others to hear, 'What ails the little man, that he should stand there staring at me like a sick calf trying to cast a spell upon the moon?' The king laughed and Jermyn bowed, as he replied, 'The moon pretends to disdain veal, doubtless in the hope of having royal beef.' The king laughed and told Jermyn to gaze elsewhere, if the moon refused to be spellbound, and the little creature left us to carry out the king's suggestion. But I shall marry Tyrconnel and make an end of it all just as soon as possible."

We returned to the palace, and I did not see my cousin during the next week. Meantime the king was growing more importunate, and one day affairs reached a terrifying climax when he intimated to Frances that if she would promise to become his wife, he would try to divorce the queen. It has been said, doubtless with truth, that the same offer was made to Mistress Stuart, now the Duchess of Richmond.

When Frances refused his Majesty's offer, which, probably, was made only for the purpose of inducing her to trust him, he asked with ill-concealed anger:—

"Do you refuse my offer because you are still thinking of Hamilton?"

"I would refuse it, your Majesty, were there no other man in the world," answered Frances, bowing and asking leave to withdraw.

When Frances told me of this extraordinary offer, I was convinced that the king had no intention of fulfilling it, but it served to open my eyes to the extent of his passion, and to assure me that he would use any means in his power, however desperate, to gain his end. Frances was in danger.

I also knew that if the king held Hamilton responsible for Frances's obduracy, means would be found of putting him out of the way, if his Majesty could but get hands on him. With this belief strong upon me, I was not surprised when Frances came to me in great tribulation, within a day or two, and said:—

"Cousin Ned, it is reported that Master Hamilton is still in London and that he has avowed his intention to kill the king. The surgeon who dressed his wounds is said to be responsible for the accusation. If he is found, he certainly will die, for the proof will be at hand, false or true. The king told me as much, and offered to pardon Master Hamilton if I would ask it in the proper spirit. But I refused, saying that I did not care a farthing what he did respecting Hamilton. You must find him, Baron Ned! Find him at once and give him warning!"

"I feel sure that Betty knows where he is," I answered. "I'll go to her to-morrow."

"Yes, she may know, and I would save him if I could," answered Frances, trying hard to hold back the tears. "I wronged him cruelly, and now I fear it is too late to make amends. I can only moan and weep, and long to ask him to forgive me and to tell him that I am not the creature he thinks I am. I would speak plainly to him for once of what I am and of what I feel for him, and then I am ready to part from him forever and to marry Tyrconnel or any one else who will give me wealth."

The following day Frances asked and received permission

from the duchess to spend the day with Sir Richard. I offered to accompany her, but she refused so emphatically that I suspected there was a purpose in her mind over and above a mere visit to her father's house.

I remember well the day. It was near the hour of ten when I saw her leave the palace by the garden door. She wore a long dark cloak, a small bonnet, and a full vizard which covered her entire face. I had never known her to wear so large a vizard, as she detested even small ones, and wore them only out of respect for the prevailing fashion. She hastened toward the King Street Gate, and I, following at a short distance, saw her take boat at the Charing Cross stairs.

After thinking over the situation, I determined to go to my uncle's house. As I had suspected, Frances was not there. After greeting Sir Richard and Sarah, I asked them, as though speaking by the way, when they had seen Frances.

"She hasn't been home for a week or more," answered Sir Richard.

"I wish she would make haste in choosing a husband, or in wheedling one to choose her," remarked Sarah. "I'll beat her in the race if she doesn't. If I should, I might furnish a new saw to the world: 'The suitor is not always to the beautiful, nor the husband to the soft of tongue.' I have a gallant."

"So I have suspected of late," I answered.

"Yes, you're right—John Churchill," answered Sarah.

"He is a fine man," I returned.

"Yes," replied Sarah, apparently very serious, though there was a twinkle in her eye. "But I'm not sure of him yet." Then with a sigh: "I would that I were. If he knows what is for his own good, he'll speak soon, as I intend to make a duke of him before he dies, and the sooner we get at it the better. A sensible conscience, prepense to its own interest, a good courtier, and a shrewd wife have made many a duke of far poorer material than my John."

I laughed, and Sir Richard smiled, but we each seemed to feel that Sarah's words were prophetic, and the future bore us out, as all the world knows.

After waiting in my uncle's parlor an hour or more, hoping that Frances would arrive, I took my leave and walked down to the Old Swan, where I found her. What happened there I learned afterward from her and from others—that is, what I did not see for myself.

After leaving Whitehall, Frances had made her way directly to the Old Swan, where she soon found Betty. At first the girl did not seem inclined to be at all cordial, but when Frances told her that she was in trouble and wanted help, Betty's kind heart responded at once. "Trouble" was the password to Betty's good graces.

"Let us go to a room where we may be by ourselves," suggested Frances. "I want to talk to you freely where we shall not be overheard."

Betty led the way to her own little parlor on the second floor and placed a chair for her guest near a window opening on the court. Frances sat down and asked Betty, who evidently intended to remain standing, to bring a chair and sit beside her.

"I would not think of sitting in your Grace's presence," answered Betty, courtesying respectfully.

"Sit down, Betty, please, and let us be friends," said Frances, coaxingly. "I am not a duchess. I am only a girl like yourself. My name is Mistress Jennings—Frances. Nelly Gwynn was jesting when she spoke of me as a duchess, and only wanted to tease you when she objected to the table linen. She is good and kind—no one can be more so."

"Yes," returned Betty. "She came back and said that the linen was beautiful and offered me money for myself, but I refused. You see I am not—well, I am not a servant. But afterward she gave me a hundred jacobusses for the poor, and I thanked her. I am very sorry that I was angry the day of the fight, but you know the great persons who come here from Whitehall are very irritating, and treat us all with contempt."

"I am not a great lady, Betty, though I live at court. I am poor and very far from happy. I am not so good as you, Betty, I'm sure, though I do the best I can not to be bad."

"Oh, you are too beautiful not to be good," returned Betty, warming up to my cousin.

"Whether I am beautiful or not I care little, for I am in great trouble and have come to you for help," said Frances. "My cousin, Baron Clyde, who is as dear to me as a brother, is full of your praises, and only the other day said that there was no woman or girl in England purer or better than you, and that he knew none in the world whom he deemed more beautiful."

The red came to Betty's cheeks, and she answered, smiling and dimpling: "Ah, did he say that of me? I deem him my very good friend indeed. Is he really your cousin?"

"Yes, he is more a brother than a cousin," returned Frances.

Immediately Betty softened and, drawing a chair close to Frances's side, sat down. After a long pause, she murmured: "Then if I may, I, too, would be your friend."

"I knew you would," answered Frances. "Now give me your hand, so that we may feel as well as see and hear each other. Ah, Betty, how soft and warm your hand is. I don't wonder that my cousin praises you. You have won me already, and I hope we may always be good friends."

"I shall be glad," murmured Betty, pressing Frances's hand, assuringly. "You say you are in trouble. In what way may I help you?"

Frances began, "You know Master Hamilton—Master George Hamilton?"

"Yes," answered Betty.

"And you would be glad to help me save him from great peril?" asked Frances.

"Yes, Mistress Jennings. He, too, is my friend and a good man."

"Yes, yes, tell me, Betty. Good, say you? I had not supposed him good, but—"

"If you supposed otherwise, you were wrong," returned Betty, straightening up in her chair, ready to do battle for her friend.

"Yes, yes, tell me, please, Betty, why you deem him good," pleaded Frances, eager to be convinced. "What has he done or left undone?"

"He has left undone all which he should not have done in so far as I know," said Betty, "and has done a great deal of good. Recently when a plague was raging along the wall from Aldgate to Bishopgate, where a great many poor people live, you know, Master Hamilton went down among them at peril of his life."

"Yes, yes," interrupted Frances, eagerly.

"He nursed them and carried food and water to them. You know one stricken with the plague is ready to die of thirst. He took care of the children, helped to bury the dead, which, you know, in case of very poor people, is done after night, consoled the bereaved, and—oh, Mistress Jennings, it was an awful sight!" said Betty, tears coming to her eyes.

"And Master Hamilton helped them?" asked Frances, hoping to keep the glorious narrative going.

"Yes, he did the work of half a score of men," said Betty. "In the disguise of a Quaker, he solicited money with which to buy medicine and to employ physicians, and did everything in his power to comfort the poor sufferers. Doctor Lilly, the astrologer, helped us. People say he is a cheat, but I wish we had more of his kind among us."

"And you helped him?" asked Frances.

"Yes, a little," said Betty, modestly. "But my father helped him a great deal with money and food."

"Master Hamilton is in danger of his life," said Frances, "and I would save him. Will you help me to find him?"

After a long pause, Betty asked: "But how shall I know that you mean fair by him? I'll see him if I can, and when you return, I'll tell you where to find him if he consents."

"So you do know where he is?" asked Frances, eagerly.

Betty did not reply, so Frances continued: "I do mean him fair, Betty. I am risking everything—my good name, perhaps even life itself, in seeking him. I expected to have to prove my good intent, so I brought with me this letter which no one save myself has ever seen, nor any one other than you shall ever see. Read it, Betty. It is one Master Hamilton sent to me from France."

Betty hesitated, but as Frances insisted, she read the letter and returned it, saying:—

"You are his sweetheart?"

"Yes, yes, Betty, in all that is best and most terrible in the meaning of the word."

Betty sat thinking for a moment, then went to the window, saying, "If you will look out the window across the courtyard, you will see a flight of stone steps leading to the cellar."

"Yes, yes, I see," returned Frances.

"If you go down the steps, you will find a door to which I shall give you the key. Enter and you will be in an empty room, the walls of which are hung with worn tapestries taken from the inn. On one side of the room you will see a tapestried panel bearing the image of St. George and the dragon. Behind the panel is a concealed door, seemingly a part of the wall, but if you will allow the tapestry to hang and will press the eye of the dragon, the door will open and you may find—your St. George."

Frances caught Betty in her arms, crying, "Let me go to him at once, at once!"

Betty and Frances went downstairs, and after waiting a minute or two, Betty said, "Now there is no one in the courtyard, and you may cross unseen."

Frances hastened across the courtyard and down the cellar steps. On reaching the outer door of which Betty had spoken, she halted in fear. But she dared not retreat, so inserting the key, she entered.

In the dim light of the room the images of faded knights, angels, saints, and dragons seemed to stand like a small army of ghosts ready to deny her passage. But soon she discovered the figure of St. George, pressed the eye of the dragon, lifted the tapestry, and entered the room of a printing shop.

While Frances had been standing in hesitation before the figure of the saint, she had heard with some alarm a rumbling noise in the room she was about to enter. The rumbling is destined, in my opinion, to go down the line of the ages, an instrument of untold good to mankind, for it was the rumbling of a printing-press.

Standing at the press, lifting and lowering it by means of a foot lever, and feeding it with broad strips of paper, stood a man in his shirt-sleeves. At an inclined desk, a type-case, stood another man setting type, close beside the press. He, also, was in his shirt-sleeves and was much older and stouter than the man at the press.

The rumbling had drowned the slight noise occasioned by the opening of the door, so that Frances stood waiting a full minute before she was observed. The stout man at the type-case was the first to see her, and when he turned, she asked, trembling:—

"I am seeking Master Hamilton. Shall I find him here?"

The man at the press then turned quickly to Frances. His face was smooth shaven, but was almost covered with printers' ink, giving him the appearance of a blackamoor. The stout man at the type-case, failing to respond, and the other being apparently too surprised to speak, Frances went to the blackamoor and, standing beside the press, was about to repeat her inquiry.

The type-case, press, and a small table, on which lay a bundle of white paper, all stood huddled together in the centre of the room, occupying a space of perhaps eight feet square.

Before Frances had gained courage to speak, a small bell rang. Immediately the stout man sprang from the type-case, ran in great haste to a chest near the wall, opened the lid and drew forth a long red cloak and a fez-shaped cap of the same color, each embroidered with signs of the zodiac in tarnished gold. He hurriedly put on the gown and cap, and again diving into the chest, drew forth a long black coat, a broad Quaker hat, a false beard, and a white wig. These he tossed to the blackamoor, then ran across the room, opened a concealed panel in the wall, drew down a lever, closed the panel, sprang to a large desk near by, sat down and began to write diligently.

These strange, rapid actions on the part of the stout man were so surprising and alarming to Frances that for the moment she did not notice that the section of the floor on which she, the blackamoor, and all the printing apparatus were standing was sinking. Almost before she was aware of the startling movement of the floor, which, after it had begun to move, seemed to fall rather than sink, it stopped suddenly, perhaps eight feet below. The floor above closed silently over her head, and she found herself alone with the inky man in almost total darkness. She was too badly frightened to scream, or even to speak, and stood in silence, awaiting with benumbed senses whatever calamity might befall her.

After a minute or two the blackamoor spoke in whispers: "Mistress Jennings need have no fear. The officers of her friend, the king, have just come to the Old Swan seeking me. The bell you heard was the alarm, sounded by Betty Pickering. Unless she is able to keep them away from here, you may perhaps hear the sheriffs presently in the room above with Doctor Lilly, the man you saw at the type-case. If they come, I trust you will remain silent, unless you are here for the purpose of betraying me."

Frances recognized Hamilton's voice, and, notwithstanding his cruel suspicion, her fear gave place to joy, for she knew that she could soon drive all doubt from his heart. His words did not even hurt her, for she bore in mind the great injustice she had done him, and remembered the good reason he had to believe that she was not his friend. She tried to speak calmly and within the bounds of propriety, but the cold words she would have spoken refused to leave her lips, and after a futile effort to restrain herself, that which was in her heart came forth, because she could not keep it back.

"Ah, Master Hamilton, you do not understand. I came to tell you that I am not what you deem me; that if you had good reason to believe me pure when we met at Sundridge, you have the same reason now. I want to tell you that when I refused to recognize you on that awful day in the Old Swan, when you fought so bravely in my behalf, I thought you were guilty of Roger Wentworth's death."

"No, no, I am not that bad," interrupted Hamilton.

"At Sundridge you made me believe that you loved me," continued Frances, unmindful of the interruption. "And now since you would not come to me, nor send me word in all this long weary time, I could not restrain myself, but, all unmaidenly, have come to you because I can in no way put my love from my heart, pray and try as I will."

She reached forth her hand in the dark and touched him. She had not underestimated her strength when she believed that by a word she could drive doubt from his heart and bring him to her feet, for in a breath she who had scorned the love of a king, and had laughed at the greatest nobles in England, was in the arms of a man on whose life the king had set a price. Her head fell back into the bend of his elbow, her willing lips gave him their sweetness, her arm was clasped about his neck, and she had forgotten all save love and the man she loved.

George said nothing, so after a little time, Frances continued: "Tell me that you know I am not the creature evil-minded persons pretend to believe I am. I might have been a duchess, with grand estates, by gift from the king, but I am not, nor ever shall be. I loathe him, and so great is my sense of contamination that when he touches my hand in dancing, I almost feel that it is a thing of evil."

"And you, whom I hear the king would marry, who, I am told, might pick and choose a husband from among the richest and noblest of the land, for whom it is said the Duke of Tyrconnel is longing, come here to this hole and throw yourself away on me, an outcast; one who makes his daily bread by labor at a printing-press, one on whose life the king has set a price? You come here to give yourself to me!" cried George, almost stunned by surprise and joy.

He held her close to him and kissed her lips, not to his content, for that would have been impossible, but till he checked himself to hear her answer. But she did not speak, and after a little time he led her, groping his way in the dark, to a box standing against the wall, where they sat down. She clasped his hand, but did not answer his question.

Supposing that her silence was without cause, and wishing an answer in words, George continued:—

"It is difficult to believe that you, who went to court to make your fortune, should refuse it when it is in your grasp and should give yourself to me."

"No, no," she answered, withdrawing her hand from his clasp and covering her face. "I do not, I may not give myself to you. But I do give you love, such as I believe no woman ever before gave to a man. I am going to marry the Duke of Tyrconnel. But when I learned how grievously I had wronged you, I would not give him my promise of marriage until I had seen you and had told you of my love, and had taken one moment of happiness before the door is closed between us forever."

This answer came to Hamilton as a chilling surprise, but a moment's consideration brought him to see that the girl was right, save, perhaps, in telling her love to a man she could not marry. His knowledge of womankind did not help him to know that her hopelessness had been a stimulant, both to her love and to its prodigal expression. It did not occur to him that what she had done and said might be the outpouring of her despair, and that even a faint hope of ever possessing him as her husband might have operated as a restraint for modesty's sake. Therefore, with unconscious perversity, Hamilton resented what Frances had done in giving him her unmeasured love when she knew that she could not give herself, and he spoke from the midst of his pain:—

"I know that I am not worthy to be your husband. Even had you not taken so great pains to tell me, but had been willing to wreck your life by marrying me, I should not have accepted the sacrifice. From the first, my love for you has been the one unselfish impulse of my life, and since I have almost lost hope of ever being worthy of you, I should not have permitted you to share my wretched life, even had you been willing. But for you to come to me and to give me your love, only to snatch it back again before I have had time to refuse the sacrifice, is cruel."

"I do not snatch my love back again," she answered pleadingly. "I could not if I would. I have given it to you for life, and it is beyond recall. It is yours forever and forever— all of which my poor aching heart is capable. Would you rather it had lain in my breast unspoken, through all the long years I have to live? You say your love is unselfish—"

"If there's anything unselfish in me," interrupted Hamilton.

"Yes, I believe it is unselfish to the extent that a man's love may be," returned Frances, defending herself. "But if it is, surely you would not deny me the joy of telling you of mine, when it is all the happiness I shall ever know my whole life through. You say, with truth, I believe, that you would not permit me to share your fate if I would, because you fear to make me unhappy. Yet you complain and say that I am cruel because I take now what joy I can at so shameful a sacrifice of womanly pride and modesty. You say that I am cruel because I cannot give you all—myself. I would share your fortunes unhesitatingly were it not that I dare not give one thought to my own happiness."

She paused for a moment to gather self-control, and when

she was more calm, proceeded with her defence: "I belong to my father and to my house, and God has appointed me to lift them from their fallen estate. I cannot give you myself, but I do give you my love for the sheer ecstasy of giving, and beg you to accept it as all that I have to offer and to give me the sweet privilege of keeping yours, which. I know is mine, that it may warm my heart in the weary years to come. I wonder if you, being a man, can understand it all. I hardly understand it myself, but this I know: I have done what I have done because I could not help it, and you say that I am cruel because you feel a part of the pain I suffer."

"No, no, I was wrong," said Hamilton, dropping to his knees before her and seizing her hand. "Forgive me and believe that my love is unselfish and that it will be yours so long as I live. All that is not evil in me, I owe to you, and I am striving to make myself more worthy of your love, even though I must surrender you to another."

"Betty told me of your good deeds when a plague was raging in Bishopgate ward," said Frances, "and Baron Ned has told me that you have changed your ways since leaving court."

"I have changed since I learned to know you," he interrupted, "and now, with my first effort to be a man, misfortunes come trooping at my heels so fast that I know not what to do nor where to turn."

"That was one reason why I came to see you," she said. "The king seeks your life because it is said that you threatened his. But you seem to know your danger, and I suppose you have been warned."

"Yes, Grammont warned me. He is a very adroit person and is my friend. He stands guard for me at court, partly because he is my friend, but chiefly, I imagine, because it is the command of his king, Louis of France. I do not want to bring Baron Ned into trouble. He is known to be my friend, and the king might have him watched, so I am using Grammont as my spy at Whitehall."

"Ah, the Frenchman?" returned Frances. "It was he who dubbed me the 'Duchess of Hearts.' He smiles graciously when we meet, but with all we hear about the wickedness of the French, Grammont has shown me greater respect than I have had from any one of the so-called gallants about the court."

"The day may come when I can repay his kindness," said Hamilton.

"But you must leave England at once," continued Frances. "The king's only show of energy comes in a case such as this. His real reason for seeking your life is that he believes you stand between him and me. You must leave England without delay."

"I mean to do so, now that I have seen you," he returned. "The desire to see you and a spirit of reckless bravado has kept me here much longer than prudence would dictate."

At that moment voices were heard in the room above. George pressed Frances's hand to enjoin silence, fearing that the sheriffs were at hand. But presently a clanking noise was heard, and George, listening attentively, whispered:—

"There is no further danger. Lilly is opening the lever panel, and soon the floor will rise."

In a moment the doctor's voice came down through the wall, asking, "Are you ready?"

"Yes," answered Hamilton. And then he led Frances back to the printing-press. Instantly the floor above their heads began to roll back, and from the depths rose Frances and Hamilton, to find Betty and me awaiting them. As they came up through the floor, Betty began to laugh, and soon I joined her, for on Frances's eyes, lips, and cheeks were black inky patches, indicating plainly the exact spots where the battle had raged. Through the ink spots on her cheeks ran furrows ploughed by tears, but, withal, my cousin's beautiful face was never more beautiful.

"They have been a-kissing," whispered Betty, seriously, leaning towards me and speaking behind her hand.

"No, no, Betty," I answered, trying to keep a straight face. But she nodded insistently, evidently much surprised and perhaps a little shocked.

By the time Betty and I had concluded this interchange of ideas, Hamilton and Frances were by my side.

"Why are you here?" asked Hamilton, turning to me and then to Betty.

"I had to bring him," answered Betty. "You told me to tell no one, but I had to tell Mistress Jennings because she cried, and I had to bring Baron Ned because he stormed and said that he knew Mistress Jennings had come to see you."

I supplemented Betty's answer by saying: "I was sure Frances had come to the Old Swan to see you, so I followed, arriving just in time to see her cross the courtyard. I sought Betty and asked her to tell me where you were and where my cousin had gone. Just then three sheriffs arrived, searching for you, and I had to wait until Betty got rid of them. Now, here I am, waiting to take my cousin home."

"But what if your cousin will not go home until she is ready, and does not desire your escort?" asked Frances.

"In that case, I should advise her to make ready at once," I replied.

"And if she does not want your advice?" returned Frances.

"In that case, I should limit my advice to a mere recommendation that she wash the ink stains from her lips, eyes, and cheeks. Master Hamilton has pretty well covered the ground with overgrown beauty patches."

Betty laughed softly, and fat old Lilly chuckled as he resumed his place at his desk.

There being no mirror in the room, Frances put her hand to her face and found traces of printers' ink on her fingers, whereupon she blushed and laughed and was so beautiful that we all laughed from the sheer delight of looking at her.

"Again Baron Ned is right, Frances," said Hamilton, offering to lead her toward the St. George door. "You must not remain. We may be surprised by the sheriffs at any moment, in which case you would suffer in reputation and I might not be able to escape."

We passed into the tapestried room, and after Hamilton had closed the St. George door, we paused for a moment before leaving. Presently I started to go, but Frances held back. I had reached the outer door and was waiting, somewhat impatiently, when Betty came up to me, opened the door, drew me outside, closed the door, and whispered:—

"Don't you understand? They would be alone a moment."

"Do you think so, Betty?" I asked, laughing at her earnestness.

"I know it," she returned emphatically.

When George and Frances were alone, she said: "I shall never again give you cause to say that I am cruel, for I shall never again see you." She tried to keep back the tears, but failed, and after a moment, continued, unheeding them, "If you could but know the joy this meeting has given me and the grief of parting, you would understand my sorrow for having wronged you, and would know the deep pain of farewell."

"I have not spoken of my love for you," said George, "because it is so plain that words are not needed to express it, and because you have known it far better than I could tell it ever since the sweet days on the Bourne Path. To speak it would seem to mar it by half expression. But it will be yours always, and I shall take it to my grave. It has been my redemption, and, as long as I live, no other woman shall enter my heart."

He fell to his knee, catching her hands and kissing them passionately, but she raised him, saying:—

"If it is your will, I shall refuse the Duke of Tyrconnel, regardless of my duty to my father and my house, and shall wait for you, happy even in the waiting, or share your fortune, be it good or ill, from this hour. Which shall it be?"

"Soon I shall be an exile, or climbing the steps of a scaffold on Tyburn Hill. This must be our farewell. Do not remain a moment longer. May God help me and bring happiness to you!" said Hamilton, answering her question all too plainly.

She drew his face down to hers and kissed his lips, till from very fear of himself he thrust her from him and led her weeping to the outer door.

When Frances came out to Betty and me, she was holding her handkerchief to her eyes and her vizard was hanging by its chain.

Sympathetic Betty lifted the vizard, saying: "Cover your face till we go to my room. Poor mistress! It must be all awry with your love, and I have heard that there is no pain like it."

We climbed the steps, and, as we were going across the yard, Betty twined her arm about Frances's waist. Wishing to comfort her by changing the subject, she said:—

"I have neither powder nor rouge in my room, but I have black patches, though I have never dared to use one, fearing to be accused of aping the great ladies."

"Betty, there are no great ladies so good and beautiful as you," said Frances, trying to check her weeping. "If I were a man, you should not go long without a chance for a husband."

"Oh, I've had chances in plenty," answered Betty, proudly. "But father says I'm too hard to suit and will die a maid. He says I want a gentleman, and—" (Here she sighed and glanced involuntarily toward me.) "He is right. I will have none other."

"Seek lower and fare better," said Frances.

"I don't know how it will all turn out," replied Betty with a sigh. The topic seemed to be alive with sighs. "A woman may not choose, and I suppose I shall one day take the man my father chooses, having no part in the affair myself, though it is the most important one in my life."

"Nonsense, Betty," returned Frances. "You are like the rest of us, and when the right one comes, you will seek him if need be—in a cellar. Take my advice, Betty, when the right one comes, help him, and thank me ever after."

When we entered the house, Frances went with Betty to her room, leaving me in the tap-room, waiting to take my foolish cousin home.

To say that I was troubled would feebly express my state of mind. All my dreams of fortune for Frances and glory for her family had vanished. I did not know at that time that she and Hamilton had agreed never to meet again, though had I known, I should have put little faith in the compact.

CHAPTER VIII

IN FEAR OF THE KING

When Frances came downstairs, she and I started home, walking first down Gracious Street, and then through Upper Thames Street toward Temple Bar. It was no time to scold her, since I was sure that she knew quite as well as I could tell her the folly and the recklessness of what she had just done. I also believed there must have been an overpowering motive back of it all, and that being true, I knew that nothing I could say would in any way induce her to repent at present or forbear in future. I might bring her to regret, but regret is a long journey from repentance. If her heart had gone so far beyond her control as to cause her to seek Hamilton, as she had done that day, it were surely a profitless task for me to try to put her right. If she, who was modest, honest, and strong, could not right herself, trying as I knew she had tried, no one else could do it for her.

Even my silence seemed to be a reproach, so I tried to think of something to say which would neither bear upon what she had done nor seem to avoid it.

After a moment or two, Betty, that is, thoughts of her, came to my relief, and I said: "If Betty were at court, she would rival the best of the beauties. There's a charm about the girl which grows on one. I have known her since she came from school in France, over a year ago, and the more I see of her the better I like her. She has grace of person and manner, is well educated, tender of heart, honest, and has wonderful eyes."

"And dimples," suggested Frances. "You might win her, Baron Ned. I should like to see you do something foolish to bring you down to my level."

There was a distinct note of sarcasm in her voice, and I felt sure that if I remained silent there was more to come. I was not disappointed, for presently, after two or three false starts, she continued:—

"I do not care to hear your comments on what I have just done. I know quite as well in my simplicity as you in your wisdom the many good reasons why I should not have visited the Old Swan to-day. I knew before I started, but I should have gone had the reasons been multiplied a thousand fold in number and cogency. Therefore, I do not care to hear your comments on the subject. I should have gone just the same had I feared that death awaited me. I had but one purpose in life, and for weeks have had but one—to see him. If I was willing to put aside the love of my father and all other considerations dear to me, nothing that you can say will do you any good or be of advantage to me."

"My dear Frances," I replied, "I find no fault with you. I am sorry you had to do it, but I know it could not be avoided. You were helpless against an overpowering motive. I am sorry for you, yet I admire you more than ever before, because of your recklessness. I have always thought you were cold, or at least that you were wise enough to keep yourself cool, but now I know that beneath your beauty there is a soul that can burn, a heart that can yearn, and a reckless disregard of consequences that on occasion may make a blessed fool of you. It is such women as you who keep alive the spark of Himself which God first breathed into man. I do not blame you. I pity you, and am lost in wondering what will come of it all."

After a long pause, she spoke, sighing: "Although you may not understand what I mean, there was a great deal of right as well as wrong in what I did. I owed to his love, which I knew to be true, an acknowledgment of mine, but more, I had wronged him grievously, and it was right that I should make what poor amends I could. But right or wrong, I did what I had to do, and I do not intend to blame myself, nor to hear blame from any one else. I am perfectly willing that the whole world should know what I have done—that is, I should be were it not for father."

"Again I say I do not blame you," I returned, "though I wish sincerely you had not gone."

"Why did you follow me, and how did you know where I had gone?" asked Frances.

I told her of my visit to her father's house and how, upon my failure to find her there, I went to the Old Swan.

"I thought it would be better that you should leave the Old Swan with me than alone," I said. "It would have been better had you taken me with you."

"Would you have gone with me, knowing my errand?" she asked.

"Yes, gladly," I answered. "When a woman deliberately makes up her mind to do a thing of this sort, she does it sooner or later, despite heaven, earth, or the other place to the contrary. I should have gained nothing by opposing you; I could at least have given color of propriety by going with you."

We walked up Thames Street till we came to the neighborhood of Baynard's Castle, where we took boat and went to Whitehall, each of us in silent revery all the way.

While I was paying the waterman, Frances ran up the stairs to the garden, and when I followed I saw her talking to the king, so I stopped ten or twelve paces from them and removed my hat. Being in their lee, the wind brought the king's words to me, and I imagined, from the loud tone in which he spoke, that he intended me to hear what he had to say. Perhaps he suspected that I had helped Frances in her morning's escapade.

"I am greatly disappointed, my angel, my beauty," said the king, "that you have taken this morning's excursion."

So he knew of her "excursion," and doubtless had instigated the visit of the sheriffs to the Old Swan.

"What has your angel done this morning to displease her king?" asked Frances, with a laugh so merry that one might well have supposed it genuine.

"What has she done this morning?" repeated the king. "She has been to visit the man who seeks the king's life. That is what she has done."

He had hit the nail squarely on the head at the first stroke, but whether his accuracy was a mere guess, or the result of knowledge, I did not know. I trembled, awaiting the outcome of my cousin's conference.

At first Frances appeared to be horror-stricken, and her surprise seemed to know no bounds, but after a moment of splendid acting, her manner changed to one of righteous indignation, touched with grief, because the king had so wrongfully accused her.

"Your Majesty horrifies me!" she exclaimed, stepping back from the king. "Is there a man in all England who would seek his king's life?"

"There is," returned his Majesty. "And you have been to visit him."

Frances denied nothing. She was simply stunned by grief and benumbed by a sense of outrage put upon her by the king. So after a moment of inimitable pantomime, she answered, speaking softly:—

"I fear a gentle madness has touched your Majesty's brain, else you would not so cruelly accuse me. You have so many weighty affairs to trouble you and to prey on your mind that it is no wonder—"

"Did you not set out this morning with the avowed purpose of going to your father's house?" asked the king.

"Yes, your Majesty," she answered soothingly, almost pityingly. "What then?"

"Did you go there?" asked Charles.

"No, your Majesty."

"Where did you go?"

"Am I a prisoner in Whitehall that I may not come and go at

will?" she asked indignantly, knowing well the maxim of battle that the best way to meet a charge is by a counter-charge. "If so, I pray leave to go home to my father, where I shall not be spied upon and suspected of evil if I but go abroad for an hour."

Her grief had changed to indignation, and she turned her face from the king, drying the supposed tears and exhibiting her temper in irresistible pantomime. The king was but a man, so of course Frances's tears and her just anger routed him. A brave man may stand against powder and steel, but he must flee before fire and flood.

Immediately the king became apologetic: "I do not suspect you of evil, but of thoughtlessness, my beautiful one," he said, trying to take her hand, but failing. "Nor have I spied upon you. I heard that you had gone to the Old Swan to see Hamilton, whom it is said you love."

Pantomime to show great grief and a deep sense of cruel injury, but the tears ceased to flow because of the fact that she was past tears now.

"I'll leave Whitehall this day!" she said, shaking her head dolefully. "I am not strong enough to bear your Majesty's unjust frown. I have tried to do right, tried to please you and the duchess—everybody, and this is my reward! I know little of Master Hamilton, having seen him only a few times in all my life. If I had no other cause to shun him, his character would be sufficient."

Again the handkerchief was brought to the eyes effectively, for the purpose of giving the king a little time in which to see how grievously he had wronged her. It required but little time for him to realize how cruel he had been, and in a moment he said pleadingly:—

Charles Major

"Your king asks your forgiveness. I do not suspect you of having gone to see Hamilton. I am convinced that I was wrong. But won't you tell me, please, why you visited the Old Swan? It is a decent tavern, I understand, but a public place of the sort should not be visited by one such as you unescorted."

"Your Majesty is right, and I thank you for the reprimand," returned Frances, drying her eyes. "But Pickering, who is the host of the Old Swan, has a daughter, Bettina, who is a good girl, far above her station. She is my friend. I went to see her this morning to drink a cup of wormwood wine with her. Now you know my reason for going."

Wormwood wine was considered a toper's drink.

Her confusion and modest hesitancy in confessing to the wormwood wine were so pretty and so convincing that the king laughed and seized her by the arm affectionately:—

"Ah, at last it is out!" he cried. "I have discovered your sin! I knew you must have one tucked about you somewhere. Wormwood wine! Absinthe! The drink of our depraved French friends! Who would have suspected you of using it?"

"Yes," murmured Frances, glad to be found guilty of the wrong sin.

"Ah, well, we'll have it together here at home," said the king, "so that you need not go abroad for it hereafter."

"No, no, I shall never again drink wormwood," protested Frances. "Betty Pickering tells me it causes vapors in the head, horrid waking dreams, and in the end incurable spasms."

"Your resolution is well taken," returned the king. "We shall seek a harmless substitute."

At this point in the conversation his Majesty looked toward me, whispered a word to Frances, and they walked down the garden path to the fountain, while I waited at Bowling Green for Frances's return. When she came back, she told me in detail all that passed between her and the king.

After they had left me, the king began to talk, and Frances seldom interrupted him save to draw him out, knowing that a talking man sooner or later tells a great deal that he should have left unsaid. This is especially true if a shrewd listener reads between his words.

"Nelly Gwynn tells me that you love George Hamilton," said the king, "and in my eyes, that is his greatest crime."

Already his Majesty had told a great deal.

"I am surprised at Mistress Gwynn's imagination and her lack of truthfulness," returned Frances. "I told her I hated him, and she herself heard me deny that I knew him when he offered to speak to me two months ago or more at the Old Swan. Mistress Gwynn kissed him. I refused to recognize him. I should say that the evidences of affection were against her rather than me."

"She says, also," continued the king, "that you believe Master Hamilton killed Roger Wentworth; that you recognized him the night of the tragedy."

"I said nothing of the sort," answered Frances, emphatically. "I saw but one man's face distinctly. Here at court I have often seen the man who killed Roger Wentworth, and I shall tell you his name if you insist. He is near of kin to your Majesty."

The king knew that she meant his son Crofts, so he hastened away from the subject.

"Yes, yes, I have suspected as much, but I beg you, Frances, to spare me the pain of hearing the truth."

"Yes, the truth is a frightful thing," sighed Frances. "Why cannot the world be made up of pleasing lies? But tell me, does your Majesty mean to say that the wretch, Hamilton, seeks your life?"

She was seeking information.

"He does, he does," returned the king. "While he was sick at the Old Swan, one standing outside his door heard him declare his intention to kill the king. When I heard of the threat, I summoned his physician, one Doctor Lilly, who, being questioned, admitted that while in a delirium Hamilton had made threats against the king's life, but that he, Lilly, had supposed the French king was meant. Lilly is a good faithful subject, and I often use his astrological knowledge, which is really great, but in this case I suspect he is trying to shield Hamilton, believing, perhaps, that the threats meant nothing because they were made in delirium."

"It is horrible to think upon," answered Frances, shivering. "But he has gone to France, and, thank Heaven, your Majesty is safe. Perhaps he has gone to kill King Louis."

"How do you know he has gone to France?" asked the king, much interested.

"I had a letter from him. He imagines he is in love with me," answered Frances, speaking in the letter of truth and with a fine air of calmness. She had received a letter from George in France, but it was before his return to England.

"Ah, indeed!" exclaimed the king. "Your news contradicts your avowal that you are not in love with him."

"Shall I be in love with all who say they are in love with me?" asked Frances, glancing up to the king.

"God forbid!" he answered. "I would have you in love with but one—one who loves your voice, your beauty, your goodness."

"Your Majesty may at least rest easy so far as Hamilton is concerned," she returned.

"But I am glad that he is out of the country, and shall see to it that he doesn't come back," said the king.

His Majesty had talked too long, for Frances had learned that his suspicions of her love of Hamilton were not allayed, despite his pretense to the contrary.

"I care not where he be so long as he doesn't trouble me," answered Frances, sighing.

"But if it is not one it is another," said the king, ruefully. "I hear that the Duke of Tyrconnel is mad for love of you."

This was a welcome opportunity to Frances, and she quickly used it. "Yes. At least, he says he is. What does your Majesty advise? Shall I marry him or not?"

"By all means, not!" returned the king, with strong emphasis. "He would take you from court. Do you return his love?"

"Well—" answered Frances, drooping her head and pausing to allow the king to fill the blank.

"But you shall not marry him," insisted the king.

"But you would not have me live a maid? Think of the humiliation of having graven on my tombstone: 'Mistress Frances Jennings, Age 85.' I'm going to marry the richest man that asks me."

"Odds fish! that's Tyrconnel!" exclaimed the king.

"I'll find a pretext for sending him to the Tower at once."

"If you do," returned Frances, laughing, "there is Little Jermyn. He will be rich and an earl when his uncle dies."

"I'll send him along with Tyrconnel," declared the king.

"And there is—" began Frances, laughing.

But the king interrupted her, "I'll send every man to the Tower that wants to marry you, if I depopulate the court."

"But here comes old Lady Castlemain," said Frances, turning to leave the king. "I can't quarrel with her, because I can't swear with her. May I take my leave, your Majesty?"

"I am sorry to grant it, but good-by," returned the king.

"Good-by, your Majesty, and thank you," returned Frances, grateful for much that the king did not know he had told her. Then she came to me and told me what the king had said, not omitting her conclusions based on what he had left unsaid.

Frances and I walked over to the park, where we stood for a time watching the Duke of York and John Churchill playing pall-mall, but the day growing cold, we soon continued our walk over to the Serpentine, where we found Tyrconnel and several other gentlemen riding. Tyrconnel dismounted and, leading his horse, came to us. He took no notice of me, but bowed to Frances, saying:—

"I hear it from the king himself that Mistress Jennings has been calling on her friend, George Hamilton, at his lodgings in the Old Swan."

"And if so, is it a matter of which you have any right to speak?" asked Frances, smiling.

"I have a right to withdraw the proposal of marriage I so foolishly made," he retorted.

"Yes, my lord," answered Frances, laughing softly. "But you need not be angry if I am not. How fortunate for me that I had not accepted." Then turning to leave and looking back at him: "May we not still be friends, my lord? You have friends at court who are as bad as I, even if what you say be true. You say it is true; the king says it is true; therefore it must be true. Two men so wise and honest could not be mistaken in so small a matter, nor would they lie solely for the purpose of injuring a woman. No, it must be true, my lord, and I congratulate you on your timely withdrawal."

We had not taken fifty steps till Tyrconnel gave his horse to a boy and came running after us, infinitely more eager to retract the withdrawal than he had been to withdraw his proposal. He protested by all things holy his total disbelief in the scandalous story, and begged Frances not to remember what he had said in jealous anger.

"Be careful, my lord. Do not make another mistake," said Frances, laughing in his face. "I did visit the Old Swan this morning, and the king told me less than thirty minutes ago that Master Hamilton lives there. It is said by those who claim to know that he is in France, but they must be wrong, and I must have seen him. The king says I did, and he can do no wrong. I neither deny nor affirm, though I fancy that my real friends will not believe me guilty of the indiscretion."

"I do not believe it," protested Tyrconnel. "I know you are all that is good."

"Thank you, my lord," returned Frances. "If I am good, I remain so for my own sake. As for the gossips, they may think what they please, talk about me to their hearts' content, and go to the devil for his content, if he can find it in them."

Seeing that Tyrconnel wanted to speak with Frances alone, I drew to a little distance for the purpose of giving him an opportunity to press his suit, in which I so heartily wished him success.

It is uphill work making love to a woman whose heart is filled to overflowing with love of another man, and I was sorry for poor earnest Tyrconnel as I watched him pleading his case with Frances. He was not a burning light intellectually, but he entertained a just estimate of himself and was wise enough not to take any one of the daintily baited hooks that were dangled before him by some of the fairest anglers in England. But manlike, he yearned for the hook that was not in the water.

I followed Frances and Tyrconnel back to the palace, and when they parted at the King's Street Gate, he asked me to go with him to the sign of the King's Head and have a tankard of mulled sack and a breast of Welsh mutton right off the spit.

Tyrconnel's speech was made up of an amusing lisp grafted on the broadest Irish brogue ever heard outside of Killarney. It cannot be reproduced in print; therefore I shall not attempt it. But it was so comical that one could never rid one's self of a desire to laugh, be his Lordship ever so earnest. As a result of this amusing manner of speech, his most serious words never produced a thoughtful impression on his hearers. It is said that the king once laughed when Tyrconnel, in tears, told him of the death of his Lordship's mother.

Arriving at the King's Head, Tyrconnel chose a table in a remote alcove of the dining room. After the maid had brought us the mulled sack and had gone to fetch the mutton, his Lordship began earnestly, but laughably, to tell me his troubles, and I did my best to listen seriously, though with poor result.

"I want to marry your cousin, baron," he said. "Yes, yes, go on. Laugh! I don't mind it. I know you can't help it. But listen. I want to marry her because she is beautiful and because I know she is good. But if she is in love with Hamilton, as report says she is, I should not want to inflict my suit upon her. I know that at best I am no genius, but I am not so great a fool as to seek an opportunity to make myself appear more stupid than I am. Of course she can never marry Hamilton, but a hopeless love clings to a woman as burning oil to the skin and is well-nigh as impossible to extinguish. Therefore I beg you tell me. Shall I beat a retreat and take care of my wounded, or shall I continue the battle?"

"I should not trouble myself about the wounded," I answered, reluctant to evade the truth, for he was an honest soul, very much in earnest.

"But do you speak honestly?" he asked, mopping the perspiration from his face with the tablecloth. "She laughs when I speak seriously, but I have hoped that it was because of my damnable manner of speech rather than my suit. Tell me, what do you think about it? Is she in love with Hamilton?"

Charles Major

His appeal was hard to resist, but I answered evasively in the spirit if not the letter of a lie: "Thus much I know. My cousin has seen very little of Hamilton—so little that it appears almost impossible for one of her sound judgment and cool blood to have fallen in love with him. I can swear that she has not, nor ever has had, a thought of marrying him. She had better kill herself."

"Ah, that's all true enough," he answered. "And now that he is in disgrace, with a noose awaiting him on Tyburn, it is of course impossible for her to marry him. But you see, my dear fellow, she may love him. Nelly Gwynn says she does."

"Yes," I replied. "Nelly set the story afloat. Her tongue is self acting. But she had no reason to do so save in her imagination and her love of talking. Half the troubles in life are caused by your automatic talkers."

I then told him of my cousin's visit with Nelly to the Old Swan, laying emphasis on Frances's refusal to recognize Hamilton, but saying nothing of the fight that followed.

"I am glad to learn the truth, if it is the truth," lisped his Lordship, musingly.

"If you would know the real danger to Frances, you must look higher," I said, cautiously refraining from being too explicit. "There is one whom my cousin scorns, but from whom she is in hourly peril. There is no length to which he would not go, no crime, however dastardly, he would not commit to gain his end. I watch over her constantly, and although my fear may be groundless, still I believe that her only safety is to marry at once and to leave court with her husband."

"But you say she despises him?" he asked.

"Yes, she even hates him. Still she is in great danger; perhaps in danger of her life. We all know that crimes have been committed by this person—crimes so horrible as to be almost past belief. You remember the parson's daughter who jumped from a high wall and killed herself to escape him."

"You are her guardian, baron. Let me be her watchdog," said Tyrconnel, leaning eagerly across the table toward me. "And if I am so fortunate as to win her love by constant devotion, she shall be my wife."

I offered my hand as a silent compact, and we finished our mutton almost without another word.

Two days after my interview with Tyrconnel, George Hamilton's *News Letter* appeared, containing a vicious attack on the king, which angered his Majesty greatly and seemed to arouse anew his suspicion that Hamilton was not in France, some one having told him on a mere suspicion that George was the editor of the *News Letter*. His Majesty accused Frances of falsehood in having told him that she had not seen Hamilton and that she believed he was in France, but she becoming indignant, he again apologized.

Frances's account of the king's state of mind alarmed me, and I determined to see George as soon as possible and advise him to leave England at once. I was delayed in going, but on a cold, stormy day at the end of a fortnight I found my opportunity, and took boat for the Old Swan, not minding the snow and sleet, because I was very happy knowing that I should see Betty. I had of late done all in my power to keep away from her, but the longing had grown upon me, and I was glad to have an honest excuse to visit Gracious Street.

I have spoken heretofore of my engagement to marry Mary Hamilton, and my passion for Betty may indicate that my heart was susceptible, if not fickle. But aside from Betty's Hebe-like charms of person and sweetness of disposition, there were other reasons for my falling off respecting Mary. While she had promised to marry me, still there was a coldness, perhaps I should say a calmness, in her manner toward me, and a cautiousness in holding me aloof which seemed to indicate a desire on her part for a better establishment in life than I could give, if perchance a better offered. My suit had not prospered, though it had not failed, since she was to be my wife provided she found no more eligible husband within a reasonable time.

Dangling blunts the edge of ardor; therefore I soon found myself noticing beauty elsewhere and discovered none that could be compared with that of Betty Pickering of the Old Swan. It is true she was, in a sense, a barmaid, and equally true that I had no thought of marrying her. Still it was significant even at that early time that my mind reverted to the fact that Edward Hyde, Lord Chancellor of England and Earl of Clarendon, had married an innkeeper's widow, whose daughter became the mother of two queens.

While this was true, still I respected Betty less than I admired her and far less than she deserved, never entirely forgetting her station in life nor ceasing to recognize the great distance between us.

When I entered the Old Swan, Betty greeted me with a smile amid a nest of dimples, and led me upstairs to her parlor, so that we might talk without being overheard. I sat down on a settle, and Betty took her place beside me. Her hands rested on her lap, giving her an air of contentment as she turned her face toward me and asked:—

"Have you come to see Master Hamilton?"

"Yes," I answered, "and you."

"And me?" she asked, looking up with a curious little smile. "In what way may I serve you?"

"By sitting there and permitting me to look at you," I answered.

"Oh, is that all?" she asked, laughing softly.

"And by smiling once in a while," I suggested.

"Who shall smile? You or I?" she queried, glancing slyly up to me.

"Oh, you, by all means," I returned. "There is no beauty in my smile, while yours—"

"Come, come, Baron Ned," she interrupted, looking up to me pleadingly. "My smiles are honest, and that is all that is needful in my case. So don't try to make me believe they are anything more. Don't make a fool of me by flattery."

"Don't you like flattery, Betty?" I asked.

"Yes, of course I do," she returned, smiling and dimpling exquisitely. "But it is not good for me. You know I might grow to believing it and you."

"But it is true, Betty, and you may believe me," I answered, very earnestly, taking her hand from her lap.

She permitted me to hold her hand for a moment, and said:—

"I am so desirous of keeping my regard for you and of holding your regard for me that I am tempted to tell you I fear it will all change if I find you inclined to doubt that I am an honest girl."

"I do not doubt it, Betty," I answered. "I know you and respect you, and you shall have no good cause to change your regard for me, if you have any."

"Frequently gentlemen are rude to me in the tap-room, and I submit rather than make trouble by resenting it, but you have always been respectful, and—and I have appreciated it, Baron Ned. Father says I need not go to the tap-room hereafter, but may direct the maids in the house, now that I am growing old—near twenty."

"Twenty?" I asked. And she nodded her head proudly.

"Yes."

"I thought you were still a child," I remarked.

"No, no," she returned, looking up to me open-eyed and very serious. "I am a woman."

"Yes, a beautiful child-woman—the most beautiful in all the world," I said, grasping her hand and holding it a moment till its fluttering ceased. "And I am jealous of every other man who comes near you."

I saw that my remark had offended her, so I continued earnestly: "I meant it, Betty; I meant it. I was not jesting."

Betty sighed, looked quickly up to me, half in doubt, half in inquiry, and was about to speak, but closed her lips on her words and leaned forward, her head drooping eloquently. Her gentleness, her sweetness, and her beauty were so tempting that I could not resist their charm. Again I caught her hand, and it trembled in mine as she tried faintly to withdraw it. I tried to check myself but failed, and I put my arm about her waist. Then, after a mighty effort to stay my words, I said pleadingly:—

"Ah, Betty, I love you. Please, please, Betty, believe me, and—and—just one kiss."

"No, no," she cried pleadingly, trying to draw away from me. "It could not be honest between us. You are a nobleman—I, a barmaid. Your friendship is very dear to me. Please let me keep it, Baron Ned, and let me keep my regard for you. Let there be at least one man whom I do not fear. You know there can be nothing honest between us, and if it be possible that one so lowly as I can deserve your respect, let me have it, Baron Ned, let me have it. Let me keep it, for it is the dearest thing in life to me."

There was such deep entreaty in her voice that it touched me to the heart, and I drew away from her immediately, saying:—

"I do know there can be nothing honest between us, Betty, and knowing it, have suffered. What I have said to you is little compared to what I feel and to what I would say. I can't help it that I love you, Betty, but you shall never have cause to fear me. Do you believe me and do you trust me, Betty?"

For answer she held up her lips to me. What she had refused on my request, she gave of her own accord, saying:—

"There, Baron Ned. Now, if you really respect me, you will know that I trust you, for I am not a girl to do this thing wantonly. Perhaps I should not have done it at all, but you must know that I could not help it. If you care for my friendship or are concerned for my happiness, I beg you never tempt me to repeat my folly. There is no other man, but now you must know after what I have done, that there is one—yourself. But there can be nothing but friendship between us, Baron Ned, and oh, that is so much to me! Let me have what happiness I can find in it!"

"But I love you, Betty, and I know that you love me," I answered, unable to restrain my tongue.

She did not speak, so I asked, "Do you not, Betty?"

"No," she answered, shaking her head dolefully. But I knew she did not tell the truth.

Presently she asked. "Do you want to see Master Hamilton?"

I answered that I did, and she said I might go to the printing shop, where she was sure I should find him.

She rose and started toward the door. I called to her, but she did not stop, so I ran after her, saying:—

"Have I offended you, Betty?"

"No," she answered, drooping her head. "But I am very unhappy, and I want to be alone so that I may cry. You know it is much harder to forego the thing one wants but may not take, than it is to do without the thing one wants but cannot take. Yearning for the impossible brings longing, for the possible anguish."

And I remained silent, almost hating myself.

I went to the tap-room with Betty, and the courtyard being vacant for a moment, I ran across and down the steps to see Hamilton.

I had tried to see Frances that morning at Whitehall, but failed, being told that she had gone to visit her father. I had stopped at Sir Richard's house, but Frances was not there, and I half suspected I might find her with Hamilton.

I found Hamilton at his printing-press, and after I had told him of the risk he ran by remaining in London, he said:—

"I have been making an honest living from my *News Letter* and am sorry to give it up, but I fear trouble will come very soon if I continue to publish it. The king has a score of human bloodhounds seeking me. It is rather odd, isn't it, to hear a man of the house of Hamilton talking about making money by work, but of all the money I have ever touched, that which I have made honestly from the *News Letter* has been the sweetest. The work has been a delight to me, even aside from the fact that it gives me an opportunity to abuse the king. Lilly tells me that the king asked him to consult the stars concerning my threats against the royal life. The result was favorable to me."

"It is strange that the king should be duped by a palpable humbug," I remarked, supposing that George would agree with me. But, no! He turned on me almost fiercely:—

"Lilly is not a humbug! Of course he humbugs the king, but everybody does. I have known him to do some wonderful things by the help of his astrological figures, conjunctions, constellations, and calculations."

"Nonsense! All humbug, I tell you!" I asserted, somewhat disgusted.

"No, it is not all nonsense," he insisted. "A poor woman lost a sum of money ten days ago. Lilly set a figure and told her where to find it."

"And of course she found it?" I inquired incredulously.

"Yes, she found it," returned George. "And Lilly would not accept a farthing for his service. Two months ago a child was stolen from its home in Devonshire, and the parents came all the way to London to consult Lilly."

"And of course they found the child?" I asked.

"They did. It was with a band of gypsies who made their headquarters at a place called Gypsy Hill, Lambeth," returned Hamilton, provoked by my scepticism. "He learns some very curious truths from the stars."

"The stars!" I exclaimed contemptuously. "He is a shrewd observer of men and of things about him, and when he guesses right, I venture to say he finds his inspiration much lower than the stars."

"Perhaps he does," returned Hamilton. "Of that I cannot say. But this I know. He can put two and two together and make a larger sum total than I have ever seen come from any other man's calculations. He is learned in every branch of knowledge, and I respect his wonderful conclusions, asking no questions about his methods."

"Very well, I'll not dispute with you if you admit that he receives even a part of his knowledge from substellar sources. But while we are alone I want to ask you, and I want you to tell me the truth: has Frances been here to-day?"

"No! Tell me, for God's sake, tell me quickly! Why do you ask?" he exclaimed, turning to me in alarm. "Of late I have been haunted with the fear that she is in danger of violence from the king. He is capable of committing any crime—has committed many, as we all know! Why do you ask about

Frances, Baron Ned?"

"Because she is not at Whitehall nor at her father's house, where the duchess said she was going. She never goes any place else, and it only now occurs to me to be alarmed."

"Only now?" he demanded angrily. "What have you been doing? I supposed you were watching over her. A fine guardian, upon my word! Where is she? Carried off by the king, of course! What else have you expected from our friend at Whitehall? If harm comes to her, I'll kill him!"

He threw off his printer's cap and apron, hastily cleansed his face and hands, put on the gray beard and wig, took his broad hat and long coat from the chest, and started toward the door, bidding me follow.

"Where are you going?" I asked.

"To Whitehall," he replied. "You to learn, if you can, where Frances is; I to form my plans what to do in case you do not find her. You must go to the river ahead of me and take a boat. I'll follow in another. We should not be seen together. You stop at Sir Richard's house, and if she is not there, go to Whitehall. Then come to me at the house of Carter, the Quaker. You know where it is—just off King's Street, not far from the Cross."

I followed Hamilton's suggestion. I did not find Frances at Sir Richard's house, so I hastened to Whitehall, where I learned that she had left shortly before noon, saying that she was going to spend the afternoon and night at home. It was near the hour of three o'clock when I had started up the river, from the Old Swan, and a snowstorm was raging which became violent before I reached the palace.

Charles Major

While I was talking to one of the maids in the parlor of the duchess, a page came to me and whispered, "A lady is waiting for you at Holbein's Gate, and wishes you to go to her as soon as possible."

I suspected that the lady was Frances, so I hastened to the gate and found, not my cousin, but Betty. I knew her the moment I saw her, despite the fact that she wore a full vizard and a long cloak. I also knew that nothing less than a matter of great urgency would have induced the girl to call for me at the palace.

The snow, which had been falling all day, was now coming in horizontal sheets, laden with sleet. The wind was blowing half a gale, and the weather was turning bitterly cold, yet Betty had come to seek me, despite weather and modesty. Eager to hear her errand, I led her toward Charing Cross, and when we were away from the gate, asked:—

"What brings you, Bettina? I know it must be a matter of great urgency that has induced you to venture forth in this terrible storm. What can I do for you?"

"Nothing for me, Baron Ned," she answered, taking my arm and huddling close to my side for protection against the storm.

"For whom, then? Tell me quickly," I asked.

"I fear Mistress Jennings is in trouble," she answered. "Soon after you and Master Hamilton left the Old Swan, a girl came to me in my parlor and told me that as she was passing a coach standing in front of Baynard's Castle two hours or more ago, a lady called to her from the coach window and told her to tell me that Mistress Jones was in great trouble; that she had been seized by two men who were carrying her away. She said the lady was bound hand and foot, and that immediately after she had spoken, two gentlemen came from Baynard's Castle, entered the coach, and drove toward Temple Bar. The girl said she followed the coach till she saw it turn into the Strand beyond Temple Bar; then she came to see me."

"Did the girl say at what hour she saw the lady, Mistress Jones?" I asked. "She probably did not catch the name Jennings."

"She said it was two hours or more before she saw me," answered Betty. "That would make it perhaps between one and two o'clock. I ought to have questioned her more closely, but I feared to delay telling you, so I left her in my parlor and came to see you as quickly as possible."

"Brave Betty! Sweet Betty!" I exclaimed, rapturously. "I could find it in my heart to kiss you a thousand times as a reward for your wisdom."

"And I could find it in my heart to be content with other reward," she answered, though her words took a different meaning from the gentle pressure she gave my arm.

"But tell me," asked Betty, "do you know where Mistress Jennings is?"

"She is not to be found," I returned. "Beyond a doubt the lady in the carriage was my cousin. You say it was perhaps one o'clock when the girl saw her?"

"Yes."

"It is after three now, nearly four, and will soon be dark. We must hasten."

We fairly ran to the Quaker's house, where we found Hamilton, who, forgetting his sacred calling, lapsed into the unholy manner of former days and used language which caused Betty to cover her ears with her hands. We did not, however, allow his profanity to delay us, but hastened to the Cross, expecting to take a coach for the Old Swan. But none was to be found, so we went to the river, where we were compelled to take an open boat with a steersman and one oarsman. We made poor headway, having to beat against the wind and the tide, so George and I each took an oar. After a time the man at the steering oar said that he would row if George or I would steer the boat, but neither of us knew the river and therefore could not take his place.

Betty said that she knew the river, having kept a small boat since she was strong enough to lift an oar, so she took the steering oar, and with four sweeps out we sped along at a fine rate. I shall never forget that water ride. We seemed to be pulling uphill every fathom of the way. The black, oily waves, with their teethlike crests of white, rose above our bow at every stroke of the sweeps, and when I looked behind me it seemed that we must surely be engulfed.

The snow, driven by the wind, swirled in angry blasts, and the damp, cold air chilled us to the bone. Our greatest danger would be when we came to land at the Bridge stairs, for the tide was pouring in through the arches of the Bridge and was falling in a great cataract just below the foot of the stairs. One false stroke of Betty's steering oar when we came to land, and our boat would be swamped. But she clung to the oar and brought us safely to the stairs within a fathom of the breakers.

We ran up Gracious Street and found the girl waiting in Betty's parlor. But Betty had told us all there was to be learned, so we gave the girl a few shillings and sent her home.

"What shall we do?" asked Betty, feeling that she had earned a right to couple herself with Hamilton and me by the pronoun "we."

"I'll go to see Lilly," said Hamilton. "He lives in the Strand, not far from Temple Bar."

"Why do you wish to see him?" I asked.

"He will tell us where Frances is and how to find her. Will you go with me?" asked Hamilton.

"Certainly," I responded, though I considered the visit a waste of time.

"May I, too, go?" asked Betty, with the double motive, doubtless, of helping and seeing. Lilly, engaged in his incantations, would be an inspiring sight to her.

"No, no, you may not go with us," answered Hamilton.

Betty's eyes looked up to me entreatingly, so I took up her cause, and suggested:—

"Lilly may want to question her about what the girl said."

"You are right," returned George. "Wrap yourself up well, Betty, and come along. We'll take a coach to Lilly's."

A porter soon brought us a coach, and Betty, having explained to her father where and why she was going, climbed in with George and me, and we were off.

CHAPTER IX

KIDNAPPED

We found Lilly at home, eager to help us. He asked many questions relating to my cousin's life and her friends at court, to all of which I made full answer in so far as I knew, including an account of the king's objectionable attentions. I suspected that the Doctor would make more use of the knowledge he obtained from me than of that to be received from the stars, but I did not care how he reached his conclusions if he could but tell us how and where to find Frances.

Lilly questioned Betty also, and when he had learned all that she knew, he left us seated in the parlor while he went to his observatory to set a figure. In the course of ten minutes he returned and gave us the result of his calculations, as follows:—

"I believe I can tell you where Mistress Jennings is, and how she may be found," he said, speaking and acting as one walking in sleep. "But your failure to tell me the exact hour of her birth lends uncertainty to my calculations. I have all the particulars concerning the nativity of a man whom I shall not name. I have read the stars many times for him and on many subjects. If he is connected with the disappearance of

Mistress Jennings, you will find her at a place called Merlin House, six leagues from Westminster and half a league from the Oxford Road."

Here his eyes began to roll and he seemed to be under a spell. He made strange, weird passes in the air for a time, then became rigid, his face upturned and his arms uplifted. Betty was frightened and drew close to my side, grasping my arm.

After perhaps a minute of silence, Lilly began to speak again in low sepulchral tones: "I see a house in the depths of a forest dark and wild. It is surrounded by a high wall. In the east side of the wall is a double door or gate of thick oak, which you will find locked and barred. The house is of brick, save a tower at the southeast corner, which is of stone three stories high. To reach the house, you must travel on the Oxford Road a distance of six leagues and two furlongs, where you will find a broken shrine, erected hundreds of years ago to the Blessed Virgin. The shrine is on the left side of the road as you travel west, one hundred paces back, on the top of a low hill surrounded by a bleak moor. The shrine has gone to decay, but it holds a sacred relic of the Blessed Virgin."

Betty, who was a Catholic, crossed herself and murmured an Ave. Lilly continued:—

"On the apex of the shrine there is a broken cross. The night is dark and you may pass without seeing it, therefore I shall direct you how to find it. A short distance this side of the shrine the road turns sharply to the left, just before crossing a bourne which is six leagues from Westminster. After you have crossed the bourne, bring your horses to a walk, and when you have counted a number equal to the sum of seven times the square of eleven, counting as the clock ticks, halt, and you will find the shrine on a hillock in a bleak moor. You may easily see it, as it will be dark against the snow. Neither rain nor snow touches it, and the storm spares it. It has been abandoned by men hundreds of years, therefore the Blessed Virgin protects it from further decay."

He seemed to be a long time coming to the house, but after another pause, he continued:—

"Half a league beyond the shrine a narrow road branches to the south. Take it, and soon you will be in the midst of a forest, dark and wild. The road will be dim and difficult to follow in its windings, but your horses will keep the way and will take you to a gate in the midst of the forest. Enter by the gate and follow the road winding among the trees till you reach the double door or gate in the wall. The house will be dark save in the third story of the stone tower, where you will see a star beaming in the window. Raphael, my familiar spirit, will hold the star for your guidance. In the room of the star, you will find the person you seek. Delay not!"

He stopped speaking, bent forward, breathed upon a gold plate covered with mystic signs which rested on a table, rose to an upright posture, again became rigid, stretched out his hands with face upturned, and whispered in tones almost inaudible:—

"Come thou, great Raphael, spirit of rescue, and help me this night in a righteous cause. In the name of Jupiter, the father of the gods, Mercury, his son, and Psyche, the spirit of the stars!"

He stood dazed for a moment, as though just awakened, then turning quickly to me, said: "Lose not a moment's time. Hasten at once to the rescue. I am sure my directions will lead you to her whom you seek."

Betty, George, and I gathered our hats and cloaks, and George, turning to me, said:—

"We must find a light coach and four good horses. The road will be heavy with snow, and we must be prepared to travel rapidly."

"Father has four good horses, as strong and swift as any in London," suggested Betty. "He has a light coach, too. Let us return to the Old Swan and prepare to start at once."

"Betty, you are too wise for one of your age and sex," said George. "But without your wisdom, I don't know what we should have done this night. Let us go immediately."

Our coachman put his horses to a gallop, we reached the Old Swan in a short time, and within less than half an hour, a porter informed me that a coach and four were awaiting us in the courtyard. Pickering lent us greatcoats and rugs and all things needful to keep us warm. He did not know the exact reason for our journey, but had learned from Betty that it was undertaken in an affair of great moment, involving my cousin's safety.

George and I each carried a heavy sword and a pistol in addition to two hand guns, primed and charged, which lay in a box on the coach floor. The drivers on the box were each armed with a sword and a pistol. They had been reluctant to leave the kitchen fire to face the storm, but when they had a hint that a fight was possible, and when Pickering offered them a guinea each, they changed their minds, quickly wrapped themselves in greatcoats, and were on the box when we came out. George stopped at the inn door to have a word with Pickering, and while they were talking I climbed to the top of the front wheel of the coach to give instructions to the drivers. I told them to drive at a moderate gait down

Candlestick Street and the Strand till they reached Charing Cross; then to turn up towards Saint-Martin's-in-the-Fields and take the crooked road across the Common till they reached the Oxford Road. When on the main highway, they were to travel at full gallop.

"How long is the journey, sir?" asked one of the drivers. "I ask so that I may know how fast to drive the horses."

"Between six and seven leagues," I answered.

"Ah, they can go that distance at a good pace if we on the box don't freeze to death," he returned, buttoning up his greatcoat, bringing the rug tightly about him and drawing on his gloves.

I sprang from the wheel and started to enter the coach just as George left Pickering, but when I put my foot on the step, I saw a small man sitting in the furthest corner of the back seat.

"Come, come, what are you doing here? And who are you?" I asked, stepping into the coach for the purpose of pulling the fellow out.

I was greeted by a soft laugh and this answer: "I am sitting here, and my name is Betty Pickering."

"My God, Betty, you can't go with us," I exclaimed, making ready to help her out of the coach.

But she put her hand over my mouth to silence me and whispered, "The men on the box must not know me."

Betty pushed me backward out of the coach, came out herself and led me to George, who, by that time, was halfway across the courtyard.

"Who are you?" cried George, surprised to see the little man beside me, for Betty was in greatcoat, trousers, and boots.

"I am Betty, and Baron Ned says I shall not go with you."

"No, no, Betty," answered George. "See the snow, the sleet, and the storm. It is freezing and the wind cuts like a knife. It would kill you to go with us."

"Think a moment," she answered, whispering, so that her words might not be overheard by the men on the box. "Mistress Jennings may need the help of a woman, but in any case you shall not have the coach and horses if I don't go."

"Does your father know?" I asked.

"Yes, yes, come on! We are wasting valuable time," answered Betty, starting toward the coach.

George and I were helpless against Betty's will, so we said nothing more, and she climbed into the coach, taking her former place at the left end of the back seat. George followed, taking the middle place next to her, and after giving the word to start, I followed George, taking the right hand corner, thus leaving him between Betty and me, an arrangement that did not at all please me. But my disappointment was short lived, for hardly was I seated till Betty spoke in tones plainly showing that she was pouting:—

"I want Baron Ned to sit by me."

George laughed, he and I changed places, and when I was settled beside Betty, she caught my hand, giving it a saucy little squeeze, and fell back in her corner with a sigh and a low gurgling laugh.

When we had climbed Gracious Street hill, we turned into Candlestick Street and drove along at a brisk pace, George and I watching the houses to note our progress.

After passing Temple Bar, the street being broader and the night very dark, we could not distinguish the houses save when a light gleamed over a front door now and then, and were not sure where we were until we saw the flambeaux over Whitehall Gate scintillating through the falling snow.

Before reaching Charing Cross, one of the drivers lifted the rug which hung across the front of the coach between us and the box and asked:—

"Did you say, sir, to take the road across the Common from Saint-Martin's-in-the-Fields?"

"Yes," I answered.

"Then, sir, have your pistols ready, for it is the worst bloody stretch of road about London for highwaymen, though I doubt if they be out on a night like this."

"You're not afraid?" I asked.

"Devil a bit, sir! I'd rather fight than eat, but I thought maybe your honors would rather eat."

He cracked his whip, and soon we were over the dangerous ground, travelling along on the Oxford Road at a fine gallop. On reaching the open country the wind gave us its full force, there being no doors to our coach, and soon our rugs were covered with snow. But George and I were wrapped to our chins, and Bettina nestled cozily down in her corner untouched by the storm.

After leaving Westminster, we had no means of knowing our rate of progress, for there were no houses near the road, and, if there had been, we should not have known them. The drivers kept the horses in a strong trot, at times a vigorous gallop, and I judged that we were making nearly three leagues an hour. At that rate it would require perhaps two hours to reach the shrine mentioned by Lilly.

We had instructed the men on the box to watch for a sharp bend in the road just before crossing a bourne, and we, too, began to watch soon after leaving Westminster. After what seemed to be a long time, George asked me to make a flare in my tinder box, while he caught a glimpse of the face of his watch. This I did under the rug, and, much to our disgust, we found that we had been less than twenty minutes on the road, so provokingly had time lagged.

After our disappointment we lay back in the coach, determined to ignore time, and thereby perhaps hasten it. In truth, time's lagging was not unpleasant for me, in one respect, at least, for Bettina was by my side. I found delight in keeping her well tucked about with rugs, so that not even a breath of the storm nor a flake of snow could reach her. She wore a great fur hood which buttoned under her chin, almost covering her face and falling in a soft warm curtain to her shoulders and bosom. She was warm, and aside from our great cause of anxiety, I believe, was happy. I wished a hundred times that George were in another coach, though had he been, I well knew that I should have said a great deal to Betty which on the morrow would have been regretted, both for her sake and my own.

Just at a point when time seemed to have halted, the driver lifted the rug hanging behind him, and said:—

"Here is the bend, sir, and yonder is the bourne."

Presently we knew by the breaking of the ice and the splashing of the water that we were crossing the bourne, and when we were over, George called to the driver, directing him to allow the horses to walk until the order came to stop.

George dropped the front curtain, and turning to Betty and me, said:—

"Now, let us count as the clock ticks to the number 847, and when finished, we shall be at the shrine."

"We are more apt to find a bleak moor and a sharp blast of wind," I suggested.

While under the spell of Lilly's incantations, I had almost accepted his absurd vaporings, but cooler thought had brought contempt, and I had begun to look upon our journey as a very wild goose chase indeed.

"We have found the sharp turn in the road and the bourne," said George, "and I see no reason to doubt that we shall find the shrine."

"Lilly may have passed over the road and may know that the shrine is here; but when we find it, what will it prove?" I asked.

"It will prove nothing, though I am willing to stake my life that we find Frances in Merlin House."

"Count!" exclaimed Betty, sharply. In our discussion, George and I had forgotten to count, but Betty had been counting under her breath as the clock ticks, and we took her number and started with it.

We all reached the number 847 almost at the same second, when we stopped the coach, and sure enough, there by the roadside, on a small rocky hillock surrounded by a bleak moor, was the shrine. Even from the road we could see the fragment of a cross projecting above the one piece of wall left standing. One would hardly have taken it to be a shrine unless the fact had been suggested, but with the thought in mind, the fragmentary cross was convincing evidence. Had its sacred quality been suspected during the time of Cromwell, not one stone would have been left upon another, but no one knew that it was the Virgin's shrine, therefore it was not disturbed, but stood there, black on a field of luminous white. We all saw it at the same moment. I was content to view it from the coach, but George went to examine it, and returned, saying:—

"It is a shrine. Part of the cross still remains surmounting a fragment of a wall."

He climbed into the coach and was about to give the word to start again, when Betty spoke up, hesitatingly, pleadingly but emphatically:—

"Please wait a moment. I want to see it."

I followed Betty when she got out of the coach, and, as we approached the shrine, she exclaimed: "Doctor Lilly was right! There is no snow on the shrine. The Virgin protects it. There must be a relic beneath the stones!"

We climbed a little hillock and after standing before the shrine for a moment, Betty said, "Please return to the coach and leave me alone."

"Why, Betty?" I asked. "You may speak plainly to me. I think I know your motive."

Charles Major

"I want to offer a little prayer to the Virgin here at her broken shrine—a prayer for your cousin and for you—and for me."

I knelt with her, and after Betty had finished her simple invocation, we rose, and I, who at another time would have laughed at the prayer, felt the thrill of her whispered words lingering in my heart. I seemed to know that we should rescue Frances, and I also knew that my love for Bettina would bring me nothing but joy, softened and sanctified by sadness, and to her nothing of evil save the pain of a gentle longing.

Betty felt as I did, for when she rose she said, "Now we shall find Mistress Jennings, and, Baron Ned, I shall fear you no more."

"Have you feared me?" I asked, touched to the quick by her artless candor.

"Yes," she answered, sighing. "Though I have feared myself more. You are so far above me in every way that it is no wonder I am bewildered when you say—say—that you—. You know what I mean."

"Yes, Betty," I answered quickly, feeling that she had more to say.

"I was bewildered in my parlor at the Old Swan to-day," she said, hanging her head. "Your opinion of me must have fallen."

"No, no, I understood, Betty, I understood, and I dare not tell you how much my opinion has risen because I would say more than would be good for you or for me," I answered reassuringly.

"But you must remember that a girl has impulses and yearnings at times, and she should not be too harshly blamed if she sometimes fails to beat them down. But now it will all be different. The Blessed Virgin will help us, and our conflict is over."

Betty and I started back to the coach, both feeling the uplift of our answered prayer. Probably we were the only devotees that had knelt before the shrine in hundreds of years, and the Virgin had heard our supplication. It was a proposition I should have laughed at and held to scorn prior to that time.

After leaving the shrine, it was only a few minutes till the coach turned to the left into a narrow road, and we were approaching the end of our rough journey. We continued to travel at a brisk trot and came to the forest, "dark and wild," of which Lilly had spoken. Thus far his "calculations" were correct, and I was beginning to take hope that they would continue so to the end. After half an hour on the winding road through the forest, the drivers halted at the gate of which Lilly had spoken, and in ten minutes more drew rein beside the high brick wall surrounding Merlin House.

Without the least trouble we found the gates or doors in the wall, and truly enough, they were of "thick oak" so strong that we could not feel them vibrate when we tried to shake them, and so firmly locked in the middle that we almost despaired of opening them. The wall was too high to scale, and for a moment it looked as though our journey had been in vain. But Betty's keen wits came to our rescue.

When George and I had examined the gates and had almost despaired of opening them, Betty undertook an inspection of her own, and presently called our attention to a hole, perhaps four inches in diameter, in each gate, which was hidden by round curtains of wood hung within, so completely closing up the holes as to make them invisible save on close examination. She suggested that we pass the trace chain through one hole, draw it out through the other, hitch the horses to the two ends, and pull down the wall if the gates refused to give way.

Her plan was so good that the horses soon opened the gate, though it required a strong pull from all four of them to do it. Betty and I were the first to enter, George following close at our heels. The two drivers, who had taken the horses back to the coach, hitched them to a tree and soon followed us, bringing the long leather reins to be used as climbing ropes if necessary.

Hardly had we entered the gate till we saw a starlike gleam of light in a window of a room in the third story of the tower, as Lilly had predicted. While I was convinced that the light came through a hole in the curtain rather than from a star held by Raphael to guide us, still my scepticism was rapidly turning to awe.

We were speaking of the light when two great dogs came bounding out of the darkness and attacked us. I drew my sword, a sharp, heavy blade, and being much frightened, began to swing it heroically in every direction. Fortunately one of the dogs happened to be in one of the directions, and I split its head. The other dog attacked Betty, but George ran to her rescue and finished the animal before it had time to bark.

Having vanquished the dogs, we hastened to the tower and stopped beneath the window of the star. We had hoped to attract Frances's attention by casting pebbles against the window-pane, but we had counted without our ammunition. We could find no pebbles, the snow being at least a foot deep.

A thick vine, probably an ivy, covered the front of the tower, and George attempted to make the escalade by climbing. He would have denuded the wall had he continued his efforts, for the vine broke, not being strong enough to bear his weight.

"Let me try it," whispered Betty, taking off her greatcoat, hood, gloves, and boots and tossing them to the ground.

I objected to her risking her pretty neck and limbs, but she insisted that she could make the ascent easily, and George agreeing with her, I reluctantly consented.

Brave little Betty at once began the ascent, I standing under her to break the fall if she should take one. When she had climbed five or six feet from the ground, the vine broke and she fell, landing gracefully on her feet. Instantly she was at it again, for Betty had a will of her own greatly disproportioned to her size. Again the vine broke, and when I picked her up I found that she had lost her breath by the fall, but she laughed as soon as her breath returned, and was in no way discouraged.

In a moment she tried again, despite my protest, saying she would go more slowly and use greater care in choosing the larger vines. This time she was determined to succeed, so she again tied the leather reins about her arm, grasped the vine, and within two minutes was standing on the upper coping of the second-story window, her waist on a level with the sill of the window of the star.

The wind howling through the trees and around the corner of the tower made so great a din that at first we did not hear what Betty said to attract Frances's attention, but presently, the storm lulling for a moment, we listened intently and heard her say:—

"It is Betty Pickering."

We supposed she spoke in response to an inquiry from within, and we were right, for almost instantly the curtains parted, the window opened, and we saw Frances standing in the light of Raphael's star—a candle.

Up to that time I had been incredulous of Lilly's wisdom, and while I had hoped to find my cousin, I had little faith in the result. But now conviction came with a shock and, notwithstanding my joy at seeing Frances, I found myself forgetting where I was in wondering whether Lilly were a god, a devil, or merely a shrewd charlatan who had obtained his wonderfully accurate knowledge from something that had happened in the past wherein the king was concerned, or from some one who knew where Frances had been taken.

I was awakened from my revery by hearing George call in a low voice to Frances, telling her to fasten the ends of the leathers to a bedpost or a heavy piece of furniture, and asking her if she could come down hand under hand. She answered that she could and took the end of the reins from Betty. After a minute or two spent by Frances back in the room, she reappeared, tossed her cloak down to us, climbed out the window, and stood for a moment beside Betty on the lower window cap. I heard Betty encouraging her, and presently Frances began her descent, reaching the ground safely. George would have been demonstrative, but I interrupted him, saying:—

"Be ready to help me catch Betty in case she falls!"

Betty started down, but George called to her, telling her to climb into the room, loosen the reins, and throw them out.

"But how shall I go down?" asked Betty, whose nerve was

deserting her.

"You must come down as you climbed up—by the vines," returned George.

Betty climbed in at the window, and presently the leathers fell at our feet. In a moment she reappeared, put one foot out the window, hesitated, and called to me:—

"I'm afraid, Baron Ned. It seems so far, looking down."

George started toward the coach with Frances, leaving me and one of the drivers to care for the girl who had saved our expedition from failure.

I could help Betty only by encouraging her, so I spoke softly: "Be brave, Betty. Go slowly. Don't lose your head."

"It is not my head I fear to lose; it is my footing," she answered, sitting on the window-sill, one foot hanging outside.

"But you must come, Betty," I said encouragingly. "Now say a little prayer to the Virgin, and you'll be all right."

I saw her bow her head and cross herself, and the prayer giving her strength, she climbed to the lower window coping and began her descent on the vine. When halfway down she fell, and though I caught her, partly breaking her fall, I knew that she was hurt. I helped her to her feet, and she said breathlessly:—

"I'm all right. I'm not hurt."

But when we started toward the coach, she clung to me, limping, and began to cry from pain. When I saw that she was hurt, I caught her up in my arms and carried her to the coach, followed by the driver, bearing the reins and Betty's hood, cloak, gloves, and boots. Frances was already inside the coach, and George was about to follow her, when I came up with poor helpless Betty, and somewhat angrily ordered him to stand aside while I made her comfortable. Frances began to soothe Betty, whose tears flowed afresh under the sympathy. By the time George and I were in the coach, the drivers were on the box, but before we started one of them lifted the curtain and said:—

"I hear them moving in the house."

"Make the more haste," I answered.

"Shan't we stay for a fight, sir?" asked the driver, evidently disappointed.

"We'll have it later on," said George, and the next moment the coach was turned and we were on our homeward road.

When we reached the Oxford Road, the horses started at a smart gallop, and we began to hope that we had not been discovered by the inmates of Merlin House. But soon we heard horses galloping behind us. After a consultation, George and I concluded to stop the coach. Frances and Betty were much alarmed, and begged us to try to escape by whipping the horses. But I knew that our pursuers, being on horseback, would soon overtake us, and I was convinced that nothing could be gained by attempting flight. I have seen a small dog stop a larger one by waiting for it.

So we waited, and when our pursuers, a half score of men on horseback, came up to us, we met them with a fusillade of powder and shot, which persuaded them to allow us to go our way and evidently made them content to go theirs, for we saw nothing more of them.

On the way to London, Frances told us briefly the story of the day. She had started to her father's house and had left the river at Baynard's Castle stairs. It was near one o'clock when she left her boat, and the snow, which had been falling for an hour or more, covered the ground. When she reached the head of the narrow street leading to Upper Thames Street from the river stairs, she found a coach waiting for her. The driver touched his hat and asked if she was Mistress Jennings. When she answered that she was, he said I had sent him to watch for her and to take her to Sir Richard's house, the snow being deep and the storm violent. My name and Sir Richard's fell so glibly from the fellow's tongue that she, suspecting nothing, entered the coach. Within three or four minutes the coach stopped, but she thought nothing of it, supposing the way was blocked.

While waiting, two men wrapped to their eyes in greatcoats came up, one on either side of the coach, entered, threw a cloak over her head, and bound her hand and foot. Immediately the coach started, but presently it stopped again, and Frances had an opportunity to speak to the girl who had come to see Betty. Fortunately a buttonhole in the cloak which the men had thrown over Frances's head happened to fall over one of her eyes, and thus enabled her to see the girl.

* * * * *

When our pursuers turned back, we reduced our speed, so that the journey might be easier for Betty, who had moaned at every jolt, and when the coach went smoother she fell asleep.

After we had all been silent for a long time, Frances said:—

Charles Major

"I have been thinking it all over, cousin Ned, and if Master Hamilton, that is, George, wishes it, I will go with him, regardless of consequences. I am tired of the fight."

"What?" I cried, startled almost to anger.

"Do not run me through, Ned," cried Hamilton. "This is the first intimation I have had of her purpose, and to save myself from slaughter at your hands, I hasten to say that I will not accept her sacrifice. It were kinder in me to kill her than to marry her."

We all laughed to cover our embarrassment, and George said ruefully: "The king, I fear, will settle the question without consulting us. De Grammont tells me that his Majesty believes I am in London and that he is eager to give a public entertainment on Tyburn Hill, wherein I shall be the principal actor. Now our beloved monarch's hatred will be redoubled, for he will suspect that I helped in the rescue to-night."

"Do you suspect him of being privy to the outrage tonight?" asked Frances.

"I know it. There is no villainy he would not do, provided it required no bravery," said George.

"But we must not let the king know that we suspect him," I suggested. "He may be innocent of the crime. I shall know the truth before to-morrow night."

"Did you see him at Merlin House?" asked George, turning to Frances.

"No," she answered. "It seems that the drivers of the coach lost their way. The horses were poor beasts, and, owing to many halts on the road, our progress was slow. When I first entered the house, an old woman led me to the room in which you found me. The ropes on my wrists and ankles had been removed soon after I left London, but I was not allowed to remove the cloak until after the old woman had closed the door on me. Then I sat down so stunned that I could hardly think. But it seemed only a few minutes till I heard dear, brave Betty at the window. You must have come rapidly."

When we told Frances our side of the story, how Betty had come to Whitehall to see me and had been the real leader throughout it all, Frances leaned forward and kissed the girl, saying:—

"God bless her, and you, too, Baron Ned. She is worthy of you, and you have my consent."

In further discussing Frances's journey, she said that the men who were with her in the coach were masked and that she did not know them, but she was sure neither was the king. They did not speak, save to tell the driver to travel slowly to avoid reaching the house too far ahead of the "other coach."

The other coach, which Frances said she heard enter the gate, arrived not more than ten minutes before we reached Merlin House, and it is probable that we were undisturbed in our rescue because of the fact that supper was in progress.

It was nearly three o'clock by George's watch when we reached the dark clump of houses standing west of Covent Garden, and within less than half an hour we were in the cozy courtyard of the Old Swan.

Pickering was waiting for us, having kept vigil alone since midnight. When he saw me carrying Betty from the coach, he ran to us with a cry and snatched her from my arms. We followed him into the house where we found him weeping over the girl, and kissing her hands as she lay on a bench near the fire.

"What have you been doing? Have you killed my little girl?" he asked sorrowfully.

"I hope not, Pickering," I answered. "She had a fall of not more than eight or ten feet, and although I fear she is hurt, I am sure the injury is not serious, as I caught her and broke the fall."

"Let us take her to bed," suggested Frances.

George went to fetch Doctor Price, the surgeon, and I carried Betty upstairs. I laid her on the bed, and after I had talked a few minutes with Pickering, explaining to him the events of the night, and telling him of Betty's glorious part in our success, I went downstairs to wait in the tap-room for George and the surgeon.

Presently they came, and George and I followed the surgeon to Betty's door, where we waited in the hallway outside to hear his report. Presently Frances came out to tell us that Betty's injuries were no greater than a few sprains and bruises, and that the surgeon said she would be well in a few days.

I could have shouted for joy on hearing the news, but restrained myself, and suggested to Frances that she go at once to her father's house and that I go to Whitehall to be there before its awakening.

If I learned that the king had been absent during the night, I should know with reasonable certainty that he had been privy to the outrage perpetrated on Frances. If he has been at the palace all night, he might be innocent of the crime.

"In neither case will I return to Whitehall," declared Frances, indignantly, when I spoke of the possibility of the king's innocence.

"But you must," I replied insistently. "We must say nothing of your terrible experience. Publicity of this sort ruins a woman's fair name, but the result in this case would be far more disastrous. Fear will drive the king to further acts of villainy to protect himself if he learns that we suspect him, and your life and mine, as well as George's, may be in peril. I shall go to my bedroom in the Wardrobe, and no one shall know that I have not been there all night."

Frances seemed stubborn, but knowing her danger, I continued: "Let us have a conference with your father and your sister. I deem it best that we let it be known abroad that you were at your father's house all night. Since the king did not see you at Merlin House, he may come to suspect that his agents kidnapped the wrong person. Later on you may leave court with honor; now you would leave in disgrace. Right or wrong, the king can do no wrong, and even were it known that he had kidnapped you, every one would laugh at you as the victim of a royal prank. Many would say that you were willing to be kidnapped, and the court hussies would rejoice at your downfall."

Frances and George saw the force of my argument, and we agreed to act accordingly, George, of course, having little to do in the premises save to remain hidden.

In a few minutes Pickering brought us a coach, and Frances and I drove to Temple Bar, where I dismissed the coach and walked with my cousin to her father's house.

I went in with Frances, and we aroused Sir Richard to tell him of his daughter's experience, and of the plan of action agreed upon, though we did not mention the king's name, leading Sir Richard to believe that we did not know the guilty persons.

Sir Richard and Sarah readily agreed that secrecy was our only means of saving Frances from ruinous publicity. Sarah especially grasped the point and cleared the situation of all cloud by suggesting:—

"My sister has been here ever since yesterday noon, as my father, John Churchill, and I will testify."

That was a very long speech for Sarah, but it was a helpful one. I, too, might add my testimony and thus furnish enough evidence to convince any reasonable person that Frances had not been kidnapped, but had remained safe and well in her father's house through all this terrible night.

Just as soon as our plans were completed, I left my uncle's house and took another coach for Charing Cross, dismissed the coach, ran down to Whitehall, and climbed over the balcony to my closet, glad to find myself once more at home. I did not permit myself to sleep, but rose at the usual hours and was at my post ready for duty when the others arrived.

I soon learned that the king had been away from the palace all night, having left in a coach near the hour of five the preceding afternoon, so that he must have been not far ahead of George, Betty, and me on the way to Merlin House. When I learned that he was away, and that I would not be needed that morning at the Wardrobe, I went to seek Frances.

Before ten o'clock, the hour at which the maids assembled to greet the duchess in her closet, Frances was on hand, looking pale, and explaining that she had been ill at her father's house over night.

Near the hour of four that afternoon, while I was looking out the window, I saw a coach approach from the direction of Charing Cross, and seemed to know that the king was in it. I hastened to Frances and told her to station herself where the king could see her before he went to his closet, and perhaps speak to her. I stood near by, and when the king entered I noticed him start on seeing Frances. When he came up to us, she smiled and made so deep a courtesy that one would have thought she was overjoyed to see him.

The king stopped before us for a moment, saying, "We have had a terrible storm, baron."

"Indeed we have, your Majesty," I answered, bowing, "though I have not so much as thrust my head out-of-doors save to go down to Sir Richard's yesterday evening to fetch Mistress Jennings home."

"Did she come—I mean, would she face the storm?" asked the king.

"No, no," answered Frances, laughing. "Why face the storm to return to Whitehall when the king was away? I remained with my father, and was so ill that a physician was called at seven o'clock."

"I hope you are well again," said the king.

"Not entirely. But now I shall be," she answered, laughing.

"You mean now that I am at home?" asked the king, shaking his head doubtfully.

"Yes, your Majesty."

"If your heart were as kind as your tongue, I should be a much happier man than I am."

His Majesty sighed as he turned away, and the expression on his face was as an open book to me, knowing as I did that he had just failed in perpetrating an act of villainy which would have hanged any other man in England.

One of the king's greatest misfortunes was his mouth. He could never keep it closed. A secret seemed to disagree with him, physically and mentally; therefore he relieved himself of it as soon as possible by telling any one that would listen. Knowing this royal weakness, I was not at all surprised to learn, two or three days after our adventure, that it was being talked about by the court.

One evening at the queen's ball, my Lady Castlemain, a very cat of a woman, came up to a group consisting of the king, the duchess, Frances, myself, and three or four others who were standing near the king's chair. Elbowing her way to the king, near whom Frances was standing, Lady Castlemain said:—

"Ah, la Belle Jennings, tell us of your adventure Sunday night!"

"Of what adventure, la Belle Castlemain?" asked Frances, smiling sweetly.

"Why, when you were kidnapped and carried to a country house for the night," returned Castlemain, with a vindictive gleam in her eyes and an angry toss of her head.

"I kidnapped Sunday night?" asked Frances, in well-feigned

surprise. "No such romantic adventure has befallen me."

"Yes, kidnapped Sunday night," returned Castlemain, showing her teeth. "Of course you were kidnapped! I'm sure nothing would induce so modest a lady as the fair Jennings to go of her own free will. She would insist on being taken by force. Ha! ha! Force!"

She laughed as though speaking in jest, but her real intent was plain to every one that heard her. Frances, too, laughed so merrily that one might have supposed she considered it all a joke, and her acting was far better than Castlemain's.

"But one must keep up an appearance of virtue and must insist on being kidnapped," said Frances, banteringly. "It not only enhances one's value, but excuses one's fault. All these little subterfuges are necessary until one reaches a point where one is both brazen and cheap."

Castlemain's life of shame at court had long ceased to be even a matter of gossip, but at this time she was notoriously involved with one Jacob Hall, a common rope dancer. Therefore my cousin's thrust went home.

"So you admit having been kidnapped?" asked Castlemain, with little effort to conceal her vindictiveness.

"Sunday, say you?" asked Frances.

"Yes, Sunday noon, in the public streets, and Sunday night in a country house," returned Castlemain.

"Let me see," said Frances, pausing for a moment to recall what she had been doing at the time of the supposed kidnapping. Then turning to the Duchess of York, who stood beside her, and who, she felt sure, would catch the hint and help her out, she asked, "Were we not playing at cards in your Grace's parlor Sunday afternoon?"

"Sunday afternoon?" repeated the duchess, quite willing to thwart Castlemain's design. "Yes, my dear, Sunday afternoon. Yes, we began just after dinner, and it was almost dark when we stopped. Don't you remember I said, after we had lighted the candles, that I wished my husband could afford to give me wax in place of tallow?"

We all laughed except the king, who became very much interested, and of course, excepting Castlemain, who was rapidly losing her head in anger.

After the duchess had spoken, the king asked, with as careless an air as he could assume:—

"At what hour, sister, did Mistress Jennings leave your parlor?"

"I think it was about four o'clock," replied her Grace. "She asked permission to spend the night with her father, and Baron Clyde called about four o'clock to escort her. Was not that the hour, baron?"

"Yes, your Grace," I answered, bowing. "I accompanied my cousin to her father's house, returned later to fetch her back to the palace, but she did not care to face the storm, so I remained till ten o'clock, returned to Whitehall, and slept till morning. Here is another witness," I continued, laughing, as I turned to John Churchill, who was standing near the king. "Step forward, Churchill, and testify. I left him making his suit to one of the most interesting ladies in London."

The king turned with an inquiring look, and Churchill answered: "Yes, your Majesty, it is all true. I was making my suit until near the hour of eleven, when Mistress Jennings, who was ill, told me it was time to go home. If she was kidnapped Sunday night, it was before five o'clock or after eleven."

I flattered myself that we had all done a neat bit of convincing lying in a good cause.

"Odds fish!" mumbled the king, pulling his chin beard, evidently puzzled.

"Odds fish!" exclaimed Frances, mimicking the king's tone of voice and twisting an imaginary beard. "Some one has been hoaxing Jacob Hall's friend."

It was a bold speech, but Frances carried it off splendidly by turning to the king and speaking in mock seriousness:—

"Your Majesty should put a check on Rochester and the wags. It is a shame to permit them to work upon the credulity of one who is growing weak in mind by reason of age."

The country girl had vanquished the terror of the court, and all who had witnessed the battle rejoiced; that is, all save the king and Castlemain. She glared at Frances, and her face, usually beautiful despite the lack of youth, became hideous with rage. She was making ready for another attack of words, if not of finger nails, when the duchess interposed, saying:—

"Evidently some one has been hoaxing you, Lady Castlemain. Mistress Jennings was not kidnapped Sunday nor any other day. She has been with me constantly of late, excepting Sunday after four o'clock, and she has accounted for herself from that time till her return to my closet."

Castlemain was whipped out, so she turned the whole matter off with a forced laugh, saying:—

"It was that fool Rochester who set the rumor afloat."

After standing through an awkward minute or two, Castlemain bowed stiffly to the king and the duchess, turned away from our group, and soon left the ballroom.

When Castlemain was gone, we all laughed save the king. Presently he left us, and I saw him beckon Wentworth and Berkeley to his side. I followed him as though going to the other side of the gallery, but walked slowly when I approached him and the two worthy villains. I was rewarded by hearing his Majesty say:—

"Odds fish! But you made a mess of it! You got the wrong woman! Who in the devil's name did you pick up?"

I could not stop to hear the rest of this interesting conversation, but two days later I heard from Rochester, who had it from Wentworth, that the following occurred:—

"We thought we had her," answered Berkeley, nodding towards Frances, "but the woman wore a full vizard and was wrapped in furs to her ears, so that we did not see her face."

"Do you suppose we could have made a mistake?" asked Wentworth.

"You surely did," answered the king. "She has established an alibi. At what hour did you leave Baynard's Castle?"

"Near one o'clock," returned Berkeley.

"One o'clock! She was playing cards with the duchess till

four," exclaimed the king, impatiently. "You picked up the wrong woman. But I'm glad you did. I suppose the lampooners will get hold of the story and will set every one laughing at me. Kidnapped the wrong woman and lost her! Odds fish! But you're a pair of wise ones. I see I shall have to find me a new Lord High Kidnapper."

The king was right concerning the lampooners, for soon they had the story, and he became the laughing-stock of London, though Frances's name was not mentioned.

It is a significant index to the morals of our time that the king's attempt to kidnap a woman in the streets of London should have aroused laughter rather than indignation.

As it was, the kidnapping episode brought no harm to my cousin, but she did not want it to happen again, and so was careful to take a trusted escort with her when she went abroad thereafter.

CHAPTER X

AT THE MAID'S GARTER

Betty was confined to her room during the greater part of the next month, and Frances visited her frequently. Notwithstanding my vows not to see Betty, I was compelled to go with Frances as her body-guard. I even went so far in my feeble effort to keep my resolution as to suggest Churchill as a body-guard, but Frances objected, and the quality of my good intent was not enduring. So I went with my cousin, and the joy in Betty's eyes whenever we entered her room was not the sort that would come because she was glad to see Frances.

* * * * *

During the first week of Bettina's illness she was too sick to talk, therefore we did not remain long with her. But as she grew better our visits lengthened, and my poor resolutions grew weaker day by day because my love for the girl was growing stronger and stronger hour by hour.

On one occasion while Frances's back was turned, Betty impulsively snatched up my hand and kissed it, dropping it instantly, blushing intensely and covering her tracks by humming the refrain of a French lullaby. I longed to return the caress, but did not, and took great credit to myself because of my self-denial. Betty understood my sacrifice and appreciated it, feeling sure that she need not thereafter restrain herself for the purpose of restraining me.

During those times I was making an honest effort to do the right by this beautiful child-woman and to save my own honor unsullied from the sin of making her unhappy for life through winning her love beyond her power to recall; and my effort toward the right, like all such efforts, achieved at least a part of the good for which I strove.

One day after our visit to Betty's room, Frances asked me to take her to see George. I suspected that she had seen him frequently, but was not sure. I objected, but changed my mind when she said:—

"Very well. I prefer going alone."

I shall not try to describe the scene between them. We found George alone, and she sprang to him as the iron springs to the magnet.

I knew then, if never before, that there could be no happiness in this world for her away from him. Whether she would find it with him was impossible for me to know, but I saw that she was in the grip of a mighty passion, and I could only hope that a way would open to save her.

Hamilton's fortunes would need to mend a great deal before he could or would ask her to be his wife, for now he was at the bottom of the ladder. He lost no opportunity to impress this disagreeable truth upon her, but his honest efforts to hold himself aloof only increased her respect and love for him. It not only convinced her that notwithstanding his past life, he was a man of honor capable of resisting himself and of protecting her, but it gave him the quality so irresistible to a woman—unattainability.

Taking it all in all, my poor beautiful cousin was falling day by day deeper into an abyss of love from which she could in no way extricate herself. In short, level-headed Frances had got far out of plumb, and, though she struggled desperately, she could not right herself, nor could any one help her. I fully realized that the small amount of self-restraint and passivity she still retained would give way to disastrous activity when the time should come for her to part with George and lose him forever. But I could see no way to save her unless I could induce George to leave England at once, for good and all.

At times the fates seem to fly to a man's help, and in this instance they came to me most graciously that same day in Whitehall, in the person of my friend the Count de Grammont.

Soon after leaving Frances in the maids' apartments, I met that most interesting gentleman roue, his Grace de Grammont, coming from the king's closet. As already stated, he had been banished from the French court by Louis XIV because of a too great friendliness for one of the king's sweethearts, and was living in exile in London till Louis should forgive his interference. The French king really liked De Grammont and trusted him when his Majesty's lady-loves were not concerned, so the count had been sent to England in honorable exile, and was employed in certain cases as a spy and in others as a means of secret communication between the French king and persons connected with the court of Charles II.

When De Grammont saw me, he came forward, holding out both hands in his effusive French manner, apparently overjoyed at finding a long-lost brother.

"Come with me, my dear baron," he cried, bending so close to me that I feared he was going to kiss me. "Come with me! You are the very man of all the world I want, I need, I must have!"

"You have me, my dear count," said I, "but I cannot go with you. I am engaged elsewhere."

"No, no, let me whisper!" He brought his lips close to my ear and continued almost inaudibly: "You may please me. You may help a friend. You may oblige—a king."

The last, of course, was the *ne plus ultra* of inducement according to the count's way of thinking, and he supposed the mere suggestion would vanquish me. Still I pleaded my engagement. He insisted, however, repeating in my ear:—

"Oblige a king! A real king! Not a flimsy fool of bourgeois, who makes of himself the laughing-stock of his people, but a real king. I cannot name him now, but you must know."

We were in a narrow passage leading to the Stone Gallery in Whitehall. He looked about him a moment, then taking me by the arm, led me to the Stone Gallery and thence to the garden. I wanted to stop, but he kept his grasp on my arm, repeating now and then the word "Come" in whispers, till we reached a lonely spot in St. James Park. There he halted, and though there was not a living creature in sight, he brought his lips to my ear and breathed the name, "'Sieur George Hamilton."

I tried not to show that I was startled, but the quickwitted, sharp-eyed Frenchman read me as though I were an open book, and grasping my hand, cried out:—

"Ah, I knew you could tell me. It is to rejoice! I knew it!"

"Tell you what, count?" I asked.

"Tell me where your friend and mine is, or if you will not tell me, take to him a letter. I have been trying to find him this fortnight."

"I cannot tell you where he is, my dear count—"

"Of course not! I do not ask," he interrupted.

"—But I may be able to forward your letter to him. I heard only the other day that he was in France."

"Of course, of course, he is in France! Not in England at all! Good, good! I see you are to be trusted. But I must have your word of honor that the letter will be delivered."

"I shall send it by none but a trusted messenger," I answered, "and shall return it to you unopened unless I am convinced beyond a doubt that it will reach our friend."

"Good, good! Come to my hotel. I will trust you."

We went to De Grammont's house, and after taking great precautions against discovery, he gave me a small wooden box wound with yards of tape and sealed with quantities of wax. I put the box in my pocket, saying:—

"I accept the trust on my honor, dear count, and though the package bears no name nor address, I shall deliver it to the person for whom it is intended."

De Grammont said he knew nothing of the contents of the box except that it contained a message for a friend, and I believed him.

When I left his house he came to the door with me, murmuring: "My gratitude! My gratitude! Also the gratitude of my king, which I hope may prove of far greater value to your friend than my poor offering of words."

I lost no time in seeking George, except to make sure that I was not followed. I trusted De Grammont and felt sure that the box he had given me contained a personal communication from no less a person than Louis XIV of France, but I wanted to take no risk of betraying Hamilton by leading De Grammont or any one else to his hiding-place.

Since Frances's providential escape, the king had suspected the right persons of her rescue. At least he suspected Hamilton, and was seeking him more diligently than ever before. His Majesty had not shown me any mark of disfavor, but I feared he suspected me, and was sure he was not convinced that Frances's alibi had been proved by unsuborned testimony. If he was sure that she was the one who had been kidnapped, his suspicious nature would connect George with the rescue, and would lead him to conclude that Hamilton must be in England.

A maid of Lady Castlemain's told Rochester, who in turn told me, that the king had again set his men to work searching for Hamilton. That being the case, George was in danger, and should he be found by the king's secret agents, who, I understood, were prowling all over England in the hope of obtaining a reward, his life would not be worth a week's purchase.

George knew the risk he ran by remaining in England, but it was a part of his reckless courage to take delight in it. Later on this recklessness of disposition induced him to take a far

238   Charles Major

greater risk. But of that in its turn.

*   *   *   *   *

After supper, I found Hamilton in his bedroom, which was connected by a hidden stairway with the room of the sinking floor. He wore his Quaker's disguise, and on the table beside him were the Bible and a few theological works dear to the hearts of his sect. I gave him the box, telling him its history. The letter was brief and was written in cipher.

George translated it thus:—

"MASTER GEORGE HAMILTON:

"Monsieur le Grand wishes you to pay him a visit immediately."

"DE CATANET."

"You probably know Monsieur le Grand?" I asked.

"Yes," he answered, "and I shall visit him without delay."

"In Paris?" I asked, not quite sure that Monsieur le Grand was King Louis of France, and not desiring to know certainly.

"In Paris," he answered, giving me to understand by his manner that he must tell me nothing more definite of Le Grand's identity.

"Don't tell me what you know of the business this letter refers to, but tell me whether you know," I said, hoping that George might at least tell me it meant good fortune for him.

"I cannot even conjecture the business upon which I am wanted," he said, "but I hope that it may give me an opportunity to be of service to the writer."

Thus I was relieved of the disagreeable task of trying to induce George to leave England, and was very thankful to escape it.

After a long silence, during which he read the one-line letter many times, he asked:—

"Are you willing to bring Frances to me early to-morrow morning, if she will come?"

"Doubtless I can," I answered. "Her willingness to come has been shown all too plainly of late; but ought I bring her?"

"Yes. It will be the last time I shall ever see her unless good fortune lies in this letter, and for that I hardly dare hope. You know that when a man's luck has been against him for a long time, it kills the very roots of hope and brings him almost to doubt certainty. Soon after I have seen my friend, Le Grand, I shall write to you in cipher, of which I shall leave you the key. If I see a prospect of fortune worthy of Frances, I shall ask her to wait a time for me, but if my ill fortune pursues me, I shall never again be heard from by any one in England. Are you satisfied with the conditions?"

I gave him my hand for answer, and told him I would bring Frances to him early the following morning.

I hastened back to Whitehall, and coming upon Frances unengaged, asked her to go to her parlor with me. When she had closed the door, she turned to me, asking:—

"What is it, Baron Ned? Tell me quickly. I know there is

something wrong with George."

"Will you go with me early to-morrow morning to see Betty—very early?" I asked.

Her eyes opened in wonder, and she answered, somewhat amused: "You have been acting as my guardian for a long time, cousin Ned, and now I think I owe it to you to return the favor. You should not see so much of Betty. I know you mean no wrong to her, but you will cause her great suffering if you continue to see her, for you must know that already the girl is almost mad with love of you. Yet you cannot marry her."

"Nor can you marry some one else," I retorted, almost angrily, for a man dislikes to be prodded by a painful truth.

"Ah, well, I suppose we are a pair of fools," she said.

"You're right, Frances," I answered philosophically, "and the only consolation we can find lies in the fact that we know it."

"Most fools lack that flattering unction," returned Frances, musingly.

"Perhaps you will take more interest in this matter when I tell you that it is not Betty I propose to see," I answered. "I am deliberately offering to take you to see some one else who is about to leave England."

She stood on tiptoe and kissed my lips for answer, then sank into a chair, covering her face with her hands to hide the sudden tears.

I went to the window and waited till she was calm. I longed to comfort her by telling of the faint prospect of good fortune that lay in Le Grand's letter, but I hesitated raising a hope which might never be realized.

At the end of five minutes I went to her and said: "Let me ask the duchess to excuse you for to-night, and in the morning I'll meet you on Bowling Green stairs, at, say, seven o'clock."

"I'll be there," she answered, smiling through her tears.

The next morning we took boat, and the tide running out, made good speed to the Bridge, hastened to the Old Swan, and found George in his printing shop awaiting us. I remained in the old tapestried room, leaving Frances and George to say their farewells. In the course of a few minutes he called me in. He had donned his Quaker disguise, and on the floor near him was a small bundle of linen. Frances was weeping, and George's voice was choked with emotion.

"Well, at last, Baron Ned, you are to be rid of me," he said, glancing toward the bundle at his feet.

"What are your plans of escape?" I asked.

"I shall work my way down to Sheerness, where I hope to find a boat for The Hague or the French coast. Lilly, who seems to know everything, past, present and future, came last night to tell me that the king has fifty men seeking me in various parts of England, especially the seaports, and has offered a reward of two hundred pounds for me, dead or alive, preferably dead, I suppose. If I go direct to Sheerness and try to take a boat, I am sure to be examined, and I'm not prepared for the ordeal. So I intend to preach my way down the river and induce the king's officers to send me abroad by force."

And so it happened with George in Sheerness. He was on the dock exhorting vehemently against the evils of the time, laying great stress on the wickedness of the king and denouncing the vileness of the court. Two of the king's officers tried to silence him, but failing, ordered him to leave England by a certain Dutch boat then waiting in the harbor with its pennant up. He protested and struggled, but at last was forced aboard, raving against those godless Balaamites, the clergy of the Established Church, who, with the devil, he declared, were behind his persecution.

So well did George play his part that a collection was taken up among the passengers of the Dutch boat to help the good man so vilely put upon. There was a sweet bit of irony in the fact, learned afterwards, that the officers who forced George aboard the Dutch ship were at Sheerness for the purpose of winning the two hundred pounds reward offered for his capture.

The goodness of God occasionally takes a whimsical form.

A month later I received a letter from George, written in cipher, which I here give translated:—

"DEAR FRIEND:

"I reached Paris three weeks ago and was received by Monsieur Le G. most graciously. Although I cannot give definite news, I hope for great improvement in my fortune soon, and perhaps may write you more fully thereof before the week is spent."

"Good fortune has but one meaning for me, of which you already know. I beg you to say to one that a letter from her hand would give me greater joy than she can know, and that I would now send one to her if I felt safe in so doing. Please send all letters in cipher, addressed: 'Monsieur le Blanc, in care of 'Sieur de Catanet, at the sign of the Double Arrow on the Rue St. Antoine, counting nine doors from the street corner nearest the Bastile.'"

"Your friend,

"LE BLANC."

When George wrote that he hoped for good fortune, I knew he had sound reason to expect it, for he was one who never permitted a mere possibility to take the form of hope, nor hope, however assuring, to take the aspect of certainty. Knowing this to be true, I found great joy in the letter, and when I told Frances, she did not pause even to give me one smile of thanks, but broke into a flood of tears and seemed to take great happiness in her tribulation.

I told Frances that we should answer the letter at once, and suggested that she have hers ready in my hands the following day, if she wished to write one. I also suggested that we meet in Bettina's parlor, where Frances's letter could be rewritten in cipher. We trusted Bettina as we trusted ourselves, and when we told her the good news, she clapped her hands for joy, laughing, yet ready to weep, and was as happy as even she could be, which was very happy indeed.

After we had talked, laughed, and cried a reasonable time in Betty's parlor, Frances handed me her letter, which was a bulky document, well taped and waxed.

"It will require a week for me to translate this," I remarked, weighing the letter in my hand.

"What do you mean by translating it?" she asked in surprise.

"I must write it out in cipher. Hamilton directed that all letters should be sent in that form," I answered, amused at her alarm.

"No, no!" she cried, snatching the letter from me, pressing it to her breast and blushing to her ears. "You shall not see my letter!"

"Why?" I asked.

"Because," she answered.

"That is no reason," I replied. "Of course you have written nothing that you would not want me or your father to see?"

"Well, yes, I have," she returned emphatically. "A great deal. Would you, Betty, want any one to see such a letter written by yourself?"

"I suppose I could write a letter which I should want but one person in all the world to see," returned Betty, arching her eyebrows.

"To whom would it be directed, Betty?" I asked, to tease her.

A faint expression of reproach came to her eyes, but after a moment of pretty hesitancy, she answered boldly:—

"Since you are so unwise as to ask, I'll answer in like folly. The letter could be directed to but one person in the world—you."

I had received more than I had expected, and though I longed to make a suitable return, I dared not for the sake of my vows, so we all remained silent, and somewhat embarrassed, for a minute or two.

Turning to Frances, I said: "If you don't want me to read your letter, I'll give you the key, and you may make it into cipher." But after examining the key, she declared that she could never learn to use it, and I suggested that she write a shorter letter in terms fit for a modest man to read.

The next day she handed me a shorter letter, saying that she had cut and pruned it till there was nothing left worth sending, but I assured her that George would think otherwise.

When I read the letter, my eyes were opened to the fact that there was more fire in Frances's heart than I had supposed any woman capable of holding in subjection. But that is a mistake often made by men.

This was my cousin's "cut and pruned" letter:—

"DEAR ONE:

"Baron Ned says my letter must be short, so I smother what remnant of modesty I have, covering nothing with the veil of circumlocution, but telling you plainly what I know you want to hear. I love only you and am true to you in every thought, word, and deed. I long for you, yearn for you, pray for you, and be your fortune good or ill, I would share it and give you a part of the bliss of life which you would give to me."

"So I pray you, do not desert me in case your present hope of good fortune fails you, but let me know at any time, and I will go to you, and will go with you wherever you will take me."

"You will say, I fear, that none but a crazy woman would write such a letter as this, but if that be true, the world doubtless is and always has been populated by maniacs, and

I pray God always will be. I pray you, remember, in judging me, that you are you and that I am but a woman by whom the good or evil of life is reckoned in the measure of her love; her joy or misery being only a matter of down weight or light weight more in the love she gives than in that which she receives. Remember, also, that in this letter I must condense when I might easily be prolix, and that after all is written, probably I shall have left unsaid the very thing I most wished to say. But these three words will tell it all and bear repeating: I love you.

"FRANCES."

And this from my sensible cousin! What would it be if her heart were not balanced by a wise head?

Our letters being written, I became alarmed about posting them in London, not knowing when a messenger would start for France, nor who he would be. The next day Frances and I talked it over, and she suggested that as the king and most of the court were about to visit Bath for a season, and as neither she nor I cared to go, we should take the letters to Dover, cross to Calais, and post them in France.

I sprang at the idea, but immediately sprang back, saying: "But it is not entirely proper for us to travel to Calais together, even though you are my sister-cousin."

"We may take father," she suggested. "Sarah wants to visit Lady St. Albans, and she can go if we take father with us. And, Baron Ned; I have another suggestion to offer. Let us take Bettina."

I sprang at that proposal and did not spring back. So we went first to my uncle, who said he would go with us, and then we went to see Bettina. She had recovered from her sprains and bruises, although she was still pale and not quite strong.

When Frances asked her to go with us, she answered, "Ay, gladly, if father consents."

Pickering, who was sitting with us at the time in Bettina's cozy parlor, turned to me, laughing, and said:—

"You would suppose, from Betty's remark, that I am master here, but the truth is my soul is not my own, and now her modest request for permission is made for effect on the company."

Betty ran to her father, sat on his knee, twined her arm about his neck, and kissed him as a protest against the unjust insinuation.

"You see how she does it," said Pickering. "No hammer and tongs for Betty; just oil and honey."

"And lots and lots of love, father," interrupted Betty.

* * * * *

Well, our journey was soon arranged on a grand scale. Pickering lent us his new coach, just home from the makers in Cow Street. It was cushioned and curtained and had springs in place of thorough-braces. It also had glass in the windows and doors; a luxury then little known in England even among the nobles. There was a prejudice against its use in coach windows because of the fact that two or three old ladies had cut their faces in trying to thrust their heads through it.

The new coach was a wonderful vehicle, and Frances and I, as well as Betty, were very proud of our grandeur. Pickering sent along with the coach and horses two lusty fellows as drivers, and gave us a hamper almost large enough to feed a company of soldiers. I was to pay all expenses on the road.

Almost at the last hour Sir Richard concluded not to go, but insisted that Frances, Bettina, and I take the journey by ourselves. As Pickering offered no objection, Frances shrugged her shoulders in assent, I shrugged mine, and Betty laughed, whereby we all, in our own way, agreed to the new arrangement, and preparations went forward rapidly.

By the time we were ready to start, the king, the duke, the duchess, and many ladies and gentlemen of the court circle had gone to Bath, thus giving us an opportunity to make our journey without the knowledge of any one in Whitehall; a consideration of vast importance to us under the circumstances. Some of our grand friends at court might have laughed at our taking the journey with an innkeeper's daughter, in an innkeeper's coach, but Frances and I laughed because we were happy.

There are distinct periods of good and bad luck in every man's life, which may be felt in advance by one sensitive to occult influences, if one will but keep good watch on one's intuitions and leave them untrammelled by will or reason. At this time "I felt it in my bones," as Betty would have said, that the day of our good luck was at hand.

All conditions seemed to combine to our pleasure when, on a certain bright spring morning, Betty, Frances, and I went down to the courtyard of the Old Swan, where we found the coach, the horses, and even the drivers all glittering in the sunshine.

There was ample room in the back seat of the coach for the three of us, so Betty took one corner, Frances made herself comfortable in another, and I took what was left, the pleasant place between them.

After Betty had kissed her father at least a dozen times, and had shed a few tears just to make her happiness complete, the driver cracked his whip and away we went, out through the courtyard gate, down Gracious Hill and across London Bridge before a sleepy man could have winked his eyes.

At first we thought we were in haste, but when we got out of Southwark and into the country, the dark green grass, the flowering hedges, the whispering leaves of the half-fledged trees, the violets by the roadside, and the smiling sun in the blue above, all invited us to linger. So we told the driver to slow his pace, and we lowered every window in the coach, there being no one in the country whose wonder and envy we cared to arouse by a display of our glass.

There was not room in Betty's little heart for all the great flood of happiness that had poured into it, so presently, to give it vent, she began to sing the little French lullaby we had so often heard, whereupon Frances and I ceased listening to the birds, and I was more thoroughly convinced than ever before that there were at least distinct periods of *good* fortune in every man's life.

Before reaching Gravesend, we halted at a grassy spot near the river bank, where we ate our dinner. When the horses had rested, we set off for Rochester, in which place we expected to spend the night at the Maid's Garter, a famous old inn kept by a friend of Pickerings.

I had noticed a twinkle in Pickering's eyes when he directed us to go to this tavern, but did not understand the cause of his merriment until I learned that by a curious old custom, a maid seeking entrance for the first time must contribute one of her garters before being admitted. The worst feature of the usage was that the garter must be taken off at the door, and then and there presented to the porter, who received it on the point of his official staff.

After entering Rochester, we went to the Maid's Garter and at once drove into the courtyard, as the custom is with travellers intending to remain all night.

When we left the coach and started to climb the steps to the great door, we found the landlord and his retinue waiting to receive us. Frances was in the lead, and when we reached the broad, flat stone in front of the door, the head porter stepped before her, bowed, and asked humbly:—

"Is my lady maid or madam?"

Frances looked up in surprise, and he repeated his question.

"What is that to you, fellow?" asked Frances.

"It is this, my lady," returned the porter. "If my lady be a maid, she must pay me one of her garters as her admission fee to this inn. If she be madam, she enters free. It is a privilege conferred on the Maid's Garter by good St. Augustine when he was Bishop of Canterbury, so long ago that the memory of man runneth not to the contrary."

"What nonsense is this?" asked Frances, turning to me, and Bettina asked the same question with her eyes. I explained the matter, and Frances, turning to the porter, said:—

"I'll buy you off with a jacobus or a guinea."

"Not a hundred guineas would buy me off, my lady," answered the porter, bowing, "though I might say that a shilling usually goes with the garter."

"Well, I'll send you both the shilling and the garter from my room," said Frances, moving toward the inn door.

"The garter must be paid here, my lady. The shilling may be paid at any time," returned the porter, with polite insistence.

Frances was about to protest, but Betty, more in sympathy with the eccentric customs of inns, modestly lifted her skirts, untied her garter and offered it to the porter, telling him very seriously:—

"I am a maid."

The porter thanked her gravely, whereupon Frances, turning her back on the audience in the doorway, brought forth her garter, gave it to the porter, and we were admitted.

Our supper, beds, and breakfast were all so good that they reconciled Frances and Bettina to the payment of the extraordinary admission fee, and when we left the next morning, curiosity prompted them to pass near the garter rack in the tap-room, where garters were hanging which had been taken from maids whose great granddaughters had become great grandmothers. The garters that had belonged to Frances and Bettina, being the latest contributions, hung at the bottom of the rack, neatly dated and labelled, and, as I left the room, I overheard Bettina whisper to Frances:—

"I'm glad mine was of silk."

We made a short drive to Maidstone, where we stopped over night. The next day a longer journey brought us to Canterbury, where we spent two nights and a day, visiting the cathedral both by sunlight and moonlight; the combination of moonlight and Bettina being very trying to me.

From Canterbury we drove in the rain to Dover, where we lodged at that good inn, the Three Anchors, to await a fair wind for Calais.

During the next three days the wind was fair, but it was blowing half a gale, and therefore the passage was not to be attempted. Though I was enjoying myself, I was anxious to post our letters, as mine gave a full account of several matters at court concerning which I knew George ought to be informed.

Among other news, I told him that King Charles had sent a messenger into France carrying a personal letter to King Louis, asking his help in finding the man Hamilton, who had threatened Charles's life. I also suggested in my letter that the king of France was trying to buy the city of Dunkirk from King Charles, and that because of the friendly negotiations then pending, Louis might give heed to our king's request. In that case, it might be well, I thought, for Hamilton to leave France at once.

With this urgency in mind, I suggested to Frances and Betty that I cross to Calais alone, regardless of the weather, leaving them at Dover till my return. But they would not be left behind, so we all set sail on a blustery morning and paid for our temerity with a day of suffering. In Calais we posted our letters, having learned that a messenger would leave that same day for Paris, and two days later we returned to Dover.

Our journey home was made in the rain, Bettina sleeping with her head on my shoulder a great part of the way. And I enjoyed the rain even more than I had enjoyed the sunshine.

We reached London nearly a week before the king's return, so that nothing was known of our journey at court.

CHAPTER XI

"ALL SUNSHINE MAKES THE DESERT"

Whatever faults Whitehall may have had as a place of residence, dulness was not among them. There were balls, games with high stakes, theatres, gossip, scandals, and once in a long while an affair of state to interest us. In order to interest the court thoroughly, an affair of state must have involved the getting of money for the privy purse; that is, for the king's personal use, for out of it the courtesans were fed and gambling debts were paid.

The time of our Dover journey was one of extreme depletion in the privy purse. The king had borrowed from every person and every city within the realm who, by threats or cajolery, could be induced to part with money. But now he had reached the end of his tether.

When matters were thus in extremis, some one, probably Castlemain, suggested the sale of England's possessions on the continent, chief of which was the rich city of Dunkirk, situate on the French side of the Straits of Dover. This fortified city, within a few leagues of Calais, had cost the English nation heavily in blood and gold to gain, and still more heavily to hold, but its value to England commercially and politically was beyond measure.

Since Queen Mary had lost Calais, Dunkirk was the only important foothold England had on continental soil; therefore it was almost as dear to the English people as the city of London itself. Because of its importance, it was greatly coveted by the French king, who shortly before the time of our journey to Dover had made overtures to buy it.

Charles turned a deaf ear to King Louis's first proposal to buy Dunkirk, not because he loved the city, or cared a farthing for its value to his people, but because he feared the storm of indignation its sale would raise. The Lord Chancellor objected to the sale of Dunkirk, and tried to show Charles the great folly of entertaining the offer. He was the only wise, honest man in the king's council, and, by reason of his wonderful knowledge of mankind, was called "the Chancellor of Human Nature." But the king needed money, so after a time he listened to Berkeley, Crofts, Castlemain, and others of like character, whose strongest argument consisted in accusing the king, most offensively, of being afraid of his people.

"Are you not king?" asked Castlemain. "Does not Dunkirk belong to you, and may you not sell that which is your property? Are not these dogs, the people, your slaves, your property? Yet you stand in cowardly fear of a rabble which quakes if you but crook your finger. A like fear of his subjects cost your father his head. The people will crawl before you if you kick them, but let them see that you fear them, and you will learn that there is no cruelty like that of the good people."

De Grammont, the French exile, called attention to the French king's successful tyranny, declaring that his master would sell Paris if he chose. De Grammont was acting secretly in the French king's interest.

A weak man easily finds logic to justify the course he desires to take, so Charles turned a deaf ear to Clarendon, and, listening to Castlemain, announced that Dunkirk was for sale. As expected, a strong protest came from the people, but no one is so stubborn as a fool in the wrong, so Charles remained firm in his determination.

Finding that protest would avail nothing, the people of London offered to buy Dunkirk, and began to bid for it against the French king. Louis, knowing that London was a rich city, and believing that its people would run up the price of Dunkirk to an exorbitant figure, took counsel with himself—his only adviser—and determined to employ other means than gold alone to obtain the coveted city.

My first definite knowledge of the French king's new plan to buy Dunkirk at his own price came in a letter from Hamilton, which reached me at Lilly's house two or three weeks after my return from Dover. Like the others, it was written in cipher, but, translated, was as follows:—

DEAR FRIEND:

"Your warning letter reached me nearly a week ago, and I thank you for your watchfulness. I had full information of King Charles's design upon my life from no less a person than Monsieur le Grand himself, who showed me the letter asking that I be returned to England."

"I explained to Monsieur le Grand that the English king sought my life, not because he is in fear of me, but because he thought I stood between him and a lady who despises him. While Monsieur le Grand was much in sympathy with the English king's grievance, his contempt for Charles, his regard for me, which seems to be sincere, and his longing to possess Dunkirk all induced him to laugh at the request, the nature of which he had imparted to no one save me.

"My account of the lady who despised King Charles's love gave Monsieur le Grand a new idea, and suggested a method of purchasing Dunkirk which he hopes will save the heavy cost of bidding against the citizens of London. I had no hint of what he intended till one day he took me to his closet and began to question me."

"'Do you possess the love of the lady who despises King Charles?' he asked."

"'I do, your Majesty,' I answered."

"'Do you know you possess it?' he asked."

"'As well as a man who is not a king may know,' I returned."

"'Tush, tush! Kings are no more certain than other men.'"

"'I know I possess this woman's love,' I said."

"Would she be willing to make a great sacrifice to help you?"

"'Anything that I should ask,' I replied."

"'Ah, I see, I see! Should ask? I take it there are certain sacrifices you would not ask,' returned the king. 'We here in France would say that your position was Quixotic. However, your King Charles is a weak fool, easily imposed upon. Is the lady quick and resourceful in expedients, calm and thoughtful in emergencies, and silent on great occasions?'"

"To all of which I answered, 'Yes.'"

"'Surely the lady is not La Belle Jennings?' asked the king."

"'Yes,' I replied."

"'In that case you are the very man I want, and your lady-love can help me buy Dunkirk. It is easy to lead a fool to do the wrong thing, and I'm sure La Belle Jennings will find a way to gain her end and ours. If, through her, you induce King Charles to sell Dunkirk to me on my own terms, I'll make you its governor and a rich man. I'll put you in a position to marry this paragon, Mam'selle Jennings, if, as I take it, lack of fortune is all that stands between you. I do not mind telling you now that De Grammont had given me full information concerning the king's view of La Belle Jennings and your relations to her before I wrote my first letter, inviting you to visit me.'"

"I am loath to undertake so mean an office as that of inducing King Charles to sell an English city, but I cannot save Dunkirk, and I may profit by helping what I cannot prevent. So I beg you broach the subject to Frances, cautioning her for me to take no risk, and if she is willing to use and to hoodwink the man who would not hesitate to take her life, let me know, and I shall write to you again with further instructions."

"With gratitude,

"Your friend,

"LE BLANC."

I sought Frances, and when I told her the substance of George's letter, she was almost wild with joy.

"Am I willing to try?" she exclaimed, laughing while tears were hanging in her eyes. "I am not only willing to try, but am determined to succeed. Ay, I'd sell England itself in the same cause. Of all the men I have ever known, this king of ours is the greatest dupe. Since the return of the court to Whitehall, he has been growing more importunate every day. He seems to have lost what little wits he had, and does and says the silliest things one can imagine."

"And you do not fear attempting to lead him on to sell Dunkirk? You do not fear going too near the precipice?" I asked, wishing to weigh her self-confidence more by the manner of her reply than by her words.

She laughed and answered: "There is no precipice, cousin Ned; nothing to fear save kidnapping, and I am always guarded against that danger; nothing to do of which I need feel ashamed, save the acting of a lie, and surely one may lie to the father of lies without sin."

"But the lie may be recognized," I suggested, "if one be too bold about it."

"My lie will go little beyond a smile or two. The king's vanity will do the rest. He will make himself believe that I mean more than I say."

Frances and I felt that we were traitors to our country in helping the French king, but we knew that in the end he would buy Dunkirk from our spendthrift monarch, and that out country's loss would be no greater by reason of our gain. Therefore I wrote George as follows:—

"DEAR FRIEND:

"The Duchess of Hearts is eager and confident. Write at once, giving full directions.

"YOUR FRIEND."

Frances added a postscript in cipher, but I shall not translate it.

One morning, some three weeks after sending my letter, Frances came to me in my closet in the Wardrobe, and I saw at once she was in great trouble. Her eyes were red with weeping, and the woebegone expression of her face would have been amusing had I not known that some good cause was back of it. As soon as she entered I saw that she was going to speak, but closets in Whitehall have ears, so I placed my finger on my lips to enjoin silence, and spoke loud enough to be heard if any one was listening:—

"Ah, Frances, I forgot that I had promised to go with you to your father's this morning. Wait for me at Holbein's Gate. I'll be there in ten minutes."

Within the promised time I found Frances at Holbein's Gate, and we walked up to Charing Cross, thence down the Strand toward Temple Bar.

"What is the trouble, Frances?" I asked, anxious to hear her news, which I feared was bad. She was in great distress, and I saw that a flood of tears was ready to accompany her tale of woe, so I said hurriedly: "Don't cry. Laugh while you speak. You will attract less attention."

She tried to laugh, but the effort was piteous and became a failure, as she said:—

"George Hamilton has sailed for Canada, and my heart is broken."

Again she tried to smile, but the smile never reached her eyes, for they were full of tears.

"How do you know?" I asked, almost stunned by the news.

She tried to stay her tears, but failed, and answered between sobs: "Last night at the queen's ball, the king showed me a letter sent by order of the French king, saying that George had sailed from Bordeaux for Canada nearly a fortnight ago. I could not help showing my grief, and the king, who was boisterously happy, said: 'Now you will forget him and listen to me.' I smiled, but it was a poor effort, and he smiled, showing his yellow fangs as he left me. I pray God that I may never be called upon to hate another man as I hate him."

"I can hardly believe that George has gone to Canada without notifying us," I said.

"Yes, I fear it is true," she returned. "But if I am ever so fortunate as to find him again, I intend to go with him whether he consents or no, regardless of father and all the world. Just as soon as I learn where he is in Canada, I will go to him. You will take me, won't you, Baron Ned?"

"I'll not give that promise," I answered. "But I am sure there is something back of King Louis's letter of which we do not know. Surely George would not have sailed without notifying us."

"He may have feared to betray himself by writing," she suggested, "since King Charles had asked King Louis to detain him."

"That is true," I returned. "But the occasion must have been urgent indeed if he could not have sent us word in some manner."

But I could find no comfort for her, for I really believed that George had gone to Canada, and there was a certain relief to me in knowing that he had passed out of Frances's life.

After along silence this feeling of relief found unintentional expression when I said:—

"Time heals all wounds, Frances. One of these days you will find a man who will make amends for your present loss, and then—"

"No, no, Baron Ned. Your words are spoken in kindness, but what you suggest is impossible. Perhaps if there had been fewer obstacles between us, or if I had not misjudged him so cruelly, I might have found my heart more obedient to my will."

The only comfort I could give my beautiful cousin was that a letter would soon come explaining everything. In default of a letter, I promised to go to Paris and learn the truth from George's friends, if possible.

Frances did not go back to Whitehall that day, but remained at home, pretending to be ill of an ague.

At the end of a week, Frances not having returned to Whitehall, Sir Richard was honored by a visit from no less a person than the king, accompanied by the duchess and a gentleman in waiting. The visit was made incognito.

As a result of this royal visit, which was made for the purpose of seeing Frances, a part of Sir Richard's estates near St. Albans were restored to him, and from poverty he rose at once to a comfortable income of, say, a thousand or twelve hundred pounds a year.

Immediately all of Sir Richard's hatred of Charles II fell away, and once more the king shone in the resplendent light of his divine appointment.

While Frances estimated the king's generosity at its true value, she was glad her father had received even a small part of what was his just due, and although she knew the restoration had been made to please, and, if possible, to win her, she was glad to have spoiled the royal Philistine, and despised him more than ever before, if that were possible.

Sir Richard's good fortune brought a gleam of joy to Frances, but it also brought a pang of regret, because it had come too late. Her only purpose in going to Whitehall had been to marry a rich nobleman and thereby raise the fallen fortunes of her house. Now that reason existed no longer, and if George were here, she could throw herself away upon him with injury to no one but herself. But George was not here, and liberty to throw herself away had come too late to be of any value.

Every day during the fortnight that Frances remained at home, she asked if I had any news from court, meaning the French court, but using the form of inquiry to avoid acquainting her father and Sarah with the real cause of her solicitude.

But my answers were always, "Oh, nothing but Castlemain's new tantrum," or "The duke's defeat at pall-mall."

Frances was the last girl in the world, save, perhaps Sarah, who I should have supposed capable of languishing and dying of love, but the former she did before my eyes, and the latter I almost began to fear if news did not reach us soon from George.

Betty came up to see Frances nearly every day, and the kissing and embracing that ensued disgusted Sarah.

"Now, if Frances were a man, I could understand it," said Sarah. "The little barmaid must be tempting to a man, being pretty and—"

"Beautiful, Sarah!" I interrupted.

"Yes, beautiful, if you will."

"Her eyes—" I began, again interrupting Sarah.

"Oh, yes!" cried Sarah, impatiently. "Her eyes are fine enough, but their expression comes from their color, their size, and their preposterously long eyelashes. Black long lashes often give a radiance to the eyes which passes for expressiveness, and I doubt not—"

"Nonsense, Sarah!" I cried, half angrily. "Bettina's eyes are expressive in themselves. As you say, their soft dark brown is the perfection of color, and they certainly are large. But aside from all that, their expression is—"

"There is no intellect in them!" cried Sarah.

"There is tenderness, gentleness, love, and truth in them," I answered, with as careless an air as I could assume.

"Yes, there may be for a man, but I insist there is no real intellect."

"Well, Sarah," I answered, showing irritation despite an effort to appear indifferent, "it is my opinion that the possession of great intellectual power by a woman is the one virtue with which men, as a rule, find themselves most willing to dispense. It gives her too great an advantage."

"Yes, a soft, plump figure like Betty's, long lashes and red lips, surrounded by dimples, are apt to please a fool."

"But they're good in their way, Sarah, you'll admit—excellent!" I retorted sharply, caring little if she saw that I was angry.

"And men are fools, so there! Not another word about the barmaid!" cried Sarah, dismissing the subject with a wave of her hand.

But men, too, sometimes like to have the last word, so I remarked: "The mother of the Duchess of York was a barmaid, at least, a barmistress."

"Yes, but is that any reason why Frances should be kissing this one? Doubtless your friend Betty finds men enough to do the office."

"Sarah!" I cried, springing to my feet, now thoroughly angry. "If you were a man, I'd give you the lie direct!"

Sarah began to laugh and clapped her hands, saying: "I was leading you on. I suspected you were fond of her. Now I know it."

But Sarah's remark, being so near the truth, did nothing to allay my anger, so I told her she was a fool, and went into an adjoining room, where I found Frances and Bettina luxuriating in tearful sympathy.

I walked home with Bettina, and she invited me to go to her parlor to have a cup of tea. To see Bettina boil the tea (steep it or draw it, she said was the proper phrase) was as pretty a sight as one could wish to behold, and when she poured it out in thin china cups, handing one to me and taking one herself, her pride in following the fashion of modish ladies was as touching as it was simple and beautiful. It was almost more than my feeble resolutions could withstand, so when I was about to leave I had a great battle with myself and was defeated, for I seized her hands, and although I said nothing, she knew what was in my mind, so she hung her head, murmuring:—

"If you are willing to make me more unhappy than I am."

"Not for the world, Bettina," I answered, rallying against myself. "Goodnight."

"Good night. Now I know you are my friend," she answered softly, holding my hands for a moment, then dropping them suddenly and turning from me.

I have refrained from speaking of Mary Hamilton of late, partly because I did not see her frequently at this time, and partly because the shame I felt at the time of which I am now writing comes surging over me whenever I touch upon the subject. Not that I did anything of which I need be ashamed, but because I remember so vividly my motives and desires that the old sensations return, even at this distant day, as a perfume, a strain of music, the soft balminess of spring, or the sharp bite of winter's frost may recall a moment of the past, and set the heart throbbing or still it as of yore.

After leaving Bettina, I went back to Whitehall and dressed for a ball which the queen was giving that night. It was an unfortunate time for me to see Mary. My heart was full, not to overflowing, but to sinking, with my love of Bettina and her love of me. There was nothing I would not have given at that time to be able to take her as my wife. I should have been glad to give my title, estates, and position—everything—to be a simple tradesman or an innkeeper so that I might take Bettina with happiness to her and without the damning sin of losing caste to me.

It was true the king's brother had made a marriage of comparatively the same sort, but it is almost as impossible for a prince to lose caste as it is difficult for a mere baron to keep it. Bettina would not be happy in my sphere of life, nor could I live in hers, so what was there for me to do but to keep my engagement with Mary Hamilton and, if I could, lose my love for Bettina.

* * * * *

The queen's ball was to be held that night at St. James's Palace, and I was glad to have the walk from Whitehall across the park. The night was perfect. A slim moon hung in the west, considerately withholding a part of her light that the stars might twinkle the brighter in their vain effort to rival Bettina's eyes. The night wind came to me, odor-laden from the roses, only to show me how poor a thing it was compared with Bettina's breath upon my cheek and its sweetness in my nostrils. Now and then a belated bird sang its sleepy song, only to remind me of the melody of her lullabies, and the cooing dove moaned out its plaintive call lest I forget the pain in her breast while selfishly remembering the ache in my own. Then I thought of what the Good Book says about "bright clouds," and I prayed that my pain might make me a better man and might lead me to help Bettina in the days of her sorrowing, which I knew were at hand.

Soon after I had kissed the hands of the king and the queen, I met George's brother, Count Anthony Hamilton. He had never been friendly to his younger brother, and had ceased to look upon him as a brother at all after his disgraceful reformation. Then when the king turned against George, Anthony, good courtier that he was, turned likewise, and there is no bitterness that may be compared with that of an apostate brother.

After we had talked for a minute or two, Count Anthony asked if I knew anything of "the fool," as he was pleased to call his brother.

"I know nothing of your brother George, my lord, if it is him you mean."

"He is no brother of mine, and if you wish to become a member of our family, you will cease to consider him your friend," returned his Lordship, making an effort to conceal his anger.

I was not in the mood to take his remark kindly, therefore I answered warmly:—

"Shall my entering the ranks of your noble family curtail my privilege of choosing my own friends?"

"No, with one exception," he replied.

"The honor of the alliance is great, my lord, but I shall not consent to even one exception at your dictation. Your sister, my future wife, loves her brother, and if she does not object to my friendship for him, your Lordship oversteps your authority, as head of your house, by protesting."

He turned angrily upon me, saying: "You have been paying your court with lukewarm ardor of late, Baron Clyde. Perhaps you would not grieve if your friendship for a family outcast were to bar you from the family."

"If your Lordship means to say that I wish to withdraw dishonorably from my engagement with your sister, I crave the privilege of telling you that you lie!"

I never was more calm in my life, and my words brought a cold smile to Hamilton's lips.

"My friend De Grammont will have the honor of waiting on you to-morrow morning," he answered, bowing politely.

"I shall be delighted to see his Grace," I answered. "Good night, my lord!"

Here was a solution of my problem in so far as it concerned my engagement with Mary Hamilton, for if I killed her brother, she would not marry me, and if he killed me, I could not marry her. The fact that a gleam of joy came to me because of my unexpected release caused me to feel that I was a coward not to have broken the engagement in an honorable, straightforward manner rather than to have seized this opportunity to force a duel upon her brother. It is true I had not sought the duel deliberately and had not thought it possible one second before uttering the word that made it necessary. Still it was my act that brought it about, and I felt that I had taken an unmanly course.

After leaving Count Anthony I walked across the room to where Mary was standing at the outer edge of a circle of ladies and gentlemen who surrounded De Grammont, listening to a narrative in broken English, of his adventures, fancied or real, I know not which, but interesting, and all of a questionable character.

When I spoke to Mary, she turned and gave me her hand. I had not expected the least display of emotion on her part; therefore I was not disappointed when the smile with which she greeted me was the same she would have given to any other man. But Mary was Mary. Nature and art had made her what she was—charming, quiescent, and calm, not cold, simply lukewarm.

"I have seen little of you this last month," said Mary, taking my arm and walking with me away from De Grammont's group. She might have remarked with equal emotion that Cromwell was dead or the weather fine. She did not wait for an explanation of my absence, but continued with a touch of eager hesitancy and a fluttering show of anxiety, "Have you had news recently of my brother George?"

Of course I could not tell her the truth, so I answered evasively: "I suppose you have heard the news spread throughout the court that he has gone to Canada? Doubtless you can tell me more than I know."

"That is all I know," she answered. "When he went, or where, I have been unable to learn, for George is a forbidden topic in our household and seems to be the same at court. What has he done, baron? I have heard it hinted that he threatened to take the king's life. Surely he did nothing of the sort."

"If he did, it was in a delirium of fever," I answered, hoping that she would cease speaking of George and would ask a question or two concerning myself.

But no. She turned again to me, asking, "Did you hear him?"

"I have been told that the accusation comes from his physician, and perhaps from one who was listening at his door," I answered, avoiding a direct reply.

"I suspect the informant is a wretched little hussy of whom I have heard—the daughter of the innkeeper," remarked Mary, looking up to me for confirmation.

"Suspect no longer," I answered, with sharper emphasis than I should have used.

"Do you know her?" she asked.

"I do not know a 'wretched hussy' who is the daughter of the innkeeper," I answered sullenly. "I know a beautiful girl who watched devotedly at your brother's bedside, day and night, and probably saved his life at a time when he was deserted by his sisters and his mother."

"We often find that sort of kindness in those low creatures," she answered, unaware of the tender spot she was touching, and ignoring my reference to George's sisters and his mother.

Naturally Mary was kind of heart, but her mother was a hard, painted old Jezebel, whose teachings would have led her daughter away from every gentle truth and up to all that was hard, cruel, and selfish in life. A woman in the higher walks of life is liable to become enamelled before her twentieth year.

While I did not blame Mary for what she had said relating to Bettina, still I was angry and longed to do battle with any one who could fight.

After we had been together perhaps ten minutes, some one claimed her for a dance, and she left me, saying hurriedly in my ear:—

"I'll see you soon again. I want to ask you further about George." She had not a question to ask about me.

She was not to see me again, for I asked permission of the queen to withdraw, and immediately left the ball.

While I was crossing the park on my way back to Whitehall, the wind moaned and groaned—it did not breathe. The stars did not twinkle—they glared. The nightingales did not sing —they screamed. And the roses were odorless. Perhaps all this change to gloom was within me rather than without, but it existed just the same, and I went home and to bed, hating all the world save Bettina, whom I vowed for the hundredth time never to see again.

The next day at noon De Grammont came to my closet, where I had waited for him all morning.

"Welcome to you, dear count!" I cried, leading him by the hand to a chair.

"Perhaps you will not so warmly welcome me," he returned, "when you learn my errand."

"I already know your errand, Count Grammont, and it makes you doubly welcome," I answered, drawing a chair for myself and sitting down in front of him.

"Ah, that is of good," he returned, rubbing his hands. "You already know the purpose of my visit?"

"Yes, I do, my dear count, but any purpose would delight me which brings the pleasure of your company."

"Ah, it is said like a civilized man," he returned, complimenting me by speaking English, though I shall not attempt to reproduce his pronunciation. "How far better it is to say: 'Monsieur, permit to me,' before one runs a man through than to do it as though one were sticking a mere pig. Is it not so?"

"True as sunshine, my dear count," I returned. "There's a vast difference between the trade of butchering and the gentle art of murder."

De Grammont threw back his head, laughing softly. "Ah, good, good! Very good, dear baron! The sentiment is beautiful and could not be better expressed—in English. You should have been born across the channel."

"I wish I had been born any place, not excepting hell, rather than in England," I answered.

"True, true, what a hole it is," returned the count, regretfully. "The Englishman is one pig."

He saw by the expression of my face that while I might abuse my own countrymen, I did not relish hearing it from others, so with true French tact he held up his hand to keep me from speaking till he could correct himself.

"Pardon, baron, I forgot the 'r,' The Englishman's affectation of a virtue he despises makes of him a prig—not a pig. Non, non! Mon Dieu! Not a pig—a prig! Is it not so?"

"True, true, count," I returned, unable to restrain a laugh. "It is the affectation of virtue that makes frank vice attractive by comparison."

"Ah, true, true, my dear baron. May I proceed with my errand?"

"Proceed, count."

"Monsieur le Comte Hamilton begs me to say that he was called away from London early to-day on the king's business, but that he will return in four weeks. When he returns he will do himself the honor to send me again, asking you to name a friend, unless you prefer to apologize, which no gentleman would do in a case of this sort. You said, I am told, that Monsieur le Comte lied. If you admit that he did not lie, of course you admit that you did. So, impossible! There must be to fight!"

"Do you know, count, the cause of my having given Count Hamilton the lie?" I asked.

"I did not inquire," he answered smilingly. "To me it was to carry the message."

"George Hamilton is your friend, is he not?" I asked.

"Yes, but far more, he is the friend of my king, and will make entreaty with my monarch for my return to France," answered De Grammont.

"It was because of Count Hamilton's insulting reference to his brother that I used the ugly word," I returned.

"A-ah, that is different!" Then recovering himself quickly: "But I undertook the mission. It is to finish. Monsieur George Hamilton? My friend? My king's friend? If it had been known to me! But you have the message of 'Sieur le Comte."

After a short silence he said, "When Monsieur le Comte Hamilton returns, I shall ask him to relieve me of this duty."

As De Grammont was leaving my closet, he paused at the door, and, after a moment's hesitancy, whispered:—

"You may expect a letter from France soon. It will come from M. l'Abbe du Boise, who I hope will come soon to London on the business of my king. You know him not—M. l'Abbe?" The eyebrows lifted questioningly. "No? You soon will know him, yet you will not know him. You and perhaps a lady may help him in his mission. I, too, shall help him, but I, too, know him not. Yet I know him. If he succeed in his mission, he will be rich, he will be powerful. And I? Mon Dieu, my friend! If he succeed, my decree of banishment from Paris—it will be to revoke. I may return once more to bask in the smile of my king. You must not speak; the lady must not speak; I must not speak when Monsieur l'Abbe comes, nor before. It is to silence. Stone walls have one ear."

"Two, sometimes, count," I suggested, laughing.

"Yes, I should have said one ears! Non, non! I forget this damnable tongue of yours! When I arrive to great interest, it is to talk faster than it is to think, and—" A shrug of the shoulders finished the sentence.

"Let us speak French hereafter, my dear count," I suggested.

"Mon Dieu, mon Dieu! It is to me more of pain to hear my sweet language murdered than to murder yours," answered Grammont, seriously.

"Ah, but I speak French quite as well as I speak English. Perhaps I shall not murder it," I replied.

"Perhaps? We shall try," he said, though with little show of faith.

I began speaking French, but when I paused for his verdict, he shrugged his shoulders, saying:—

"Ah, *oui, oui!* It may be better than my English." But notwithstanding his scant praise, we spoke the French language thereafter.

The count bowed himself out and left me to decipher, if I could, the problem of M. l'Abbe du Boise. Presently I discovered the cue. The Abbe was George Hamilton, and for the moment my heart almost stopped beating. If he should come to England on the French king's business, which could be nothing more nor less than the Dunkirk affair, and should be discovered, there would be a public entertainment on Tyburn Hill, with George as the central figure.

When I found a spare hour, I hastened to see Lilly and came upon the good Doctor among the stars, as usual. There was a letter for me from Hamilton. It was short and in cipher:—

"DEAR FRIEND:

"This is to tell you that M. l'Abbe du Boise will soon be in London. He will be the guest of M. Comte de Grammont.

"You do not know him. Please call on him when he arrives. Tell the Duchess of Hearts that he will want to see her. Ask her to be ready to help him. He goes to buy Dunkirk for the French king, and his success will mean good fortune for me.

"Your friend,

"LE BLANC."

After reading the letter, I felt sure that the Abbe du Boise was George Hamilton. I could hardly bring myself to believe that he would be so foolhardy as to visit Whitehall, though I knew the adventure was of a nature likely to appeal to his reckless disregard of consequences. I knew also that, if successful, he would win the reward without which life had little value to him.

I was sure that Hamilton had fully weighed the danger of his perilous mission, and that he was deliberately staking his life on a last desperate chance to win fortune and Frances Jennings.

Though perhaps Lilly was a charlatan in many respects, he was to be trusted; still I did not feel that it was my place to impart George's secret to him, though I had in mind a plan whereby he might be of great help to the Abbe du Boise in influencing King Charles. The king consulted him secretly in many important affairs, and I was sure that if the good Doctor should be called in by his Majesty in the Dunkirk affair, the stars would tell a story in accord with our desires if we made it to Lilly's interest.

However, all of that must wait for the Abbe du Boise. Of one thing I was sure; I must tell Frances at once so that she might be paving the way to the king with her smiles. It would be a disagreeable task, but I knew she would do it gladly, and I also knew that no woman could do it better.

While I had expressed my doubts to Frances concerning Hamilton's emigration to Canada, I had not felt entirely sure there was nothing in it, and she, womanlike, taking the worst for granted, had accepted it as true. But the coming of the Abbe du Boise changed everything, and when I saw her at her father's house and told her of my suspicions, and showed her Le Blanc's letter, she was so greatly alarmed that she said she would rather know that George had gone to Canada than to fear his return to England under the circumstances.

"The dastardly king will take his life if he comes," she said.

"I admit the danger," I answered, as hopefully as possible, "but I believe, if George comes, he will be able to take care of himself."

"Danger!" she exclaimed. "It is certain death! George will find no mercy."

"If he is caught," I answered. "But the letter from King Louis will convince King Charles that Hamilton is in Canada and will throw our jealous monarch off his guard. Perhaps Hamilton will be safer than we suppose. He speaks French like a Parisian, but, above all, he is cool, calm, and thoughtful in danger. The London merchants will be far more dangerous than the king."

"It does seem that we are guilty of treason to our country in thus helping France," she said. Then laughingly, "But I'll go back to the palace at once and begin my task of wheedling the king." She paused for a moment, then continued hesitatingly, "Do you suppose it possible that George would doubt me afterwards?"

"Impossible," I answered, with emphasis that seemed to reassure her.

"I am doing it for him," she continued with a sigh. "God knows I would do almost anything in the same cause. But I do not know men, and I fear it is possible that he will doubt me after I have succeeded. Let us go to see Betty. She is restful to me, and always soothes my nerves. But besides, I want to have her help. I'll introduce her to the king—"

"No, by God, you'll not introduce her to the king! I'll explode the whole affair, and Dunkirk may go to the devil before you shall introduce Betty to the king," I answered.

"Yet you are willing that I should meddle in the dangerous affair? Evidently you love her more than you love me?"

"Only a few hundred million times more," I answered sullenly.

"Is it that way with you, my dear brother?" she asked, coming to me as I stood gazing out the window, seeing nothing save Bettina's face. Frances put her hand on my shoulder and said coaxingly: "Forgive me. No harm shall come to her through me."

Of course I was sorry that I had allowed myself to become angry, and at once made my apology as well as I could.

"Let us go to see Betty, anyway," said Frances. And I assenting, she went to fetch her cloak, hat, and vizard.

But when she returned, I had changed my mind and declined to go, telling Frances that I must see Bettina no more.

"Why?" asked Frances.

"Because I would not win a love from her which I cannot accept."

"Baron Ned, there are few men who would be so considerate."

But I required little coaxing, and when Frances had made ready for the journey, I buckled on my sword, which I had left standing in the corner, took my hat from the floor, and started out with her.

While walking from the Bridge to the Old Swan, I remarked to Frances, "My engagement with Mary Hamilton is likely to be broken by her family."

"Why, Baron Ned?" she asked in surprise.

"Count Hamilton has challenged me to a duel, to be fought when he returns, and you see, if I kill him or if he kills me, well—" I answered, shrugging my shoulders.

She was much alarmed at my disclosure, but was reassured when I made light of the affair, probably because there was no danger in it to George Hamilton, and, perhaps, because if I should kill Count Hamilton, George would inherit the title and estates.

"But poor Mary! She will grieve," said Frances.

"I think you need waste no tears for her sake," I answered. "She is a fine, pretty little creature, who will take what comes her way without excess of pain or joy. She is incapable of feeling keenly. God has been good to her in giving her numbness."

"No, no, cousin Ned, you are wrong!" she returned. "Life without pain is not worth living. I have heard that the Arabs have a saying, 'All sunshine makes the desert.' God is good to us when he darkens the sun now and then and gives us the sunshine afterwards."

"Perhaps you are right, Frances," I returned. "But you and I are in the cloud now, and a little sunshine would be most welcome."

"Not enough sunshine to make a desert," she answered.

"Ay! But enough to make a garden," I returned, as we climbed the narrow flight of steps leading to the private entrance to the Old Swan.

When we paused at the door, Frances said, "Your garden is at hand." And when she opened the door, there stood Betty, and I was in Eden. The moist glow of her eyes, the faint blush of her cheeks, the nervous fluttering of her voice, spoke more eloquently than all the tongues of Babel could have spoken, and I could not help comparing her welcome with that which Maxy Hamilton had given me at the queen's ball.

Bettina led us to the parlor, and while we were drinking a cup of tea, we had the great pleasure of asking and answering questions of which we always had a large supply in reserve.

When it was time to go, Bettina walked down to the Bridge with us. As it was growing dark, Frances suggested that I walk back to the Old Swan with Betty, which I did, she taking my arm of her own accord, and both of us very happy, though we spoke not a word, for fear of saying too much, save "good night" at the door.

"Good night at the door!" God gave its sweetness to youth right out of the core of His infinite love.

CHAPTER XII

A PERILOUS EMBASSY

Four or five days after our visit to Bettina, I met De Grammont at Charing Cross, and he surprised me with an invitation to his house that night to meet Monsieur l'Abbe du Boise at supper.

"The king and a dozen other gentlemen will be present," he said, "but there will be no ladies. Monsieur l'Abbe, being of the church, is not a ladies' man, and besides, ladies have sharper eyes than men, and might see much that is intended to remain unseen."

The count's remark seemed to settle the question of the Abbe's identity, and I hastened to Frances with the news. She assured me that she was ready to die of fright, but showed no outward sign of dissolution, and when I complimented her on her power of self-control, said:—

"Fortunately, I am part hypocrite, and can easily act a part."

"You have a hard one ahead of you," I returned, "and will need all your strength before it is played to the end."

* * * * *

I was on hand early at De Grammont's supper, but found several gentlemen ahead of me, awaiting, with the count in his parlor, the arrival of the king. Soon after I entered the room, De Grammont presented me to the Abbe. I was convinced at once that he was not George Hamilton. His beard, worn a la Richelieu,—a mustache and a tuft on the chin,—was snow white, and his hair, which was thin, hung in long white waves almost to his shoulders. He walked with a stoop and wore spectacles, the glasses of which were slightly colored. Being an ecclesiastic, though not a priest, he wore no wig; but he was of the Order of the Cordon Bleu, and wore, in addition to his badge and blue ribbon, a sword beneath his long coat. It was the first time I had ever seen an ecclesiastic wearing a sword, though it has since become common in France, where there are many "Abbes" who are neither priests nor in orders.

The Abbe spoke poor English, therefore the conversation was carried on in French, much to the annoyance of some of our guests, who pretended to a greater knowledge of that language than they possessed.

Soon after my presentation to the Abbe, the king arrived, and we all went out to the supper table, where the Abbe's chair was on the king's right, with De Grammont on his Majesty's left. After the king had been seated a moment, he rose and asked us to be seated; so we took our places, all save the king dropping our hats beside us on the floor because of his Majesty's presence.

I sat next to De Grammont, almost opposite the Abbe, and had a good opportunity to observe the French emissary. The king's French was excellent, and the dinner conversation was carried on largely between him and the Abbe. All subjects were discussed, but the Abbe adroitly avoided Dunkirk and seemed to prefer talking on religious and philosophical topics, in which he took the liberty to disagree with the king in many respects, politely though positively.

I listened attentively, hoping that some tone of the Abbe's voice, a pose or a gesture, might reveal George Hamilton, if it were he, in the most excellent disguise I had ever seen. But nothing of the sort occurred, and before the dinner was over, I was still more convinced that whoever the Abbe du Boise might be, he was not Hamilton.

After dinner came the heavy wines, of which the Abbe did not partake, and of which De Grammont and I drank sparingly. All the others, including the king, were gloriously drunk long before the night was over.

While smoking our pipes, the king, who was eager to get his hands on French money, told the Abbe that he hoped to see him, with his credentials, at Whitehall on the second morning following at ten o'clock, and the Abbe said he would leave his credentials with my Lord Clarendon, and would be at Whitehall at the hour suggested by the king, for the purpose of making the French king's offer.

Most of the guests went home between two men, very late at night, but fortunately I was able to walk home by myself.

I was both glad and disappointed not to find George in the gown of the Abbe. I was glad because of the risk he would have taken had he come to England, yet disappointed in missing what would have been the most picturesque, daring personal exploit of English court history. But on the whole it was better as it was.

The next morning the king sent for me to come to his closet, and asked if I knew one Lilly, an astrologer. I answered that I knew little of him personally, but had heard much of his wisdom and learning.

"Yes, yes, but you know where he lives, do you not? On the Strand, a dozen houses this side of Temple Bar?" asked the king.

"I have seen the house often, your Majesty," I replied.

"Good! Now listen attentively to what I have to say," returned the king, graciously taking my arm and leading me to a window overlooking the river. "I hear from De Grammont that the Abbe du Boise is a firm believer in the teachings of astrology. I want you to arrange, without letting any one know that my finger is in the pie, to take Lilly to see the Abbe, or the Abbe to see Lilly. I'll whisper a word in your ear. The stars will tell our friend, the Abbe, a story to suit our purposes. The French king and his ambassadors will find their match in me, I warrant you. I have bought Lilly, body and soul—with promises." The king shrugged his shoulders and whispered: "With promises, you understand, Baron Ned, with promises. Now give him a chance at the Abbe."

Charles laughed and chuckled in self-gratulation, not the least suspecting that he was talking to the wrong man and playing into the French king's hand. I bore in mind the fact that the king had bought Lilly with promises, and I determined to buy the good Doctor with ready gold.

"I'll try to carry out your Majesty's commands," I answered, apparently doubtful of my ability. "But of course you would not have me insist, if the Abbe seems disinclined to consult Lilly."

"No, no! Odds fish, man, no! But find a way to bring them together, and your reward will come later. I choose, you for this little piece of business because you are in no way connected with the affair between the French king and me, and because I know you are to be trusted."

I to be trusted! So was Brutus!

"I shall do my best, your Majesty, and if I fail, I shall notify you at once," I said, taking my leave.

I hastened to De Grammont's house, which at that time was over near the Mall, and told the count what the king had said.

"Ah, that is good!" cried De Grammont. "A fool, who knows himself to be a fool, is likely to be wary, but one who deems himself wise is the easiest dupe in the world. I'll see Monsieur l'Abbe. Wait."

De Grammont returned in a few minutes, saying that the Abbe would go with me to see Doctor Lilly, and I suggested that I return for him in three hours.

I went back to Whitehall, where I found Frances, and told her to be at Lilly's house on the Strand within three hours, to meet the French king's ambassador, and to receive the instructions which George's letter had intimated the Abbe would give. I told her, also, that the Abbe was not the person we had expected to see.

The evening before, she was ready to die of fright because we believed that the Abbe was George Hamilton, and now, since I had found he was not, she was ready to die of disappointment—so she assured me.

At the appointed time, De Grammont, the Abbe, and I took the count's barge and went down to the water stairs nearest Temple Bar, where the Abbe and I left De Grammont and walked up through the crowded streets to Lilly's house.

Owing to the crowded condition of the street, the Abbe and I found no opportunity to exchange words until we were before Lilly's house.

Lilly was at home, I having sent word of our coming, so when we knocked, the servant opened and directed us to the waiting parlor, saying that the Doctor would soon come down.

We started upstairs, I in the lead, the Abbe following ten paces behind. When I entered the room, I found Bettina and Frances sitting by the street window. They came to me quickly, and Frances explained Bettina's presence.

"I did not like to come here alone, so I asked Betty to come with me. She is to be trusted."

"You need not assure me of that," I answered, taking Betty's hand. "I already know it. I am glad you—"

But here I was interrupted by a soft cry from Bettina, and by a half-smothered scream from Frances, both of whom deserted me suddenly and ran toward the door I had just entered. Turning, I saw Frances with her arms about the Abbe's neck, and Bettina clasping one of his hands. I thought the two had gone mad, but when Bettina saw my look of surprise and inquiry, she dropped his hand, came to me, and asked:—

"Did you want us to pretend that we did not know him? If so, you should have told us."

"But you don't know him," I declared.

"Perhaps I don't," she returned, laughing softly and shrugging her shoulders, "but evidently your cousin does. If

Charles Major

not, she should take her arms from around his neck."

"But she is mistaken," I insisted.

"She seems to be convinced," answered Bettina, with a curious little glance up to me, half laughing, half inquiring. Evidently she was doubtful whether I spoke in jest or in earnest.

Frances still clung to the Abbe, her head resting on his shoulder, so I started toward her, intending to correct her mistake. Bettina, seeing my purpose, caught me by the arm, saying:—

"Don't you really know?"

The Abbe turned his face toward me, and when I caught a glimpse of his eyes without spectacles, I recognized George Hamilton, and almost choked myself in smothering a cry.

Frances turned to me, asking indignantly, "Why did not you tell me?"

"Because I did not know," I answered, hardly able to believe the truth.

But we had important business before us, and I knew that we should prepare for it before Lilly came in. So George, Bettina, Frances, and I went to a window at the far end of the room to hold a consultation.

"Since I did not recognize you, perhaps Lilly will not," I suggested. "I trust the Doctor, but perhaps we had better leave him under the impression that you are Monsieur l'Abbe du Boise and give no intimation of the truth."

"I had not hoped that my disguise would deceive you, Baron Ned," said George, "but since it has, it is just as well that we leave Lilly in the dark if we can."

"But he will know. The stars will tell him," suggested Bettina, opening her eyes very wide.

"The stars will tell him what he is paid to hear," I remarked. Then turning to Frances, I asked, "How is it that you were able to recognize him?"

"By his eyes!" exclaimed Frances and Bettina in concert.

"That gives me a valuable hint," said George, hastily adjusting his colored spectacles. "Now, how about it?"

"I still should know you," answered Frances.

"Not I!" exclaimed Bettina.

Presently Lilly came in, and I presented him to Monsieur l'Abbe du Boise and explained the presence of Frances and Bettina by saying:—

"A friend of ours in France has asked Mistress Jennings to render what aid she can to Monsieur l'Abbe, and she is here at my request to receive his commands."

"It is good!" exclaimed Lilly. "She has the king's ear if any one has, and the ear is very close to the mind. What may I do to serve Monsieur l'Abbe?"

"If I may see you privately—the baron and me—I shall tell you how you may serve me," answered the Abbe.

The Abbe and I excused ourselves to Frances and Bettina,

and went with the Doctor to the room which he called his observatory, where we came to the point very quickly:—

"I want to buy Dunkirk for my master for the sum of one hundred thousand pounds," said the Abbe, by way of starting the consultation.

"But London has already offered that sum," returned Lilly, "and stands ready to pay more."

"In payments," suggested the Abbe.

"Yes," returned Lilly. "But I see no way of bringing the king to accept the sum you offer unless—unless Mistress Jennings can persuade him."

"She may be able to do so," answered the Abbe, shrugging his shoulders. He spoke very bad English throughout the consultation. "But the stars, too, may be very persuasive with King Charles. To be plain, he will probably consult you, and if—"

"I am to see him to-night. That is why your visit was postponed until to-morrow," interrupted Lilly.

"That is as I supposed," remarked the Abbe. "Now, if I buy Dunkirk for one hundred thousand pounds, you shall receive two thousand pounds within ten days after signing the treaty, and Baron Clyde will be my surety."

"Two thousand pounds?" mused Lilly. "That is rather a small sum in so great a transaction."

"I doubt not the purchase may be made without the help of the stars if you feel that two thousand pounds is too small a sum to be considered," returned the Abbe.

"No, no," said Lilly. "I understand that you wish me to set a figure and work out the solution of this affair, and if I learn from the stars that it is to King Charles's interest to accept your offer of one hundred thousand pounds for the city of Dunkirk, I am to receive—"

"If King Charles accepts!" interrupted the Abbe.

"Ah, I see! Yes, yes, of course," returned Lilly. "I shall go to work immediately and set my figure. Of course I do not know what I shall learn, but I shall be glad to learn from the stars that which will enable me to advise the king according to your wishes. Two thousand pounds are two thousand pounds, and the word of a king is but a breath."

"What will the king give you for setting the figure and working it out? What does he usually pay you in important affairs?" asked the Abbe.

"Ah—eh—I—I—In truth," returned Lilly, stammering, "the king, who is so liberal with his lady friends, is—what shall I say?—close with me, save in promises. He buys folly at the rate of hundreds of thousands of pounds a year, while he pays for knowledge with large promises, and now ten shillings and again five. On one occasion I assured him that he would not fail if he attempted to put through a much-cherished plan of carrying a lady to the country against her will. He was much pleased and gave me a guinea, but borrowed it a week afterward, and—and still owes it."

George turned quickly to me, but, remembering that he was the Abbe du Boise, said nothing. But I caught his meaning and, turning to Lilly, asked:—

"Do you refer to the occasion of a certain kidnapping in which Hamilton and I consulted you?"

"Yes," returned Lilly.

"And you allowed it to be carried out without telling us?" I asked indignantly.

"I did not know who the lady was till you came to me for help," he answered.

"And you were able to put us on the right track to find her because of knowledge gained from the stars?" I asked, with a sharp note of sarcasm.

"No, no," he replied coolly. "Why trouble the stars for information that may be had as easily and more definitely elsewhere?"

"Then why did you not tell us the true source of your knowledge?" I asked warmly.

"Because I had neither right nor desire to betray the person most actively engaged in the affair. To have done so might have cost me my life. I gave you the information you asked, and you saved the lady through my help, without which you would not have known where to turn. You would have been helpless. You paid me ten guineas. Were my services worth the fee?"

"Ah, richly," I returned, beginning to see the whole matter of astrology in a new light.

"Then why do you complain?" he asked. "A man, naturally, wants to know where his meat comes from, but knowledge, like a diamond, is good found anywhere."

"I beg your pardon, Doctor Lilly," I answered, waving my hand as a substitute for hauling down my colors. "I turn you over to Monsieur l'Abbe once more."

"I think we understand each other," remarked the Abbe. "You say the king has employed you to set a figure, and that you are to take the solution to him to-night?"

"Monsieur l'Abbe is correct," returned Lilly.

"I hope the stars may see fit to advise the king to accept my first offer, for it will be the last," said the Abbe. "Possibly the stars may show that in case King Charles sells Dunkirk to London even for a much larger sum than I shall offer, he may be compelled to spend the money and a great deal more in defending the city."

"True, true," agreed Lilly.

"Possibly the stars may indicate that King Louis loves war," continued the Abbe. "They may show that if King Charles refuses my master's offer, England may be compelled to give up Dunkirk for nothing, or spend a vast deal of money and blood in defending it. If the French king lays siege to Dunkirk, the English people will force King Charles to take one of two courses—defence or abdication. In the latter case he might lose his head, as his father did before him. Furthermore, if King Charles refuses my first offer, my master will withdraw, in which case London also will withdraw. Is it not possible that the stars may tell you all this?"

"The conditions you suggest are so probable that one hardly need ask confirmation of the stars, and so reasonably to be expected are the events you predict that, beyond question, stellar revelation will be in accord with your desires. But the stars will say what they will say, and I shall give King Charles the truth from whatever source it comes," said Lilly, lifting his head in righteousness and posing as the

Charles Major

embodiment of truth.

"That is all I can ask," returned the Abbe, rising to close the interview.

"All exceedingly reasonable—reasonable," answered Lilly, bowing.

We returned to the parlor, where we found Frances and Bettina awaiting us, not patiently, if I could judge by their looks. I asked Lilly to allow us to occupy the room undisturbed for an hour while the Abbe gave certain instructions to Frances, but the Doctor did better for us. He took us to a room enclosed in glass on the roof of his house, where we could be by ourselves with the sun and the sky overhead, and all London beneath us.

To this day I am not sure that Lilly did not know Hamilton, but if he did, he concealed his knowledge completely, feeling, doubtless, that it would be a dangerous bit of information to himself and of no benefit to any one else. If George should be discovered by the king, Lilly could honestly disclaim knowing him. If affairs turned to our desire, the Doctor could lose nothing by his ignorance whether pretended or real. So I doubt not he thanked us for the imposture, if he discovered it.

It is needless to say that Bettina, Frances, George, and I were very pleased to be together once more. We spent a delightful hour in Lilly's observatory, where we made our plans for the following day, which will unfold in the order of their occurrence. A great deal of the time we were all talking at once, but for some strange reason we were all silent when George said laughingly, though nervously, that the French king had sent word to Frances that we would pay her ten thousand pounds if George's mission proved successful.

Having anticipated the possible necessity for quick action at the proper time, George had brought with him two copies of a treaty, written in Latin. He brought also plenary authority from the French king, under the great Seal of France, authorizing Monsieur l'Abbe du Boise to sign, execute, and deliver the treaty on the part of France and to receive in return the treaty to be executed by the English king. He also bore authority to make and deliver to King Charles a bill of exchange on Backwell, the goldsmith, for the purchase money of Dunkirk. Thus all would be ready for immediate conclusion the moment King Charles accepted the French king's offer.

That night near the hour of one o'clock, Lilly called by appointment to see me at De Grammont's house, coming from Whitehall, where he had been closeted with the king for three or four hours, explaining to his Majesty the message of the stars as read by the light of two thousand pounds.

"I explained to his Majesty," said Lilly, "that in all my calculations and observations, Mars intruded with alarming persistency in conjunction with King Louis's star. I tried to show him that the recurrences of this untoward conjunction were so rapid and constant as to denote war at a very early date if conditions were not affected at once by the intervention of the messenger, Mercury, whose sign fortunately accompanied each unfortuitous conjunction. The king, though pretending to be learned in the noble art of astrology, asked me to translate my solution, and I did so, almost in the words of Monsieur l'Abbe this afternoon."

"Thank you," remarked George.

"No, no, do not thank me," said Lilly, disclaiming all credit. "What Monsieur said was so reasonable and fitted so aptly to the probable conditions of the future, read in the terrestrial light of the present, sound reason, that it was hardly necessary to ask the stars. But in compliance with the king's request, I set my figure and found, as usual, that the revelations of the stars coincided with the dictates of reason. It is true the stars sometimes forecast events which seem almost impossible in view of present conditions, but the questioner of the heavens who does not use his reason to help his interpretation of the stars is, to say the least, far from wise."

"Yes," interrupted the Abbe. "But come to the point! What did the king say?"

"He did not entirely accept the message of the stars," returned Lilly. "He does not seem to object to war. He says there is no time when it is as easy to raise money from the people as in times of war. I suggested that money in the nation's treasury was not in the privy purse, where the king most wants it. But he said it was only a short journey from the treasury to the privy purse, and—well, I agreed with him. If you want to convert a vain, stubborn fool to your way of thinking, don't let him know what your way is."

"So the stars have failed?" asked the Abbe.

"No," returned Lilly, "they have put the king to thinking, but more, they have sowed the seeds of fear, a plant which grows rapidly in a coward's heart by night."

"But not rapidly enough to suit our purposes, I fear," returned the Abbe.

"Yes," insisted Lilly. "If the king's inclination can be changed, fear will sweep aside all other considerations in a moment, and he will accept the one hundred thousand pounds which you will offer to-morrow morning. But in case the king does conclude to accept the French king's offer, the iron will at once take on a white heat, and—well, iron remains at white heat only a short time. You must be ready to act quickly when the proper moment comes, or London will spring between you and the king."

"I shall be ready," returned the Abbe. "The king shall be inclined to our proposition before another day is past."

"Shall I tell you what the stars predict concerning the signing of the treaty?" asked Lilly.

"Yes, yes," I answered eagerly.

"I have found Venus in conjunction with—" began Lilly.

"Oh, damn the stars!" cried the Abbe, most uncanonically. "Tell me what you think about it!"

"The stars tell me that the treaty will be signed to-morrow night—that is, to-night, this being the early morning," answered the Doctor, persistently maintaining his attitude of stellar interpreter.

"Very well. Good night, Doctor," said the Abbe. "And may the shadow of your discretion never grow less."

A moment later I conducted Lilly to the door, and when I returned to De Grammont, who had not spoken a word during the entire interview, he shrugged his shoulders and said:—

"Sacrament! What a wise man a fool may be! It is to admire!"

"I doubt if any man is beneficially wise unless he be in part a fool," said the Abbe, and I closed the symposium by remarking:—

"Folly tinctures wisdom with common sense, illumines it with imagination, and gives it everyday usefulness. But best of all, it helps a man to understand the motives of other fools who constitute the bulk of mankind."

"Ah, baron," said De Grammont, yawning. "It is all doubtless true. Who would have expected to find so much cynical wisdom in an Englishman? But let us to bed!"

Hamilton and I were up by five o'clock the next morning, in consultation. He was for dropping the matter in so far as it involved Frances, but I insisted that while it was a disagreeable task for her, she was wise with a woman's wisdom, calm with a woman's calmness, and bold with a woman's boldness, which knows no equal when the motive springs from the heart rather than the head.

We discussed the matter in all its phases, and then I went to the palace to see Frances. When she arose, I was waiting to tell her that the Abbe would see the king at ten o'clock and to ask her to wait in the anteroom of the duchess's parlor. If Charles accepted the French king's offer, I should pass by her wearing my hat, and she would know that her help would not be needed. If the king refused, I should carry my hat in my hand, and she could take her own course with Charles.

"Do you fear?" I asked, being myself very much afraid, for we were dealing with an absolute monarch, devoid of conscience, devoid of caution save when prompted by cowardice, but plenteously imbued with venom in his heart and all things evil in his soul.

"I fear?" cried Frances, tossing her head defiantly.

I thought surely no woman ever was as beautiful as this one, in whose heart there was no fear, no doubt of self, no faltering in the face of danger. I asked her to tell me of her plans, and she answered:—

"I have no plan save to see the king. Then the plans will come of themselves."

CHAPTER XIII

FRANCES DELIVERS THE TREATY

George went to the Shield Gallery in Whitehall at ten o'clock the next morning, where he found his Majesty, the Lord Chancellor, and a half score of the king's creatures, including Berkeley, Wentworth, Crofts, Jermyn, and others of like quality.

These were the men with whom George had to deal. He was known intimately to each of them, and was hated most heartily by all save the Chancellor.

When George entered the Gallery, the king took his seat in a great chair of state on a dais at one end of the room, while his counsellors ranged themselves on either side. I, with a dozen other gentlemen, had been commanded to be present, not as advisers, but as attendants on the king to give dignity to the occasion.

George, having been sent to England secretly, had brought no retinue, since it was desired by every one connected with the affair that his presence should attract as little attention as possible and thus avoid alarming London. When George went to Whitehall, he was accompanied only by De Grammont and a gentleman of the count's household.

While George knelt before his Majesty, asking leave to speak for the French king, his master, I could not help thinking of the strange contiguity of antagonisms so frequently observed in one's journey through this life, nor could I help wondering what would be the fate of the bold man kneeling before the king if his Majesty could but see through the Abbe's disguise.

But I had little time for reflection, since George was not one who allowed matters to drag. On receiving permission to speak, he rose and went to the point at once in badly broken English, which I shall not try to reproduce.

"I shall not take up your Majesty's time with idle words," said the Abbe, glancing at a written memorandum which he held in his hand. "My master, King Louis, sends greeting to his royal brother, and hopes that no cause of difference may ever arise to darken the blue sky of peace that now hangs over two kings, potent as are your Majesty and my master, and two nations, happy, rich, and powerful as are the noble realms of France and England. Believing the possession by either monarch of cities or territory within the other's realm to be a constant menace to this much-desired peace and amity, my master, the king of France, sends me, his humble ambassador, with plenary authority, the instrument of which now lies with your Majesty's noble Lord Chancellor, to make offer to your Majesty of the great sum of one hundred thousand pounds for the good city of Dunkirk, which is on territory contiguous to my master's domain."

"The great sum of one hundred thousand pounds!" demanded Charles, contemptuously. "Does your master consider one hundred thousand pounds a great sum to pay for so great a city as Dunkirk?"

"It is a great sum to pay, your Majesty," returned the Abbe, with meekness in his manner, but boldness in his words, "when it is considered that the king of France might have the city of Dunkirk for the mere taking, did he not love your Majesty."

"Might have it for the mere taking, say you?" cried Charles, with a flash of imitation fire. "Odds fish, man! What do you suppose we should be doing while he was taking it?"

"Sending ships across the Channel at a great cost in money and life to your people, your Majesty," coolly, though meekly, answered the Abbe.

"Of that my people will not complain," answered Charles, still burning a pinch of red powder. "Their blood and their gold will be given gladly to defend my possessions abroad. My people are brave and do not fear death for the sake of their king, I would have you to know, Sir Abbe."

"Noble praise, your Majesty, and beautiful in the mouth of a king who stands ready to march at the head of his own army, and to help fight the good fight of his own cause," returned the Abbe, bowing with deep humility.

"Sir, your words are bold and are in no way mitigated by your humble mien!" exclaimed the king. "If you have no other offer to make, the audience will end, at least for the present."

"May I crave one moment more?" asked the Abbe.

"Yes, but be brief," returned the king.

"My instructions, your Majesty, are to leave London not later than sunrise on the day after making my king's offer. That will be to-morrow morning, when I shall hasten back to Paris, whence no other messenger will come. Twenty thousand troops are now within three hours' march of Dunkirk. Your Majesty's ships cannot reach the city in time to save it. I beg to say that I have delivered the entire message intrusted to me by my august master, and therefore crave your royal permission to withdraw."

The king lifted his right hand in assent, and the Abbe moved backward, bowing himself from the room. De Grammont, who had come with him, met him at the door, and immediately they went to the count's house. When they were gone, the king dismissed all save his counsellors, and I being at liberty to leave, hastened to her Grace's anteroom. As I passed the door, my hat in my hand, I bowed to Frances, who was watching me intently. She smiled, glanced significantly toward my hat, nodded her head to let me know that she understood, and I passed by, glad that she had the courage which I so sadly lacked.

Evidently Frances lost no time in doing her part with the king, for two hours later a page came to me in the Wardrobe, saying that the king wished to see me immediately. I made all possible haste, and when I entered the king's closet, he said:—

"Close the door, Clyde," but seemed unable for the moment to say more.

He could not hide his excitement, and presently began telling me in a peremptory manner that he had a very delicate piece of business for my hands. He did not seem to feel sure of his ground, and spoke with a bravado altogether unnecessary, as though he would say I should do his will whether it suited me or not, rather than in words of respectful command. I could see easily that his bravado was assumed for the purpose of forestalling any objection on my part. Of course he did not suspect for one moment that I surmised what he wanted, or his words would have been: "Odds fish! To the Tower with him!"

After several stammering efforts, he began: "I want you to see Du Boise, whom you will find at De Grammont's house, and tell him that I accept the offer he made this morning. I understand he brings the treaties from France already written. At eight o'clock this evening they are to be placed in the hands of your cousin, Mistress Jennings, together with the bill drawn on Backwell of Lombard Street, for the sum of one hundred thousand pounds. Deliver my message immediately and secretly. Let no one know that I have spoken to you on the subject. After you have seen Du Boise, go to Mistress Jennings and give her word from the Abbe designating where and at what hour she is to receive the documents. I suggest eight o'clock, that they may not be in her possession too long. But wait a moment!"

He went to a writing desk standing near the river window, beckoned to me, and continued excitedly, "Sit here and write at my dictation."

I sat down before the desk, took a quill, and awaited the king's pleasure. After a moment's thought he dictated as follows:—

"To MONSIEUR L'ABBE DU BOISE,

"Ambassador Extraordinary from his Majesty, King Louis of France:

"Out of love for my royal brother, King Louis, and for the purpose of maintaining the peace and amity now existing between the glorious realms of England and France, I accept his Majesty's offer to purchase the city of Dunkirk, communicated to me at this morning's audience. You will therefore place in the hands of the bearer, Baron Clyde, two copies of a treaty consummating this transaction which I understand you have already written out. With said copies you will also place a bill drawn in the sum of one hundred thousand pounds on one, Edward Backwell, goldsmith, Lombard Street, with whom I am told the funds lie, and for which this writing shall be your full acquittance.

"The treaties shall be fully executed by you on the part of your master, in accordance with the terms of your instrument of authority now resting with my Lord Chancellor. When said treaties and said bill come to me, the treaties will be signed, and the copy intended for your master will be returned to you this evening so that you may carry out your instructions by leaving at dawn tomorrow morning. To the which I give my reluctant consent and request that you leave England without further ceremony, believing that your duty to your master mounts superior to the mere observation of courtly usage in formal leave-taking.

"Signed by the king's own hand,

"CHARLES R."

"You will see your cousin immediately after your consultation with Du Boise, and arrange to deliver the documents to her hands privately at the hour of eight o'clock."

"I beg your Majesty's indulgence for one question," I said, assuming as well as I could a reluctant manner.

"Yes, yes, but be quick," returned the king.

"It is this," I continued stammeringly. "Is my cousin to deliver the documents to you after the hour of eight o'clock?"

"That is no affair of yours, and your question is impertinent," answered the king. "Obey my commands and keep your lips sealed, if you would oblige your king, save trouble to yourself, and perhaps be rewarded. Hear me, Clyde! I will brook no interference in this matter. Do you fully understand?"

"Yes, your Majesty. To obey the king's command is the highest duty I know," I answered, hanging my head.

"Ah, that is better. Now you may go," said the king, motioning his hand toward the door.

Frances had been expeditious in doing her part, and I was wondering what she had done to work so great a change in the king's mind in so short a time. So I made all haste to see Du Boise in order that I might the sooner see my cousin and question her. I found Hamilton downcast, but when I gave him the king's letter, his gloom turned to anger.

"No, no!" he cried, springing from his chair. "Never! Never! Frances is buying the king's complaisance, God knows at what price! It shall not be! The cur! The coward! I'll kill him before the hour arrives!"

"Listen to me, George," I insisted, "and for once in your life, don't be a fool. You will ruin us all if you lose your head at the moment when success is waiting for us. You, yourself, suggested this plan, and, thanks to my cousin's courage, it is working out beautifully. I don't know what she has to propose, nor what she is going to do. I know nothing of her plans, but I trust her. Can't you?"

"Yes, yes, I trust her," he replied, growing more calm. "But I do not trust him. She will go to him alone, expecting, doubtless, to escape, but she does not know the risk she is running."

"Do not fear for her," I answered assuringly. "She will be prepared to defend herself. Make all things ready, and I'll go to learn of Frances's plans. You may be sure she will provide some way for her own protection. When a woman of brains sets out to hoodwink a man, he usually gets what he deserves, even though he be an absolute king."

"Well, be off, and back again at the earliest possible moment," said George, resigning himself, under compulsion, to the hard conditions the situation imposed.

When I left Hamilton, I hastened to Frances and found her expecting me. She told me her story in a few words:—"The treaty and the bill of exchange, I believe you call it, are to be placed in my hands to-night at eight o'clock," she said. "I am trembling now, but I shall be calm when the time comes. I am to take the documents to the king's closet at nine o'clock, and am to enter by way of the privy stairs from the river."

"Yes, yes, I know," I answered, and then I told her briefly of the king's orders.

"You to bring me the papers!" she exclaimed, laughing softly.

"Yes," I answered. "It completes the jest, if it prove to be one. But tell me, what do you propose to do when you go to the king's closet?"

"You see it was this way," she began, sitting down and smoothing out her skirts; "I so arranged it that I met his Majesty soon after I saw you pass with your hat in your hand. He was ready enough to take me for a walk in the garden, and when he fell under the influence of the sun and the flowers, he began, as usual, to protest his love. I gave him full rein,—full rein, Baron Ned,—and after he had

Charles Major

talked and protested a great deal, I told him that he might prove his regard for me if he would. He asked me in what manner, and said that he would do whatever I asked.

"'It is this, your Majesty,' I answered hesitatingly. 'By accident I met the Abbe du Boise at Lilly's house yesterday. It seems he had heard of the kind friendship your Majesty has shown me, and doubtless hoping to use me, offered me ten thousand pounds if I succeeded in inducing your Majesty to accept the French king's offer for the city of Dunkirk. Ever since my interview with him, I have been trying to see your Majesty, hoping that you might find the information useful, and desiring your Majesty to know that I was to receive the money in case you accepted, else I might seem false to my king.'"

I laughed and said: "I knew you would be able to wheedle him. A little woman with a big motive is like faith, in that she can move mountains."

"Yes, yes, it is easy enough," she answered. "He took my hand, and I permitted him to hold it for a moment, then withdrew it, you know, as though impelled by modesty. After duly hanging my head and casting down my eyes in a very spasm of shyness, I told the king that I hoped he would accept the French king's offer, and reminded him that it might avert the terrible consequences of war, in addition to putting ten thousand pounds in my poor empty little purse. He said he would put the ten thousand there for me, but I refused, saying that I had never before made a request of him, and that if he did not see fit to grant this, I should never make another, but should leave Whitehall at once."

"Ah! the little woman with a big motive pouts if the mountain moves too slowly. I should like to have heard you talking to him," I said.

"And perhaps you would have spoiled it all," she answered. "We walked down the path for perhaps three or four minutes, but at length the king spoke, stammeringly, and said that if I would bring the treaty to his closet this evening at nine o'clock, he would sign it."

"The dog!" I exclaimed.

"After a long pause, I answered hesitatingly, telling him that I could not accede to his request, and that I withdrew my petition, craving permission to leave Whitehall to-morrow. Thereupon he fell into an ecstasy of entreaty, and when we parted he was very happy, for I had promised to take the documents to him at nine o'clock. He said I was to come to the privy stairs leading from the river to his closet and go up to him for his signature and seal, when he would execute the treaty immediately and send it by a trusted messenger to the Abbe du Boise."

"Ah, but how will you get away from the closet?" I asked.

"If he will permit me to be the messenger, I can easily escape, but for fear he will not, you and George shall act as my watermen. Have a boat waiting for me near the garden stairs at nine o'clock, and we'll go by river to the king's private stairs. I'll go by myself to his closet and will come back to you by some means with the signed treaty. And, Baron Ned, have Betty with you. A woman is always braver with a woman alongside, and Betty always brings us good luck. Then, too, she can steer the boat; she knows the river as she knows her father's house. Remember, nine o'clock, and be sure that Betty is with you."

I went back to George, and when I told him of Frances's plan, he said:—

"If she does not return from the king's closet as soon as we shall have reason to expect her, we'll fetch her and make a page of history by leaving a dead king."

"In which case the English people would hang us and then bless us. It is their fashion. We should be as immortal as Guy Fawkes," I answered; laughing to keep my courage up.

George stood in revery for a moment and answered as if he were speaking to himself:—

"But what will happen if we are overpowered in the king's closet? He always keeps a ruffian guard in his ante-chamber."

"In that sad case, Frances must kill herself and we shall die fighting unless we preferred Tyburn Hill a day or two later," I answered. "It is all as plain as day. Why do you not forget that failure is possible? I have never known you to stand in doubt; why do it now on the eve of victory?"

"Frances! Frances! Frances! She is why I stand in doubt. My own life is not worth a farthing, but I have no right to bring her into this frightful peril."

"She has no fear, and the sooner you drive it out of your heart the better it will be for our cause."

"I suppose you are right, Baron Ned," he responded with a sigh; "if we go at this without fear or doubt we can't fail. Go ahead, my friend. May God forgive us if we are wrong and help us in any case." And I left him hurriedly, lest I should be infected with his deadly fear.

I next saw Betty, much to my delight, and of course she was eager to help us.

"Know the river?" she exclaimed, in answer to my question. "I know it as well as I know Gracious Street. I have shot the arches of London Bridge with the spring tide going out, and there is many a waterman who would not dare try it. If need be, I'll take you through the middle arch, where the flambeau hangs, and land you at Deptford or Sheerness, or Holland, I care not which." So there was no fear in her heart. If courage was the touchstone of fortune, we were sure to win, for there was no fear in any heart save George's, and ordinarily he was the bravest of us all.

When all arrangements were made, even to engaging a small boat, which was to wait for us at Westminster stairs, I took to my bed for the rest of the day. At six o'clock I received the treaties and the bill of exchange from Hamilton and delivered them to Frances. Then I went to fetch Bettina.

Grammont had offered to go with us, when we explained what we were to do and the danger in doing it, and we were glad to have him and his sword, for we might find ourselves in straits where we should need both. He and Hamilton were to meet me at the head of King's Street. Each of us was to carry a long sword and to have a pistol, charged and primed, in his belt.

After leaving the parchments with Frances, I hastened to bring Betty up to Whitehall, and, shortly after eight o'clock, met Du Boise and De Grammont at King's Street arch, all of us wearing full vizards.

We walked down to the boat, De Grammont frequently taking notice of Bettina, for, despite her full vizard and an enveloping cloak, she was far too attractive not to rivet his attention.

When we reached Westminster stairs, we found the boat

awaiting us. We did not want the watermen to go with us, so I bought the boat and dismissed them.

We entered the boat, and when Bettina took the stern oar, De Grammont asked:—

"Who is she—the lady on the stern thwart? Can she steer the boat? Does she know the river?"

"Yes, to all of your questions, count," I answered.

"'Yes' doesn't answer the first question," he returned.

"It isn't to be answered," I replied curtly, and he returned with an apologetic "Pardon!"

Just before nine o'clock we took Frances aboard at Whitehall Garden Stairs and drifted slowly down to the king's privy stairs, from which the narrow flight of steps rose to the king's closet in the story above.

When we drew up at the privy stairs, Frances stepped out of the boat to the landing and whispered:—

"I shall arrange in some way to return, just as soon as the king signs the treaty, but if you hear me scream, come to my rescue. I am prepared to defend myself, and shall give the signal only when I must."

After climbing the narrow steps, she entered the king's closet and found him alone. Almost at the same instant she caught the sound of heavy steps in the adjoining room and heard the clang of steel on a bare oak floor. This demonstration was made, I suppose, by the king's order, for the purpose of intimidating Frances lest she prove rebellious.

In response to her frightened look of inquiry, the king said, "Only a half dozen troopers whom I always keep in my anteroom to be at hand if needed."

"A wise precaution, your Majesty," returned Frances, bringing herself together as quickly as possible. "Here are the copies of the treaty, your Majesty, and here is the bill on Backwell. The Abbe du Boise instructed me to ask your Majesty to sign his copy of the treaty immediately and return it to him. He waits in a boat at the foot of the privy stairs, and is anxious to go down the river to his ship before the tide turns."

"Waits at the foot of the stairs?" exclaimed the king. "Odds fish! What is he doing there? But it shall be done at once. I had the Great Seal brought to me, so that I might fully execute the treaty without delay. I supposed the Abbe would desire its immediate return as soon as the money was paid."

"Yes, your Majesty," answered Frances, growing short of breath from excitement, "he is waiting below for it."

The king sat down at his desk, signed the treaty, affixed the Great Seal, returned the parchment to its envelope, and, turning to Frances, said:—

"Now, the first kiss, my beauty!"

"Not now, your Majesty. Please wait till I return," she answered, taking the treaty from the king's hand without his leave. "I do not want to disarrange my vizard till after I have returned the parchment to the Abbe. I fear the watermen will recognize me."

"Who is in the boat with the Abbe?" asked the king.

"His servant, a French gentleman, and two watermen. He insisted on bringing me, reluctant, doubtless to trust me with the parchments and the bill," she answered, lying with the ease of a Lombard Street hosier.

But the king, growing suspicious because of her haste, caught her by the arm, saying: "You remain here. I'll return the treaty."

She drew her arm from the king's grasp and started so hurriedly toward the door that the king took alarm and followed her, crying out:—

"I tell you I'll send the packet by other hands. You remain here."

She did not stop, so he caught her again by the arm, and spoke sharply: "You are to remain with me. Do you hear? I'm not to be played with. I'll send the packet—"

But she broke from his grasp, hastily opened the door, and found herself not at the head of the privy stairs, but in the king's anteroom, surrounded by a half dozen men in armor one of whom attempted to seize her. Instantly she sprang back to the king's closet, screaming, not as a signal to us, for she had forgotten our agreement in that respect, but in genuine fright.

Her screams brought George, De Grammont, and myself to the door at the head of the stairs in less time than one could count ten. We drew our swords, and I tried to open the door, but found it locked.

"The oars! The heavy oars!" whispered De Grammont.

I ran down the stairs to the boat and was about to ask Bettina to hand me the oars, when she, anticipating me, whispered:—

"I heard some one call for the oars, so I threw them out. There they are!"

There they were, true enough, halfway up the water stairs, ready for my hand, because of Betty's quickness.

In less than ten seconds I was at the top of the stairs again, and within twenty seconds more we had battered down the door with our heavy ash oars. In the king's closet we found Frances, surrounded by men at arms, and the king crouching in a corner, barricaded by small pieces of furniture.

George fired his pistol, and one of the six men fell, whereupon several pistol shots were fired, filling the small room with powder smoke, but injuring no one so far as we knew. De Grammont found an opening in another man's armor, and four stood between us and Frances. Then the real fight began—four against three. This would have been heavy odds in an open field, but it was not so formidable in a small room almost dark with smoke. Above all, the troopers were fighting for pay; we were fighting for life.

The four men charged us fiercely, and while we were fighting just inside the room, Frances worked her way from behind our antagonists toward the battered door and was about to make her escape when one of the king's men struck her a cowardly blow with the hilt of his sword, and she fell to the floor at the head of the stairs.

"You and Hamilton take her to the boat," cried De Grammont, speaking to me, but continuing to fence, as though by instinct. "I'll hold the door till you call; then I'll run. The next best thing to fighting is running."

I regretted the use of Hamilton's name, as it would betray his presence, if overheard, which otherwise would not have been suspected, all of us being well masked. But I had no time to waste in vain regrets, so George and I lifted Frances from the floor and helped her down to the boat, leaving De Grammont just outside the battered door, defending himself nobly against four armed men and keeping them inside the king's closet. He seemed to be enjoying himself, for he was laughing, bowing, parrying, and thrusting, as though he were at a frolic rather than a fight. There is but one people on earth in whose blood is mingled fire and ice—the French.

When we reached the water, we found that the running tide had carried the boat a short distance down-stream, but Bettina was standing on the stern thwart, bending this way and that in her endeavor to scull back to the landing by means of the steering oar. Every drop of blood in Bettina's plump little body was worth its weight in triple fine gold to us that night, for she brought the boat back to us without delay, and George helped Frances aboard while I ran to the foot of the privy stairs, shouting loudly:—

"Come on, Berkeley! Come quickly!"

Usually I think of the right thing to say a fortnight after the opportunity, but this once the name Berkeley came to me in the nick of time, and I evened my score with its possessor for many a dirty trick he had put upon me. To suspect was to condemn with Charles, and I knew that if he heard me call Berkeley's name, that consummate villain would suffer the royal frown. And so he did, never having been able to explain, nor deny, satisfactorily to the king, his presence at the head of the privy stairs that night. But to return to the fight.

De Grammont heard my summons, came down the stairs

three steps at a time, and sprang into the boat from the landing.

"The oars! The oars!" cried Hamilton.

"Death is between them and us!" cried De Grammont.

"Let us go!" cried Betty. "I'll scull the boat with the steering oar!"

There was not a man in the boat who knew the art of propelling it with one oar. Truly Betty was our salvation that night.

I shoved the boat off, Betty turned its head down-stream, and away we shot. We were not ten paces from the water stairs when five men came running from the privy stairs to the landing. I recognized the king, who was in the lead. As they reached the water edge of the landing, I heard a splash. Majesty, in his eagerness to overtake us, had gathered too great headway and had landed, if I may use the word, in the water.

The other men, being in armor, were compelled to doff their iron before jumping in to save the king. The night was dark, but we were so near the landing that I saw two of the men begin to throw off their armor, and presently I heard two splashes, followed quickly by two pistol shots in our direction. In our direction, I say, because both of the balls struck our boat.

After the pistol shots, all was quiet, but I knew that one of the king's barges, with a dozen men at as many sweeps, and a score of men at arms, would soon follow us. I made my way to the stern thwart of our boat, where Betty was sculling for dear life, taking her course diagonally across the river toward

Charles Major

the Southwark bank. After we had passed the swift current in the middle of the river, which I thought she had been seeking, I asked:—

"Why do you not keep to the centre, Betty? You are making toward the other bank."

"Yes," she replied, with what breath she could spare. "We'll find a stand of boats tied to poles almost opposite Temple Bar stairs. There we may take a pair of oars. I'm afraid I can't hold out at this much longer."

We soon found the boat stand, and, with little ceremony, appropriated a pair of oars, leaving a crown on the thwart of the rifled boat.

Hamilton and I quickly adjusted the stolen sweeps in the oarlocks, Betty sat down on the stern thwart, guided the boat to the swift water of the centre, and immediately we sped toward London Bridge at a fine rate. Presently, as we had expected, we heard the rapid, regular stroke of the sweeps in the king's barge, and in a few minutes it was so close behind us that we could see the men at the sweeps. When they saw us, they fired their pistols at us, but we did not hear the bullets splash in the water, so we knew they did not have our range.

My greatest fear of the bullets was for Bettina's sake, she being in the rear and more exposed to the enemy's fire than we who were at the sweeps, but I could not leave my oar to take her place, nor could I have steered the boat had I done so, being unfamiliar with the river. All I could do was to hasten our stroke, which George and I did to our utmost, and soon the welcome beacon over the centre arch of London Bridge came into view, dimly at first, but brightening with every stroke of our sweeps. As we approached the Bridge,

De Grammont nervously called our attention to the danger ahead of us.

"Yes, we'll take the middle arch, and I shall enjoy seeing the king's barge follow us," I answered, with what breath I could spare.

"Take the middle arch, and the tide running as a river in flood?" cried De Grammont, speaking French, being too excited to sort out English words. "Never! Never! Let me out!"

"Do not fear, count," I answered. "Our pilot—"

"Our pilot! Ah, sacrament! We are lost! Our pilot is a mere girl!"

"But a wonder, count, a wonder. There is no waterman on the river in whose hands we should be safer," I replied, expressing my confidence in stronger terms than it really deserved. To shoot London Bridge when the tide was running out, as it then was, would give pause to the hardiest waterman. A misstroke of the steering oar, the slightest faltering in the hands that held it, the mere touch of the boat's nose against the jagged rocks and logs of the pier, and all would be lost.

We could not stop to put De Grammont on shore, and presently recognizing that fact, he sat down in resignation in the bow of the boat, remarking with a sigh, as though speaking to himself:—

"Ah, the beautiful land!"

By that time the flambeau was blazing not two hundred yards ahead of us. The current had caught us, and the waves

Charles Major

of the running tide came almost to the gunwale of the boat. Bettina had risen to her feet, leaving her hat, vizard, and cloak in the bottom of the boat, and was standing on the stern thwart, her back towards us and her face up-stream. Behind us, perhaps three hundred yards, came the king's great barge, ablaze with torches. The men in the barge had ceased firing, supposing, probably, that we should be forced to land above the Bridge, and should then become an easy prey. But we had Bettina with us; they had not. Besides ours, there was not another one in the world.

On came the flambeau over the middle arch. It seemed to be coming toward us rather than we going toward it. Nearer lowered the black dim outline of the houses on the Bridge, with here and there the flicker of a candle in a window, magnified to starlike brightness by distance.

Clearer and clearer came the dash and the splash, the roar and the turmoil of the waters pouring through the terrible death's door, the middle arch. Yet over the middle arch was the only flambeau on London Bridge, placed there because it was the broadest of all the spans, and we dared not attempt to pass under the Bridge in the dark.

But worse than the middle arch ahead of us was the king's barge following close behind us. It, too, was in the current, though its twelve sweeps could easily have taken it ashore. I suppose that pride and eagerness to overtake us prompted its captain to follow in our wake. At any rate, he continued and was narrowing the distance between us with each stroke of the sweeps. When I asked Bettina if she thought they would attempt the arch, she replied:—

"I hope not," then laughing softly, "—for their own sakes. The royal barges are not built to shoot the bridge."

As we approached the bridge, Betty turned her eyes backward toward it every few seconds, taking her bearings and bringing the boat's nose now a little to the right, now to the left, and again holding it straight ahead.

When we were within twenty yards of the middle arch, she told us to cease rowing, and we obeyed, leaving the boat in her hands.

The roar of the falling waters, tumbling in a cataract on the further side of the Bridge, frightened me, but if Betty heard it she did not fear it, for she began to sing the plaintive little French lullaby we had so often heard, and De Grammont, leaning forward, touched me on the back as he whispered:—

"God gives us an angel to steer our boat."

The next moment the water caught us in its mighty suck, just under the upper edge of the arch, and almost before we were aware that we had started through, our boat made a plunge on the lower side, the perilous moment was past, and we were floating in comparatively still water two score yards below London Bridge.

Then Captain Bettina resumed her seat on the stern thwart, and we dipped our oars.

We were turning about to get under way again, when De Grammont cried out:—

"Mon Dieu! They are lost! There they go under! Ah, Jesu!"

We all turned our eyes toward the Bridge, but were too late to see the barge. It had sunk in four fathoms of water, and every man aboard had gone down with it.

We backed water, resting on our oars, and presently the overturned barge came to the surface and floated past us, telling its sad story, "Perished in a bad king's bad cause,"—a story written on almost every page of the world's history.

A short distance below the Tower, we met a large boat belonging to the ship in which George had come from France, which was waiting off Sheerness to take him back. The boat had been plying between Deptford and the Bridge, looking for George, since early evening. We recognized it by its long sweeps, and when we hailed it, we received the password and drew alongside.

All this time Frances had been allowed to sit in the bottom of the boat, she having assured us that she had taken no injury, but as we approached the French boat she arose, and when I asked her if she was hurt, she said, "No."

When I asked her if she had the treaty, she replied, holding out her hand to George:—

"Yes, here it is. It would have been a pity, indeed, to have lost it after all our trouble."

As we drew alongside the French boat, Hamilton whispered to Frances:—

"You have nothing to fear from the king. This affair shows him in a light so ridiculous that he will not care to make it public, and besides, he will not want to return the hundred thousand pounds. You will be safe in London, and I shall write to you just as soon as I return to France. If King Louis's reward proves to be what I expect, I pray you come to me, for, after this affair, I dare not set my foot in England."

At that moment we touched the other boat, and the Frenchmen

grappled us to hold us alongside. George had risen and was about to step aboard, when Frances, catching him by the arm, drew him back and sprang aboard the French boat ahead of him, saying:—

"I shall not wait for a letter. I am going with you now."

George followed her into the other boat, and as it drew away, I saw him bending low to kiss her hand. Then he shouted "Good-by!" and soon we could see nothing but the black water between us.

Betty began to weep, and after a moment I began to swear, for I did not like to see my cousin go off in this manner. De Grammont relieved his mind by a shrug of his shoulders, took the oar that George had abandoned, and without a word we started up-stream again.

CHAPTER XIV

HER LADYSHIP'S SMILE

We landed at the Old Swan stairs below the Bridge on Lower Thames Street, and went to the end of the Bridge, where De Grammont waited till I had taken Bettina home.

When I returned to the Bridge, the count and I took coach, and after a rapid journey across silent London, I arrived at the palace just as Old Tom of Westminster was striking eleven.

I climbed over the porch to my closet and reached there none too soon, for I was hardly in bed when my door opened and in walked the king followed by two men bearing candles. I pretended to be in a deep sleep and when aroused sprang from my bed seemingly half dazed and ready to defend myself, till the king spoke, when, of course, I was humble enough.

"How long have you been here?" demanded the king.

"All night I suppose, your Majesty; what time is it now?"

"Past eleven!" the king answered.

"In what may I serve your Majesty?" I asked.

"By telling me the truth!" he said, glaring at me and whining out his words. "Do you know anything about the attack on my closet this evening?"

Nothing is ever gained by denying, so I took a leaf from woman's logic, and answered his question by another.

"An attack on your Majesty's closet?" I cried. Then after a long pause, and with a manner of deep injury, I demanded: "Has anything untoward befallen my cousin? I carried out your Majesty's instructions without objection or protest. I intrusted her to your care, and it is my right and my duty to demand an account of her and to hold your Majesty responsible for her welfare."

He looked at me for a moment with a hang-dog expression on his face, but he could not stand my gaze, so he turned on his heel and left the room without another word.

He was not convinced of my guilt, nor would he believe me innocent. Evidently the royal verdict was "not proven." But in any case I knew that my favor at court was at an end.

During the next week I constantly importuned the king to tell me what had become of my cousin, and intimated my intention to make trouble in terms so plain—for I knew the king's favor was lost to me—that my Lord Clarendon was instructed to offer me a sum of money to say nothing more about the matter. I agreed to accept the money, it was paid, and I remained silent.

Frequently the difference between an acted lie and a spoken lie is the difference between success and failure. Then, too, the acted lie has this advantage; there is no commandment against it. We should congratulate ourselves that so many pleasant sins were omitted on Sinai.

At the end of a week after our great adventure I went to the country, and within a fortnight returned to find that my place in the Wardrobe was taken by another, and my place in the king's smile by the world at large; at least, it was lost to me.

When a wise courtier loses his king's smile, he takes himself out of his king's reach. Therefore I cast about in my mind for a London friend who would like to possess my title. I thought of Sir William Wentworth, rather of his wife, and suggested to her that for the sum of thirty thousand pounds I would resign my estates and title to the king, if Sir William would arrange for their transfer to himself. The transfer directly from me to him was not within the limits of the law. It could only be made through the king by forfeiture and grant. But the like had happened many times before, and could be accomplished now if the king were compensated for his trouble.

Wentworth broached the subject to our august sovereign who, in consideration of the sum of ten thousand pounds "lent" by Sir William to his Majesty, and because he was glad to conciliate a prominent citizen of London, that city being very angry on account of the sale of Dunkirk, agreed to the transfer, and the baronetcy of Clyde with the appurtenant estates passed to the house of Wentworth, where, probably, they brought trouble to Sir William and joyous discontent to his aspiring lady.

Aside from the fact that I knew the king's ill temper was cumulative, I had received a hint, coming through Castlemain's maid to Rochester, that if I remained in England, the king would despoil me. Then, too, I had other reasons for making the sale. I was sick of England's fawning on a poor weak creature, as cowardly as he was dull, and almost as dull as he was vicious, and longed to flee to the despotism of strength as I should find it in France under Louis XIV. There was still another reason, of which I shall speak later.

Three days after the consummation of my sale to Sir William Wentworth, Count Hamilton returned, and, learning of the manner in which I had disgraced myself, withdrew his challenge, sending De Grammont to tell me the sad news. He would not honor me by killing me.

"Why did you sell your title and estates?" asked De Grammont.

"I have several good reasons, my dear count," I answered. "The first is that I should have lost them had I not sold them. While the king does not know that I was connected with the fight on the privy stairs, he doubtless suspected it, for I have lived in the royal frown ever since. The second reason is that I hate Charles Stuart, and, admiring at least the strength of your king's tyranny, desire to live in France. King Louis says he is the state, and by heaven, he is! Charles Stuart knows that he is nothing, and he is right!"

"Give me your hand, baron!" cried De Grammont, a smile of satisfaction spreading over his face. "I now tell you my secret. No one else knows it. The purchase of Dunkirk has bought for me the smile of my master. I have been recalled to Versailles. I return to La Belle France within a fortnight! Come with me! I'll show you a king in very deed, and promise furthermore that his smile shall be for you!"

"I can't go with you, my dear count," I returned gratefully. "But I promise to see you soon in Paris. I suppose you will take with you the elder Mistress Hamilton, to whom I understand you have long been plighted in marriage, or will you return for her?"

"O-o-oh! Return for her, dear baron, return for her!" answered the count, shrugging his shoulders.

To close the chapter of De Grammont's life in England, I would say that he kept the secret of his recall to France, and one night after dark left his house near the Mall, taking a coach to Dover without saying to Mistress Hamilton when he would return.

But Mistress Hamilton had two brothers still in England, Count Anthony and James, who, catching wind of De Grammont's exodus, took horse and a small escort, made all possible speed, and came up with De Grammont's coach some six or eight leagues east of London.

Count Anthony rode up to one door of the coach, while James brought his horse to the other.

"Good morning, count," said Anthony, bending down to the coach window.

"Good morning, my dear count," returned De Grammont, blandly.

"Is there not something you have forgotten, count?" asked Anthony.

"Odds fish! Yes! I forgot to marry your sister," answered De Grammont, appropriating the king's oath, and apparently astounded at his own forgetfulness. "Thank you, dear count, for reminding me. I'll go back to London and do it at once."

"Your parole?" asked Anthony.

"Yes, the word of a De Grammont," answered the count, whereupon the Hamiltons lifted their hats and galloped home, knowing certainly that De Grammont would follow.

De Grammont reached London soon after sun-up, and, true to his word, married Miss Hamilton, blessed his stars ever afterward for having done so, and gave her no cause for unhappiness save a French one.

Soon after the sale to Wentworth, I received a letter from George telling me that King Louis had not only made him rich, but had appointed him Governor of Dunkirk, with promise of further advancement. George said, also, that the French king, having heard of my part in the Dunkirk transaction and my disgrace with my king, had offered to advance my interest if I would go to France. In a postscript to the letter, which was much longer than the letter itself, Frances told me how she and George had been married immediately on landing in France, and were living very happily in Paris, where they would remain until George should take up the government of Dunkirk.

So it had all fallen out just as one might have expected to find it in a story-book. George had been proved by Fortune's touchstone, and her Ladyship had chosen him for her smile. He had won the long odds.

What remains to be told is simply the denouement of my own affairs.

* * * * *

At the time of my transaction with Wentworth I said nothing to Bettina about the sale of my title and estates, but when I heard that our friends were safe and happy in France, I went down to the Old Swan, with more fear than I should have thought possible, to broach a certain matter, which was very near my heart, to Betty and her father.

I knew that in so far as Betty herself was concerned, I should find no trouble, but I also knew that I might find difficulty in persuading her to leave her father, for duty was a tremendous word in Betty's vocabulary.

When I reached the Old Swan, policy and fear each told me that it would be safer to attack Betty and her father separately. The odds of two against one, in this case, I feared would be too great for me to overcome. So I led Betty to her parlor,—rather she led me,—and after a preliminary skirmish, I told her I had come to see her on a most important piece of business.

"I'm glad to see you, whatever brings you, Baron Ned," she answered, smoothing out her skirts in anticipation of an interesting budget of news.

"But I'm no longer 'Baron Ned,' Betty," I informed her.

She asked a hundred questions with her eyes and eyebrows, and I hastily answered them by telling of the sale to Wentworth.

"Ah, I'm so sorry," she answered, "and I'm so glad, too, that I could cry. You don't seem so much above me nor so far away."

"That was my chief reason for selling my title and estates," I answered, reaching forward and taking her hand, which for the first time she did not withdraw. "I sold them, Betty, for a large price, but my reason for so doing was one that could not be measured by money. I want you for my wife, Betty, and my title, at least, stood between us. I should have given it away if I could not have sold it, because I want you, Betty, more than anything else in all the world."

"Ah, please don't, Baron Ned!" she cried, bringing her handkerchief to her eyes. "It can't be. I'm not so selfish as to take you at your word."

I was sitting on the cushioned bench by the wall, and she was in a chair facing me, within easy reach, so I caught her wrists and drew her to me, whispering:—

"Sit here, Bettina, by my side, and tell me why it cannot be, for I pledge you my honor I am not to be denied." She resisted for a moment, but at last sat down beside me, and I put my arm about her, despite her fluttering struggle. "Now, tell me why, Bettina. I need not tell you that you have my love. You know it without the telling."

She nodded her head "Yes," and covered her face with her hands.

"And am I wrong in believing that I possess your love?" I asked.

She shook her head to indicate that I was not wrong, and the little gesture was as good as an oath to me. After her confession, she would not dare to resist me, nor did she, save to say pleadingly:—

"Please, Baron Ned, it cannot be."

Tears were trickling down her cheeks, and I could see that she was in great trouble.

"I do not ask you to come to me now," I said, "but you may take a long time, if you wish—a day, or two, or even three, if you insist. But Betty, I am not to be refused, and you may as well understand now and for all that you are to be my wife. But tell me, Betty, what is your reason for denying me at this time?"

She dried her eyes, sat erect, and answered in a voice full of tears: "Well, you are so far above me that the time might come when you would be ashamed of me."

"Nothing of the sort, Betty. Drop that argument at once. You know you do not mean it. You are not speaking the exact truth. There is no sweetness, no beauty, like yours."

"Do you really mean it, Baron Ned?" she answered, smiling up to me.

"Yes, yes, every word and a thousand more," I answered.

"But I am so unworthy," she said.

"You're pretending, Betty," I answered, and I argued so well that she abandoned her position.

"Now, give me another reason, Betty," I demanded, feeling encouraged by the success of my first bout. To this she answered with great hesitancy, murmuring her words almost inaudibly:—

"I could not leave father."

That was the reason I had feared, and when I drew away from her, showing my great disappointment in my face, she took one of my hands in both of hers, saying:—

"Not that I should not be happy to go with you anywhere, but you see I am all the world to father. He would die without me."

Here, of course, I might expect tears, nor was I disappointed. I, too, found the tears coming to my eyes, for her grief touched me keenly, and her love for her father showed me even more plainly than I had ever before known the unselfish tenderness of the girl I so longed to possess. It was hard for me to speak against this argument of hers; for it was like finding fault with the best part of her, so for a little time we were silent. After a minute or two, she glanced up to me and, seeing my great trouble, murmured brokenly:—

"If you think I am worth waiting for, and if you will wait till father is gone, I will go with you, and your smallest and greatest wish alike shall be mine. And when you become ashamed of me, I'll—"

"I'll not wait, Betty," I answered, ignoring the latter half of her remark. "I have a far better plan. I am going to France, and you and your father shall go with me."

"Ah, will you take him?" she cried, falling to the floor on her knees, creeping between mine, and clasping her hands about my neck. Her sweet, warm breath came to me like a waft from a field of roses, the fluffy shreds of her hair tingled my cheek, thrilling me to the heart, while the touch of her hand and the clasp of her arm carried me to heaven.

Then she laid her head on my breast, her lips came close to mine, and she murmured with a sigh:—

"Now, Baron Ned, as you will."

I told Betty to call Pickering, and when he came in I related my story. I told him how Betty and I were of one mind, how George had prospered in France and had invited me to share his good fortune, how I wanted to go to France and to take Bettina with me, and how I wanted him to sell the Old Swan and go with us to the fair land across the Channel, where his wealth would give him station such as he deserved.

Immediately he objected, saying that the scheme was impossible. He said that he could sell the Old Swan for a great sum to Robbins, of the Dog's Head, and that all he possessed, aside from the inn, was in gold, lodged with Backwell, but for all that, my plan could not be considered for a moment.

"My dear Pickering, hear my side of the case," I insisted, determined to win this last bout as I had won the others. "You love your daughter and would be unhappy if she were to leave you alone in the world?"

"Indeed I should be," he answered firmly. "I will not consider your suggestion. I will not. I will not."

"She is more generous than you," I returned, "and refuses to leave you, though she would be very unhappy if you force her to remain."

"I suppose you think so," he replied sullenly.

"I know so," I answered, "and can prove it by Betty." Betty nodded her head "Yes," and I continued: "You will not be unhappy in France with us. You will be happy. Yet you refuse to be happy save in your own stubborn way, even though you bring grief to the tenderest heart in the world. But come, come, Pickering! This will not do! I tell you, I'm not to be refused!"

Pickering lapsed into stubborn silence, and as there is no arguing with a man who will not argue, I determined to take another course; so I spoke sharply:—

"Since you will not be reasonable, I have another plan to suggest: I will give up my prospects of fortune in France, and will live here in this rotten Old Swan as long as you live, never taking Betty from your side. If you do not give her to me under these conditions, I will take her away without any conditions. Eh, Betty?"

Betty hung in the wind for a moment, then nodded slowly:—

"Yes."

Pickering covered his face with his hands for a moment, then looked up to me and asked:—

"Would you do that, baron? Would you come down from your high estate to our lowly condition for the sake of my poor little girl?"

"Yes, Pickering," I answered.

Then after a moment's thought, he said: "I'll sell the Old Swan and go with you to France."

Betty took my hand, then she grasped her father's, drew him down to her and kissed him.

So Betty and I were married in the little chapel at the Southwark end of London Bridge, and off we went to our friends in France, where God blessed us and we were very happy. We had all been tried by the Touchstone of Fortune, and had won her Ladyship's smile! May God comfort those on whom she frowns!

NOTE

Baron Clyde seems to be the only writer of the period of Charles II who mentions the part taken by George Hamilton and Frances Jennings in the sale of the city of Dunkirk, but, of course, the particulars of that disgraceful affair would have been kept a secret from all save those who participated in it.

It is said that Nell Gwynn, John Churchill, and Sarah Jennings were younger than Baron Clyde indicates. Therefore there are many discerning persons who hold that he was "idealizing" when he wrote of them being at court at the time Dunkirk was sold.

There appears to be some ground for the criticism.

But in all essential respects the baron's history is held, justly, to be true to facts and conditions, and that, after all, is the main thing. Exact truth is evasive; therefore the virtues of approximation are not to be deprecated.

ABOUT THE AUTHOR

 **Charles Major** (July 25, 1856 – February 13, 1913) was an American lawyer and novelist.

Born to an upper-middle class Indianapolis family, Major developed in interest in both law and English history at an early age and attended the University of Michigan from 1872 through 1875, being admitted to the Indiana bar association in 1877. Shortly thereafter he opened his own law practice, which launched a short political career, culminating in a year-long term in the Indiana state legislature.

Writing remained an interest of Major, and in 1898, he published his first novel, When Knighthood Was in Flower. The novel about England during the reign of King Henry VIII was an exhaustively researched historical romance, and became enormously popular, holding a place on the New York Times bestselling list for nearly three years. The novel was adapted into a popular Broadway play by Paul Kester in 1901, premiering at the Criterion Theatre that year.

Major continued to write and publish several additional novels, to varying degrees of success, as well as a number of children's adventure stories, most set in and around his native state of Indiana. Charles Major died of liver cancer on February 13, 1913 at his home in Shelbyville, Indiana.

Choose from Thousands of 1stWorldLibrary Classics By

A. M. Barnard	Booth Tarkington	Edward Everett Hale
Ada Leverson	Boyd Cable	Edward J. O'Biren
Adolphus William Ward	Bram Stoker	Edward S. Ellis
Aesop	C. Collodi	Edwin L. Arnold
Agatha Christie	C. E. Orr	Eleanor Atkins
Alexander Aaronsohn	C. M. Ingleby	Eleanor Hallowell Abbott
Alexander Kielland	Carolyn Wells	Eliot Gregory
Alexandre Dumas	Catherine Parr Traill	Elizabeth Gaskell
Alfred Gatty	Charles A. Eastman	Elizabeth McCracken
Alfred Ollivant	Charles Amory Beach	Elizabeth Von Arnim
Alice Duer Miller	Charles Dickens	Ellem Key
Alice Turner Curtis	Charles Dudley Warner	Emerson Hough
Alice Dunbar	Charles Farrar Browne	Emilie F. Carlen
Allen Chapman	Charles Ives	Emily Bronte
Alleyne Ireland	Charles Kingsley	Emily Dickinson
Ambrose Bierce	Charles Klein	Enid Bagnold
Amelia E. Barr	Charles Hanson Towne	Enilor Macartney Lane
Amory H. Bradford	Charles Lathrop Pack	Erasmus W. Jones
Andrew Lang	Charles Romyn Dake	Ernie Howard Pie
Andrew McFarland Davis	Charles Whibley	Ethel May Dell
Andy Adams	Charles Willing Beale	Ethel Turner
Angela Brazil	Charlotte M. Braeme	Ethel Watts Mumford
Anna Alice Chapin	Charlotte M. Yonge	Eugene Sue
Anna Sewell	Charlotte Perkins Stetson	Eugenie Foa
Annie Besant	Clair W. Hayes	Eugene Wood
Annie Hamilton Donnell	Clarence Day Jr.	Eustace Hale Ball
Annie Payson Call	Clarence E. Mulford	Evelyn Everett-green
Annie Roe Carr	Clemence Housman	Everard Cotes
Annonaymous	Confucius	F. H. Cheley
Anton Chekhov	Coningsby Dawson	F. J. Cross
Archibald Lee Fletcher	Cornelis DeWitt Wilcox	F. Marion Crawford
Arnold Bennett	Cyril Burleigh	Fannie E. Newberry
Arthur C. Benson	D. H. Lawrence	Federick Austin Ogg
Arthur Conan Doyle	Daniel Defoe	Ferdinand Ossendowski
Arthur M. Winfield	David Garnett	Fergus Hume
Arthur Ransome	Dinah Craik	Florence A. Kilpatrick
Arthur Schnitzler	Don Carlos Janes	Fremont B. Deering
Arthur Train	Donald Keyhoe	Francis Bacon
Atticus	Dorothy Kilner	Francis Darwin
B.H. Baden-Powell	Dougan Clark	Frances Hodgson Burnett
B. M. Bower	Douglas Fairbanks	Frances Parkinson Keyes
B. C. Chatterjee	E. Nesbit	Frank Gee Patchin
Baroness Emmuska Orczy	E. P. Roe	Frank Harris
Baroness Orczy	E. Phillips Oppenheim	Frank Jewett Mather
Basil King	E. S. Brooks	Frank L. Packard
Bayard Taylor	Earl Barnes	Frank V. Webster
Ben Macomber	Edgar Rice Burroughs	Frederic Stewart Isham
Bertha Muzzy Bower	Edith Van Dyne	Frederick Trevor Hill
Bjornstjerne Bjornson	Edith Wharton	Frederick Winslow Taylor

Friedrich Kerst	Hayden Carruth	James Branch Cabell
Friedrich Nietzsche	Helent Hunt Jackson	James DeMille
Fyodor Dostoyevsky	Helen Nicolay	James Joyce
G.A. Henty	Hendrik Conscience	James Lane Allen
G.K. Chesterton	Hendy David Thoreau	James Lane Allen
Gabrielle E. Jackson	Henri Barbusse	James Oliver Curwood
Garrett P. Serviss	Henrik Ibsen	James Oppenheim
Gaston Leroux	Henry Adams	James Otis
George A. Warren	Henry Ford	James R. Driscoll
George Ade	Henry Frost	Jane Abbott
Geroge Bernard Shaw	Henry James	Jane Austen
George Cary Eggleston	Henry Jones Ford	Jane L. Stewart
George Durston	Henry Seton Merriman	Janet Aldridge
George Ebers	Henry W Longfellow	Jens Peter Jacobsen
George Eliot	Herbert A. Giles	Jerome K. Jerome
George Gissing	Herbert Carter	Jessie Graham Flower
George MacDonald	Herbert N. Casson	John Buchan
George Meredith	Herman Hesse	John Burroughs
George Orwell	Hildegard G. Frey	John Cournos
George Sylvester Viereck	Homer	John F. Kennedy
George Tucker	Honore De Balzac	John Gay
George W. Cable	Horace B. Day	John Glasworthy
George Wharton James	Horace Walpole	John Habberton
Gertrude Atherton	Horatio Alger Jr.	John Joy Bell
Gordon Casserly	Howard Pyle	John Kendrick Bangs
Grace E. King	Howard R. Garis	John Milton
Grace Gallatin	Hugh Lofting	John Philip Sousa
Grace Greenwood	Hugh Walpole	John Taintor Foote
Grant Allen	Humphry Ward	Jonas Lauritz Idemil Lie
Guillermo A. Sherwell	Ian Maclaren	Jonathan Swift
Gulielma Zollinger	Inez Haynes Gillmore	Joseph A. Altsheler
Gustav Flaubert	Irving Bacheller	Joseph Carey
H. A. Cody	Isabel Cecilia Williams	Joseph Conrad
H. B. Irving	Isabel Hornibrook	Joseph E. Badger Jr
H. C. Bailey	Israel Abrahams	Joseph Hergesheimer
H. G. Wells	Ivan Turgenev	Joseph Jacobs
H. H. Munro	J. G.Austin	Jules Vernes
H. Irving Hancock	J. Henri Fabre	Julian Hawthrone
H. R. Naylor	J. M. Barrie	Julie A Lippmann
H. Rider Haggard	J. M. Walsh	Justin Huntly McCarthy
H. W. C. Davis	J. Macdonald Oxley	Kakuzo Okakura
Haldeman Julius	J. R. Miller	Karle Wilson Baker
Hall Caine	J. S. Fletcher	Kate Chopin
Hamilton Wright Mabie	J. S. Knowles	Kenneth Grahame
Hans Christian Andersen	J. Storer Clouston	Kenneth McGaffey
Harold Avery	J. W. Duffield	Kate Langley Bosher
Harold McGrath	Jack London	Kate Langley Bosher
Harriet Beecher Stowe	Jacob Abbott	Katherine Cecil Thurston
Harry Castlemon	James Allen	Katherine Stokes
Harry Coghill	James Andrews	L. A. Abbot
Harry Houidini	James Baldwin	L. T. Meade

L. Frank Baum	Paul G. Tomlinson	T. S. Arthur
Latta Griswold	Paul Severing	The Princess Der Ling
Laura Dent Crane	Percy Brebner	Thomas A. Janvier
Laura Lee Hope	Percy Keese Fitzhugh	Thomas A Kempis
Laurence Housman	Peter B. Kyne	Thomas Anderton
Lawrence Beasley	Plato	Thomas Bailey Aldrich
Leo Tolstoy	Quincy Allen	Thomas Bulfinch
Leonid Andreyev	R. Derby Holmes	Thomas De Quincey
Lewis Carroll	R. L. Stevenson	Thomas Dixon
Lewis Sperry Chafer	R. S. Ball	Thomas H. Huxley
Lilian Bell	Rabindranath Tagore	Thomas Hardy
Lloyd Osbourne	Rahul Alvares	Thomas More
Louis Hughes	Ralph Bonehill	Thornton W. Burgess
Louis Joseph Vance	Ralph Henry Barbour	U. S. Grant
Louis Tracy	Ralph Victor	Upton Sinclair
Louisa May Alcott	Ralph Waldo Emmerson	Valentine Williams
Lucy Fitch Perkins	Rene Descartes	Various Authors
Lucy Maud Montgomery	Ray Cummings	Vaughan Kester
Luther Benson	Rex Beach	Victor Appleton
Lydia Miller Middleton	Rex E. Beach	Victor G. Durham
Lyndon Orr	Richard Harding Davis	Victoria Cross
M. Corvus	Richard Jefferies	Virginia Woolf
M. H. Adams	Richard Le Gallienne	Wadsworth Camp
Margaret E. Sangster	Robert Barr	Walter Camp
Margret Howth	Robert Frost	Walter Scott
Margaret Vandercook	Robert Gordon Anderson	Washington Irving
Margaret W. Hungerford	Robert L. Drake	Wilbur Lawton
Margret Penrose	Robert Lansing	Wilkie Collins
Maria Edgeworth	Robert Lynd	Willa Cather
Maria Thompson Daviess	Robert Michael Ballantyne	Willard F. Baker
Mariano Azuela	Robert W. Chambers	William Dean Howells
Marion Polk Angellotti	Rosa Nouchette Carey	William le Queux
Mark Overton	Rudyard Kipling	W. Makepeace Thackeray
Mark Twain	Saint Augustine	William W. Walter
Mary Austin	Samuel B. Allison	William Shakespeare
Mary Catherine Crowley	Samuel Hopkins Adams	Winston Churchill
Mary Cole	Sarah Bernhardt	Yei Theodora Ozaki
Mary Hastings Bradley	Sarah C. Hallowell	Yogi Ramacharaka
Mary Roberts Rinehart	Selma Lagerlof	Young E. Allison
Mary Rowlandson	Sherwood Anderson	Zane Grey
M. Wollstonecraft Shelley	Sigmund Freud	
Maud Lindsay	Standish O'Grady	
Max Beerbohm	Stanley Weyman	
Myra Kelly	Stella Benson	
Nathaniel Hawthrone	Stella M. Francis	
Nicolo Machiavelli	Stephen Crane	
O. F. Walton	Stewart Edward White	
Oscar Wilde	Stijn Streuvels	
Owen Johnson	Swami Abhedananda	
P.G. Wodehouse	Swami Parmananda	
Paul and Mabel Thorne	T. S. Ackland